KAT AMONG THE PIGEONS

A Kat Shakespeare mystery

e.c.saunders

First published in 2012 by Lulu.com

ISBN 978-1-291-15832-8

A CIP record for this book is available from the British Library

katamongthepigeons@gmail.com

FOR GLYN

'Well, that's the end of the film.
Now, here's the meaning of life."

(Monty Python, The Meaning of Life)

CHAPTER 1

Kat did not hear the explosion. It was only when she saw the building shudder that she realised the lower floors must have blown. Nobody else appeared to have noticed anything yet.

Her gut instinct was to move back, but she knew she'd not get away with it with everyone watching, waiting for it to go pear shaped. Outwardly confident, she made do with a surreptitious wipe of damp palms down her sides, forgetting she was in her posh frock.

Earlier that day she'd squeezed in amongst the mayor and other pillars of the community as they had posed smirking for the cameras and posterity on the roof of Julie Andrews Towers.

Now, safely back on terra firma, the silent implosion came as a disappointment after the raucous klaxons and communal countdown leading to the moment when she had triggered the explosives. Not a bang, nary a whisper. It seemed ages before she caught the tell-tale whiplash crack, followed by the thin coil of dark smoke that spiralled up from the roof, signalling secondary blasts on the upper floors. More smoke puffed out from the sides. There was a cloud of dust and the subdued iceberg crackle of displaced concrete as, trailing kite-tails of bunting, Julie Andrews House imploded in a huge, arthritic curtsey.

Kat Shakespeare, after thirty-two years on Planet Earth, had managed to acquire a raft of unusual, often eccentric, life skills. Blowing up a tower block was definitely a first.

The awed silence of the crowd watching the ugly Seventies' concrete flats collapsing as languidly as a sand castle was broken by a flight of boys who, as if to compensate for the lack of whizz-bang, began circling the field with arms wide, making NATO airstrike noises.

'Hic, hic, hooray,' the mayor giggled, quickly covering up her faux pas with a ladylike cough when she remembered where she was.

From the flushed faces of the councillors and guests on the viewing podium, it was obvious that Her Worship was not the only one who had overindulged. There had been a long wait after their return to ground level while Health and Safety did what they do on such occasions. As fuses were checked for the umpteenth time the VIPs had been downing enough complimentary Cava to sink an armada.

Across the road at the bus stand a woman in a ketchup-coloured sari doled out free 99s from a Krishna Ices van to those not fortunate enough to have been invited to form the mayor's entourage. Girl Guides going all out for their hostess proficiency badge skipped about the field, pressing beakers of dilute orange squash on spectators.

The designated safety zone was crowded. It would have been more so had Kat not dispatched the estate's sizeable army of asthmatics both real and imagined to the Holiday Inn, where they'd be out of range of any dust fall-out and where an 82-inch HD screen had been installed.

On the red-carpeted podium beside Kat, Mel Dickson was dressed to kill in a floaty affair. Given her build, only someone as confident as Her Worshipful the Mayor could carry off an outfit like that. Levering herself from her gilt chair she inclined her expense-account hairdo and jangled a cluster of Indian bangles at a group of musicians in colourful blankets and Tibetan beanies. Los Paranoias, a mariachi band from Bognor Regis, picked up their cue and began punching out *"I like to be in Amer-ikah"* with much enthusiasm.

The residents' representative joined in, from his perch beside the mayor, pushing discordance to new levels.

'Cheethuth, somethink's landed on me boat,' he choked, adjusting the peak of his John Lennon cap which had failed to prevent a feathery drift from settling on his face. Dipstick thin in a filing-cabinet grey pin-stripe polyester suit, Cosmo King had the lined face of someone who had spent most of his life on a high-octane nicotine regime.

'Dust and feathers won't kill you,' Kat said, carefully edging out of range of the blast of extra-strong mint that had caused his temporary lisp.

It was unfortunate the mint had failed to hide evidence of his having eschewed the council's wine and and shored up beforehand with gin.

'Feathers? Try pulling the other leg. It ain't dust, neither.' He squinted up at the sky. More debris landed on his face. 'I don't Adam 'n' Eve it,' he said, in an attempt at cockney humour, although everyone knew he couldn't have found his way north of the River, let alone to within hailing distance of Bow Bells. King's faux-cockney image was about as credible as Dick Van Dyke's chimney sweep.

He glanced around to check the reaction, but all eyes were on the ugly building biting the dust. The media were getting all the shots they could ever want or need of a tower block being demolished by someone a deal more photogenic than the ubiquitous middle-aged white male in navy blue suit and hard hat.

They all knew the ignition had been fired by implosion experts, engineers, working behind the scenes. The showboating, however, went down well with residents who expected something besides free compost bins and seven-day library opening for their council tax.

Soon it was all over, bar the shouting. A few media folk remained, aiming cameras and iPhones randomly, without skill or fervour, but appreciating that it was names and faces that sold papers and provided them with second homes, kids' private schools and ski trips.

Kat straightened her spine, released her breath in a controlled whoosh, donned a confident smile and ignored her overheated feet. She'd lost a heel earlier and had been forced to ditch her smart sandals. It was her own fault. Had she worn sensible shoes from the start, the heel wouldn't have snapped as she hurtled out of the rent-free council flat that was home for the duration of her contract. She'd had to rummage through half-emptied removal boxes for an alternative. With only three pairs of shoes, excluding flip-flops or trainers, to her name, she ought to have been able to lay hands on something better than a pair of charity shop trainers, but she wasn't getting into a lather about upsetting any fashion gurus. Nobody was going to be looking at her feet today. With this redevelopment contract sufficiently lucrative to have taken the Inland Revenue off her back, despite sweaty trainers and a ticker tape of detritus, she was beginning to enjoy herself.

King continued to jig around like a demented stick-insect. It must have slipped his mind that the event was going out live over the internet. He seemed more concerned with the stuff floating onto them than the spectacle of the huge building being brought to its knees.

'Glad you made it down from the roof this morning without mishap,' whispered Mel Dickson, whose first initiative upon being appointed that year's mayor had been to copy the British royal family by taking lessons in speaking without moving her lips. A wise investment which enabled her to avoid the problems encountered by political colleagues who had their often imprudent asides lip-read to become meat for the tabloids.

Mel, as if to prove she had nerve endings of steel in her feet, was perched on designer heels high enough to let her see above rooftops without a ladder: pricey Christian Louboutins, judging by the trademark glossy red soles. Kat's centre of gravity was a little lower, courtesy of minor-designer barefoot technology trainers from Christian Aid, with their Grip-Tight anti-slip stick-ons.

'Don't you dare,' said Mel, catching the young community organiser smirking at the hundredweight of mayoral bling which was weighing down Bickeridge's premier citizen. 'It was Buggins's turn.'

'Muggins, you mean.'

'I wouldn't go that far,' Mel said. 'We all have to do it. It's not exactly living dangerously, and it's only for a year, after all. I get waited on, wined, dined and chauffeured, and travel first-class as befits my elevated station. Politics isn't only about fiddling expenses, or bungs for dodgy planning decisions. How about you? I haven't seen you for what? Two, three years? I couldn't gossip while we were up on the roof this morning. There was all that media stuff going on. Then you sloped off down the emergency stairs with that redhead in the Armani suit. What was that all about?'

'Neither of us fancied getting into the lift again,' Kat said. 'The upward journey was bad enough without doing the trip in reverse.'

The BBC had forecast the hottest April in thirty years. It had already hit thirty by mid-morning when Kat had been the last to board the lift waiting at the bottom of the condemned building. By the time she had been pressed into the wall of overheated bodies being transported to the mayor's roof-top photo-call, her hair had reverted to damp ringlets, and perspiration in the small of her back was trickling into her pants.

She shuddered, recalling that lift ride. Seconds after the machinery had lurched into noisy action, the lift's single fluorescent light had sizzled and died, to a chorus of groans and colourful expletives.

'That's politicians for you, keeping us in the dark,' somebody had sniggered.

'We've had worse than busted lights in here, darlin', retorted the gravel voice of a smoker, to a burst of strained laughter.

As the crowded, darkened lift had wobbled upwards, she was almost overcome by the overworked body spray and flatulence fighting for dominance with industrial-strength disinfectant. Despite the squeeze, however, she managed to wriggle around to face the other way, and was relieved to catch instead a faint whiff of expensive cologne.

There were worse ways to begin a job than putting on a posh frock to front the demolition of a tower block. Despite the recession, Kat had been lucky. Freelance work had been plentiful. It was only recently, as housing authorities began to fall foul of the cutbacks, that work had started to taper off. The job offer from Bickeridge Borough Council to trouble-shoot their down-at-heel Sir Patrick Moore Estate and speed it through a multi-million makeover had come at the right time for her bank balance. Her appointment had tied in nicely with the council's right-on, PC image. Racially ambiguous, she was their ideal poster child: single, female, same vintage as the condemned building, facts made much of in the council's press releases. In addition, and to the relief of the media-savvy politicians, she was not exactly bog ugly, although one councillor had been heard to comment that a photo-friendly disability would have been a bonus. Politicians never learn that you can't have it all.

It wasn't until the lift door scraped open and the man had asked for his arm back that she had noticed him in the shaft of light cutting through the doorway. Red hair overdue for a trim, he had the type of face you saw in glossy magazines escorting a willowy blonde. She took in the distance runner's build, rangy, enough muscle to avoid being skinny, nothing too showy. His lightweight summer suit could have paid off her mortgage arrears. Everything about him said posh – private school, Oxbridge, silver spoon – the whole cliché. Dark, thick lashes that were too good to be wasted on a man, and quite incongruous on a redhead. He'd smiled. She'd gawped.

'My arm? No rush; when you're ready,' he'd said.

Kat had nudged the cogs in her brain back into gear.

'I'm sorry,' she apologised, cheeks burning.

He was lucky she wore her nails short; propelled by the crowd, they had been moving out of the lift with her fingers sunk into his arm. It couldn't have been any more embarrassing. Yes it could. Her other hand had been clamped to his backside. She let go, flustered. Not too flustered, however, to notice the faint web of lines at the corners of his eyes, or the scatter of freckles where the sun had caught the fair skin.

She was letting herself get side-tracked, a sure sign that her social life was in a lean period. She needed to get out more.

'They say every journey is an opportunity to make new friends and get closer to people,' declared Mr Charm.

She gave him a glance that said he was talking bollocks.

'Closer to what? Packed into that death-trap, I doubt any of us had thoughts of becoming closer to anyone other than our Maker.'

Why was it always the ones with the nicest arses who tended to talk out of them?

'Never mind,' he had reassured her. 'The trip down'll be a doddle.'

'You think?'

It occurred to her that she might have been well advised to have drawn up a will before undertaking such a hazardous trip. However, with nobody to whom she could leave her overdraft, her microscopic flat, and the meagre sticks of furniture constituting her worldly goods, it wasn't worth the hassle.

The big question du jour, given her reluctance to use the lift again, appeared to be how the heck was she going to get down from that roof?

CHAPTER 2

Earlier that day, anybody who was anybody in Bickeridge had joined the mayor's entourage on the roof of Julie Andrews House to admire the panorama stretching from the Epsom racecourse in Surrey to beyond the 2012 Olympic Stadium in East London.

Below, well outside the danger zone, a fair had set up. Faint screams drifted up from children intent on annihilating each other in a state-of-the-art playground amongst the new cottage-style houses. In a garden where grass had not yet emerged someone was pegging out a line of football kit. Half a mile off the estate, two hooded figures guided by a third on crutches were pushing an upright piano uphill along the high street, causing a traffic jam and a tail back reaching beyond Sainsbury's.

In the haze that merged with the City of London's skyscrapers Kat could see the towers of the Barbican Centre, which had been the model for the Patrick Moore Estate. She had not set foot on the estate until that week although she had once driven through its canyons without stopping, half expecting a band of Apache to be lying in ambush. Afterwards she had claimed her car doors had locked themselves, sensing danger.

When it was built, back in the Seventies, someone had jokingly dubbed it 'The Moor' for the number of inhabitants rumoured to have served time on more institutional 'Moors' elsewhere. The post office people had given up demanding that they use the full name or bothered to put the 'e' on the end of the surname.

'I liked the way you sailed out of that lift,' Mel had murmured after the redhead had turned away to take photos with a swish-looking camera. 'You began with all the poise of a catwalk model. Such a shame you had to take a trip over that air vent.'

'I was tempted to administer a sharp elbow between that bloke's ribs when I heard him cover up a laugh,' Kat replied. 'But I had second thoughts after I'd seen what my sneeze had done to his posh shirt; he was covered in my make-up. I didn't look too closely to see what other unmentionables I might have deposited on his clothes. I decided I'd probably made us quits.'

Mel laughed. 'You might as well make the most of the view while you're up here.' she said. 'There aren't that many places you can see landmarks as far apart as the Epsom grandstand and Canary Wharf just by swivelling your head. When I was a kid, we used to come up here every Guy Fawkes' night just to get a free show of the firework displays half-way across London.'

The redhead had attempted to be sociable, asking how the view compared with that from the London Eye, the popular South Bank landmark which was rotating a few miles to the north, reflecting the sun. The single occasion Kat had been on the Eye she'd queued for an hour in rain. When she had finally elbowed her way into a thirty-person pod, she'd shared it with a bunch of French teenagers who had hogged the windows and squinted through the drizzle at the stainless-steel metropolis whilst making disparaging remarks about *les fous anglais*.

When she glanced down, she had the same tingle in her ankles now that she'd had then. But she was seeing more than she had from the Eye.

'Being twenty floors up and on top of a hill gives us the advantage,' she had said in reply to his comment about the view from the Eye. 'Hi, I'm Kat-with-a-K Shakespeare,' she added, diverting attention away from her surname and thus avoiding the predictable jokes.

'Hello, Kat-with-a-K. I'm Jack Ashton-with-two-As.'

Kat was tempted to point out that Smart-Arse made it four As, not two. She caught the quick gleam in his eye, and suspected he was ahead of her on that one. Best not to encourage him. She had an uneasy feeling that Mr Ashton found her amusing rather than attractive.

Mel had no such reservations. Seeing Ashton's VIP badge, the mayor had switched into practiced politician's mode, lipstick smile bright enough to warn ships off rocks.

'Mr Ashton, hello, I'm Mel Dickson, mayor of Bickeridge. I'm so glad you could be with us today. I do hope you're enjoying the view.' Mel had raised social gushing to an art form.

'Thank you, Madam Mayor, I'm impressed. I imagine the only place in South London with a better view must be the flight path into Gatwick,' he joked, glancing up at an Airbus or two circling overhead.

Had he been a local, Mr Smart-Arse Jack Ashton-with-two-As-or-four would know Gatwick used a more southern approach, over Kent.

Turning to correct him, Kat had been discomfited to see him aiming his swish Leica in her direction. Quickly swivelling around, she had gazed up at the jets stacking for Heathrow, and pondered upon the meaning of life, the universe, everything. And hoping she was showing her best side. That had been two hours ago. Now she brought her thoughts back to the present as she heard Mel talking to her.

'Health and Safety had kittens when you shot down those stairs earlier on,' Mel said as they watched the building disintegrate.

'Why? The stairs weren't roped off,' Kat replied. 'When they called time on the roof, I suspect the chatty Mr Ashton was casting around for an alternative to the lift as much as I was. Imagine the strain on the chain or whatever it is they use to hoist those things up and down. I'm sure I heard bits falling off as we came up.'

'Those stairs were for bona fide emergencies,' said Mel. 'What was he saying about your shoes?'

'Shoes? Trainers, you mean. I had hoped nobody would notice. I broke a heel as I came out, and changed into the first thing I could lay hands on. I'm still not unpacked. He said that given my footwear I shouldn't have any trouble keeping up, going down twenty flights, but that I was welcome to hang on to him if I needed help. Can't make up my mind if he was being sarky, or kind and sensitive, or cocky and patronising. But I wasn't going to look a gift horse in the proverbial, so I let him do the blokey thing and escort me down the stairs.'

'I'm surprised he's not here on the platform with us; he had a VIP badge,' Mel said.

'He's over there with that big copper in the flash uniform,' Kat replied, chinning her head towards a blue Land Rover, scruffy enough to cart sheep in, which was parked between a vandalised playground and the charred remains of a sports hut. On a nearby rectangle of concrete shuttering, men in orange vests and hard hats circled a silent cement mixer. The policeman's medals were catching the sun. He was a big man, beginning to show the sort of body fat that comes with business lunches and charity dinners. Someone with clout, the sort who addressed conferences, issued press statements, and did a lot of public speaking.

'The guy in the flash uniform's our local police head honcho, Liam Grant,' Mel said. 'But I've no idea who the fanciable redhead is. What was his name – Ashton? Since he took the trouble to introduce himself, I imagine you hadn't met him before, either.'

'Nope, never set eyes on him. I thought he was one of your lot, part of the council's setup. Dashing down those stairs didn't leave us any time for the social niceties. As soon as we reached ground level, off he went with his camera, and I didn't see him again,' Kat said. 'Oh, yuck. What's this?' She batted at debris that had flown into her mouth, in the process shunting into Mel, whereupon the mayor's centre of gravity shifted, sending her sideways into a man with more chins than were strictly necessary. He weebled into Cosmo King, the skinny residents' rep.

The two men wrestled against the ceremonial rope guard-rail before disengaging. The lightweight Cosmo immediately righted himself on the podium and adjusted his aviator shades. The other bounced like a space hopper in slow motion over the side and onto the faux grass no-man's-land around the podium.

'Bloomin' pantomime,' he grunted, hoisting himself back onto the platform. He must have fallen onto the only patch without a cosmetic covering of Astro-turf. There were stains on his cream trousers.

'Sod it!' Mel swore, flapping at a drift of feathery parachutes. 'My outfit's dry-clean only. Cost a blooming fortune. I wasn't expecting this.'

It was a view clearly shared by her colleagues. Hanging onto their plastic champagne flutes, they cowered under handbags, newspapers, whatever they could lay hands on. The finance director had whipped a large plastic bin liner meant to be for collecting litter afterwards over his head. He had torn a pair of holes at eye height.

'This is going to play havoc with everyone's clothes,' Mel protested. 'That'll mean more dodgy compensation claims in the council pipeline by mid-day tomorrow.'

'Oi, due respect, an' that, Mel, but 'ow about less rabbit, and a bit more getting around to doing something about the muck that's coming down on us all?' Cosmo King interrupted, in a linguistic misadventure that combined Sarf London and Cockney, all dropped aitches and glottal stops; they'd need subtitles if he kept it up.

'It's pretty,' Kat protested, admiring the snow-shaker effect.

'It's bird poop and seed and Lord knows what else, They may have emptied the place of pigeons but they were too bone idle to shovel up thirty years' worth of shit,' Mel muttered.

Behind them on the podium someone whimpered as a ticker tape of detritus landed.

'The fuss some people make over a little bird poop,' Kat said.

'Hey, fair does; it's feathers and bones, too,' Mel replied.

'Should've blown the dirty beggars to kingdom come years ago,' snapped King. 'Sod it, I'm havin' a fag.' Ignoring the tobacco ban, he lit up a cigarillo.

‘I want to go home,’ wailed a minuscule Brownie who had been waiting to present the mayor with a bouquet. She and her flowers were taking a hammering.

There were signs of activity at the Land Rover. The big policeman pocketed his phone, stuck a flashing Kojak light on the roof, and drove off. The redhead, Ashton, he of the swanky camera, seemed to have disappeared at the same time.

‘The Lord giveth, and the Lord taketh,’ Mel said with a heavy sigh.

‘Pervert,’ Kat laughed. ‘Come on, Mel, let's get this show under cover.’ She turned to the VIPs, some of whom seemed shell-shocked. ‘Ladies and gents, looks like the band’s going to keep on playing, but now might be a good time to take to the lifeboats.’

The councillors gazed like sheep seeking guidance, seeming alarmed at the prospect of making a decision without the benefit of a PowerPoint presentation. The officers, deadpan, dark suits, pale faces, were slumped in their hired gilt chairs, a discount offer from a wedding cancellation. Their body language implied that this was nothing to do with them.

Cosmo King was the first to show some gumption.

‘Dunno about you lot; I’m gettin’ a drink down me ferret.’ Clearing his throat noisily he did a pantomime dragon act of blowing smoke through his nose in an attempt to avoid inhaling feathers.

‘Gangway,’ bellowed an old woman who had been dozing in a garden recliner on the grass nearby. She wore a flowered Laura Ashley dress topped with a squashy straw hat that seemed to be advertising a Spanish donkey sanctuary. As everyone headed for the Maurice Mickelwhite Community Centre, people stepped out of range of the handbag she held in front of her like a weapon of mass destruction.

Not to be outdone, the skinny residents’ rep leapt up to get ahead but was too late to stop something nasty landing on his cigarillo. Kat caught the scent of barbecued poultry as he pushed past her.

CHAPTER 3

Concertina doors between the Maurice Mickelwhite Community Centre's hall and bar lounge had been opened to make one large room. The place was packed. With the council picking up the tab everyone was making the most of it.

Thirsty after all those feathers, Kat paused in her sideways shuffle towards the food. A vat of colourful liquid with fruit flotsam ebbing and flowing across its surface was being wheeled around on a trolley by an early-thirty-ish streaked-blonde squeezed into faux-zebra-skin leggings that would have been best left on the animal. The glass bead decoration on her cropped tee-shirt co-ordinated with her body piercings. She seemed familiar. Kat recalled Mel saying that on the Moor almost everyone was related.

'I wouldn't, if I were you,' warned the barman, flashing yards of expensive dentistry as he raised his voice above the babble. 'Shardonnay's fruit punch has been known to unblock drains. The mayor said you'd prefer red.'

'Sounds good,' Kat said. 'Thanks.'

The sheep dip Cava the council had supplied earlier clung to her taste buds. She watched him pour a generous measure of Rioja out of a bottle whose mesh sleeve suggested it might be head and shoulders above the supermarket plonk she was used to. As he poured, his turned-back cuffs revealed a square-faced designer watch.

'Here's gaffer tape for your frock,' he offered. 'If I didn't know what they cost, I'd swear that was an early McCartney.' He must either read the fashion magazines, or spend his down time shopping for dresses.

Kat didn't need her attention drawn to the pigeon mess on her eBay bargain. The image in the bar mirror said it all.

'Gaffer tape?' She eyed the glossy black spool.

'Wrap it round your hands, works like a clothes brush. Of course, I might be wrong and you could be hoping to make a fashion statement with feathers and unmentionables,' he said. 'Shame to let a nice frock go to ruin. By the way, those trainers lend a certain *je ne sais quoi*.'

'Yeah, well,' she laughed. 'I lost a heel, and the only thing I could find quickly were these. Thanks, er?' she squinted at his staff badge: *Barry Farthing*. 'Thanks, Barry. I'll sort it out in the ladies' once I've caught my breath back.

'Tape's here when you want.'

'Thanks,' she said, as he went back to shaving skin off lemons.

'Nibbles?' offered Shardonnay, the blonde in the zebra outfit. 'Home made, no preservatives; tinned salmon and peanut butter, peanut butter and anchovy, and smoked salmon special.'

Not if it came with peanut butter or anchovies, it wasn't special. Even on their own, peanut butter and anchovies were, like Marmite or boiled sheep's eyes, an acquired taste. Kat politely accepted a plate of canapés: smoked salmon special, with a strawberry garnish, a beetroot and horseradish bruschetta, and mashed aubergine blini with half a stuffed olive on top. Could have been worse. Nibbling delicately at the bizarre offering, she surveyed the crowd. Most of the media had taken off. No surprise, given the eccentric catering.

It was her first opportunity to examine the place. Well past its sell by, the Maurice Mickelwhite Community Centre was showing its age in the water-marked ceiling, abstract 1970s wallpaper and health-hazard carpet. She'd give odds on the multicoloured tablecloths hiding an all-over pattern of cigarette burns on the laminate tops.

There were faces she recognised, although few aside from Mel were from personal acquaintance. Guests sipped the home-made punch and chatted as they strolled around the exhibition of photos and posters showing how the estate had evolved from skylark heaven at the turn of the century to early between-the-wars airport and thence to award-winning Seventies housing which had ended up as a crumbling heap of leaking walkways and rusting trusses. Sixties blueprints showed plans for an eighteen-hole golf course complete with club house, five-star hotel and championship pool, although there was no evidence it had gone further than the design stage before the council had changed colour and the housing idea had taken over. Pictures from the roof of the now-defunct building, as well as the shots of today's demolition, were on display. In a close-up of a laughing Kat, folk not knowing any better might think the cleverly-out-of-focus shower was bridal confetti.

Guests had settled into fixed clumps. Apart from the mayor, nobody made an effort to circulate. No rush. Kat would discover who they were, in time. She wondered if the redhead would turn up. She squeezed with care through the tangle of mums, and toddlers in pushchairs. Small children made her uneasy. She had an idea she was lacking any maternal instinct. When she'd arrived at the children's home after the accident, traumatised, refusing to speak or eat, the nuns had given her a doll. It was the worst thing they could have done given the circumstances, but they weren't to know. They watched her, reassured, as she dutifully fed Tiny Tears its bottle and changed its nappy when it peed out the contents, and wiped its face when it cried to order. After a week, their vigilance relaxed, whereupon she had dropped Tiny Tears into the duck pond and watched the bubbles as it sank. Like mother, like daughter.

She glanced down at the pigeon mess augmenting the peacock pattern of her one posh frock and decided it was time to head for the cloakroom. Offloading Shardonnay's nibbles, which could have been recycled for building dry-stone walls, in a pile of used plates, she trusted that nobody, particularly the canapé queen herself, had seen. When someone grabbed her elbow she swung around, fearing she'd been sussed. It was Cosmo King, too preoccupied with his own problems to notice her manoeuvre with the canapés.

'Blimey, feels like me froat's bin cut,' he croaked. He grabbed a glass of punch off the trolley and chugged it down without breaking stride. A nanosecond later, he reared up, wide-eyed, spluttering.

'Gordon Bennet, what's in it, creosote? I'm gettin' a proper drink,' he gasped, rushing to the bar.

Shardonnay rolled Bollywood eyes at the nicotine ceiling and shook her head, exasperated, causing the rest of her to bounce. Her piercings set up a racket like a drawer-full of cutlery.

Kat continued across the room. Catching the wail of sirens she glanced out and saw it had begun to rain. A police car raced by, and in its wake, the vintage fire engine that had been crawling with small boys earlier. They were followed by the Pied Piper chimes of the ketchup-coloured ice cream van. There was no sign of the lorry convoy that had been carting rubble to landfill. Up and down the road there was evidence where, loaded to the gunnels, they'd broken off tree branches.

The podium had lasted the course, but the red carpet, AstroTurf and wooden planking had not, and children were dismantling the scaffolding. In the gravelled car park, three hoodies, one using a crutch for a bat, were lobbing stones at an animal sprawled motionless on a fence.

'Those ASBOs'll be the death of me,' King said, shedding flaky pastry crumbs from one of Shardonnay's sweetcorn vol-au-vents. Kat caught a hint of canned mushroom soup.

They watched as the boys tried to bounce the animal off the fence. A broken brick clanged as it ricocheted off a manhole cover, skimmed the fence, bounced on a plastic Euro-bin and hit an invisible object. There was a shriek of indignation from behind the fence. Doubled over, the trio ran off guffawing, led by the one on crutches. The animal remained so motionless it might have been an abandoned fur coat. An ambulance wailed by. At the podium, children continued dragging scaffolding away with lengths of yellow plastic clothes-line.

'It's the TV people again. I'm off for a shufti,' bellowed Cosmo King through a racket now augmented by the heavy engine growl and thunk of helicopter rotors. Parts of the room were vibrating.

'Reminds me of the blitz, sir,' said a fragile old gent in a too-large fleece who'd been propped up at the bar.

'Spritzer? Yes, sir, coming right up,' replied Barry who, in a lull, had been bidding for vintage Piaf records on eBay.

Across the room, Mel waggled her head towards the disabled loo. A handwritten sign on the door read: *'Reserved for Mayors and Disabled'*. Kat reckoned it must work on a similar basis to executive airline lounges, and took the mayoral head-waggle as an invitation to join her.

It was tough on anyone else needing a pee, but the sign meant they had the cloakroom to themselves. Cracked basins, fly-blown mirrors, and raised floor tiles. Kat whipped her posh frock off to soak in the one basin with a working plug. It wasn't every day she dressed for work in anything other than jeans and T-shirt. Then again, it wasn't every day she was photographed blowing up a London tower block.

'Thanks for flagging up this job for me,' she said. 'Much appreciated. The cuts were beginning to bite. I was about to get behind with the mortgage on the world's smallest flat and was contemplating cancelling my membership of the British Film Institute.'

'Blimey O'Reilly,' said Mel. 'Times must be bad for Miss Film Buff Extraordinaire. I thought you earned big bucks in your job.'

'Yeah, I do, as a general rule, but only as long as I keep in gainful employment. Work's been slacking off, lately. Before the advance on this contract, my bank balance was so low I swear it could have kissed the pavement without bending. It was nearing the stage where my accountant was about to suggest I took up busking on the London Underground for a living.'

'You could do this job with one hand tied behind your back,' Mel said. 'The Moor's going to be a doddle after the miracle you worked at Tower Hamlets last year.'

'It was touch and go, there, for a while, but thanks.' Kat turned back to the mirror. 'Oh, dear. Hello, Kung-Fu Panda,' she muttered.

Seldom bothering with anything more exotic than lip balm or kohl eyeliner, Kat had trowelled on enough makeup that morning to re-grout a house. The idea had been for it to stay on long enough for the picture session. Amongst the junk in her capacious tote there would in all likelihood be a few bits of make-up but could she be bothered?

'Your eyelashes have gone walkabout,' said Mel.

'I've not tried them before. One must have come adrift when I sneezed over that chap in the lift. Blessed things are about as much use as a dead parrot.' Kat picked the remaining lash off her cheek and binned it. Her hair, straightened to within an inch of its life earlier that day, was in tight Bride-of-Frankenstein-encounters-live-socket curls. The pigeon muck was an interesting add-on.

'That highlight-lowlight combo suits you,' she told Mel, checking for debris before using Barry's gaffer tape to attach her dress to the dryer. Lucky the fabric was so wrinkle-resistant it could be run over by a London bus without coming to any harm.

'My hairdresser charges a fortune for these multi-streaks,' Mel replied. 'I shall miss the perks when my mayoral year is up. Watch that drier. The blast is hot enough to launch a space probe, and you have to hit the button every thirty seconds or it'll grind to a halt.'

'Thanks for the warning,' Kat replied, smoothing Mel's Peach Creme onto her face. The mayor's minder always carried a vanity case of cosmetics and creams. Anything less would be slumming it.

'Good of you to let me use your stuff,' Kat said. Standing back, she frowned at her reflection. 'I'm too dark for anyone to mistake me for an English rose; it's given me a Co-op Funeralcare look.'

'Stick blusher over it,' Mel said without interrupting her feather plucking. 'Ow, my blessed arches are falling faster than share prices in these heels, but I don't dare slip them off. I did that at a charity do last month and some joker puked in them.'

'You're barking, buying such expensive shoes. Anyone's welcome to puke on mine,' Kat laughed. 'As long as I'm not in them.'

'Luckily they were only market stall knock-offs. But thanks for the sympathy. Not,' Mel said. 'I'd never admit it in public, but that pigeon mess was a hoot. I suspect the press will hang us out to dry.'

'Why? The council had the publicity it wanted. PR wise, I'd say the day's gone well. We didn't write off any *live* pigeons,' Kat reasoned. 'Is that a Gucci?' She'd focused on Mel's handbag.

'I wish,' Mel indicated the 'h' in the name under the faux bamboo handle. 'Another market-stall knock-off.' She glanced in the mirror, where a crack in the glass made both their faces lopsided. 'Listen, do me a favour? The press don't know that we first met when you sprung me from jail. I thought, maybe, as it's been so long, and in view of my position as Mayor and magistrate, you might like to, how can I put it?'

'You mean, don't mention the war? Or, to put it another way, peace demo, in case the media gets wind?'

'No, peace demo's cool. It's my sojourn in the nick I was thinking of. For myself, I don't give a monkey's. But it wouldn't go down too well among the citizenry if it was known that their duly-appointed mayor had been incarcerated in a police cell, albeit briefly.'

'What police cell?'

'Atta girl. I owe you.' Mel checked her watch. 'I must circulate. Let's have a proper drink together next week. In the mean–'

There were raised voices outside, a woman's shriek and the crash of a tray of glasses hitting the deck.

'Buggeration,' muttered Mel in language unbecoming a holder of civic office. 'What's wrong *now*?'

CHAPTER 4

Kat was wriggling into her still-damp dress as they rushed out into the community hall, where Cosmo King was holding forth, his cap and shades still in place.

'Yeah, I told you, but you were yakkety-yakking and not payin' attention. They've found a dead body in the rubble, right under Julie Andrews' bloomin' arse.'

Kat groaned. Pigeons aside, it had been going well until now. Not counting that morning's lift ride from hell. Or her broken heel. Or Shardonnay's catering. *But apart from that, Mrs Lincoln how did you enjoy the play*? Okay, not such a good day, then.

Overcoming the urge for an early night, she told herself that such scenarios such as this were included in the small print of her job description. She couldn't recall ever working on a site where they'd uncovered anything before, but she'd bet it would interfere with her schedule. They might have found a missing Battle of Britain pilot. The estate had, after all, been built on the site of an old aerodrome.

'You're not making sense, Cosmo. Slow down,' she begged. 'What do they think it is? Archaeological, Roman, Anglo-Saxon burial ground?' Watching him jerk from side to side made her dizzy. 'Sit down. Get him a drink, somebody.' She pushed a chair towards him.

'Not alcohol: never give alcohol for shock,' piped up the plummy tones of one of the opposition party councillors. She wore a pleated shiny taffeta dress that must have taken a skivvy all day to iron.

'I don't think he's in much danger, Councillor,' Kat reassured her. She doubted Cosmo King was in shock. She'd soon reached the conclusion that the self-appointed residents representative was more thick-skinned than a stand-up comedian. It looked like he was enjoying every minute of it.

'Pardon me,' the woman snapped. 'I've been an extra on *Casualty*, so I do have some medical expertise. But since you seem to know better, I'll let you get on with it. Then we'll see.' Without waiting for a response she stormed off, little feet going like a wind-up toy.

'We're not on telly, and this ain't Time Team.' King spoke rapidly. 'This is a live one. Well, not live, but ya know what I mean. One of the JCBs picked it up with the rubble. The police have closed the site, Gawd 'elp us. I wouldn't be surprised if there's more.'

Kat shivered although her hands were perspiring. King must have his wires crossed. If, as he claimed, it was not an ancient burial, the likely alternative was that it was the result of some long-ago gang-related incident from the Moor's murky past.

The Sir Patrick Moore Estate, aka the Moor, was an anomaly straddling the boundary between South London suburbia and the Surrey merchant banker belt. To the police and emergency services, pizza deliverers, and to politicians canvassing for support every fourth year, it was Comanche Territory, a place best avoided. However, despite its maze of concrete blocks and waterlogged walkways it was no inner city slum ghetto, despite stories about how, when they'd hit pay dirt by winning a Euro grant worth millions to rebuild the estate nine years earlier, the chief planning officer and the council's deputy leader had taken bets on how long it would take for the first of the bodies to surface. Bodies which according to local legend may have ended up in unmarked graves during the South London gang wars of the early seventies. However, bang went any chance of a payout after the wily politician did a runner to the Algarve with the takings and the wife of his chief planning officer, one step ahead of the Fraud Squad. The subsequent scandal forced political change upon the council, after which no more was said, heard, or seen of body parts ancient or modern.

Voices tailed off. Eyes darted around the room. It was as if people expected someone other than King to step forward and explain what was happening, but like actors in some dire television soap, they'd missed their cue.

In the silence Kat heard the fridge thermostat in the kitchen click off. Two of the hoodies sneaked into the room aping cartoon burglars and loaded up with food. Nobody else had noticed. Giggling, the two ran off with their booty to join their mate who had been keeping lookout, lounging on his crutches against the mobile phone equipment cabin.

'I thought those sirens was the television people come to do some more filming for The Bill,' someone whispered.

There were murmurs of agreement. The run-down estate had always generated an income as a location for gritty detective dramas. Typically, whenever the genuine Bill arrived, everybody headed for the hills, but if it was film trucks and Range Rovers loaded up with uniformed actors they'd rush out demanding food, cash to keep the kids quiet, or jobs as extras. Sometimes all three.

'No, mate, it's the real McCoy.' King jiggled his left foot. 'They put barriers across, vans, blockin' the view. Half the blooming Met's over there. So I come back here.'

'Are you sure someone's actually been killed?' Kat hoped he was wrong. 'What exactly did they say?'

'Just that they'd found human remains,' King admitted. 'I reckon someone might have followed you and the ginger bloke down those stairs this morning and got themselves trapped when the place went up.'

'Nobody followed us. We checked everyone in and out; there was a roll-call, if you remember.' She stopped.

Electronic arrangements of Vivaldi's Four Seasons, The King's Speech theme and several versions of ABBA songs had broken out around her. The news had buzzed around the estate. People were receiving calls from their nearest and dearest.

King had used words like *killed* and *died*, but there was a subtle difference. Kat couldn't believe anyone had been caught in the blast. She hoped it was a false alarm and the police activity would turn out to be part of a TV night shoot, after all, although she was inclined to think not. In huddles around the room, those whose loved ones were safely located competed to come up with grisly scenarios to explain what might have happened. Nobody had any idea who, if anyone, could have been caught in the blast. It was unfortunate that by the time the body had been discovered in the debris, much of the rubble, together with any clues or evidence it might have contained, had already been on its way to landfill. Guessing games would have been useless. When it became apparent that no further information was likely to be forthcoming that night, people began to drift away, bringing the civic celebrations to an end.

One of the last to leave, Cosmo King was continuing to insist someone must have been stranded on the roof after that morning's mayoral photo-call. The huffy opposition councillor in the permanent pleats suggested it might be a suicide by 'some care in the community creature who hadn't taken their medication'. King disagreed, but they were united in their blame of the council's ruling party for allowing anyone onto the roof in the first place.

'Time for bed said Florence,' Barry carolled, flashing his faux-designer watch. 'Go home, or there'll be nothing left to drink but Toilet Duck and it'll all be my fault as usual.'

'A doggy bag?' said Kat, as he handed her a plastic container.

'Welcome to the Moor,' he said. 'Cake: I made it, not Shardonnay, so you're okay. Cheer up. The sugar will make you forget your troubles. Listen, don't worry. It'll turn out to be a communications cock-up. Par for the course, around here.'

Mel agreed. 'Cosmo exaggerates. At worst, it's much more likely to be a passer-by just knocked out by flying debris. I'd better go. I'm staying at my gran's tonight. We'll talk tomorrow.'

Mel had sent her mayoral entourage home. The old lady with the straw hat and aggressive handbag, grandma, at a guess, seemed to be enjoying the drama and was reluctant to leave until Mel told her the booze had run out. With her was an obese young man with fluttery eyes and an institutional haircut who seemed content to go along. Barry ushered them out and set the alarm.

'Want to share a brolly?' he asked Kat. He lounged against the doorjamb, ankles crossed, brimmed hat angled, umbrella on shoulder, posed. Such a pity the cameras had gone home.

'London may appear romantic at night in the rain,' he said. 'The rest of us don't.'

'Speak for yourself,' Kat said. 'I'm fine. My flat's right here.'

'Not as here as you think. There's a ruddy great builders compound in the way. You won't find your way through the mess. You don't know what you might walk into in the dark. I need the exercise; I'll keep you company.' He walked beside her.

Floodlights made the demolition site resemble the entrance to Eurotunnel. The police chopper had gone. The rain was stopping. The air was muggy with the faint baby-sick, herby, burnt-popcorn aroma of high-rise home-grown. Pre-dawn raids regularly uncovered hash farms in bedrooms and sheltered balconies. The super-glued letter boxes, dark blinds, permanently closed windows, sophisticated security systems, and electricity cable sneaking from street lamp to bedroom window were a dead giveaway.

Rounding a corner they came across the three Asbo kids sharing a smoke. Hooded-up against drips from the overhead gutter, the boys sprawled on a sofa sprouting its innards. They were surrounded by car batteries and cooker parts, and were showing great sense in using discarded piles of the local freebie Bickeridge Bugle for cushioning.

'When shall we three meet again?' carolled the one with the crutches. His teeth were encased in an insane orthodontic Meccano set.

'Yeah,' chipped in the curly one. *'In thunder, lightning, or in rain?'*

'I'm hallucinating,' Kat whispered to Barry.

'Naw, Petal. It's your surname that's done it,' Barry explained. 'You ain't heard nuthin' yet. They're on a drama workshop programme for young offenders. This term it's *Macbeth*. Their first attempt was *Hamlet*. They had a spot of bother with that one when they rustled up a real skull for poor Yorick. The Bugle ran a front page asking what was wrong with society that unruly teenagers can desecrate graves. It was picked up by the media. The National Theatre's press officer went on TV and claimed it was traditional to use the skull of a real person when they did Hamlet. Not to be outdone, Party Poppers in the town centre contacted the Beeb to say it was one of their plastic glow-in-the-dark novelty skulls. Red faces all round. Party Poppers made a killing at a fiver a throw. Skulls were turning up all over the place. The boys started a scrapbook. They're doing *West Side Story* next. Lord knows what they'll come up with. Don't play up to them or they'll never stop.'

'Night, boys,' she and Barry chorused.

'Good night, Kate,' the boys sang out.

Kate? Leave it. She wasn't prolonging the agony by correcting them.

'Night, Bazza,' trilled the trio, sharing their roll-up under the tarp.

'Bazza?' she asked, when they were out of earshot.

'Hangover from my football days.'

'Football? Really?'

'Just because I dress well doesn't mean I'm a bad footballer,' he said, picking a careful path through dog mess. The poop bins were overflowing with disposable nappies and beer cans. At the end of the alleyway they passed a piano. Someone had been practicing nail art on the keys. There was a red fire bucket on the top containing a bunch of plastic flowers. They crossed the main road.

'That was another life. Before I got beaten up I was a rugby fly half. I've put on weight since then and I keep a lower profile these days. Remind me to tell you about it when we know each other better.

'I'll hold you to that,' she said. 'If someone really has been caught in the demolition it's going to make the news in a big way. The newshounds will be all over the estate like flies on cows.'

'Not much we can do about that,' said Barry. 'I wouldn't worry too much about it. Meantime, d'you want anything to help you sleep?' He stopped as they reached her stairs.

'No, thanks,' she laughed. 'I'll make do with a cup of tea, some of your cake and a bath. All at the same time.'

'Good. Get some sleep, Petal. Worse things happen.'

'Not if you're the poor bugger in the demolition,' she replied.

'Yeah. See you tomorrow. Sleep tight.'

She let herself into the flat. The stuffiness after being closed up all day failed to hide the scent of eau de pigeon she brought in with her. Forget the tea. A bath, glass of Merlot and a chunk of Barry's cake would sort that. She had glimpsed Red Maraschino cherries and cream through the opaque plastic container. Dumping her tote, she placed the cake on the tiny hall table and levered off her trainers.

A furtive scuffling sound from behind the living-room door sent what felt like a chorus line of ants tap dancing along her spine. The metallic taste of fear rose in her throat. Grabbing her bag from the floor she rummaged for a weapon. Big girls don't need tazers if there's an aerosol handy. She once knew a woman who never went out without her super-hold hairspray. Fully armed, she flung the living-room door open, ready to deodorise to death any burglar face on.

Something the size of a tank slammed into her. Light exploded across her eyes, like watching a fast-moving 3-D movie without special glasses. For a weird moment, before everything went black, she thought she was being attacked by a troop of winged monkeys. Wrong again. That had been Dorothy and Toto.

CHAPTER 5

Detective Inspector Jack Ashton had been stuck on twenty-three across for fifteen minutes, despite the boost from a second Danish. They hadn't rolled home until dawn from planning Liam's stag bash. Now he wanted a caffeine kick-start, but all he'd had was grief from Liam's new Japanese halogen-powered all-singing, all-dancing coffee machine. It was going to take someone with a degree in electrical engineering and months of training to operate it.

Superintendent Liam Grant, bridegroom-to-be, old school friend, joint owner with Ashton's twin sister of the piece of wizardry that had arrived gift-wrapped two days earlier, had disappeared, along with everyone else at Bickeridge nick. The prison van had also long gone. The cells in the basement were empty apart from a leftover from last night who, judging by the repeated caterwauling of *'Yellow submarine, yellow submarine, yellow submarine,'* hadn't sobered up in time for court. Discounting a few civilians in admin there was no-one in the building aside from a world-weary sergeant attempting to repel boarders in reception. Ashton had the place to himself. Officers were tied up with yesterday's skeleton from the Moor estate.

Liam Grant's disappearance had scuppered Ashton's plans and he was hacked off. He had a limited number of leave days to finalise the nuptials. It had all gone adrift when the superintendent became caught up in case briefings, leaving his best man, Ashton, with a half-completed Telegraph crossword for company and an invitation to help himself to coffee. Fat chance, when neither he nor anyone else could work the machine. The actor whose coffee was hijacked by glamorous models in the TV commercial had things easy.

Stretching, he rotated his neck, then swivelled in the superintendent's Mastermind chair to gaze out of the sash window.

Bickeridge nick was a suburban Old Scotland Yard, all red brick and white horizontal stripes. It faced the town hall, which had been recycled from an old cinema, Monumental Pictures. No inspiration there, or from the two blue lamps on their red-brick pillars outside his window. In the street below, damp umbrellas jabbed blindly for space between plastic-swathed buggies skidding across the lights. It would have made a good picture. A trail of empty buses splashing back to the garage had him regretting leaving his camera at home that morning. He'd captured some good stuff yesterday. They'd forecast a heat-wave again. The radio had talked of a hose-pipe ban this morning despite the rain bucketing down. Wrong sort of rain, apparently. Probably the same wrong sort of rain that was stopping play in Ahmadabad.

'A domestic break-in, madam?' he heard through the open door. 'I've no-one here at the present time,' the duty sergeant said as Ashton doodled matchstick men on gibbets amongst the scribble of anagrams in the newspaper margin.

'Could you come to the station to make a –? Oh. Should I send medical assistance? No, I see, best not,' continued the sergeant. 'I'll ask the community support team to call round.'

Yawning, Ashton gave up on the matchstick men, returning to twenty-three across and tried to shut out the desk sergeant's voice.

'Kat, with a K. Right, I've got that,' the voice broke in.

Ashton stopped in mid yawn, almost dislocating his jaw. When Liam Grant had been too busy to attend the mayor's rooftop photo-call the previous day, and given that rain had also stopped yesterday's play, Ashton, at a loose end, had used the superintendent's invitation, hoping it might turn into an interesting photo opportunity. Which it had.

Up on the roof, he had sussed that the woman's reluctance to get back into the lift had been as great as his. The upward journey had been bad enough, particularly when the machine jolted to a stop after her gigantic sneeze had exploded like an aeroplane-loo flush. He had been convinced it'd damaged the mechanism and would mean they'd have to be winched to safety by the fire brigade. However, before he'd had time to get on his mobile to call for assistance, the doors had scraped open. Afterwards, amongst the Technicolor drift of make-up which her sneeze had left on his shirt he'd found a fake eyelash which, for one panicked moment, to Liam's amusement, Ashton had mistaken for a spider.

The plans for his twin's marriage to his best friend had been the main item, aside from lunch together, on today's agenda. Not much else was going on. He couldn't even look forward to a television replay of yesterday's cricket from Ahmadabad since they'd had rain for two days on the trot.

He slid his loafers off the desk. Balancing his chair on its back legs he found he could eavesdrop better. It'd do him good to get out, never mind that he wasn't on his own patch. Nor could he by any stretch be considered dressed for the job, lolling about in a casual shirt, chinos, and no socks. If he was lucky, it might pass for undercover in this neck of the woods. The locals could probably do with a little help.

Abandoning twenty-three across, he strolled into reception, where, if the lugubrious officer behind the mesh-strengthened security screen felt any surprise at the visiting police inspector's unsolicited offer to help out on a simple domestic break-in, he wasn't letting on.

'Yes, sir. Always good to get down to the coalface.'

Liam had once told him that the local constabulary, on the rare occasions they ventured into the Moor, went mob handed, heralding their arrival with full 'blues and twos', shorthand from when police cars were blue and had flashing Kojak lights and two-toned sirens, and counted on the troublemakers being sufficiently warned by the noise to have gone underground by the time they arrived. It saved on paperwork.

The sergeant didn't have much in the way of options. It was a simple domestic break in, after all. No reason why an off-duty copper from another division couldn't help out if nobody was available.

'I'll try to raise the estate sergeant or one of the constables,' he said. 'Get them to meet you there, sir.' Which roughly translated meant he'd get someone there in time to prevent Ashton making a pratt of himself.

'Thank you, Sergeant. Could you tell the superintendent when he shows,' Ashton said over his shoulder. 'I'm nicking his wheels.'

CHAPTER 6

Ashton parked Liam's Land Rover in full view on the main road opposite the address the sergeant had given him for Kat-with-a-K. Her flat was the first in a block of units built at first and second level above ground floor fly-tipped garages. The place was a dump, the only sign of life a plastic bag performing elegant cartwheels on the pedestrian deck. Graffiti on the stairs and boarded-up windows reinforced his view that schools had given up teaching spelling years ago. They didn't spend time on anatomy, either, judging by the artwork.

The walkway was wide enough to drive a road through, but the paving was cracked and weeds grew up to the boarded front doors. With the addition of a few sandbags he could have been in Beirut.

The community support sergeant had beaten him to it.

'You found us all right then, sir,' she said as she answered his cheerful shave-and-a-haircut knock.

'Yes, no problem, thank you, Sergeant,' he said, trying not to stare at the officer's fringe while trying to decide whether or not it had been painted on under her little Lego bowler hat.

The flat was small: narrow hall, door leading into a bathroom. a kitchen whose window overlooked the deck, L-shaped living room and a bedroom. Windows in both would have looked across the road at the Community Centre if the builders' compound hadn't blocked the view.

In the living room clothes were dumped haphazardly on a sofa draped with a multicoloured knitted blanket, a sagging wing chair, and a wicker theatre basket used as a table. In a corner an old-fashioned three-tiered wooden hostess trolley struggled to remain upright under an ancient television attached to an equally ancient video player. Books covered the floor, the bookcase having collapsed onto a carpet of lime green shag-pile that needed a mow.

There were no pictures or ornaments apart from an old-fashioned desk toy, a perpetual motion cradle with steel marbles that knock each other and need a little push to set them off: clack-clack-clack. Someone with a sense of humour, a steady hand, and time to spare, had painted a face on each of the five balls – Grumpy, Happy, Sleepy, Bashful, and Dopey. The flat was bereft of potted plants, although she might have been trying to grow something on the kitchen windowsill, and there were enough palm trees on the wallpaper to reforest the Amazon basin.

In the kitchen, Kat-with-a-K sat scrunched at the strawberry patterned Formica table. Ashton didn't need his police training to deduce that she might not have made it into bed last night. No more had he, but he'd been at a party into the wee small hours, whereas she looked like she might have spent the night in a ditch. Her eyes were closed. She still wore yesterday's dress, now looking as limp as its owner. Today's fashion accessories were a pair of dark bags under her eyes and the bruise coming up on her forehead.

'Hello,' he said, warrant card held out as a votive offering.

As she sat up her dress rode up, failing to cover her thighs. Nice. She noticed his glance and straightened her clothes before placing her hands on her lap: Miss Prim. Her bare feet looked a lot better now that she had shed yesterday's disreputable footwear. She can't have imagined they'd ever have lent the perfect finishing touch to her dress.

'Your feng shui's gone to pot,' he quipped, wondering if he'd pronounced it correctly. Feng shui didn't get much of an airing around police stations. He couldn't tell if the stare he got was because he'd mangled it, or because he sounded pretentious. He suspected the latter.

'We weren't properly introduced. DI Jack Ashton, filling in for the locals. They're busy investigating the human remains that have been found.' He placed his warrant card on the table, face up.

'A policeman?' she said, with the dazed expression of a daytime TV quiz contestant trying to make sense of random consonants and vowels before a jingle signals their time is up. 'I didn't... never mind. Sorry: my brain's fuzzy.' She frowned, rubbed the side of her forehead, wincing as she came across the shiner. 'I don't want to sound ungrateful, but could you whisper? Got a headache.'

'I'm sorry to hear that,' he said.

'Thanks,' she said. 'Bad karma, I expect.'

'Well, you do seem to get your share of bad luck. This is two days on the trot: the lift, the pigeon muck, and a break-in. Maybe you should stay indoors for a while, keep a low profile.'

He didn't as a rule joke or spout insensitive garbage to the victims of crime. Lottie and Liam's pre-wedding palaver must be rotting his brain.

'Low profile?' She snorted down her nose at him, 'You mean leave my clothes on a beach, get a new identity, and go hide up a gum tree with Shergar and Lord Lucan. Don't think so. I've got a job to do.'

Miss Kat-with-a-K didn't appear to suffer fools. He'd asked for that snub. Given his outfit and all the flannel about feng shui, she must think him as camp as a Christmas cracker.

The squeak of rubber soles heralded the arrival of the community support team. He shifted further into the kitchen. They sounded keen. He supposed it must make a change from chasing library fines or nicked hubcaps while their colleagues were having the time of their lives investigating the business across the road. If they hung around the accident-prone Kat-with-a-K there was a good chance of enough excitement to last them a lifetime.

The quartet wore short-sleeved pale blue shirts under identical regulation stab vests, and utility belts that bristled with enough equipment to storm Baghdad. For all the notice Kat took of their ID, they could have flashed their supermarket loyalty cards. Ashton did a quick check that no-one had. He leant in to examine her bruise.

She flinched. 'What the–'.

He expected her to shoot off another stinger, but she sank back.

'Sorry, bad hair day. Don't mind me. It's only a bump.'

'If you say so,' he said. 'Head injuries can be deceptive. Sergeant, bell the incident site, get a medic over here.'

'Yes, sir,' said the sergeant. She'd been staring across the deck, wondering if all this activity would mess up her holiday. An overfilled skip, boarded-up flats and acres of grey slab was no competition for herds of wildebeest sweeping majestically across the plain.

A cell phone propped on the windowsill suggested opportunities for a signal inside the flat might be limited. Luckily the sergeant chanced on a live spot straight away. Meanwhile, the constables clattered about the flat sounding like boy scouts loaded up for a cross-country hike, their utility belts jangling each time one of them bent to peer into, under, over or behind furniture.

Ashton smiled slightly as he watched Kat hoist herself upright again whilst she attempted to keep her thighs modestly covered.

'Shall we get to work?' he asked. 'Or do you want to hang on for the medic?' He scanned the kitchen. 'Can I get you a coffee?'

'Sorry, pot's broken. There's green tea somewhere.'

'Never mind. We'll manage without.' He eyed the broken glass on the cork tiles. 'Comfortable? Then we'll begin. From the top.'

Kat eyed him, and remained waiting.

'Would you like to begin?' he asked.

'What about making some notes?' she said.

Whenever Ashton saw a television copper reach for his little notebook, he switched channels. He couldn't stand robotic investigating officers who automatically began scribbling away in the regulation pocket-size spiral jotter. He never used one. All his work was in his camera, but he was meant to be on leave: today was for talking about wedding stuff, then lunch with the happy couple. It was a long time since he'd done the scene-of-crime notebook-and-interview routine. Not wishing to disappoint the lady, he took out his diary hoping she wouldn't recognise it as such if he kept a hand over the cover. As he took out his classy faux-silver pen, he caught an exchange of eye-rolling between Kat and the sergeant which suggested that real-ink pens might be a touch pretentious on the Moor.

'Tell me what happened,' he said, examining his diary which was masquerading as a police notebook. The otherwise blank page appeared to consist only of a list of suit measurements for Liam's wedding ushers. He glanced up, to check she hadn't sussed him for a fraud, but her eyes were closed. He coughed gently.

On the point of dozing off, Kat straightened up.

'I came in, heard a noise, went to look, and bam, wham, kapow, I got zonked,' she said, sounding happier now he was making notes.

He jotted down *"Bam, wham, kapow, zonked, Batman fan?"* on the first empty page with enough care to suggest his notes were destined to be used as evidence in a landmark murder trial at the Old Bailey.

'My eyes are gritty,' she complained.

'Medic'll be here soon,' he said. 'How about a cold flannel?'

'Naw. I'm all right, thanks.'

'Okay. Everywhere's boarded up. Are you the only one still here?'

'The whole of this side's empty, sir, due for demolition,' said the sergeant. 'In my humble opinion, anyone living here on their own must need some bottle.' Deadpan, having said her piece, she returned to gazing out of the window.

'Yup, sometimes necessity is the mother of bottle. However, this place comes rent free with the job. I'm on 24-hour call,' Kat explained. 'The council says my being here will deter vandals.'

'Why would they think that?'

'That's the theory, anyway. I'm not going to argue with them while I can rent out my own flat and live here for free: beats spending a fortune on petrol. My car's not exactly the latest eco-model.'

That ageing rust bucket he'd passed on the way in must be hers, but he decided to pass on that. Not so, the sergeant.

'Is that your car downstairs with half a garden shed on the back? Looks like it's had a good kicking,' the woman officer chipped in. 'It's never going to get through its MOT.'

'It's a classic eighties wood-trim Mini Traveller, and it is MOT'd. In my line of work I can't go around splashing out on posh wheels.'

'What work *do* you do,' Ashton asked. No job deserved this place. However, if she wasn't earning much she'd be glad of a freebie.

'I'm a Tenants' Friend.'

'Tenants what?'

'Friend. It's shorthand for all sorts: negotiating community rights, dishing out advice, liaising with the authorities, sorting out race or gender issues, trouble-shooting,' she explained. 'This project was going down the pan while they wasted time arguing about everything from roof tiles and front door colours to which end they have the bath taps. I've got four months to whip it into shape or they lose their funding.'

'I wish you luck,' said the sergeant, a sceptic.

'Sounds as if you'll need it,' Ashton added. 'Back to this break-in. You arrived home.' His pen spurted dollops of ink over the table. 'Sorry about that. Have you a pencil I could use?'

Kat passed him a packet of wipes and indicated a green and purple *Votes for Women* mug bristling with pens on the microwave.

Ashton saw that unlike the coffee pot, the mug was in one piece. In fact, there were no broken ornaments, no emptied or splintered drawers, no ripped upholstery, no upended or smashed furniture. No sign of forced entry. Not the signature of a classic break-in. The general untidiness he put down to her being out all day and half the night. He didn't think of her as the type to be lolling around waiting for Hello magazine to call. Pity her cafetière was broken, because he could have murdered a coffee right now. He finished mopping up the ink. The place needed proper kitchen furniture. An electric socket dug into his back when he sat down. The flat might have been fitted out for some aged pensioner with a decreasing bone mass. Ashton could have touched both walls at once without stretching. One of his legs had gone to sleep. Where had the medic got to?

'How did you leave this place yesterday?' he asked.

'In a hurry. I don't obsess about tidiness,' she replied.

Must've been some hurry, Ashton thought. Who knows what microbes and bacteria the place was fermenting.

'Life's too short for housework,' she said, giving him a narrow-eyed welfare benefit officers' glare. 'It's not as if I expect anyone to perform open heart surgery here.'

'With all respect, it is a bit of a mess.'

'Yeah, well, it's not usually this bad. Must've done something wrong to justify all this bad karma coming at once.'

Although Ashton didn't know his karma from a cabbage he wasn't admitting to that gap in his education.

'I'd kill for a coffee,' she said. 'I bought some yesterday but there's nothing to make it in. C'est la blooming vie, n'est ce pas? Anyway, where was I? Yes. When I came to, I took headache stuff and I rang the police station.' She leant back against the wall and closed her eyes.

She was coping well. Her clothes and her hair were a mess, she had a massive shiner, but she could still spout clichés in execrable French and joke about karma, Lord Lucan and missing racehorses. He stretched his legs in the economy class space under the little table and hoped the medic arrived soon. It tickled him that with her desk toy with its five painted dwarf faces, once Doc arrived, they'd soon have the full cast under Miss Sneezy's roof. As he turned aside, trying not to laugh, he saw she had an old-fashioned enamel tea kettle.

'Listen, why don't I make coffee? Failing all else, I'll use the kettle.' He ignored the sergeant's throaty imitation of an automatic rifle. 'You stay there. I'll do it. Where do you keep the biscuits?'

'I don't. Never eat them.'

'I do, and you need sugar and carbs. What else have you got?'

CHAPTER 7

The community support team were rooting around in corners and cupboards as if they were trying to find something worth donating to the Oxfam shop. Kat nursed her bruise and watched Ashton make coffee. There seemed to be a dead yak in her mouth. Not surprising, after a night spreadeagled alongside her collapsed IKEA bookcase.

She had a vague memory of coming to once or twice during the night and making feeble efforts to get upright, but that it had set her off on a roller coaster. She had been better off where she was. When she did wholly surface, it had been daylight. Comfortable though it had been on the floor, if she stayed there much longer she risked some joker drawing a chalk line around her. Placing one foot in front of another with great care she had shuffled half-way down the hallway before becoming entangled in her bag. The usual string of profanities had made her feel no better, but it had at least proved she was alive.

She'd rummaged around in her tote for a strip of Codeine, a leftover from a holiday haul, where chemists weren't fussed about prescriptions. The fridge-cold milk hit her fillings when she'd washed them down. Her one injury seemed to be a sore head. The flat appeared more damaged than she. There wasn't much to steal. No self-respecting burglar would want her stuff: wardrobe and decor by Oxfam or Christian Aid, ditto her ten-year-old telly. Bureaucracy had obliged her to report the break-in so as to get a crime number for the council's insurers. Now her flat was crawling with coppers and cloudy with fingerprint powder.

Expecting an overweight pair of community constables on her doorstep, the redhead's arrival had come as a bonus. Yesterday, given his VIP badge, camera, and chat-up line, she would not have been surprised to learn that he was part of the council's PR or press machine rather than a policeman. He'd settled into her kitchen pretty fast, too.

The moment he turned the tap on, the airlock had set up a staccato hammering that had nearly ripped the radiators off the walls, but he seemed to know from instinct where to bang the pipe to get water. In the absence of biscuits, his radar had homed in on Barry's cherry cake. He was right: she needed a caffeine and sugar pick-me-up; her head felt pumped full of cavity-wall insulation.

He gave her the first slice of cake, cut smaller pieces for his mates, and, no surprise, helped himself to a larger chunk which he demolished before the coffee had brewed. She was about to take her first mouthful when a belt of the electronic door chimes made her jump, and her nose hit the cake. Wordlessly, Ashton handed her the wet wipes to get rid of a cherry large enough to raise funds for Comic Relief.

The medic who squeezed through the narrow hall had push-bike handlebar eyebrows which had long given up any idea of following a line above the eyes. He must have been nearing retirement age, but he would never be out of work as long as kids believed in Santa.

'Cake? Lovely, thanks. Let's go to it,' he said cheerfully, gloving up. He prodded her head with surprising gentleness for someone with hands the size of Christmas turkeys, all the while keeping up a barrage of questions without waiting for answers. How did she feel? Did she have any trouble staying awake? Was there any dizziness, any nausea? Had she a headache? Had she put any money on the Grand National winner last Saturday? Could she see two of him, or hear whistles or bells or invisible armies whispering in her head? Could she recite her mobile phone number from memory? She couldn't? No matter; most people couldn't, either. How about her bank account sort code and PIN number? Very funny. Not. Fifteen minutes later, he'd almost done.

'No head-stands for a while; other than that, you're all right,' he advised. 'A minute or two more, while I give your hair some attention. Don't wriggle, woman, I'm not hurting you.'

Giving up the struggle to get comfortable at the table, Ashton had moved away to lean against the wall. Back braced against the corner, he was oblivious to the large spider working its way down from the ceiling. He finished his second chunk of cake and continued drinking his coffee with the concentration of someone focused on survival.

'Great cake,' the medic mumbled through a mouthful. 'You're not a cordon bleu cook, by any chance?' Crumbs floated down above Kat's head, breaking her concentration on the spider.

'Do what?'

'Cake. Home-made,' he said. 'Cordon bleu cookery class?'

'No, I'm a one-ring, one-pan, ready when the smoke alarm goes off, more cordon noir than bleu,' she said, and saw the inspector smirk.

'They left this place a tip,' the doc mumbled through cake crumbs.

'Actually, it's hard to say what's different from when I went out yesterday,' she admitted. She turned. 'By the way, did they really find a body last night? Or is that a figment of Cosmo King's fevered imagination? I gather nobody's been reported AWOL on the estate, you know. Do you think someone was caught up on the roof or in the building by accident? Perhaps it was a suicide getting in before the last high-rise disappeared,' she said in a non-stop string.

Ashton finished his third slab of cake. 'I'm afraid that's confi–'

'Let the poor wee girl out of her misery,' the doctor said as he swabbed her head. 'Yes, they did find remains. You needn't worry about accidents, suicides or serial killers on the loose or anything remotely threatening. The poor soul they found is long gone. The man's a skeleton, must have been there for years. They'll have their work cut out, identifying him. I would have only been a houseman at St George's then, didn't go into general practice until later, so I don't know him. They say he's probably a victim of the Seventies' gang wars.'

'A skeleton? So that's why nobody's reported anyone missing,' she said. 'Some of the locals were convinced it was one of them. The press have been shouting the odds about the estate being unsafe at night.'

'There's nothing for you to worry about. Let's concentrate on your break-in,' said Ashton. His hair had fallen forward. She watched him flip it back without pausing in his scribbling in what was clearly not a regulation police issue notebook.

'There's a sticky substance in the lounge,' the sergeant called from the living room. 'I'll give CSO a bell.'

The sergeant was either a congenital optimist, which Kat doubted, or she still hadn't realised the significance of the phone parked on the kitchen windowsill. Unless she hit the right spot, as before, she would never get a signal through all that reinforced concrete. The flats were built to withstand a nuclear blast.

The turbaned PC went off and came back almost immediately with a diminutive Crime Scene Officer in a paper suit that failed to disguise her advanced pregnancy. Nobody offered to help carry her shiny metal case. Ashton put his notebook away and together they went into the living room, or as the sergeant would have it, lounge.

Siamese-twinned with the medic still excavating in her head for Tutankhamen's lost treasures, Kat shunted into the hallway to eavesdrop.

From the sound of it the inspector didn't think the stains were blood; the sergeant disagreed. The CSO was silent, aside from an occasional grunt which could have been assent, dissent, or the onset of labour.

In an effort to see what was happening, Kat shuffled her chair almost into the room.

'You haven't been carrying bits of that car up here to repair, have you?' Ashton asked. 'Or got any friends with motorbikes?'

Kat remained silent; none of that merited an answer

'Sir, you're right,' said the sergeant, louder. 'It's oil, not blood.'

'Yep,' Ashton replied. 'It's oil, it's even on the –'

There was a high-pitched scream. They froze.

'I've been attacked.' One of the constables reversed at speed from the bedroom, rubbing a streak of blood on the back of his hand. 'There's a stonking great gorilla the size of Kong under the bed.' The young PC's eyes were huge in a face drained of blood.

A gorilla? Even with her minimalist decor, Kat doubted there was enough space in that flat for anything bigger than a Chihuahua.

'Don't exaggerate. It's a scratch,' said the doc. 'One patient at a time. I'll see to you in a minute.'

'Get a grip,' muttered the sergeant, a lady clearly a trifle short on compassion.

They all flinched as something streaked out of the room and into the kitchen. A well-worn plastic panel set into the wooden fascia under the kitchen window gave a sharp clatter and began walloping to and fro. Kat caught a glimpse of a blurred ginger fur coat vaulting the rubbish skip and disappearing over the edge of the walkway. Man or beast, as it disappeared, it gave a rude hand sign. But that may have been a trick of the light, or a result of the bang on her head.

'There you go,' the doctor said, repacking his bag. 'I'll give you some solvent for the diesel. From the state of all those books on the floor, you must have frightened the animal off the the bookcase and the whole lot went flying. You're lucky it was only the furniture that attacked you. Monkeys can have a nasty bite.'

'I've no doubt the lady would've bitten it back,' said Ashton, knife sharp after all the sugar and caffeine.

'Inspector,' interrupted a so-far silent PC, older than the others. He had the appearance of a bank clerk who might have taken up law enforcement late in life. 'There's been talk of a monkey roaming the estate. Apparently escaped when the house moving began. It wasn't a problem so we've not interfered. It's never attacked anyone before.'

'It's gone feral and we've not interfered? You're kidding.'

'No, sir, animals are the council's job, not ours, unless they're involved in a crime. Looks like it's been living in the old boiler house, from the amount of diesel it's trailing around.'

'Can I have a tetanus booster, doc?' the injured constable said. He was struck by an idea. 'I won't get AIDs off it, will I?'

Kat shunted to the window. Apart from the glister of paw marks in a symphony of diesel and coffee grounds the deck was empty. In her peripheral vision, she saw Ashton return to the kitchen table.

'Hey, that bloody orang utang's nicked my cake,' he roared. His police colleagues gaped at him as if he'd sprouted two heads.

Ashton sans cake acted as a signal for the others to wolf theirs. Once it had gone, they trailed across the deck and down the steps. Ashton, however, seemed reluctant to depart.

'I've enjoyed our little tête a tête, but your mates are waiting for you, Inspector,' Kat urged.

'All in good time. Can I call someone for you, family, girlfriend, boyfriend, to come over here?'

'No, I'm fine. The cause of the problem has gone now, and I'm reviving fast, thanks to your coffee.'

'You're sure?' He tore a page from his notebook and scribbled on it. 'Here's my number. The quickest way to contact me is by my mobile. Or leave a message for me at the station.' He handed her the page.

As their fingers brushed she felt the hairs stand up along her arm. She saw he was aware of the effect this had. Mr Charm didn't half fancy himself. As she caught his eye, an unexpected jolt in her gut sent her early warning system on alert. Shields up, she told herself. Get a grip. Take the man's piece of paper, say thank you nicely and goodbye. End of story. She really did need to get out more often.

CHAPTER 8

Kat changed into leggings and an XXL *Feed Audrey Two* tee-shirt and was thinking of popping out to Lal's mini-mart for cleaning materials when there was a burst from the doorbell. Busy day.

'You must be absolutely shattered, Petal,' Barry said, with more than a touch of the drama queen.

He was accompanied by two buggy-mums, their pushchairs top heavy with bags and bundles.

Kat smiled sweetly, groaning inwardly when she saw they'd brought their duvet-swaddled infants along. Shardonnay, yesterday's canapé queen, her battery of piercings jangling like wind chimes, was first in. She was followed by a girl in her early twenties who Kat recognised as the part-time manager of the estate's housing office.

'Heard what happened on the bush telegraph. We've come to help clear up. Nary a word, Petal. I insist,' said Barry. 'I am such a lemon; what am I like, not coming to your door last night? I feel awful. If I hadn't swanned off, I might have stopped Winnie making such a mess.'

'Winnie?'

'Winston, as in Churchill. Chimp with attitude. Victory sign when he's happy, Vee-off when he's not. He also blows a fine raspberry,' he said. 'First, let's get you tidy.'

'Wow,' Karen breathed, hauling her over-laden buggy into the sitting room. 'Ain't half a mess.' The younger girl's make-up and hair was pure Addams family. However, unlike Shardonnay, Karen was without piercings and still had her own eyebrows.

Shardonnay hoisted her multicoloured bundle out of its buggy. Half way across the room she tripped, sending it airborne.

Kat reacted instinctively, lunging forward in a nifty one-handed rescue to find she'd saved a bag of dusters. Time to see an optician.

'Blimey, is that a real telly or a double decker bus?' said Karen, gaping at the vintage television perched on an old wooden hostess trolley in the corner.

'Shall I take this for you?' Kat, not to be caught out twice, reached for Karen's bundle of cloth, only to jerk back in alarm. Not rags: a pink, solid object swathed so rigidly in Baby Gap that its limbs stuck out like the horns of a nautical mine.

'That telly'd get you into the Antiques Road Show,' Karen said.

Meanwhile, everyone was pretending that their new community organiser to whom the council was paying a small fortune had not made a fool of herself. Karen had brought along a Tweenies DVD.

'The slot on this machine's too big,' she exclaimed.

She was bewildered when Kat explained that the TV had been manufactured before DVDs were invented. Reluctant to let them use her laptop to play the disc Kat rummaged amongst the still half-full removal boxes and came up with a Magic Roundabout video whose psychedelic colours were guaranteed to keep Baby Gap occupied.

With Karen on wallpaper and Barry on curtains, the tropical islands, palm trees, and parrots soon took on a whiter shade of pale. Shardonnay, whose recent incursion into cordon bleu cookery classes at the local adult education institute had given her a heightened awareness of hygiene, was convinced that close contact with sofa or carpet might risk a new pandemic, and said so.

'Give us the keys for your van, Baz,' she said. 'I'll pop down the road and see if there's anything worth scrounging from the emergency furniture store.

By late afternoon, not only was the place cleaner than an operating theatre but Kat had acquired a replacement sofa and a rug. Barry lit joss sticks to offset the aroma of Jeyes disinfectant.

'Oh, dear, it's a bit beige and boring and TV-makeover-ish,' Barry said, eyeing the scour-cleaned furnishings. 'Needs something to liven things up a bit, don't you agree? Try under the sideboard at my place.'

This time Shardonnay came back laden with a fringed gypsy shawl, a brightly coloured Mexican rug and a pair of exotic embroidered cushions with glass insets that a small child had probably laboured over in some foreign sweatshop.

'So, girls, what larks, eh? They say that skeleton's likely to have been under those flats for donkey's years,' Barry said as they washed down another of his endless supply of cakes with a pot of tea. His cake. His tea pot. His Earl Grey.

'Yeah,' said Shardonnay. 'It's pissing my dad off. He keeps banging on about someone being trapped on the roof but nobody's taking a blind bit of notice. He's an embarrassment. I'm not the first kid who thinks they were swapped at birth. I worked my socks off when I was a kid, doing a paper round to pay for a DNA test and prove Cosmo wasn't my real dad. I'd seen it on Oprah. But I never managed to save enough.'

'Think positive, Shaz,' Karen said. 'As long as you don't get DNA tested, you won't know. If it said you were Cosmo's, you'd be gutted.'

'Yeah. You're right.'

'What'll you do if Winnie pops in again?' Barry asked.

'Again? Well, I doubt we'll be going clubbing together.'

'Don't be horrid,' Barry said. 'If it wasn't so un-PC, a chimp could be an icebreaker at parties. Be company. Useful as man-bait, too.'

'Man-what?' They chorused.

'Bait, man bait,' said Barry. 'What man could resist a girl with her own pet monkey? You could put him on a lead, like a dog.'

'I can think of better ways to spend my time than taking a bloke walkies on the end of a lead,' said Kat.

'Not the bloke. The monkey,' Barry said. 'A monkey who is, by the way, fully house trained.'

'Hah, he can be as house-trained as a Swiss cheese plant for all I care,' Kat replied. 'I don't do pets.'

'Bet you never even had a pet as a child.'

'No, you're wrong. I had a mouse once. I'd just begun to get interested in the cinema, so I called him the Cooler King, because he kept escaping – you know the one I mean? He was too stupid to know when he was well off. One day when he went walkabout, so did the school cat. Which just goes to show something or other. If that ape crosses my path again, I'm having him made into a pair of winter boots.'

'Gotta catch him first, Petal,' said Barry. 'He's knife sharp.'

As she waved her new friends goodbye she suspected they were laughing at her.

Her laptop was blinking: she had mail. She also had a meeting with politicians and developers at the council offices. Before she unleashed her undisputed organisational skills on the unsuspecting inhabitants or checked her email, her priority was to work out a rescue strategy for the project. The councillors would want to know what she had in mind for the next three months. Ideas she had in plenty. First step in any strategy: write a list. Kat was an obsessive list maker. She liked drawing up lists and working out problems via diagrams. Without a list, a plan, a script, or a story board, things could so easily go pear shaped. She needed an aide memoire, a mental SatNav, a chart, any kind of chart – flow chart, bar chart, pie chart, weather chart. Computers were all very well. But.

She fetched pad and pencils to make notes. There was no point in letting ideas swirl around without shape or form. Ideally, to get ahead of the game and bring the project back on schedule, she'd like to empty all the flats at once and park the tenants out of the way. Decks cleared, she'd race ahead with demolishing the empty properties and building new homes. Not impossible. Worth following up.

It didn't take long to tape sheets from a flip chart onto the kitchen wall as a template. She set up the kitchen table with her laptop facing her action plan. An hour's web search, forays into Facebook, a Tweet or twenty, two emails to a travel company, a live chat set-up for some serious wheeling and dealing. Covered in pink post-its and red marker, the wall chart soon resembled someone who had cut himself shaving.

After emailing Cosmo King, she bundled the bedding and clothing that had suffered the outrages of her simian intruder into a big plastic plaid bag and carted it to the Coin-Op Washeteria on the way to her meeting. She didn't do the launderette thing too often. Anyone with half a pulse would be hard-pushed to come up with anything more boring than watching a washing machine go through the whole shebang. However, she had learned the hard way that if she left the machine to its own devices she'd find her stuff in a wet heap on the floor or some moron would have stolen her underwear. She had her laptop and a folder of paperwork to keep her occupied while her clothes tossed and turned their way through the full wash and dry cycle.

She arrived at her meeting with the developers in clean underwear and a cloud of washing powder. The first made her feel better, and the second took her and everyone else's mind off the tobacco smell that permeated the committee room.

It was late by the time she returned, delayed by the water company having dug up half the roads trying to identify a leak. Lal's Mini-Mart was battened down for the night. Subedar Lal Bahadur Gurung – nobody went the whole nine yards – would be tucked up, safe in the bosom of his family above the shop; she could have banged on the bemedalled ex-Ghurkha's door. However, given that she wasn't, by anyone's standard, one of the world's big spenders, getting him to open up for her would have been taking advantage. She could have detoured via the big supermarket on the bypass, but didn't fancy going out again. Should have kept back some of Barry's cake.

The light in the fridge had blown. Not that it mattered since apart from a tub of re-frozen mint choc chip, there was nothing of gourmet interest. Today's treasure trove comprised half a bottle of fizz-free fizzy water, a banana with measles, a few black olives, a jar of barbecue sauce with green fur, the remains of a pack of bacon off-cuts, an overlooked morsel of red onion. In the chiller drawer was a hundred-pack of IKEA tea lights, a pair of sheer stockings and the last third of a thin-sliced white.

She had enough to make a toasted bacon butty. If she hadn't guzzled all the cheese slices in the car yesterday she could have made Croque Monsieur, more continental than a plain old-fashioned fried-bread sandwich. In the spirit of healthy eating, she added the onion, flinging on a liberal handful of fresh basil and parsley from her little window box, and some anonymous little leaves that had seeded themselves there. Every little helps. Dumping the barbecue sauce she topped it off with a burger bar ketchup sachet from her collection, for the extra vitamins, as well as a sprinkle of dried Italian garlic seasoning to keep her cholesterol from going through the roof. Crowned with the two olives that turned out to be dried prunes, it could almost have passed as a bacon pizza. Shame about the cheese, lack of. A melted topping would have been good.

Deciding not to break the habit of a lifetime and go without pudding, she fried the banana and ate it with the ice cream. She left the stockings and candles for another day.

A flick through the TV promised a dreary night of mutilated female body parts on BBC 1, and females with subtitles on the receiving end on BBC 2. The Late-Night Classic on Channel 4 was often worth watching. Not tonight: bleak Swedish landscape, more subtitles, and the dreary intricacies of a chess game with the Grim Reaper amongst the malevolent forces of the plague didn't suit her mood.

At the other end of the scale were comedy classic re-runs. She had missed last night's offering. Tonight it was Are You Being Served. The vacuum cleaner, predictably also Swedish, offered more in the way of entertainment. Sprawled on her clean sofa with a glass of one-Euro Calais Merlot, she settled for a DVD on her laptop. Around about the time the tortured, thumbless, Willem Dafoe begins to explain to the disfigured Ralph Fiennes exactly why he's been hunting him she gave up the battle to keep her eyes open. She'd watch it through to the end without falling asleep, one of these days.

CHAPTER 9

The metre-wide digital projection on her ceiling showed two am when she awoke to a hissing sound. Her throat was dry, her eyes itched. She smelt gas. Hoisting her legs over the side she began to make a sleepy lurch for the kitchen but shot back into bed when her feet touched the cold laminate of the bedroom floor. As her brain began to adjust to being awake, she was not so sure. Wasn't modern gas treated to smell like cat's pee? And in any case, the flat didn't have gas installed. Most council flats were all-electric these days, dating from a well-documented gas explosion in a London tower block in the Sixties.

Rotten bananas? She'd discarded the skin on the draining board. Unlikely. The noise might be compressed air brakes down the street. Nothing to do with her. She yanked the sheet back over her head.

Psssssss..ssss.

Still there. Too early to be street cleansing. Maybe a tap left running, or the shower. She couldn't be arsed to check. In a flat awaiting demolition, a little flood wasn't going to hasten the end of civilisation.

Psssssss.......ssssshhhh.

The noise came from outside her front door. With most of the block emptied of tenants, she had no neighbours. This time of night, it was going to be some drunk. Or those Asbos letting off party sizzlers. She would have to sort it out or she'd never get back to sleep.

Pssssssssss....ssssss.

She stumbled out of bed, veering off to retrieve her *Audrey Two* tee shirt from the ironing pile. Not the latest in glamour wear, it was better than opening the door in the buff. The letter box began clattering a tinny tattoo. Padding barefoot down the hall, she rehearsed the string of expletives she would unleash on the yobbish trio.

'Psssst... You there?'

That didn't sound like the boys. She slipped the bolt.

'I've been here ages, trying to wake you.' Mel said.

Kat thought her friend had never looked so daft as now, on all fours, down at letter-box level like that, but she sounded sober enough. Her Worship glanced furtively over her shoulder. 'Can I come in? We don't want everyone gawping.'

'Gawping? At this time of night?' Kat scoffed. 'Who are we expecting? Colonel Bogey? The Household Cavalry trooping the colour? A host of angels singing *I'm a little teapot*?'

The sole sign of life was the ape snoring half inside a wheelie bin lying on its side and minus its wheels. The animal was wearing a West Ham away strip and had a fluorescent bobble hat pulled over his eyes. Kat rubbed hers, to check she wasn't hallucinating. Otherwise, the pedestrian deck was deserted, empty aside from fly-tipped litter, a slight breeze giving momentum to an empty beer can, gentle drizzle, new moon: the usual. Plus one mad-as-a-hatter mayor.

'Can we talk?' Mel said, brushing coconut matting from her knees.

'It's two in the morning,' Kat said, folding her arms across her chest, her body language unmistakable. Finding sympathy for Mel's plight at that time of night was hard work until she remembered Mel's council was paying her for this contract. 'You may as well come in now. I'm wide awake. Don't expect too much: I forget my manners when I'm roused from my bed at this time of night.'

'Yeah. Sorry,' Mel said. 'I wanted to get something off my chest.'

Kat resisted the urge to make a crack, and instead led her friend into the living room. She'd left the TV on when she went to bed. An Open University tutor wearing a full beard was enthusing about how the moon didn't have a dark side although people might think the opposite. Huh?

'Why the secrecy?'

'Terrible day,' Mel said. 'Couldn't get away from a hairy meeting.'

That made them a matched pair, Kat thought, reminded how she had gone round in ever-decreasing circles at her development meeting. She'd achieved her aim in the end despite the councillors all having their own entrenched ideas and never listening to anyone else, largely because she had more stamina than the politicians or the navy-suited developers,. Cosmo King had arrived as they were packing up and complained that he hadn't known of the meeting, and why had be been left out of the loop? Apologies flowed, but they all knew the builders would have walked out after five minutes of the mouthy residents' rep.

'Come into the kitchen,' Kat said.

If she was going to be spending what remained of the night fighting off yawns, she might as well make tea. The light was strobing, making her eyes water. She turned it off and switched on the bulb in the extractor hood instead. Fishing out two mugs she waited for the kettle to boil.

'Builders bags, green, or Barry's Earl Grey? It's all I have,' she offered. 'Unless you prefer something stronger?'

Kat had the beginnings of a migraine, with shoals of shiny squiggles moving in from the right. Mel paced the kitchen as if it was a cage. Three paces up, three down, repeat. She shook her head.

'Whatever. The best thing about tonight's council meeting is that it's over. We had harpies heckling us all evening, claiming the new lingerie shop is too near the kids' play centre. The meeting went on forever. I had a medicinal vodka or two in the mayor's parlour afterwards.'

The kettle whistled. Kat poured hot water over the tent-shaped bags and watched it turn khaki before adding milk.

'Okey-dokey,' she said, blowing steam off her brew. 'I'm all yours. What's the problem?'

'The skeleton. Something my brother said. It's been niggling. I've heard it's male, mid thirties, been there ages, no more. I'm only the mayor: they tell me nothing,' she complained. 'Did I hear right?'

'T'would seem so. So what's the problem?'

'I'm worried,' Mel said vaguely.

Kat began to nod off.

'Oi, wakey-wakey.'

'Sorry. Running on empty. Go on.'

'Listen, and tell me what you think,' Mel replied. 'Billy wasn't making much sense last night. Sometimes you have to pick out information from the dross. It occurred to me that the body, the skeleton, I should say... well, I'm not sure how to put this.'

'What?'

'I think it might be my dad.'

'Your dad? Did I miss something back there?'

'No, well, oh, I dunno. For starters, they're having trouble identifying it, so it could as easily be him as anyone else.'

'How do you make that out?'

'My dad disappeared thirty years ago, when the foundations for that block were being laid. They'd just finished the pilings at the time,' Mel said. 'Billy remembered.'

'They'd just finished the what? You don't think you're stretching credibility a tad far?'

'No,' Mel said. 'There was a pub here in the old days, the Stargazer, where my father used to drink with his mates. One night he never came home. No sign. No message. Rumour was he'd done a runner after threats from one of the local villains, or that they'd offed him. With no mother handy, Billy and I nearly ended up in care, a fate worse than death. Gran stopped it. But it was a narrow escape.'

'Not necessarily. Some care homes are a hundred percent better than the alternative. Trust me, I – ' Kat stopped. 'Sorry. You were saying?'

'I'd forgotten you were brought up in care. D'you realise, in the ten years we've known each other, I don't think we've ever got around to talking about that. I'd heard orphanage were horrendous. You read some terrible stories.'

'No, it was fine, given the artificiality of it being a convent full of nuns. We didn't get beaten or starved or sent up chimneys. They did their best. Must have done – they got me through A-levels and into university without too much damage,' Kat said. 'However, lots of water, lots of bridges; you know me, I don't do girly chats, and I'm useless at show and tell.'

A lone wolf, Kat regarded the sordid details of her personal life as nobody's business but her own. She expected the deal to be mutual. Now Mel was digging, and Kat wasn't comfortable confiding in friends. She wasn't used to *having* friends, full stop.

'Sorry, you're right,' Mel said. 'I'm being nosey.'

'Nosey? You? Heaven forefend! You were saying?'

'Where to start? My dad disappeared, I wasn't quite two. Billy was nine or ten. We lived with my gran – old lady, big handbag, sunhat big as a beach umbrella. Remember her from yesterday? But it's been thirty years, and I imagine they've ditched the files by now. It'll be the devil of a job persuading them to look at it again, after all this time. But I can't shake a gut feeling.'

'But what are the odds he ended up under Julie Andrews House?'

'The clincher is those foundations getting filled in within days of his disappearance,' Mel said.

'Thin. Where was your mother in all this?

'I don't have any more luck with family than you. Billy was in a hit-and-run just after I was born,' Mel said. 'Six months later my mum ran off with a porn cinema manager with a polka-dot pink bow tie and a Triumph Stag.'

'A porn cinema. Oh, classic.'

'Did I mention my dad was a policeman?' Mel asked.

'Really? Hmm, look, I don't want to rain on your parade, but more than 20,000 people, including the odd copper, go walkabout each year in the London area, alone. Who else have you spoken to?'

'Nobody. I thought you'd talk to the lovely inspector.

'Why not pick up the phone and ask the police yourself?

'I can't. I'm the mayor: not terribly important in the greater scheme of things, but around here, I'm a big fish in a small pool. Everything gets into the papers. It'd be easier for you, in your line of work.'

'What exactly do you want me to do?'

'See people, chat with them, listen, but don't make it too obvious. I'm not asking you to play detective. Well, maybe, but not enough to draw attention to yourself. Do what you're best at, liaison, listening, gathering information. Pick up on what the police might say about the case, and if you hear anything, let me know. Think of it as part of your strategy to get things flowing on the estate.'

'I wouldn't count on it staying under wraps,' Kat said. 'First, police stations have more leaks than the Welsh rugby squad. Second, anything hinting of sleaze or scandal will find its way into the tabloids. Imagine the headline: '*London Bobby offed by mob is mayor's dad*'. It could run and run. You'd have the papers tapping and hacking, and squatting on the doorstep. Third, my history with the Old Bill has been a touch negative since I sprung you from jail. Over the years, we've reached an understanding: I avoid contact with any arm of the law and they ignore me: I'm the original invisible woman.'

'You're paranoid. That demo was ten years ago.'

'And they almost had me banged up for springing you.'

'Instead, they let us all go, with a caution, for which I'm truly grateful. So, pish tush.'

'Pish what?'

'It wasn't you they cautioned, it was me. A little run-in with the fuzz on behalf of a bunch of activists campaigning in a good cause doesn't count as a criminal record,' Mel said.

'Little run-in? I was negotiating on your behalf. Normally I get paid for that. It's a valuable area of expertise. It wasn't the good cause that was the problem. It was the rather adversarial manner of your campaign. They'd have had the lot of you nicked and under lock and key in a flash, given half a chance.'

'We annoyed the shit out of them, didn't we?' laughed Mel.

'You weren't behaving very peacefully, given that you were meant to be marching for world peace.'

'I wasn't, was I? I can still see you standing there like a suffragette on the steps of the police station waving your arms like a racetrack bookie' said Mel. 'D'you remember, you were on the top step so you could look taller than the rest of us.'

'I saw it on TV. They kept replaying that bit where I mouth off at that arrogant copper who was decked out like an admiral of the fleet.'

'The look on his face when he tried to grab you but went flying when you sidestepped.'

'Did well on You Tube.'

'Ah, happy days,' they sighed.

'Are you sure you want to go down this road, Mel? Your father's been gone thirty years. You could be raking up things best left alone.'

'I wouldn't ask if I had any doubts,' Mel replied.

'Fair enough, but someone's bound to come sniffing, low profile or not. Have you thought of that? Some copper will get a hefty bung for leaking it to the press, and when I make a fuss and demand an explanation they'll quote the Data Protection Act and refuse to say anything. You'd get the information quicker if you Googled it.'

'Yeah, maybe. Listen, our friendly inspector gave you his number,' Mel replied. 'Your average copper knows more criminals than the ones they put behind bars. My dad could have been bent, or just unlucky, but I don't want to put ideas into anyone's head at this stage.'

'My lips are sealed. But rest assured once the police get in on it they'll want to speak to your granny, and your brother, Billy, and it won't take long before it's everywhere.'

'I'll take that chance. I'm not sure how much they'll get from Billy. All you have to do is keep your eyes and ears open and ask a few questions,' Mel said. 'There's no risk involved. In your job, people expect you to nose around.'

Kat mulled it over. Her priority, and the main item on her agenda, was to flesh out her strategy for getting the regeneration back on its feet. There were reports to write, calls to make. Sleuthing for Mel would have to be slotted in when work permitted. She worked best under pressure. Playing detective might end in nothing. Mel could be wrong. Kat weighed her natural curiosity against the time and effort. Nosiness won. She liked poking under stones, exercising the old grey cells, solving puzzles. She may be less genteel than Marple, less shrewd than Holmes, less Belgian than Poirot, but they were only fictional. She was real. She knew her limitations. However, there was no call for her to be coy. She'd be good at it. She pictured the big moment. The cast of suspects corralled in the library – it was usually the library – while she explained how she had solved the mystery. She'd point with a great sense of drama to the guilty person, who would fall apart and confess all. People would be amazed. She'd be swamped with job offers from all points of the compass.

'I'd have no idea where to begin,' she said. 'I've never done this sort of thing before; I have no track record.'

'On the contrary. Your track record could be said to be excellent. You can honestly say you've never lost a case,' Mel said.

'Never lost a case? Trust a politician to come up with that one.'

'Say you'll help,' Mel pleaded.

'I don't know. How do we find out what your father might have been working on when he disappeared? Could it have had a bearing on his disappearance? If this skeleton isn't your father, then whose is it? How did he get there? Has he really been there for thirty years? Are we interfering in something beyond our capabilities?'

'Naw, see, you're getting the hang of it.'

'There are so many blanks to fill in,' Kat said. 'How did whoever it is get there? The base of a tower block is hardly a dirt floor you can dig up and bury bodies in when you feel like it. What else was happening that weekend? Who was around when all this was going on? The things I do for my friends! You'd better give us your dad's full name and anything else you think I should know.'

'You're a treasure,' Mel said. 'It's PC Jeff Rampart, Jeff with a J. He was the Moor's home beat Bobby, collar number, ZX801. The big question, of course, if it is him – did he fall or was he pushed?'

Kat was going to have to talk to the chatty Inspector Charm after all.

CHAPTER 10

After Mel left, Kat had curled up on the sofa for the remainder of the night. She then slept so deeply that she missed the dawn chorus of idling engines, squeaky pushchairs and the general racket of the bin men crashing and banging their dust cart.

In the shower, she found she was out of both shampoo and gel. All she had to work up a lather was a stump of Christmas soap with a brown crack down the middle the size of the San Andreas fault. The first spray of water made the bruise on her head smart, which forced her to change tactics. Detouring around the painful minefield of bumps, she gave her hair a haphazard wash. Not the shower of a lifetime. Then, as if that wasn't enough, the cooling puddle around her ankles refused to drain away. Not a good start to her day.

She crouched on all fours to investigate but was unable to shift the mesh of hair which clogged the drain. She had nothing resembling a tool kit. Eyebrow tweezers didn't count. Cutlery wouldn't do the trick. She poked through a removals box marked *Kitchen Odd & Sods* and found a pack of wooden kebab sticks. Poking around in the lumpy scumminess of the blocked drain was enough to put her off barbecues forever. She broke a dozen in the attempt to dislodge the blockage. The final stick jammed in a greasy blob bearing a resemblance to the wing of a chicken long-gone-to-its-maker. Kat yanked it up and the water ran away.

Dressed for a day of site meetings and house calls, in trainers, jeans and a close-fitting quick-getaway top without trailing bits that might be grabbed by an irate tenant or which could get snagged on something, she switched on Classic FM for some background music. Across the room she could see the email notification light on her laptop blinking like a traffic indicator. First things first, she thought, and put the kettle on. There was nothing that couldn't wait.

She took out a biro, opened her spiral pad and wrote in block capitals at the top of the page, *Things to Do*, and underlined it. After a moment she began writing:

Obtain council records of people on estate thirty years ago.
Get list from Mel of her dad's mates.
Raise subject casually on site visits/house calls on off chance.
Check architects blueprints/time frame for J Andrews House.
Mel's dad: enemies, girlfriends, debts, arrest record?
Identify/locate people working/drinking in pub that night.
How much police effort put into original investigation?
Details of case/s Rampart working on when disappeared?
If not Mel's dad, tell Mel, stop sleuthing?
Any mileage in asking Inspector A for info, given DPA issues?

The kettle boiled. She now had a replacement for the pot the chimp had broken. Barry, who understood her matinal craving for caffeine-and-plenty-of-it, had lent what he called a French press. When Kat said she thought a French press was an exercise bench for working triceps and forearms, involving weights, barbells and considerable effort from a prone position, it turned out he was talking about a coffee pot with a plunger which he'd picked up on a trip to the States.

'A *cafetière,* you mean? The Americans certainly have a peculiar way of speaking English: fries instead of chips, cookies for biscuits, buggies for prams, malls for arcades, movies for films, apartments.'

'Yeah, right,' he interrupted. 'The French are worse, with their casseroles, cafes, and chauffeurs.'

'Okay, okay. Pax,' Kat laughed.

'Hey, that's cheating. I don't know Latin,' Barry said. 'Apart from *Tempus fugit* and *Illegitimi non carborundum.*'

'Never mind. Thanks for lending it. You can call it what you like.'

As she waited for the coffee to brew she opened a pack of index cards and began to make notes, ticking off items from her earlier list. There wasn't much writing involved, given the paucity of information, but she was surprised that when she had transferred all she knew onto the cards, one item on each, she had more background data than she had realised.

Having culled what she could, discarded the bits she didn't want, and filed those which matched her idea of what she needed to know, she needed a user-friendly retrieval device for whatever level of detail was required. The human brain may be a computer, but even with her prodigious memory, Kat lacked the capacity for total recall. Naturally, the system didn't always work, even with cards and flip charts and endless lists, but her strategy of committing everything to a written format allowed her to rearrange information and see an overall pattern or shape. She'd tried using her laptop but found it wasn't as flexible as shuffling cards or paper around like a jigsaw puzzle.

She tuned in to Radio Wazzoo for the local news. There can't have been much that day; they were still banging on about the skeleton.

'... a Bickeridge Council tower block in an implosion triggered by security consultant Katharine Shakespeare.'

'I'm not a security consultant, nor am I a Katharine,' she muttered.

...there to supervise the project.' Almost right. A passing helicopter drowned out the next sentences. She turned up the volume.

'Neither Miss Shakespeare nor the mayoress, Mel Gibson...'

'Not mayoress, she's mayor in her own right,' she muttered. 'And it's not Gibson, it's Dickson, dozy so-and-sos.'

'...were available for comment. Superintendent Liam Grant of the Metropolitan Police has issued a statement.' The newsreader droned on; nothing Kat hadn't heard before: investigation begun, incident room set up, special lines opened, confirmed suspicious death, Dah-di-dah. The body had not yet been identified. There was nothing new.

Back on Classic FM they were playing a funereal piece she recognised. An ex-boyfriend, whose idea of a perfect date was a night in with a vindaloo and a war film, had made her sit through Platoon. He liked the violence, she liked the violins. The vindaloo was hot, the boyfriend not. He went his way, she went hers. She air conducted, humming along as she popped the last two pieces of thin sliced white in the toaster. Less than enough to fuel a day of site visits, house calls, paperwork and super sleuthing, but it would have to do.

CHAPTER 11

If you looked hard enough you could still see the original wall sign for Monumental Pictures in ghost-writing high on the stonework of Bickeridge town hall. Dwarfing everything in the road and built between two World Wars in the heyday of cinema architecture, it had an art deco façade with a front door big enough for a Chinese railway station.

In the majority party office on the fourth floor, a slim woman was hammering a keyboard at an amazing speed. Lemon-coloured hair scraped into a baguette and lashless eyes combined to give her a bald appearance. She was in beige: beige high-waisted skirt and matching beige ruffled blouse with a bow at the neck. It was the sort of Margaret Thatcher style that featured in long out-of-date magazines at the health centre. Magazines with engagement portraits of rich debutantes marrying into the aristocracy, expensively-schooled and Swiss-finished young ladies with a plum in their mouth, answering to Camilla or Antonia, and with a double-barrelled surname not pronounced the way it was spelt.

'How can I help you?' She stopped hammering the keyboard. Her name badge said Janet Steggles, her accent Basildon. Unable to keep her hands still, she fiddled with the enormous rock on her engagement finger as if expecting Kat to rip it off and make a dash for the border. It was obvious the girl was not going to give anything away without the go-ahead from the council's lawyers. Deaf to entreaties, she unbent sufficiently to offer an appointment in a week's time when Councillor Parsons-Green returned from a town twinning conference in Monaco.

'You can leave your number, if you wish,' she offered, casting lovelorn glances at her computer. She was either desperate to return to affairs of state or had a live chat going on Facebook.

Kat couldn't wait a week before talking to someone. She politely spurned the offer and headed for the press office. Lower in the pecking order and in the building, the media suite on the first floor was deserted but for a cheerful soul in denim dungarees who was happily occupied transferring waste paper from mesh bins into a plastic sack. He and his multicoloured knitted Rasta tam bounced to some silent rhythm being transmitted to the man's brain through a pair of earphones big enough to block out a jackhammer.

'Yo, sista. They be out,' he said. Kat suspected he was having a laugh at her expense. 'How 'bout you come back when they be in?' He emptied another basket of shredded paper into his sack and returned to jigging to the music. He knew better than to suggest she left her number for a call back at some date in the future.

The police station was across the road but there was no point in joining the lengthy queue. It was fines enforcement day: divvy up before noon and avoid a one-way trip in the prison van for another week.

In the bus home the driver had his two-way radio on, gossiping with his mates about traffic jams, moaning about working through their break, or trying to swap shifts. The passengers were making a similar racket, shouting their business and everyone else's into mobiles. Bedlam. Might as well follow the flow. Kat belled the local Bill.

'We are pursuing enquiries,' intoned an overstretched officer at the police station over a buzz of voices. No details, of course. Not yesterday's voice, either. After her break-in fiasco it was a miracle they were speaking to her at all. She'd try again later.

Mel's phone went to voicemail where an accent-less female advised that her worshipful was pond dipping with special needs children at the ecology centre. Cosmo King's phone was permanently engaged.

A small crowd had taken up residence around the Julie Andrews site. She could hear the chatter as she got off the bus: house repairs, Poundshop, phone tap scandals, last night's telly, their kids, other people's kids, fad dieting, laminate floors, they'd got everything covered. Nothing like adversity to bring out the community spirit. A cordon of police tape continued to encircle the area. The previous day's brief cloudburst had turned the road into a mud slick making the empty tipper trucks lining Warp Drive resemble a string of canal barges.

As she passed the dosser on his sleeping bags behind the bus stop, he stopped chatting on his iPhone long enough to swear at the amount she chucked into his empty violin case. Opposite, an acne'd teenager with gel-spiked hair bounced up and down with a microphone connected by umbilical cord to a Radio Wazzoo van. Parked alongside, Krishna Ices was doing a good trade. Both vehicles were on a triple yellow. A wizened lady in a white sari was positioned to signal the approach of traffic wardens from any of four directions. Inside the barricade, police were sifting rubble.

'Morning, Petal,' carolled Barry, his signature black relieved by an embroidered matador jacket. 'Take a look at this lot. There's enough tracksuits to put on our own Olympics. They're pretending to be picking up the morning paper, but I know they get them all delivered. They probably get their Big Issue brought to the house, too. Ghoulish lot.'

'Pot and kettle, Barry.'

He seemed to have splashed out on more papers than usual. She doubted many community centre customers demanded the FT or Telegraph with their beer and bar snacks. The nationals had headlines varying from *shocking find* to *satanic ritual*; anyone expecting news in the local rag was in for a wait. The Bickeridge Bugle majored in spelling errors, crap grammar, and late-appearing stories one-finger-typed by thick-as-treacle infant reporters or fed in by self-important councillors, exaggerated complaints from disgruntled council house tenants, animal stories, and the most recent examples of negligence in the local health service. The best they could rustle up that morning was the pigeon fiasco and a grainy picture of an overturned bus in the town pond. Vehicles in the pond were a regular occurrence, but London double-deckers are designed not to topple and generally don't. Less prominent on the page was a small picture of Kat laughing her head off in a confetti of pigeon poop and feathers. The photograph's soft focus made her look good.

'Hello, miss. Fancy a chip?' invited the shortest of the ubiquitous trio, the one with the curls. The boys hovered on the edge of the crowd, positioned for a quick getaway. They were stuck into a shared takeaway bag. Kat's mouth watered.

'Yeah,' said the skinny one with the pale complexion and no hair. Maybe he was having chemotherapy. She didn't like to ask. He wore low-crotch trousers with a baggy top large enough to house the other two. 'There's toe of frog or wool of bat.'

'Or tongue of dog,' finished the one with the metal orthodontics and crutches. 'Actually, we're messin' about. It's Thai sweet chili prawn.'

She returned their greeting, passing on the takeaway.

'Fair does,' said the big one. 'More for us. Ta-ra, miss.'

Curly, Chemo and Meccano: they shuffled off with their arms buried in their bran tub of takeaway.

Kat and Barry picked their way through dog mess and litter around the community centre and estate office building The semi-detached pair of bunker-grey, corrugated concrete single-storey buildings was all that remained of the Apollo Thirteen shopping precinct. The estate office windows faced the back and were covered in heavy duty security mesh. The community centre windows, looking out onto the main road opposite Kat's flat, weren't. Their shared flat roof was encircled with rusted razor wire. Cigarette butts covered the pavement. The number on the wall of the estate office had slipped and now resembled a road traffic warning for road humps. Someone had added graffiti nipples.

The remainder of the site was derelict. What remained of the public lavatories was open to the sky, affording an unimpeded view of vandalised porcelain. The boarded-up remains of the Stargazer Pub took up the whole of the other side.

Barry led her through the line of supplicants which snaked its way towards a harassed clerk in the cramped reception area at number thirteen. The luckier ones waited on pink plastic chairs, beamed upon by flattering portraits of their elected representatives, each with its own integral spotlight. The open door to what had been turned into Kat's office said *Fire Exit keep closed* and led into a converted breezeway running front to back, squeezed between the estate office and community hall. A handy short cut to the shops, it had not taken long for the council to conclude that its drawbacks far outweighed any convenience it afforded as an emergency exit. Within a week of being finished, it had been blocked up and thereafter used for storage, regardless of any Health and Safety fire regulations.

Today, daylight relied upon an obscured glass panel in the outside door. Someone had made a stab at decorating the space with lilac emulsion but hadn't finished before the paint ran out. There were two travel posters on the wall, one for the 2008 Beijing Olympics. The other demonstrated the joy of frolicking in the sand at Southend-on-sea. Kat had been to Southend. The tide went out so far she'd never found the sea. Mile upon mile of wet grey estuary mud teeming with marine life that made her toes think they were being hoovered up.

Her little 'office' held a metal desk sprouting more paper than the Bank of England, a cloth-covered typist's chair, two pink plastic-seated metal-frame chairs of a size which suggested they'd come from the infants' school, and a black Bakelite fax telephone. The clunky PC bore a luggage label indicating it was en route to or from the council's recycling centre. Smelling of mildew and tobacco, it was the sort of room where things came out at night when the lights were off and scuttled about depositing their body fluids over the furniture.

'Blimey, Petal.' Barry stared at the computer. 'Any chips in that thing must've come ready salted.'

'No problemo,' she said. 'Have laptop: will travel. I'll only be using this place as a base.'

'Buckingham Palace it sure ain't,' Barry said. 'Lucky the glass is frosted, with that salubrious view – not – of the lavs. In extremis, you can tap out an SOS on the wall in Morse code and I'll leap to the rescue like a superhero.'

'You're so kind. Which superhero had you in mind?'

'Dunno. Who do you see me as?'

'With those glasses? Clark Kent, Superman?'

'God, no. He's got such awful taste in clothes. I ask you, tights with shorts? I'm a Jones sort of person.'

'Grace, Corporal, or Bridget?'

'No, you wicked girl,' laughed Barry. 'Indiana: I've even got the hat.' He watched as she rummaged through her bag. 'Lost something?'

'No,' she said. 'I don't want to come back here today. I've stacks to do. Mobile, iPod, body spray, keys, specs, purse, tic tacs, torch, Pills, passport, driver's licence, fizzy water.'

Barry began to laugh.

Kat stopped rummaging.

'What?'

'This is the Moor, Petal, less than half a mile end to end. You're doing a couple of site visits and a few house calls before lunch, not masterminding a major expedition to deepest Africa.'

CHAPTER 12

Finishing her rounds, Kat tried the police station again. It would have been easier to get a Russian visa than get past the duty sergeant.

'Date of birth... occupation... phone number... email address... mother's maiden name...'

'Why do you need all that?' Kat asked.

'We're collecting data for our e-policing initiative, madam. There are only a couple more questions left. How do you receive Neighbourhood Watch News? Through your door, email, or other?'

This was going nowhere. She'd have to drop Ashton's name into the mix, say he was a friend. Can't get much friendlier than sneezing into his best shirt. And what else do you call a chap who's given you his confidential mobile number, even if you aren't using the information thereon? There was a pause, followed by the rustle of paper.

'Hold the line, please, madam.' The phone switched to a loop of classical piano dull enough to induce stasis. The officer returned during the third round, oozing politeness: *Yes madam, no madam, three bags full madam, I've put a call out for the inspector, asking him to contact you; have a nice day, madam.*

Too late, she realised she hadn't asked what the sergeant had meant. Would Ashton call her? Maybe he'd pop in on the off-chance of more cake. She did a quick tidy, sweeping her gym kit under the bed where it formed the nucleus of a dirty laundry collection, rammed papers and files into drawers and cupboards. A tea towel dipped in Woolite scented the room as it dried in the sun on the windowsill. The hall received a squirt of fabric freshener; ditto, the living room. Barry's joss sticks would have been overkill. She dragged a brush through her hair and was applying lipstick when Ashton's *dah-di-di-dah-dah* knock on her open front door startled her and sent lipstick swerving across her cheek.

'In the kitchen,' she carolled, simultaneously wiping the misrouted lippy with one hand and whipping on a dab of eyeliner with the other. Pays to be ambidextrous. Seconds later he ambled in wreathed in smiles and a light green suit, as sharp as a Colombian drug baron. He'd brought his posh camera with him.

'You rang?' he said. 'I couldn't find any homeless beggars to beat up this morning, so I thought I'd pop in and see how you were.'

'Good of you to come round,' she said. 'I went to the police station but it's fines day and I couldn't get near the place. I've been given some information that might help you identify the mystery skeleton.'

'Oh?' He seemed disappointed. 'Okay, well, I'm here.'

'Would you like some coffee? I've borrowed a *cafetière*. I was about to make myself a pot.'

'Good timing. I'd love a cup,' he said. 'I've given up trying to get any joy from the station machine.' He watched her make coffee. 'We've had a rush of informants but nobody's come up with anything useful. People on the estate aren't being particularly forthcoming.'

'I've got the name of someone reported missing thirty-odd years ago who was never found. They think he might have turned up here.'

'Oh, and who's that? Here, let's take that off you. Is the cake coming, too?' He relieved her of the *cafetière* and followed her into the living room, a hint of freshly shampooed hair competing with the scented chemicals she'd distributed around the flat. He sat down by the window, his Armani a perfect match for the steam-cleaned curtains.

'Help yourself,' she said. 'It's another of Barry's efforts. I can't pretend I made it myself.'

'Thanks,' he said, detaching a chunk the size of a T-bone. 'If your cooking is as bad as you claim, you're fortunate in having such generous friends. So, fire away,' he said. 'I'm all ears.'

'I thought maybe we could do a spot of horse-trading.'

He cocked an eyebrow. 'That rather depends on the horse.'

'I don't know how the police are coping, but people on the estate are chivvying me on an almost-hourly basis for information. They're also driving the housing department batty with phone calls and emails and banging on the estate office door,' she said. 'In return for the information I'm about to give you I'd appreciate anything that might stop them driving us all up the wall with their questions.'

'I can't tell you what the police are doing. Data Protection Act and all that,' he explained. 'However, I'm happy to hear what you know.'

'I'm sure you are.'

Ashton didn't know how determined she could be: didn't know he was dealing with someone who had embarked on and maintained a silent hunger strike at the age of eight. Kat had anticipated trouble, but she'd promised Mel, and she wasn't giving up.

'No, really, I'm bound by the Data Protection Act' he explained. 'I really am. Sorry.'

'There must be some smidgen you can tell me without breaking any rules that you can't live with. As for data protection, you don't appear to have much data yet. On the other hand, I have.'

She would change her mind about becoming a super-sleuth if it was always going to be such a hard slog. Let him do his own detective work. See how far he'd get. The Moor had a long tradition of not cooperating with the Law. She waited, undeterred as he gave her one of those long-distance stares they learn at police college.

'We're going round in circles,' she said. 'Why not meet half-way? I tell you what I have, and you can see if it matches your data. Then you give me just a few teensy-weensy details which won't do the investigation any damage, and I pass it on to the tenants, and stop them bothering us. I'm happy to sign the Official Secrets Act, if that's what it takes. More cake, inspector?' Teensy-weensy. Had she really said that?

He took another slab of cake and mulled over her suggestion. The major part of her total food supply was disappearing faster than the Antarctic ice shelf, yet the man hadn't an ounce of surplus fat on him.

'I'm not sure if there's anything I *can* tell you,' he said finally.

'There must be something. Listen, if my information doesn't make sense, or match up with yours,' she said, 'we won't waste each other's time. I don't know about you, but I have work to do.'

'I've enough time,' he said. 'I'm on a leave day, meant to be organising my sister's wedding. Tell me, do you blow up many blocks of flats? For my money, that has to be more entertaining than chatting about a thirty-year-old skeleton.'

'It was my first demolition,' she said. 'Part of the job description.'

'Your job description sounds intriguing. Hard work, is it?'

'Not hard so much as time intensive.' She resigned herself to having to do the groundwork chat. Eventually he would get around to telling her something useful. 'I work on a strictly binary system.'

'Howzat?'

'When I'm on a job, I'm on a deadline. I work all day, every day, and through the night if necessary, until I keel over. No time for proper meals or socialising. Between contracts I scout for work and live on cheap pasta and recycled teabags. Like all self-employed, I worry I might not find another job. Feast or famine is the nature of the beast.'

'You mean your social life happens when you're jobless but not while you're working?'

'No; job hunting takes as much time and energy as working.'

'All work and no play isn't good,' he said. 'How do your friends keep track? I'm sure you exaggerate about having no social life.'

'Not unless it's job-related,' she said. 'It's hard to make or keep friends when you're forever on the go, having to up sticks at short notice, never staying in a place long enough to put down roots.'

'What about your friend the glamorous mayor?'

'Mel? We meet mainly through work, and not that often, either.'

She supposed what she had with Mel was the nearest thing she had to friendship. The idea of anything closer was scary. As a child she had been much alone but never, as she recalled, lonely. She had grown up keeping people at arm's length. Who needed friends? She had adapted, curled up with a book, usually in the council's inspection cupboard if her mother's boyfriend was around. She learnt not to care about the lack of invitations to after-school teas or sleepovers, or when she saw other kids pairing off. Inside her head she controlled a world of her own making, from books. Other kids had a mum and a dad and an imaginary friend. Kat had imaginary adventures.

Later, in the care home she had used her pocket money wisely, graduating seamlessly from page to screen when the local library jettisoned its videos for DVDs. Her haul had carried her by wagon across America with Henry Fonda and John Wayne, and with O'Toole by camel through the Arabian desert. She'd puttered down-river with Bogart and Hepburn and chugged to Brighton with Genevieve. At ten she had thought Dietrich and Davies cool. By twelve, she'd decided *Casablanca* was neat, *Gone with the Wind* overrated, and she had sussed *Psycho* in the first fifteen minutes. *Marathon Man* had put her off dentists for life.

She could recite from memory all the movie Oscars since 1928 even if she had seen less than a quarter. The nuns were clueless about film censorship and had no idea what she might be watching. Sometimes as a special treat, they'd rent an 'uplifting' film for all the children to watch together in the dining hall. Attempts to include her in communal viewings of such anodyne offerings as *The Bells of St Marys, Song of Bernadette,* or *Mary Poppins* were met with an outward ambivalence. The good Sisters had never been sure, particularly after the Tiny Tears incident, whether Kat was in dire need of care or too disturbed to warrant it. Left to her own devices she thrived, and was free to indulge her obsession with the cinema. She preferred to learn her life from those films. Not team material, she was nonetheless respected by the other children and by the nuns for her ability and readiness to stick up for herself and for others when the need arose.

She had been tempted to tell Ashton she had never felt in need of friendship or support from anyone. In Kat's private world, aloneness was a position to be nurtured with vigour. But in order to address Mel's concerns, she was going to have to make a few concessions.

CHAPTER 13

She watched Ashton's eyes take in the wallpaper now lacking its pattern since Barry and Co's cleaning binge, the glittery cushions, the rugs, and the gypsy shawl draped nonchalantly over the sofa.

'You've made a pretty good fist of this place. It's quite different, now.' He smiled at her over his mug. 'Much more you.'

She wasn't stupid. She knew when she was being worked; it didn't make it any less effective. In return, she was happy to bestow the odd wide-eyed smile on the inspector if it got her the information she was after. She was no great beauty, but there was the smile, and her skin was good: a soft light caramel that owed more to the genes provided by her anonymous father than salon technology. Her hair, she preferred to ignore. A fish and olive oil diet would have helped, as would soft water and sunshine in some little fishing village in Mediterranean France or Spain. Fat chance, as long as she wanted to work. And right now, work was the Sir Patrick Moore estate, where the oil came in engines or deep-fat fryers, tomatoes in fast-food single-serving sachets, and the fish was as battered as the cars.

'Why the police? You're not exactly my idea of a copper.'

'I hadn't intended joining the force,' he said. 'My parents and sisters are in medicine: doctors, nurses, that sort of thing. I wanted to be a photographer, but my family wasn't enthusiastic, so I hedged my bets with a degree in forensic and photographic science. A month before finals, circumstances changed and I had to find a proper job with a decent career structure that would support a wife and child. Liam, an old school friend, was headed off into the police graduate entry scheme, so I decided I might as well join him.'

He'd mentioned a wife and child. The best ones always had a wife and kids or were gay. All part of life's rich pattern.

'I'm currently with the NPIA, responsible for forensic seminars. I still do crime scene photography. It hardly qualifies for *Photographer of the Year*, but I do manage to do enough to keep my Box Brownie from getting rusty.'

Kat eyed the two grand's worth of Leica on the table.

'Anyway,' he said. 'That's enough about me. How did you get into your line of work?' Squaring an ankle over a knee, the picture of relaxation, he leaned back in the one piece of furniture Kat had considered worth bringing from her London flat, a well-worn leather wing chair she'd rescued during the Proms from a builders' skip behind the Albert Hall.

'My line? Purely by accident,' she said. 'After I'd topped up my Latin American Studies degree with an MA in Human Rights, I was helping at a neighbourhood advice centre when the street came up for redevelopment. Homeless Ecuadorian refugees living next door asked for help. The houses were too far gone to save, but the campaign was successful. We got the developers to do a deal with the council to use empty flats nearby to re-house the Ecuadorians as a group, so the families didn't have to find new jobs or new schools for the kids and they could still support each other. The local health services and the council's workloads didn't change, because social workers and health visitors were already in place, and the council had got them off the homeless list and into permanent homes. The David-and-Goliath story ran in the tabloids. I was head hunted by an international human rights organisation. I worked for them for three years. I loved the work, but it was becoming more and more research oriented and office bound. I needed to get out and about and do my own thing. I'm not much of a team player.'

'No, I can believe that. I'd lay odds you're a single child.'

'I was brought up in a children's home. It's sink or swim there,' she said. 'I'd say you're the opposite: maybe the youngest. No, I know, you're an only boy among a bunch of sisters.' Flirtatious chit-chat was fun. No threat, no harm done: it wasn't going to lead anywhere.

'Right on both counts: youngest, or joint-youngest with a twin; three sisters,' he said.

'Doting older sisters would explain the big ego.'

'Ego? Moi? No, never. In any case, I didn't come in for much doting. The girls ganged up on me. To give you a for instance, when I was thirteen, I cycled into town to meet my friends. Everyone I passed on the way was extraordinarily friendly, cheerful, waving, smiling. It was only when I caught sight of myself in a shop window I realised that while I'd been asleep in front of the television beforehand they'd made me up with Bollywood eyeliner and blusher and glittery eye shadow.'

Kat gave a roar of laughter.

'There's worse,' he said. 'In my haste, I'd picked up my mum's bike. Pink. With a little basket on the front. Took me ages to live down.'

'Apart from that,' she spluttered. 'I bet they spoilt you.'

'No more than I deserved,' he laughed.

They were slipping into the easy, unstructured conversation of old friends, something Kat was unused to. Her line in social chit chat tended to stick to the professional or impersonal, rarely straying across the line. He was that rarity, a good listener, who made you believe you might be the most important creature they had ever met. The odds were that everyone he talked to got the same treatment. If it was a ploy, it worked.

They discovered a shared dislike of TV reality shows, shouting into mobile phones in public, coughing in the doctor's waiting room, white van drivers, cyclists belting down the high street head butting shoppers and yelling obscenities at baby buggies. Ashton was into live theatre. Kat, film buff extraordinaire, preferred wide landscapes and close ups. She told him of the videos she'd liberated in her childhood.

'By the time I was ten I'd become a film freak,' she said. 'When the other kids played ball or skipping games outside, I'd shut myself away indoors with a pile of videos – classic black and white, mostly. Later, I sussed how to get DVDs out of the library for free. I watched anything, everything, until my eyes were pure grit. I loved all those old heroines: Marlene Dietrich, Katharine Hepburn, Sissy Spacek, Sigourney Weaver, Jodie Foster, the good, the bad, the barmy. I was cynical of happy endings, always imagined it going pear-shaped after the end credits.'

'No musicals or romantic comedy?' he asked.

'No, apart from the Hepburns, Katharine and Audrey. Not Debbie Reynolds in sneakers or Doris Day in frilly pinnies.'

'Or Julie Andrews in full flow or poor Meg Ryan in anything,' he finished.

'Absolutely.'

'I like the buzz with live theatre,' he said. 'The atmosphere, the intimacy of being there with the actors. That's lacking in film. You can't connect with real people, with the audience. They don't even have film projectionists or usherettes any more, only popcorn and surround sound and no interval break when you can be sociable.'

He paused to chop off a piece of cake for himself – it was the size of a Russian tank.

'You mean the cinema's anti-social? Yep,' she said. 'But I chat and am chatted to enough at work. At home, I want peace and quiet and make-believe. Although I have been known to switch on the radio.'

'What do you listen to?'

'Not current affairs or political interviews: I lose the will to live, hearing too many axes being ground. Desert Island Discs is all right, good comedy, drama, not poetry,' she said. 'I cringe whenever I hear poetry on the radio.'

'You hate poetry, or you hate hearing it read aloud?' he asked.

'Hmm. I like some poetry, but I want to read it for myself, not listen to some stagey actor emoting. How about you?'

'Not recently. But I used to like Coleridge, and Browning, Elizabeth, and Robert.' He blushed, 'Sorry, that sounds so pretentious.'

'I wasn't going to say. You surprise me. Real live theatre, poetry. I don't think I've met a copper who's into culture before.'

'I'm under cover,' he confessed. 'That's why I'm sitting here pretending to be one of your curtains.'

She hadn't thought he'd notice, now the curtains had been cleaned of their colour, how they almost matched the pale green of his suit. He could have moonlighted as camouflage scenery in a stage set.

'How about you?'

'Some. I did Coleridge's Ancient Mariner at school,' she said. 'I love the way the old sailor hangs around trying to bare his soul. But Coleridge must have been on something when he wrote *Kubla Khan.* 'Alf the sacred river?' I ask you! Auden's stuff is good, *Night Mail*, or the one they use in *Four Weddings*.

'*Stop all the clocks, Cut off the telephone. Funeral Blues.*'

'That's the one,' Kat said. 'But I don't get much time for poetry.'

'No poetry, no social whirl. No family. All work, no play.'

'No-one to hold you back, no place you're tied down to, no-one you must answer to, no social diary to be juggled against work, no roots, no ties, no relationships, no hassle.'

Kat's attitude towards relationships was like her attitude towards Catholicism: she carried around a weight of guilt for not conforming, but blind faith and commitment were lacking. She had never been part of an "us". Her childhood showed that she was safest among strangers. In her job, she could organise, take control, communicate, go home at the end of the day and switch off for quality time. She never tried to explain that. Confidences led to sympathy, one step from pity what was a fate worse than death. Ashton must have sensed negative vibes, for he changed tack.

'Anything in the pipeline when this job finishes?'

'I don't plan ahead. Some jobs overrun. You?'

'Once I've dispatched the happy couple to their honeymoon, I'm back with my nose to the grindstone, currently in Durham.'

'What about Mrs Inspector, stuck at home with all the little inspectoreens? Aren't they fed up with you being away so much?'

'No, I'm long divorced,' he said. 'No mortgage, no debts, no dog, no cat, no exotic fish. I'm sound in wind and limb, don't do drugs, don't smoke, take a lot of exercise. I own my house outright, my job prospects are good, and my bank balance is in excellent condition.'

'Whoa, hold on. It's not a proposal I'm after, only case notes.'

That'd teach her to be nosey. He had thrown her. She fiddled with the coffee, but seeing the pot empty, she cut some cake instead. Bugger the carbs. As long as the blood could get through to her arteries, a little extra effort at the gym would see off another three kilos on her backside.

'We'd best get back to business,' she said.

'Okay. Information. This missing person. Name of?' he asked.

'First things first,' she said. 'Let's check dates. My person went missing thirty years ago. How about yours?'

'Thirty years, yes, it matches,' he said. 'But don't get carried away thinking our pooled intelligence will solve this case. I won't mislead you. I'm not assigned to the investigation, nor likely to be.'

'But can't your National Policing Agency or whatever become involved in cases, like the FBI in the States?'

'No,' he replied. 'We respond to requests for help. We don't wander in and help ourselves, or dash about catching burglars or serial killers – none of the gung-ho stuff you see on TV.'

'I accept that,' she said. 'But you probably know how things are going from your mate with the medals, Superintendent Whatsit.'

'Yeah, well,' he said, glancing at his watch. 'Talking of which, I have to meet Superintendent Whatsit in half an hour. Why don't we continue our chat over dinner?'

'You what? ' she said. 'Sorry. Too busy, but thanks for asking.'

'Tomorrow? I can pick you up around eight,' he offered.

'No, I don't think so.'

'Earlier?' he said, purposely misunderstanding.

'No. Sorry.'

'Later, then. Alternatively, we can meet at a restaurant. You choose where we go, anywhere you fancy.'

'No. Not earlier, not later, not anywhere,' she protested.

'It's the least you can do, after erupting over my shirt and scaring the shit out of me with that fake eyelash. I thought it was a spider.'

'Can't help the eyelash. I'll pay your laundry bill,' she laughed.

'That won't be necessary. You will recall that I carted you down twenty flights of stairs,' he chided. 'I could've left you to it.'

'Hah! You were no keener on that lift than me,' she retorted. 'I'd have found my own way down in the end. Seriously, I don't think the Met would want you getting pally with someone involved in the case.'

'Involved? Only peripherally, and no more than I. In any case, you weren't born when this one shuffled off his mortal coil. It's only dinner. I might have some information for you by then.'

'So you can text or email me. Or ask one of the community police to drop by.'

'Good grief, woman, I'm offering you a square meal, not asking you to elope. It wouldn't kill you to say yes.'

'Sorry, Inspector, but not only would I not want to break the habit of a lifetime, but also, in my line of business I can't afford to be seen socialising with the Bill. It'd send my street cred into overdraft.'

CHAPTER 14

That dimmed his headlights. He frowned, held her eyes for a time without blinking, as if consulting some interior agenda.

Kat calmly drank her coffee. It could have gone on forever, except that she sensed a shift in herself which he must have picked up.

'Nah, you'll make an exception, because I'm not like any other copper you've met,' he said. 'And you like me. A chap can tell. We're too old to play games, but I'll go along with it for now. By the way, you can call me Jack.'

'There really is not much wrong with your ego, is there?' she said. 'Let's get back to the body, Inspector.'

Tilting his head, he raised his eyebrows, waiting.

'What? Oh, all right, let's get back to the body, *Jack*.'

'If we must. You can change your mind about dinner any time, you know,' he said. 'Nice restaurant, Italian, Chianti bottle candles, check tablecloths, hand-painted walls, mandolins, fresh pasta, You won't find a pizza, frozen chip or bottled sauce anywhere on the premises.'

'Sorry, no, but thank you for asking.'

'Oh, well,' he sighed, resigned. 'Okay, let's get back to work, see how far we can get. It is a skeleton, male, matches your time frame. There were no clothes or artefacts with the remains, so they might have a problem in establishing his ID.'

'No clothes?' She peered down into her cold coffee, now thicker than Marmite, and shuddered.

'There was nothing. They're sifting through the debris for buckles, buttons, coins, stuff like that,' he said. 'Bramshill holds records of missing persons worldwide. If that fails, we might get lucky with dental records. Your missing person was reported at the time?'

'Yes, and there was a a search, but it came to nothing.'

'Name of?' he said. 'Come on, I'm not going to broadcast it from the top of an open bus.' Ashton leaned back, runner's legs stretched out.

She explained, without mentioning Mel. He didn't interrupt.

'Right,' he said. 'For a missing copper the investigating team would have left no stone unturned. There is another man missing from that time, name of Delaney. Could be him. Or anyone else, for that matter. People go off for any number of reasons. Some to escape problems, or change their lives. Some imagine they'll land up on a beach, being rubbed with sun oil by bronzed beauties. In reality, a few lucky ones end up running a third-rate B&B in Westcliff-on-Sea. Most end up in a ditch, years later, with nobody left to remember them.'

'But no-one's come forward with any names apart from this Delaney character,' Kat said. 'Let's for the sake of argument put him aside for a while and stick with PC Rampart.'

'Is there any suggestion he might have done a romantic flit?'

'Nobody's mentioned any girl friends.' She'd have to ask Mel.

'I'll check the files,' he said. 'I'd be surprised if they didn't do that then. He lived with his mother, you said. She still around?'

'Yes, but Mel hasn't mentioned any of this to her, yet.'

'Mel Gibson, the mayor?'

'Yes. By the way, it's Dickson,' she corrected. 'Not Gibson. Everyone gets it wrong. Jeff Rampart was her father.'

'I imagine a politician with a missing copper for a father might receive some unwanted media attention. What about the rest of the clan, brothers, sisters, aunts, uncles, second cousins twice removed?'

'Only an ex-husband who's not around, two of them, rather, a brain-damaged brother in sheltered accommodation, and a grandmother.'

Ashton frowned. 'Councillor Dickson thinks her father was murdered and buried under those flats?' Giving up on the coffee he put a dollop of icing into his mouth and leaned back, fingers intertwined behind his head, deep in thought.

'I won't ask if the woman's given to flights of fancy,' he said. 'I'll have to take your word that she's sane.'

'Thank you,' Kat said. 'What does the forensic report say?'

'Wish it were that simple,' Ashton replied. 'You watch too much television. It'll take weeks to get results. Real crime labs are windowless cubicles in basements with metal desks and a patchwork of equipment held together with Selotape or Blu-tack. There's never enough time or technicians to cope with the volume of work and even then it may not be possible to get DNA from what little we have.'

'Nothing to suggest he died somewhere else?'

'Nobody sane would keep a body lying around on the off-chance of a lorry load of ready-mix concrete turning up. There was construction everywhere in the seventies. They'd have been spoilt for choice.'

'The local police think it's an old gangland execution,' she said.

'I'm dubious,' he said. 'There's no evidence of slice'n'dice.'

'Slice-in-what?' she asked.

'Gang executions generally show signs of torture or are minus limbs. They're not squeamish about employing a blow torch or chainsaw before they shove the bits in with the frozen peas in the chest freezer before burial, to make our job more difficult.'

'Ugh!' It was enough to put her off soft scoop forever.

'He had injuries to the vertebrae and head,' Ashton said. 'The lab's working on it. Question is, did he fall or was he pushed?'

'Clever man to cover himself with twenty floors of reinforced concrete,' she said. 'What do I tell Mel?'

'Tell her not to be optimistic. We're chasing Delaney, and three others of similar age and height who disappeared at the same time. Rampart and Delaney are the best bet because they're local.' He glanced at his watch. 'I must go; have to be somewhere.' He rose, drained his coffee. He had a smudge of cream on his chin.

Kat reached over and wiped it off, then licked her finger. The intimacy of the gesture struck her too late. Ashton gave a wicked smile, his eyes holding a hint of speculation. Her face burnt with mortification.

'I can't believe I just did that,' she stammered.

'And I was saving that bit for later,' he said. 'Now you've turned down dinner, I'll starve to death; it's no fun eating out alone.'

'You'll survive,' Kat said. She was tempted to change her mind about dinner. It was eons since she'd been out to a good restaurant. Or a bad restaurant, for that matter.

CHAPTER 15

Mel came knocking at Kat's door before Ashton's brake lights had disappeared. Today she was strawberry blonde with henna highlights, clearly making the most of the perks before her mayoral year ended.

'Do I smell coffee? Wouldn't mind a cuppa. Shove the kettle on,' she said, nose up like a Bisto Kid as she strode into the kitchen.

'Oh, silly me,' Kat said. 'Here was I, worried I'd be stuck in an empty flat with nobody to talk to.'

'Fat chance.' Mel was loaded with folders. 'Is that one of Barry's cakes? Not much left, is there.' She glanced into the living room. 'Looks better now the colour's gone. Sorted out that monkey yet?' She eyed the chair and broomstick wedged across the pet flap. 'Obviously not.'

'I can't open a window or he's in like a flash. I wonder if I could persuade Environmental Health to take the creature to a refuge or drop it over the Surrey border during their next fox dump.'

'Fox dump? Nobody's meant to know about that.'

'But everyone does. There must be a sanctuary nearer than Somerset. That aside, what brings you here?'

'I saw the inspector leaving. By the way, you know that big flash copper he was with, Liam Grant, top dog at our local nick? Well. he's engaged to Ashton's sister. Oh, you must know all this by now. Ashton's twin sister, Charlotte, known as Lottie, is a paediatric consultant motivational psychologist, whatever that is. Ashton's on leave but normally he's based at some police college up North,' she said.

'Gosh, you have been busy. Slow week in politics?'

'Don't be ungrateful when I'm going to such trouble to improve your social life,' Mel retorted. 'Seeing as he's made two house calls in as many days, I reckon he fancies his chances. Anyone else would have told you to take your information down the cop shop.'

'You're incorrigible,' Kat said. 'He's a policeman, for Heaven's sake. The sky could fall in and kill the whole population of Planet Earth before I'd fancy a copper. Particularly one who thinks he's God's gift.'

'From where I'm standing, he's entitled to be confident of his own charms,' Mel said. 'You should watch your body language. That smug smile you had when he left was a dead giveaway. He seemed chirpy, too.' Mel poked a digit into the cake for some cream.

'You've gone puce.' Mel's laugh would damage someone's health one day. 'Did you talk about my dad or was it a social call?'

'Mel, you are impossible. Yes, we talked about the case.' She did not mention Ashton's dinner invitation.

'Good. Maybe we'll get somewhere. There's a pretty good chance he'll help, given that he's after more than cake and case details,' said Mel. 'It sure ain't your hairdo.'

'I had a steam after the gym this morning. This is my sporty look. You could do with some exercise, yourself,' Kat sniped.

'Exercise? Hush, there's no call for foul language. Go wash your mouth out with chocolate. On the other hand, give us some cake,' said Mel, laughing. 'I don't understand why you people jig about on treadmills and rowing machines. Exercise doesn't make you lose weight, only encourages you to eat more.'

'Better than jogging in petrol fumes and rain,' said Kat.

'Us townies can live with fumes, but gyms have a sweat-and-dirty-socks-based ecosystem all their own. Take my advice, get thee to a hairdresser,' Mel advised. 'Kool Kutz does home visits.'

'Is that the girl who does the senior citizens? You must be joking. Her idea of haute coiffeur is a Coco the Clown perm and a pink rinse,' Kat laughed. 'I don't trust hairdressers. I'll stick to my pinking shears.'

'Your hairdo must limit your sex life,' Mel said. 'Pinking shears?'

'Kitchen things. Forget hair. I need to focus on work, not complicate my life with a man. I'm like a camel – I can go a long time without.'

'That's water, not sex,' Mel laughed. 'According to Cosmopolitan there's a link between sex and memory loss. The more sex, the better your memory, and vice versa. When did you last have sex?'

'Can't remember.'

'There you go. That proves it.'

'Bollocks. I hate all the palaver when you dump them.'

'I wouldn't mind a palaver now and then.' Mel said, with a laugh that rattled the windows. 'A decent hairdresser could do wonders with that hair, you know. I'd hate to wake up with it. Or beside it.'

'You're not invited to. Nor is anyone else. D'you know, I swear that cake's migrating directly to your hips without passing go.'

'Yeah, yeah, there's no call to be bitchy. I'm going on a diet the day after I end my mayoral stint,' Mel said. 'Or maybe the week after. For the past year I've rarely had a sit-down meal with meat and two veg. Luckily I eat anything I can get. Equal opportunities feeding, it's called. I'm wolfing down the quiches and samosas and nuts and nibbles they dish out at functions. As soon as my term of office ends, my weight will shoot back down to normal. If you're not interested in the lovely inspector, I wouldn't mind a crack at him. What else did he say?'

Kat told her, ending up with his promise to get back to her.

'Yeah, I bet.' Mel said.

'I told him about your exes.'

'Which ones?' Mel said.

'Both.'

'Both? You're behind the times. It's four now,' Mel laughed. 'I'm a lightning conductor for unsuitable men. My trouble is I have to marry the men I sleep with. Slime bag Dickson and Randy Raoul were only the first of the few.'

'Four, you said. I'm impressed. How long do you stay married?'

'It varies. With Dickson it was four years. I gave up college and did two jobs so he could study while I did the little-wifey thing. There we were, starter mortgage, top of the range garden furniture with a heater and yards of solar lights from Homebase, me in a frilly pinny, candlelit dinners, him networking. Soon as he qualifies he trades me in for a bimbo with legs up to her armpits, cut-price silicone tits and an IQ that never reached room temperature.'

'Bastard.'

'Yup,' Mel said. 'We'd finished our Sunday roast: Asda corn-fed chicken, three different coloured veg, baked Alaska, sparkling Lambrusco, and he sits there with his feet up on the coffee table watching me iron his shirts. Then he gets up, picks up his car keys and says he can't see our relationship leading anywhere and he's calling time. We'd been married four years. He swans off, saying he'll be back in the week with a van for his stuff.'

'Cheeky sod,' Kat said.

'Yup. That, too. I'm gobsmacked. I have a rant and a cry, and open a bottle we'd bought to impress his business colleagues. I put the iron on maximum and re-do his shirts, leaving an iron-shaped scorch mark on each one. I fold them carefully and lay them gently in his wardrobe. That done, I invite the neighbours to help themselves to whatever they fancy: golf clubs, multi-gym, camcorder, stereo player with the Bose speakers I'd given him for our anniversary. That night, we had a BYO barbecue. We loaded the fire with his Nova Windsurf Board rig, his DVDs, and stuff nobody fancied and had hot dogs and fireworks. For afters, we had the top tier of my wedding cake that I'd been saving for a future Christening – wasn't gonna need it now, was I? Next day, I toddle off to the library and borrow all Stieg Larsson's books, on his card, in Swedish.'

'They're depressing enough in English,' said Kat.

'Yeah. I included the non-fiction, as well. That's even drearier. I put each of the Larsson books inside the casing of a Folio Society special edition. He wouldn't know the difference until he tried to read any of the Folio books. Finally, I reported his credit cards stolen.

'Way to go,' Kat said. 'What happened?'

'He was a bit huffy that I'd trashed his stuff. He carted off his precious Folio collection without checking. He and the bimbo then flew all the way to the Turks and Caicos Islands before discovering I'd cancelled his credit cards and cleaned out our joint account. The thick bimbo, not that thick, after all, found someone else in a week,' Mel said. 'When he got back he had the brass neck to turn up on my doorstep.'

'You didn't let him in?'

'As if! I closed the door, sold the lease and transferred the cash into a savings scheme out of his reach. The library was threatening him with court action for unpaid fines on those Larsen books. I don't know if he ever found them because me and my rucksack had gone walkabout in South America – Tierra del Fuego, Lake Titicaca, up the Amazon and down the Orinoco, Machu Picchu, Angel Falls, roast guinea pig, coca leaves, Eva Peron's tomb, Iguassu. I stayed awhile in Buenos Aires, learned the tango and married Raoul. He was gorgeous. Everybody fancied him. Trouble was, he fancied them back. He was very good when I divorced him, gave me a little villa in Spain and first-class air travel home to the UK with stopovers anywhere en route. So I came home the long way around – Oz, Thailand, India, and ended up with a Greek whose surname nobody could pronounce.'

'Makes my achievements dull by comparison,' Kat said.

'It's the way I tell it,' Mel admitted. 'Anyway, enough about me. I come with tidings. There's a fault with the radio-telecoms junction box behind the Maurice Mickelwhite. It's been, not vandalised, exactly. Rearranged, I think is the word.'

'Curly, Chemo and Meccano were there the other day,' Kat said.

'Curly, Chemo and who? You mean Mickey and his mates?'

'I shall remember to call him Meccano Mickey in future,' Kat laughed. 'They must have gummed up the works. It's a nuisance. I've only got the mobile since that mad ape broke my land line.'

'Nobody uses land lines any more,' Mel said. 'The chair of the tenant liaison sub-committee says can you let him know when you're thinking of planning the public meeting so you can explain your plans for pulling the project out of trouble In addition, the Evergreens want you to pop in to their line-dance class.'

'Thanks, I'll talk to them.'

'One more thing. I need to pick your brains. There's a mysterious twenty-five thou bar deficit at the Maurice Mickelwhite. You must've come across this sort of thing before. Any ideas?

'In cases like this it generally turns out to be down to the staff or committee members, but I can't see Barry or Shardonnay on the take, can you,' Kat said, watching Mel finger-dab cake crumbs from an otherwise empty plate. 'The cleaner doesn't have access without someone being there. That only leaves the committee. Has anyone spoken to Cosmo King or his mates about it?'

'No, but I do know that place has more lock-ins than Colditz. A dozen or more generally stay behind after Barry leaves.'

'Free drinks don't explain such a huge loss,' Kat said.

'The councillors say to leave it to the officers; the officers won't upset the apple cart in case it slows things down more,' Mel said.

'But it'll transfer to the new centre and get worse as long as there's a licence,' Kat said. 'Why not just revoke the licence? End of story.'

'They wouldn't sanction that,' Mel said. 'Otherwise we could cut our losses, write it off and count on it not happening in the new place. All that money can't go walkabout without a paper trail.'

'I'm not so sure,' said Kat. 'Who uses paperwork nowadays?'

'I was thinking of dud invoices, or dodgy off-sales,' Mel said. 'Fancy helping me again?'

'How?' Kat was reluctant to get tied up in another of Mel's schemes. She hadn't made any progress with the first yet.

'I want to stake out the community centre one night.'

'What for?' Kat asked. 'Lurking in dark doorways watching the street lights shining on wet cobbles isn't my style.'

Mel, with her ample contours, was never going to find a doorway deep enough in which to lurk.

'Maybe not,' Mel said. 'Some kids took a pop at the street lamps last week, killed all the lights in the road, which would be handy except that with my luck, they'll have repaired them and I'll be caught in the glare.'

'If they hadn't put the builders compound out there, we could have watched from my bedroom window,' Kat said. 'You can't hide in the bushes. Heaven knows what you might step in,'

'I'd end up falling flat on my mayoral face.'

'Why not sit in a car, in comfort, with coffee and doughnuts?'

'I can't use the mayor's official limo and I've no car,' Mel explained.

'Use my Mini, whip it around the corner and keep out of sight.'

Mel grimaced. 'I can't. No licence. It's been mislaid.'

'That won't matter. You're only driving across the road.'

'When I say mislaid,' Mel said. 'It's sort of semi-permanent. I overshot a red light. DVLA's hanging onto it for a while.'

'A while?'

'A year. '

'Blimey, must've been a very big red light.'

'You know how it is,' Mel said, sheepishly. 'If I so much as sit in a car alone I'll be done for no insurance or in charge without a licence.'

'Oh, don't tell me you don't expect me to lurk for you.'

'Not *for* me, *with* me. Come on, be a pal.' Mel pleaded.

Kat hated the idea of sitting in a car all night like she was auditioning for another stakeout movie.

'Give it some thought, eh?' Mel suggested. 'It could be a hoot. I'll bring coffee to keep us alert. We could park around the side, out of sight by the bins; use the down time to catch up on the gossip.'

'Oh, all right, then. When do we lurk? It is only lurking we're talking about, isn't it? Nothing more.'

CHAPTER 16

The air conditioning was on the blink again. The tobacco cloud billowing out of the Maurice Mickelwhite was enough to make a beagle blush. Grey seaweedy vertical blinds waved in the meagre draught from French windows which had been jammed open in an attempt to let in something approximating fresh air.

The lack of an entertainment licence didn't stop the blast of the Bee Gees Night Fever from the bar speakers nor did it worry the geriatric trio doing a knees up beside the ladies loo. One was in soft zip-up bootees.

Outside, a gathering of bikers were holding an ad hoc chapter meeting. Hogs and Harleys towered over retro Lambrettas. High on the agenda appeared to be a boisterous comparison of engine capacity.

'Recovered from the shock of the mystery skeleton, Petal?' Since she'd last seen him Barry had acquired the sort of lowlights that women pay their hairdresser a fortune for. He ignored the optics on the wall to pick up instead a bottle of Rioja from beneath the counter.

'No, thanks,' said Kat. 'I only popped in for a minute or two, to talk to the OAPs. I'll stick with coffee.'

'Okey-doke,' he said, fiddling with the machine. 'Coffee it is.'

'Good crowd,' Kat said squinting through the tobacco haze.

'Yeah, we're doing good business since the skeleton appeared.' Barry said. 'Are you hungry? There's stuff, if you want. Any joy with liaising, as Cosmo King would say? Mel tells me you're playing Miss Marple.'

'Trying. Nobody's been any help so far, except DI Ashton. He's not giving much away, though. What's today's special?'

The blackboard on the wall above the bar might have been written in Sanskrit for all the help it gave the serious eater.

'Today it's tuna cauli with a lemon and raspberry cooli. Shardonnay's started cordon bleu classes at the Tech,' Barry explained.

'She's put something called *taramassala* with the deserts.'

'Your guess is as good as mine,' Barry laughed.

'They haven't identified the body, yet,' she said, wondering what gossip Barry might have picked up.

'Some say they have, if you believe the dozen half-arsed rumours floating around,' Barry glanced down the bar where a couple had reached the end of their glasses and were miming death by thirst.

Kat turned her attention to the counter while he was otherwise engaged, giving a faint moue of distaste at the bowl of dried potpourri masquerading as bar snacks. Barry noticed, and slid the bowl out of reach along the counter to a tattooed couple in matching wife-beater vests. Their hands blurred as they leapt on it.

'They'll need to do DNA tests,' Kat said.

'On Shardonnay's snacks?'

'No, you daft sod,' Kat laughed. 'On this skeleton.'

'Will there be much left to DNA after thirty years?' Barry asked. He finished polishing a glass to within an inch of its life before putting it back on the shelf and picking up a new one.

'There's always dental records,' she said, watching him dust off glass number two. She was half expecting him to spit in it, Western style, and was surprised when he didn't. 'Apart from my friendly copper, how do I find out what's going on?'

'Try Precinct 13.'

'Precinct what?'

'The estate office.'

'You're kidding.'

'No, they named the shopping precinct the Apollo Thirteen, way back, and hung a dirty great number thirteen on the wall of the estate office. They hadn't finished putting the Rawlplugs in before the tenants were calling the housing office Precinct 13. The support team are very chatty. They have their tea breaks in Karen's room, next to your hidey-hole. Or you could try the bus queue. Tuesday's pension and prescription day, Thursdays it's seniors' discount on elevenses at BHS.'

'All the geriatrics seem to talk about is teenage crime, surgical operations and the state of their bowels,' Kat said.

'In that case, somewhere down the yellow brick road, you'll have to fall back on your copper. So to speak.'

'Hmm. What's the gossip? Anyone done a disappearing act?'

'I've heard not a tittle,' Barry replied. 'Well, not a sensible one. I'll keep an ear open. Why don't I make a list of anyone still around from the old days? You could talk to them. Someone might know something.' He glanced up at the clock. 'You could begin your interrogations with the bingo crowd; they're on their tea break.'

'Good thinking, Batman,' Kat said, slipping off the bar stool.

'Good luck,' Barry laughed. 'Don't expect them to remember what they had for breakfast but they'll remember stuff from thirty years ago.'

Kat pushed open the door to the adjoining room where the elderly bingo players were tucking into ham sandwiches with more dedication than lions gnawing on a fresh kill. Once they knew who she was, however, they seemed content to share with her their Jaffa cakes. They were even keener to share their views on life. She sat through tales about the cost of staying alive and the breakdown of society which they claimed was down to Greece leaving the Euro, pollution in China, war in Iraq, foreigners, politicians, and the tabloid press.

'It started with the Crossovers coming over and blocking hospital beds,' posited an aged gentleman whose red braces held him upright.

Kat quietly hoovered up Jaffas and listened politely.

'This skeleton lark,' the man said. 'The TV said it was illegal aliens.'

'They were left behind by a space ship,' volunteered an old girl who must have cat-napped through cable re-runs of ET all week. She was wearing a fluffy pink jumper and matching hair. Her shins, encased in shiny beige support hose, looked like soup bones.

'Evie Tripp, you don't half talk a load of old cobblers,' said Mel's granny, Joan Rampart.

'Aliens, my eye,' said a man in a shiny, once-good, suit.

'Don't listen to Evie,' said an elderly gent whose stroke had left him with an eye twitch and a tendency for his arm to spasm.

Kat remained at a safe distance, to avoid decapitation.

'When this place was built, a rough crowd moved in from the East End. Like the Fostocks and the Delaneys, ain't that right, Joan?' Twitchy Man said, turning to Mel's granny, which seemed to be the signal for them to gallop off down memory lane. Kat smiled with stoicism, letting tales of costermongers and Pearly Kings and Queens, street parties and cheery cockney capers wash over her while she occupied herself with a mental note of people she ought to talk to.

'Yeah, in those days they only bumped each other off,' said Shiny Suit. 'Never bothered us. Saved the police a job, an' all.'

'He's back. Bye-bye, duck,' said Mel's Gran, watching the bingo caller returning. They all headed back to the game, and Kat returned to the bar, where Barry poured her some wine despite her earlier refusal.

'Count the grape as one of your five,' he suggested.

Beyond the bingo door, however, the noise level had risen from a murmur to a strident buzz of angry shouts. Kat nudged the door open a crack to see Mel's Gran in a tussle with Mrs Fluffy Jumper.

'Gimme my pen,' the old lady shouted, enraged. 'Trust a Tripp to half-inch anything not nailed down. You thieving cow.'

'Cow? You cheeky mare,' yelled the diminutive Evie, whereupon she was immediately sent flying by the frail old granny's roundhouse punch, not having the foresight to get out of range before speaking her mind,

'That'll teach yer,' grunted Mel's Gran, satisfied.

Floored, Evie had gone face down in a Jaffa cake and acquired a chocolate birthmark. Amidst laughter, someone spoofed a countdown. On cue, she sat up and glared.

'What ya' starin' at?' she rubbed the side of her face. 'We're wasting bingo time.'

'Don't mind them,' Barry said. 'We have more suspensions for fights than a cup final.' He'd polished enough glasses for a brewery convention. 'I see they've started a house-to-house.'

'Yes,' said Kat. 'There seems to be lots of urgent spring cleaning on the estate right now. Got any ice cubes?'

'Ice? With red? Tres gauche, Petal.'

'Be that as it may, this stuff could do with some help,' she retorted, plonking cubes into her drink. 'It's almost body heat.'

'Sorry, must have used a warm glass. Want another? No? How about the tuna cauli before it goes?'

'No, thanks, I'll manage. I'll nuke a pizza later.' She'd sampled Shardonnay's cooking at the demolition party and suspected barium meal might be tastier than today's pièce de résistance.

'Give Shardonnay's cooking a couple of weeks. She only started last month, and –' He broke off at a crash of glass. 'A thrill a minute, this place. Here we go again. Gangway.'

Discarding his tea towel, Barry vaulted the counter, and darted across the room. Fly-half, he'd said. That figured.

Shardonnay had launched herself across a table at a man half her size. There was a crunch of cartilage as part of his nose made a rapid change of location. Gushing blood and snot, he held his face, swearing in words that would get triple word scores and sweep the board at Scrabble.

Everyone stopped drinking to have a look. A girl with a Croydon facelift hairdo and a sequinned tank top began hyperventilating noisily.

Barry raised his hands, signalling for calm.

'Don't worry about the blood, folks. Nose jobs always look worse than they are. She hasn't killed him,' he said. 'Not this time.'

There were some laughs and ribald remarks amid the rustle of scandalised whispers.

'He bloomin' asked for that,' Shardonnay announced, marching her injured partner out to a round of catcalls and applause. 'He's lucky it's his nose. Next time I'll aim lower and he'll be singing soprano.'

'Shardonnay and Dave have a dynamic relationship,' Barry said. 'They'll be in A & E for the day. I'm on my own. Want to lend a hand?'

'Another time, maybe,' Kat said. 'Stuff to do, worlds to conquer, and all that jazz. You handled that well. I was half expecting you to whistle Land of Hope and Glory and juggle plates on the end of your nose, too.'

'Ah, time was,' Barry laughed. 'I'm rusty.'

'On the contrary; how long since you played pro football?'

'A few years. I was beaten up by a bunch of neo fascists, ended up with too many broken bones to be able to play again.'

'That's awful,' Kat said.

'Could've been worse, Petal. As long as I keep moving, I'm fine.' He went to remonstrate with a pair of scruffs who were hitting the side of a games machine with hard, sharp slaps while their two children jumped on and off the window ledges, risking defenestration.

'Hang about, missus.' It was Cosmo King, in jeans that made Kat think he might have dislocated a hip. 'You earnin' your dollar for us? What's happening with this body they found?'

'No news so far,' Kat replied. 'Glad I caught you. We need to talk about speeding up the project.'

'Yeah,' he said. 'Read your email. Gotta do somethin' before the council yanks the plug and sidelines our grant into one of their barmy pet schemes: aerobic toilets is their latest.' He tapped the side of his nose. 'Town hall's got more leaks than the bloomin' Titanic.' He rambled on, comfortable with the sound of his own voice as Kat sipped her drink, inserting an occasional 'Hmm' and waited for him to run out of steam.

'I think my idea will solve our problems,' she said, when she could slip a word in. 'If the last tenants waiting to move were to go to Magaluf or Ibiza, emptying their flats, we can demolish and rebuild without a gap, and not waste time or money shunting people in and out of B and B.'

'You barmy? We can't afford holidays. Who's gonna pay – you?'

'No, the council,' she replied. 'A Spanish company, Olivas Travels, can do four to eight weeks in Magaluf, all-in, for less than a third of the council's re-housing budget,' she explained. 'The council flies you out to

Spain, we knock down the old and whip up new, working twenty-four hour shifts. When you get back your homes are ready. It'll be the summer holiday, kids are home, most of you aren't working so there's no lost earnings to be considered. Not only do we finish rehousing the tenants but there would be surplus houses to market to first-time buyers.'

'Hmm, I don't suppose we're gonna find any suitable temporary accommodation this side of Christmas,' he reflected. 'You might be right, girl. Glad to see you're starting to earn your keep.'

'Thank you,' Kat said. 'This is how I see it working: you go off to Spain, leaving us to demolish your old places, and get the new homes up and running. I fly out for a few days at the end to finalise things like removal vans, door colours and bathroom tiles.'

She watched it dawn on him that he wouldn't be spending six months in dodgy B&B in the lower reaches of Crawley or Croydon after all.

'All-in deal? No cost to the tenants?'

Kat nodded.

'I could prob'ly persuade them to go along with that,' he said, sounding reluctant, although Kat could see he was having a hard job hiding a smirk.

'Good. So that's sorted. Next up, those remains. Saw you chatting to the ginger copper the other day. What's he say?'

'Not much,' Kat said. 'They began the house-to-house today. All I've heard is that it's a skeleton, male, been there awhile, and they're trying to ID it. Gosh, is that the time? If you want me at your committee tonight, I ought to get a move on.'

'Oh? Yeah, ta-ra.' From King's expression, his spirit was already lounging on a sandy beach under an umbrella.

'Cheers,' Kat said, fluttering her fingers in a wave. 'See you later, too, I expect, Barry.'

'Something to look forward to, Petal,' he replied. 'By the way, are we wearing our posh frock tonight?'

'You wear whatever turns you on. I'll be in jeans.'

CHAPTER 17

That evening, en route to the residents' committee taking place in the back room, Kat hastened through the bar and tried not to inhale. With the air conditioning still out, the pungent whiff of cheap aftershave, unless Barry had been over-zealous with toilet duck, didn't quite cover the after-effect of Shardonnay's lunchtime tuna cauli which had now had all day to work its way through the building.

'We all here?' Cosmo King asked, slipping a blue plastic *Eau de Perrier* bottle into his pocket; the chances of it holding any eau were not high. He was wearing his suit again, this time with flashing Hot-Lights trainers. The room was too warm, in defence against which he had removed his John Lennon cap.

On a trestle table at the side of the room were plates of sandwiches which the heat had turned into giant toenail clippings, to which people were helping themselves.

'Ever seen those things under a microscope?' Barry murmured as Kat reached for a prawn-avocado sandwich to take the place of supper. 'They hang around sewage outlets with their mouths open.'

She changed her mind and made do with a piece of mango.

'We're all here, let's get on with it,' suggested King, in the chair, adding, as people continued chatting. 'Oi, bit of hush. Order! Order.'

He never missed *Today in Parliament*. He banged the table with his plastic water-bottle. Instead of a bang it made a dull thud but it nonetheless brought the room to sufficient order for the meeting to begin. It was no different from committee meetings the world over. First, the arguments about the veracity of the minutes of the last meeting, which more appropriately could have been called hours. Then, after much posturing by the chair, and a long debate on whether or not to permit a diversion from the formal agenda before the meeting could begin.

Kat meanwhile kept part of her brain on what was going on and busied the remainder with learning by heart the fire evacuation instructions printed at the front of the agenda. There was one light moment when after a noisy, confused argument, King with reluctance agreed to amend the records concerning their generous donation to a village in Azerbaijan. It had not been, as it purported in the minutes, for the purchase of '*stacks of porn*'; it should have read '*sacks of corn*'.

When they reached Kat's strategy to speed up the project by sending them all to Magaluf, it was clear the tenants were never going to argue against sun, sand and sangria on the council tax.

'Full board? Drinks included? What language do they speak over there? I haven't got time for Spanish lessons.'

The vote would have been unanimous, except for an opposition councillor whom Kat recognised as the weighty man who'd taken a tumble off the demolition day viewing platform, who said the barmy bunch running the council would never get away with offering a freebie on the honest, hardworking taxpayers to a bunch of council house layabouts and benefit cheats. Mel whispered to Kat that this was rich, coming as it did from the man who had wangled his expenses to cover employing his daughter as his secretary and an official limo owned and chauffeured by his son-in-law.

'Benefit cheats?' This was a sensitive issue. Since his divorce from Shardonnay's mother twenty-five years earlier, King had avoided overt employment and with it any need to pay maintenance. 'Living in council housing doesn't make us second-class citizens.'

In an attempt to avoid full-out war, Kat moved next business but was interrupted by a deafening banshee wail.

'FIRE!' King yelled, sending his chair flying in a dash for the exit. 'Come on, don't hang about. We'll get burnt alive!' He paused, as it occurred to him that if the alarm ran for more than forty-five seconds, the sprinklers would kick in and soak the new office carpet he had his eye on, come demolition day. He de-activated the sprinklers before he left.

Outside, Kat could see no flames gushing from anywhere. There was no fire. Cosmo King had been fooled by the noisy racket of dozens of car alarms going through their entire menu of electronic agony in the car park. Pulsating indicators and flashing headlights were strobing like old newsreel footage of VE Day, wails soaring high over the roofs, accompanied by the howl of the estate's dogs and by hounds further afield who must have thought fox hunting had been reinstated. People spilled onto the pavement. The Krishna Ices van, trundling home after a long day, drew in on the off-chance of sales. The ubiquitous hooded trio, now a foursome with Winnie, huddled by the car park wall, stifling their laughter and watching everyone troop out.

Once the fear of being barbecued alive had dissipated, order restored and the fire brigade turned away, there was some half-baked speculation about seismic shudders causing everyone's car alarm to activate. There was also talk of power surges, invisible lightning strikes and failed attempts by delinquents to steal from cars that may have set it all off.

The committee returned to its meeting, leaving a small band of testosterone-fuelled vigilantes tooled up with baseball bats and garden forks. For the next two hours the posse trawled Warp Drive without success for miscreants. People weren't ever that stupid. Consequently there was a noticeable shortage out-of-doors on the estate that night of teenagers, gays, anyone with a tan, Irish, Catholics, and asylum seekers. More than one Ford Pinto was left out overnight with keys in the ignition and a full tank by owners hopeful of making an insurance claim the next morning after what the press would be probably call a night of rioting.

Kat guessed the not-so-silent-three-plus-Winnie would have already gone home and be deep in untroubled sleep after having mapped out their alibis and plotted their next diversion while the vigilantes were still noisily rolling around the estate.

King told the meeting he'd agreed to hire out the big field to a fairground company for a large amount of money and would they please ratify his chair's action so they could all go home.

'We need to stockpile as much dosh as we can before the television companies decide to stop coming here to film once the place is tarted up,' he said, and called for a show of hands.

Even that was not straightforward. There were alternatives that had to be discussed, including the possibility of tying in the funfair to an estate-wide carnival. The weighty opposition councillor said he was on enough committees and wasn't prepared to fart around on any more. King ignored him and called for a vote. The female councillor nodded in agreement. Motion carried, they agreed that Kat would organise everything. That done, he banged his hip flask on the table and declared the meeting over. They hadn't got around to a discussion of the unexplained deficit in the bar takings.

Apart from the Jaffas with the elderly bingo players, the slice of mango had been Kat's only food since breakfast. Going home, she picked up two frozen pizzas at Lal's to nuke in the microwave. Cholesterol heaven. No matter: some people can eat well, stay fit, and still die. She put the second one out on the deck for Winnie. Maybe it would stop him breaking into her fridge overnight.

Turning on the TV, she poured a glass of wine. They were showing Terminator number whatever. She'd lost count. She'd missed most of it, switching on as the bad robot's body explodes and bursts open. She poured a second glass as, head and arms hanging from threads of iron, it lost its balance to fall screeching into the pool of molten metal. Several more heads and arms popped out of its body before it took the rough shape of a giant open-mouthed head. Which reminded her that she had not fixed a date for a residents' meeting to discuss her idea of sending them all off to Magaluf and putting their belongings in storage while the developers raced ahead and she hunkered down with the paperwork without interruption. She'd pretty well agreed a special deal with Olivas Travels. Now all she had to do was to get the customers on her side.

CHAPTER 18

Ashton texted that he'd passed Rampart's name on, followed by a second message to say police were taking that on board. Kat texted back her thanks and by return received a third text, repeating his dinner invitation. Not to be put off, he was suggesting the following weekend, when he would be coming south again. She texted her thanks once more, regretting she was unable to take up his offer due to work commitments.

The caretakers were still sneaking into her cubbyhole for their tobacco breaks in her absence, imagining they and their tin ashtrays were free from discovery. No point making a fuss. She made do with piling files on the furniture until it was high enough to require grappling irons to reach the top. With nowhere to sit, the smokers would have to stand between bundles of paperwork and endeavour not to send the whole lot up in flames. While in residence she left the street door ajar for air, and added Shake'N'Vac to her shopping list.

Juggling site visits, house calls and a removals timetable with carnival preparations whilst fleshing out plans for Magaluf left little time for side trips. Long days on the hoof left scant free time in her job, but she had to stay fit to work. It was mid-week before she was able to do anything about it. Her last gym visit had been over a week earlier. Grabbing a mini packet of three Garibaldis and a water bottle, she tied her door key to her trainer laces, stuffed her mobile down her running bra, and headed out. She knew she would have to plan a proper fitness regime when her jog around the estate took longer than usual.

She returned home to find her ancient Mini sharing the kerb with a flash cabriolet, a swanky mustard-yellow that would have made a pimp blush. By contrast her banger looked like a write-off in a demolition derby. The Merc's spotless interior had a control panel that could've done duty as an in-flight simulator for Airbus. An old-fashioned brass

AA badge was attached to the radiator, and she caught a glimpse of a tax disc tucked discreetly in the corner of the windscreen. No dangling dice, air fresheners, or stickers, screen or bumper variety to express the owner's identity or personality through a love for New York, whales, political ideology or sports team. She liked that.

Rounding the corner she almost tripped over Ashton sprawled on the steps, doing the crossword.

'Hello.'

There was a large brown paper bag beside him on the step.

'Whistle-stop, to bring you up to speed. I've a briefing this afternoon on a case going to the Old Bailey. I'll be shut in a stuffy room for hours, and I fancied an al fresco business lunch.' He dangled the bag. 'Free range chicken, organic goats cheese, home-grown tomato salad, olive mayonnaise, wholemeal baguette, apple juice.'

'That's kind of you,' Kat said, dismayed he might prove to be some sort of militant health nut. However, who in their right mind would turn down a free lunch, even if it came free range, un-interfered-with, organic, or even home grown? He'd brought enough to feed the five thousand. Shame to waste it.

'You shouldn't have bothered with all that,' she said, but was nonetheless glad that he had.

'Sorry. I can bring Slim Fast, Ayds and mineral water if you prefer.'

'No, don't do that.'

'Don't bring food?'

'No! Yes. Food. But no diet stuff,' she said. 'It'd be churlish of me to refuse such a feast, after you've gone to so much trouble.'

She saw him smirk as her empty stomach sent out an audible SOS. The Garibaldis were long gone. It would make a change to have food grown in real soil in the ground and not dunked in fat and fried into oblivion and that wouldn't put her on statins before she was forty.

Cross-legged atop the wooden roundabout revolving slowly in the otherwise demolished children's playground, they had the park to themselves, apart from Winnie and the three Asbos playing hockey with crutches and an empty-sounding petrol can. A dozen magpies perched, uncharacteristically silent, on the remains of the old, vandalised, climbing frame, watching for crumbs. Nobody was using the new playground nearby. No fun to be had in pushing your mates off when all they could fall on was rubber surfacing.

Across the park, three men installing a new poacher-proof community pond reached the end of their working day and began packing up.

'Let's do this again, soon,' said Ashton, as he left for his appointment. It was already half three. Long lunch hour.

Returning a couple of days later for Liam Grant's stag do he found her with her feet up on the side of the bath, putting purple polish on her toenails, waiting for her avocado and aloe vera facemask – a first, for her – to take effect. Topping it all off was her wet hair stretched over giant straighteners.

'Time off in loo? Bit early for Halloween. Best eat in today,' he suggested, between breaks when he surfaced for air during his laughing policeman impersonation. 'It'll give you time to set. If I'd known, I could have rustled up something to sup with a straw so as to not disturb the artwork. Doesn't have to be organic.' A laugh a minute, this guy.

She didn't have a vase. His flowers looked fine in the kettle.

He'd also brought lemon tarragon chicken. Crusty bread. Egg salad. Olives. Cherry tomatoes. All free range, organic, delicious. Kat didn't have any trouble eating like this as long as she wasn't expected to do the shopping, prepare the ingredients or get lumbered with the washing up afterwards. A girl could easily get a taste for pigging out on Fortnum-and-Mason-style meals-on-wheels delivered in a swish Merc.

After he'd left, she took his flowers out of the kettle to boil water. While the coffee brewed, she emptied and cooled the kettle, then returned it and Ashton's flowers to the kitchen table.

Sitting cradling her coffee, ignoring Winnie who was rooting through the rubbish bin and lining up takeaway containers and old tea bags on the draining board, she breathed in the steam, admired the flowers in the kettle, and ran over events in her head. She found herself smiling as she worked without a break for the rest of the day, speaking to developers and fielding problems, any of which could set back the project by days or months: wrong doorknobs, slow-flushing lavatories, garden shed too big, too small, wrong colour wheelie bins.

Winnie had found little amongst the leftovers worth staying in for. He slipped on a shocking pink Barbie hoody the boys had given him and went out to look for some action. When Barry cornered the four later outside Kat's flat, the boys were teaching the animal to skateboard.

'Here, give this lot to Kat,' he said, handing them a new television set and a satellite dish. 'Tell her I'll be round later with a Sim card and a DVD player.' He also handed them a bag of screws. 'These are for the ape-flap. With all those letters after your names you can work out how to do it. Can't stop now, gotta dash.'

'Where'd you get all this?' Kat asked when Barry reappeared later.

'Junk room at the community centre. People get rid of things when they move,' he told her. 'New home, time to nick something new to put in it. Don't worry, it's kosher. How're you getting on with Winnie?'

'The boys have made the flap secure, which will keep him out unless he's invited in. For the rest, the boys have it buttoned up. For which I am truly thankful.'

'Poor Winnie. You've not seen him at his best,' he told her.

'Animals are only at their best on a barbecue,' Kat retorted. 'If you're so concerned about all creatures great and small, you take him home.'

'No, my working hours are as erratic as yours. Plus, I already have a goldfish. You don't have so much as a pet rock.'

'The only way I could ever own, feed and clean up after a pet would be if you pushed me out of a window and I cracked my head on the road and was no longer able to make a sensible decision.'

'Shall I take that as a no?'

Kat was determined to call the shots. Winnie was allowed in on her terms: not at night, not when she was out or had visitors. For much of the time, she ignored the creature that stalked her and stood sentry on the deck by her kitchen window when she was home. Barry was keeping an eye on job vacancies for her for when her contract finished, and joked about more openings now she'd added demolition expert and pigeon exterminator to a CV he claimed had more varieties than Heinz. Meanwhile, Mel continued to worry about the bar deficit.

'It isn't as if the place is a great social Mecca,' she told Kat. 'Some members don't approve the drinking that goes on. The police would oppose the licence, except that it would cause a shindig.'

'You don't have to have a licence with the new place, do you?' Kat replied. 'Don't apply for one, is the quick answer. Problem solved.'

'Make the new community centre dry? We'd never get away with it,' Mel said. Politicians had to think about these things.

'Why not? Blame the slippage in the programme. Say you've run out of cash to finish the place off properly.'

'That won't make a difference to a licence application.'

'It might. One way to ensure it doesn't happen again is not to have a stand-alone community centre in the first place,' said Kat.

'I'm not with you.'

'Listen, with a tiny tweak to the plans you could put the community centre in the new leisure building with other community services.'

'It'd save money,' said Mel. 'But it doesn't solve the problem of the bar deficit that's staring at us right now.'

'No, that'll have to be written off. Councils do it all the time. Think about it: apart from the incongruity of a licensed bar being tacked onto a sports facility used by schools, imagine the opposition there'd be to selling alcohol under the same roof as the health centre, social services, a Muslim Women's Association and a day nursery.

'It wouldn't work,' said Mel. 'Once they understand the licensing implications for a multi-use facility, they'll hit the idea on the head.'

'Not if there's a financial report to explain the slippage and how things might have to be cut back for lack of cash or, alternatively, remain unfinished,' Kat said. 'Next thing, someone comes up with an attractive one-stop-shop option without mentioning licence application. They'll go for it. By the time they've moved the furniture in, it's too late to do anything about applying for an alcohol licence.'

'It might work,' Mel said. 'It's a brilliant idea.'

'Another thing,' said Kat. 'The council could recycle the space meant for the centre for properties to sell on the open market.'

'Brilliant,' Mel said. 'I'll talk to my lot. Getting it past the drinkers is another matter.' She sat back, pleased with life. 'What a brainwave. Why didn't anyone come up with that before?'

'Because you don't have freelance worker syndrome. We of the self-employed persuasion have to be lateral thinkers. We also have to think faster than folk with regular jobs if we want to keep working,' Kat said. 'I won this contract partly because the council wanted an ethnic poster child to attract media coverage for the scheme. My task is to prove I am the right person by finishing the job successfully and on time. Then it's good night, good luck and happy job hunting.'

'Ethnic poster child? You can't blame the council for making the most of a media opportunity,' Mel said. 'We're bored with men in suits putting on day-glow orange jackets and hard hats to demolish these estates. They don't even get their picture in the paper: regeneration isn't news any more. Not without some add-on. We had you. We had exploding pigeons. We had a dead body. What more do you need?'

CHAPTER 19

Despite a high police presence in and around the estate, nothing seemed to be moving on the investigation. It was two weeks since anything had appeared in the press.

Kat was kept busy. Ashton rang to report progress or lack of it. He, too, was busy with police work and with finalising plans for his sister's nuptials. He had also begun building a portfolio in response to the enthusiasm for his demolition day pictures. Kat laughing amid the pigeon 'confetti' had made it to the nationals.

The police had a dragnet around the estate. With such obvious policing, petty crime and domestic violence took a dive. At the Maurice Mickelwhite, each day brought a new stream of gossip but little in the way of solid clues. Police interviewed relatives and friends of anyone reported missing as long ago as thirty-five years earlier. The Surrey South London borders appeared to have been a popular place from which to disappear in those days.

The house-to-house was in full swing. Ashton told her of discovering a sex-and-massage parlour in one of the new houses, where the knock at the door had been answered by the wife of a senior detective.

'Not very good at detecting, was he,' Kat ventured.

Mel's granny had been brought into the picture. To supplement Barry's efforts at list making, Mel was collecting details of her father's friends on the theory that some of them might still be about. They'd have to be spoken to. Barry became exceedingly dusty on his day off, trawling the local paper archives housed in the basement of the council's mortuary. Nobody had ever had the funds or the inclination to transfer the contents to an electronic medium. He came up with little apart from confirming that April that year had been unseasonably hot, the government voted not to reinstate capital punishment after all, house prices spiralled, and Motorola announced their first mobile telephone, the size of a breeze block. Closer to home, residents had been getting hot under the collar over the new Patrick Moore estate which was going up next door despite earlier promises of an eighteen-hole golf course on the land. Bickeridge Heights residents did not welcome living alongside East Enders dispossessed by the luxury redevelopment of their dockland slums. They felt they had already taken their East End quota after the bombing of the docks during the war.

It was now thirty-odd years since Jeff Rampart had disappeared. People died, moved, or were taken out of circulation by virtue of long-term incarceration in a care home, prison or hospital. The shortlist would be limited. It would not take Kat long to do the rounds.

Ashton rang from the Old Bailey. He claimed rigor mortis was setting in through the boredom of sitting around waiting to be called.

'I'm sorry to hear that,' Kat said. 'You've no idea what sort of day I've had. Would that mine had been as quiet as yours.'

'What have you been up to, then? Anything interesting?'

'You could say that. I was trotting across the estate to my little palace of an office this morning, minding my own business,' she said.

'As is your wont,' he said.

'Look, do you want the full SP or not?'

'Sorry. Please continue. I won't interrupt.'

'Right. I bumped into this man. Or, rather, he bumped into me. *Hey, doll, do us a favour,* he says. *Grab hold of this, and make an old soldier happy*, and tries to haul a suitcase over his garden fence. I reach up to take the case, but he overbalances and both he and his luggage go flying. I wore Docs yesterday cos I was on site with the builders. But the day someone offloads a ton of high quality metal forgers' plates onto my toes, I'm in flip-flops. Doc says there's nothing you can do with toes except tread carefully, walk slowly, and cancel the tango lessons.'

'Ouch!' Ashton winced and chortled simultaneously. 'He told you to tread carefully? Can't have known you very well! He might as well tell the Pope to stop being a Catholic.'

'Ha-bleeding-ha! Let's hope you don't turn into concrete while they keep you waiting in court all day.'

He was still laughing when she ended the call.

As well as his tale of the massage parlour and the policeman's wife, rumours were flying regarding the success of the house-to-house. An indoor hash farm siphoning power from street lamps had its electricity cut off; police were in discussions with councillors who wanted the crop as green compost. Thirty men lacking immigration papers were found to have knocked a hole between a pair of semis, making a dormitory; an unmarked charabanc with barred windows carted them away, causing a number of South London restaurants to close. Despite a lack of progress with the investigation, police morale was buoyant, clear-up rates soared, and the house-to-house became a sought-after duty.

Kat had begun to make time each day for the gym. Sprinting around the park had its limitations and she was not a natural athlete. If she had to make a spectacle of herself, she preferred to keep it relatively private. She would never break the pain barrier necessary for athletic success. However, reconciled to a fitness regime, she forced herself into uncomfortable positions on gym machines, hoping to shed a few pounds along the way. She was a long way from types like Ashton who thought nothing of running ten miles in knickers and vest before breakfast whatever the weather. Kat exercised in an effort to remain reasonably fit, to avoid stiffening up and to redistribute any flab brought on by the odd litre of wine or soft scoop. And a pizza or three.

In the gym she found she was in good company. The local vicar, who turned out to be the big biker from the community centre car park, was a regular, huffing and puffing through what the equipment manufacturers claimed to be a Fat Burn programme. Kat and everyone else suspected they'd been lying through their teeth. Barry, in his signature black, worked through a programme in slow-motion that Kat recognised from Karate Kid, and always ended up perched on one leg, for a laugh. There was a Mr Muscle with prison tats, number-one haircut and what looked like fingerless greengrocers' gloves, lifting weights. He never exchanged a word with anyone and took his exercise seriously. Two skinny middle-aged women strolled side by side on treadmills, using less calories on exercise than they did keeping up a strident, uninterruptible gabfest about the week's designer clothes at TKMaxx, the price of fish at Waitrose and the happy state of the weather in Lanzarote.

Kat stared ahead and worked her heart, fake jogging a level-twenty random programme of simulated peaks and troughs, and avoided involvement in the conversational marathon by the simple expedient of wearing headphones. Nobody had ever bothered her and probably ever would, warned off by the headphones, unaware that she had generally omitted to recharge her iPod. She always paced herself to catch women's hour in the steam room afterwards, and almost always had it to herself since the TKMaxx Two claimed that sitting around in the steam brought on wrinkles.

She peeled off her swimsuit, and stretched out on the slab in a haze of heated menthol and eucalyptus to the gentle sound of pan pipes and hiss of steam. She'd barely been there for five minutes when the door opened, and remained open, creating a cold draft.

'Come in or go out,' she called. 'Or I'll have to kill you.' The door closed. The steam renewed itself in energetic puffs.

Something grabbed one of her ankles. She jerked upright, her heart jumping, banging her head. Somebody screamed. It wasn't her.

'OW! 'Ere, watch it!'

She hadn't intended bead-butting her assailant. Unable to see through the steam, she edged backwards, in the direction of the door.

'Found ya!' The woman's eyeliner had melted in the steam; vertical runnels on her face had turned her into an oversize candelabrum. Kat scooted backwards into a corner. Her assailant, fully clothed, followed, with arms out, zombie fashion, through the steam.

'Oi, where are you? You was 'ere a minute ago.'

All thought of a relaxing doze in the steam disappeared. Holding her swimsuit up in an attempt at modesty, Kat squinted through the mist.

'Stay still, will ya?' The woman squelched down beside her on the slab. The haze was too thick to see all four walls at once but Kat knew that as long as she kept scuttling along the slab away from the woman she'd reach the door. She moved; the woman followed.

'I'm glad I managed to catch you while you're not doing anything.'

This had to be one of those naked-in-public-and-trying-to-cover-her-naughty-bits dreams. Soon she'd wake up, with her clothes on. She tried getting into her swimsuit but it was wet. She gave up, and instead kept it held strategically in front of her for some gravitas.

'I'm afraid I'm not dressed for company,' she said, trying to be polite but totally pissed off. It takes a certain skill to maintain a sense of dignity while naked. Her assailant backed off, Kat's tone and body language being sufficient disincentive.

'Listen, dear, I've got a bit of a housing problem I want you to see to,' the woman said. 'But I can see you're not a morning sort of person. I'll come back later, when you're dressed properly, shall I?'

CHAPTER 20

Coming out of the gym Kat ran slap into the postman in his cut-offs and distinctive orange vest. He was remonstrating with Karen who had been kicking the post box and swearing.

The box had an Out of Order sign scotch-taped to it.

'Ugh, slugs,' spat Karen. 'Gross, or what? The box is full of slime. I've got a pile to post but there's a queue longer than War and Peace at Lal's post office counter and I'm on my todd.'

She stopped as Shardonnay hove to, lugging her week's washing from the launderette in a Kensington nannies coach-built pram.

'It was never this way when we had a proper post office,' Shardonnay moaned. 'I dunno why they had to close it in the first place.'

'Tell me about it,' grumbled the postman.

'I'm on my way to Lal's,' Kat said. 'I can take your stuff and post it for you if you like.'

A cage had been installed at the back of Lal's mini mart to replace the Moor's stand-alone post office, which had been shut down in the previous round of cuts.

Kat used her time in the queue to check her messages and to earwig on local gossip. The line was still growing when she left forty-five minutes later for her morning surgery.

Questions and complaints addressed, advice given, forms completed, wills witnessed, passports signed, repairs and requests noted, by midday all that remained was a pair of middle-aged women reeking of tobacco.

The first had orange hair and skin like an alligator. All she wanted was an oyster, not pink, bathroom suite in her new home. That was easily disposed of. She could have sorted it out with a simple phone call, but this may have been her big outing of the week. Appeased, she marched off, a 36-pack of bog rolls jutting from her wheeled tartan shopping bag.

Kat's final supplicant was the steam room woman. Make-up reinstated, and fighting the ageing process with everything available to man or mortician, she had changed since the morning into in a blue-and-white striped bathing-tent dress.

'Call me Rosie. Did Shardonnay tell you I was coming in? No? I'm only her mum. Don't suppose you've got kids yet. No, didn't think so. You don't look fed up enough.'

It took Rosie a while to cut to the chase. As the woman catalogued her woes Kat doodled a family tree and tried to work out the relationships. It seemed Rosie had three children by two husbands: Cosmo King and one Trevor Picket. Shardonnay and Charisma King's younger brother, Lee Picket, was Karen's on-off partner, making the girls effectively sisters-in-law, and Rosie the almost-mother-in-law of Karen. She was another one who seemed happy with a few well-placed grunts and nods to accompany the sound of her own voice.

Kat wondered if this garrulousness, bordering on Asperger's, was something in the local gene pool. She switched to automatic pilot, doodling matchstick people queuing at a bus stop, half listening to a history of Rosie's thirty-year sojourn on the estate.

Running out of momentum, the woman came to the reason why she was seeking Kat's help. Her current difficulties were caused, she claimed, by the council having re-housed her an unreasonable distance from her daughters.

'So, to cut a long story short, dear,...'

Would that she had, Kat thought.

'I have to move nearer to the girls,' the woman explained. 'Cos where they are, it's too far for me to visit them without the car, which is off the road right now.'

Given that the estate measured less than half a mile in any direction, a geriatric in a walking frame could cross from side to side in fifteen minutes, or circle the estate in half an hour, max. What was the woman's beef? Kat reminded herself she was there to help, not criticise someone for being too bone idle to walk a few hundred yards. She promised to investigate. Rosie gave her the girls' addresses before heaving herself to her feet. She patted her pockets, searching.

'You can't lend us a fag, can you, darlin'?'

'Certainly.' Kat said, reaching for her emergency stash. They used to be advertised as cool as a mountain stream. Nowadays, a sombre black strip on the pack warned of hell and damnation and twenty types of lingering cancerous death. Smoking wasn't fun any more.

'Menthol?' Rosie made a moue of disgust and withdrew her hand faster than if she'd been offered a rattlesnake. 'Ugh! No, ta, dear. If I want mints I'll suck a polo, thanks all the same. No disrespect. By the way, I'd get something for that smell if I was you.'

'Smell?' Kat repeated.

The woman was right. Karen must have been microwaving a fish curry lunch for one again.

'When you talk to the council about me, they might have me under any number of names, but I've gone back to my maiden name now, Delaney,' she said, repairing her lipstick and checking her eye liner before leaving.

As the woman trotted out with her trolley Kat heard her muttering about 'proper fags'. She also caught the words 'MP', 'letter' and 'papers'. It was unclear whether the woman would be writing letters of complaint to her member of parliament or to the press or both about the tobacco crisis and/or her unsatisfactory housing position; Probably all the above, if the mood took her. Whatever. Kat popped her head through the open fire door to talk to Karen, and recoiled.

'Phew, what happened?' she asked.

'Glue,' Karen replied, hammering away at her PC with such vigour that the odds for the survival of her keyboard were next to nil.

'Glue?'

'Eh?' The girl sounded confused. 'Sorry. Thought you were asking about our letterbox. It was snails; they were after the glue. Someone put glue sticks inside and laid a trail up from the pavement.'

'I can't believe anybody would go to all that trouble,' Kat laughed.

'We'll have to do something about Mickey and Co.' Karen growled.

Kat had seen them, too, Curly, Chemo and Meccano Mickey, beside the post box the other day, doing their usual weird stuff about cauldrons and newts. Social Services and drama workshop were clearly not keeping the boys sufficiently stretched.

'One of these days!' Karen stomped back into the little box kitchen, calling back over her shoulder as she disappeared. 'Kat, can you do me a favour? Something's smelling the place out. I've used so much deodorant and air freshener that I've cleared the mini mart out out. Any chance of you lending me some until I can get over to the supermarket?'

One day they'd name a hole in the ozone layer after Karen. Kat rooted out her Coeur d'Or Total Protection from her bag and left it perched artistically on Karen's keyboard. If it contained half the ingredients it claimed – extracts of tea tree, rosemary, mint, sphagnum moss and elderberries – it would be more than enough to knock anything dead. It was meant to be a body spray, but Kat had once inadvertently used it as a fly killer, causing a particularly irritating bluebottle to meet a rapid and most noisy and unhappy end.

As she turned to leave, it occurred to her that Karen might not want an economy sized deodorant left sitting on her desk looking like an unsubtle hint about her personal hygiene, so she stuck a post it on the can before putting as much distance as she could between herself and the disgusting pong in her office.

CHAPTER 21

Winnie had popped in while Kat was out and helped himself to a packet of butter and half a dozen eggs she'd not put away. In her hurry to go out she had failed to close the kitchen window. There were eggshells on the floor. The chimp was now on silent stakeout beside the fridge. He had been through the laundry basket and retrieved her grubby all-purpose tee-shirt. A splatter of free-range egg yolk down the front had been added to the stains and paint splatters. He gave Kat a swift glance and a gummy grin before turning back to work with determination at the bottom edge of the door seal with a paw. He hadn't seen the strip of gaffer tape stuck to the top, which was keeping it closed.

Kat expected the tape to prove too much for his limited talents, but the chimp must have been something of a lateral thinker. He ran a sharp claw along the join and the tape parted. A bottle of fizzy water too plump for its slot in the door shot out. Dodging the missile, he whipped upright and clawed at a bag of herb salad. Greenery joined the eggshells on the kitchen floor.

'OUT,' Kat yelled with enough force in such a confined space to risk giving both Winnie and herself concussion.

Jerking his chin and pursing his lips, the creature blew a raspberry as she chased it onto the deck. Running the salad under the tap was effort wasted, given the combination of monkey germs and the condition of the kitchen floor.

Enough was definitely enough. Winnie's days of sneaking into the flat were at an end. Kat refused to be beaten by the dearth of nearby refuges or retirement homes for delinquent apes. There was a place in Yorkshire that according to its website had cats, dogs and canaries, one Nubian goat and a number of retired horses, circus or otherwise. It had also given house room to a marbled polecat found limping across the

Gateshead Millennium Bridge. However, nothing Kat said would persuade them to take an ape from the home counties even when she offered to pay its fare.

Time to rethink strategy. Curly, Chemo and Meccano Mickey couldn't be expected to take Winnie off her hands permanently. They had lives to disorganise, folk to irritate, appointments with probation officers and social workers and, on occasion, school to attend when they could be arsed or were not suspended. Drama workshop, too. They were in trouble there after last week's dress rehearsal for Macbeth, when they'd smuggled the creature in as a fur tippet for Lady M's costume.

Winnie wasn't stupid. Sensing Armageddon, he kept out of the way. Kat checked the Yellow Pages for the nearest RSPCA, emptied one of her removals boxes, and waited.

After a couple of days on the tiles, overcome by greed or hunger, or both, for Winnie the unaccustomed aroma of egg and bacon breakfast coming from Kat's kitchen was too much,.

Waiting until the boys were off visiting their probation officer on the other side of town, Kat carried her captive to the car. She sang all the way into town, not caring that the angry, spitting head sticking out of the cardboard box on the passenger seat of her rust-bucket received some strange looks as she drove through the heavy traffic.

She had run a broken curtain pole through the top of the container as a carrying handle. When Winnie tore the box and shoved a belligerent arm through the top, she cuffed him to the pole with pink plastic party shop handcuffs. Howls of rage and protest drowned the noise of her rattling exhaust. She hauled her home-made pet transporter on the curtain-pole, big game safari style, into the pet surgery and lifted it onto the counter, which was empty aside from an RSPCA donation box, a desk bell, and a sleeping kitten pretending to be a fluffy paperweight on a stack of papers. Winnie sneezed violently. He had an allergy to cats but that was not her problem any longer. A manic parakeet paused in its demented plucking of feathers long enough to croak 'Gesundheit' before returning to plucking. The demented bird's human companion stared ahead, unblinking. Further down the line of seats a mother sat with a child clutching a plastic pet transporter. There was no clue what might be inside.

The disinfectant smell was strong but it failed to mask the odour of ape. It might have been worse had not Kat swathed his nether regions in six supermarket bags. Although if the animal had disgraced himself in the car, another set of stains would hardly have been a disaster.

The ambience in the waiting room was undertaker chic, lacking only the Arum Lilies. Utter silence. A phone began to ring in the background, its faraway tones having the echo of a lost cause.

Kat pinged the old-fashioned bronze desk bell, which was the only thing of any character in the place. No Design Centre furniture or works of art, no mood muzak, potted plants or gurgle of exotic aquaria in low-lit corners. The room was furnished in neutral easy-clean grey: grey lino, grey side table empty of ornament or magazines, grey wipe-down metal and vinyl chairs designed to cope with the constant deluges of body fluids and guts, loss of bladder or sphincter control or the projectile heaving up of other unmentionables by man or beast and everything in between. There was a short burst of barking. The phone continued to ring. Kat imagined the staff were most likely up to their Marigolds in some creature's innards. Or on their tea break. Or both.

She was tempted to dump the box and make a run for it but didn't trust the other customers not to rat her out. The phone stopped. There was the muffled sound of a woman's voice in the background. When all went quiet once more, Kat double-pinged the desk bell a second time. There wasn't much else to do, not even any out-of-date magazines to flick through. There was a notice board with pictures of missing cats and escaped cage birds, a flyer for an aged three-legged tortoise answering to the name of Trigger who had gone walkabout, homes wanted for rescued animals, obedience tuition offered, dog-walking services, dog whisperers, and meditation classes for stressed pets. Several carpenters expressed their willingness to make a variety of residences from dog kennels to dovecotes. No pets wanted ads. Pity. Nobody was offering a loving home to a house-trained skateboarding ape with a penchant for breaking into homes and stealing from secured fridges.

'Hello, who've we here?' The voice on the phone had materialised. Well into her fifties, her straight, shoulder length salt-and-pepper hair, heavy on the salt, was topped off with a fringe of surgical precision above rimless glasses. She was wearing garden gloves strong enough to yank up brambles. She smiled over the counter, speaking in that octave-too-high Minnie Mouse voice some use towards small children or old people with dementia. There was an excited snitter from the chimp.

'Hello, Winnie, long time no see; what have we been up to?'

Long time no see? Life was getting better, with the opportunity to get rid of the offensive-at-both-ends overactive piece of shag-pile.

'He's fine. Might need a bit of a clean,' she said rapidly.

'Oh, what happened?' the woman asked.

'He fell into some oil the other day. He's housetrained, likes dressing up and he can skateboard. Hours of fun for the kiddies. You'll tell whoever takes him, won't you? Must dash. Bye.' Kat made for the door,

'No, wait.' The woman gave a syrupy smile. 'This little chap is very special. We were worried when he went off. Still, he hasn't done too badly, has he? Apart from losing a bit of weight. He was taking food put out for the pigeons but he must be hungry now they've gone, poor lamb.'

'Lamb? He's a pest,' Kat rejoined. 'Actually he's an absolute nightmare. He follows me about, breaks into my flat, attacks people, wrecks the place, steals food. And he dresses up in my clothes.'

'Who's a naughty boy, then?' the assistant simpered. 'He's chosen you, dear: that's lovely. I expect you want him to have a check-up and a repeat of his Valium. His injections were up to date, last time I checked.'

Valium? Injections? Vet's bills? No chance.

'No, that's all right, he's not here for a check-up. I'm the one wanting the Valium, not him. I'd like you to re-home him, or send him to a sanctuary. Failing that, I'm sure you'd agree he should be put out of his misery. Whatever it takes, as long as I get rid of him.'

There was a tsunami of disapproval. The mother and child pair stared but remained silent. The parakeet squawked, and its owner gave a disapproving click of her tongue The kitten paperweight, disturbed from its doze on the counter, gave the room the evil eye.

'Oh, dear,' the assistant continued. 'We had him here for a while but he escaped. Three times. We tried a sanctuary. When he escaped, he let the other animals out. It caused havoc. I'm sure he'll be better behaved if he has a chance to settle into a proper home. Pets bring their own rewards. Chimps are very bright. Winnie's such an independent soul.'

'Sorry, no can do. My work keeps me on the move. My flat's tiny. No time. No room. I'll leave him here.' Kat made for the door once more.

'No, wait!' The assistant ran alongside, lugging Winnie, still in his removals box. 'We re-homed him four times. Nothing works. He always escapes and makes his way back home, but I think he's adopted you.'

The chimp was bright enough to sense what was at stake. He stood quietly, as if butter wouldn't melt. It was an Oscar-winning performance. orphan Annie, sad smile atremble. Kat wasn't taken in by such a ham.

'Listen, I'm not a pet person,' she insisted. 'I work long hours, I move around between jobs, I'm never in. He'd be lonely, neglected.'

'He wouldn't take much looking after,' the woman insisted.

Kat didn't believe a word of it. She knew she would come home one day and find him stretched out cold, the flat filled with fur balls and stale pee. Or worse. He'd invite his mates to dress up in her meagre wardrobe while she was out earning a crust.

'Is there no chance you might keep him?' the woman pleaded.

Kat had made up her mind. 'No way, sorry,' she said, firmly.

'None?' the woman asked. 'It'd be such a shame to put him down.' She stroked Winnie through the hole in the box. The ape purred like a cat. They had a good double act going.

'Nope. Sorry.'

'Poor old chap. Any chance at all?'

'Absolutely not,' Kat said, pushing the box back over the counter for the umpteenth time.

'Oh, dear.' The woman knew when she was beaten.

On her way out Kat did a half turn to say a polite 'Goodbye,' but not swivelling enough to let anyone think she would change her mind.

'Mum, is that lady leaving her monkey to be killed?' wailed the kid with the animal container.

'Shh, Alfie,' the mother replied. She gave Kat a grim stare. 'She's allowed to. It's her monkey, none of our business.'

Alfie let rip a siren wail that made the hair on Kat's neck stand up.

'Oh, for God's sake, give him back,' she sighed.

The kid switched off the howl.

'I can't guarantee he'll be properly cared for. I honestly do have a demanding job.'

'I'm sure you'll do your best, dear,' trilled the assistant.

Kat was never going to get her money refunded from the removals firm. The box was no longer in a fit state to be returned. The vet's assistant, relieved to have averted another tragedy, tore it open, whipped Winnie out, mopped him down and handed him over with a fluffy towel around his neck towel like a hairy boxer between rounds.

Kat heard sniggers from shoppers as she returned to the car with Winnie hugging her leg like a particularly ugly toddler and sucking the end of the towel for comfort. What? Were their kids so different?

It was turning into one of those days. That morning she had run out of toothpaste, bog roll and fresh food, the hot water was off, and her electronic doorbell had jammed on *Jaws* although she'd set it for *Close Encounters*. Worst of all, she'd allowed herself to be lumbered with an unwanted chimpanzee. And the day wasn't over.

Winnie hopped into the passenger seat and pulled the belt around him, good as gold. Kat wasn't fooled. Fuelled by irritation and a near-empty tank, she and her Mini achieved nought to thirty in seven seconds.

The British Motor Corporation would have expected no less. She didn't knock out any gates, fences, or flower beds, and made sure both their seat belts were sufficiently tight to thwart any inclination she might develop on the homeward journey to punch the smug creature through the windscreen.

The dark garage area beneath the flats had once been an Aladdin's cave of stolen car and bike parts. It had never been a place anyone wanted to wander around. These days it was empty. No self-respecting petty thief wanted to come home to find their cache buried under a ton of rubble, inside a council crusher or carted off to landfill. Kat usually gave the shadows a miss and parked in the road, where she could keep an eye on her car. Her insurers had full details of the vehicle, so there was no point leaving it to get stolen. The payout wouldn't stretch to a push bike. Now, ignoring the hosepipe ban, she opened the doors and washed Winnie and the car in one. The chimp shivered, got ready to make a fuss.

'My house, my rules, so shut up or ship out.'

It was a warm day. They'd dry out soon enough.

'I warn you,' she hissed through gritted teeth once they were indoors. 'You make one false move and you're finished. Understand?' She gave him a banana and put the kettle on.

Winnie treated her to a leery, yellow-toothed smile ending in a big rubbery kissing motion and turned on the television to watch Pingu.

CHAPTER 22

Life was improving. By Sunday morning, Mobile phones were working again. Curly, Chemo and Meccano Mickey were looking after Winnie, and Kat had Barry's list. She'd called in at the community centre that morning, when, with all the body language of a spy passing classified information, he'd slid a scrap of paper across the bar.

'Gosh, this is exciting,' he whispered. 'I feel like Mata Hari. Be careful not to lose this, Petal.' He walked off with studied nonchalance to serve a customer. It was only a piece of paper, for Heaven's sake. Kat skim read: it bore a resemblance to the list Mel had made from her gran's Christmas card address book. Cosmo King featured on both, as did the Delaney clan. Trevor Picket was there, too: quite a family affair.

For the crowd at the Maurice Mickelwhite the mystery was last week's news. They were now focussed on the carnival, growing more ambitious with the addition of a parade with drum majorettes and marching bands. Anyone claiming a gram of talent for anything legal had entered the preliminary heats for an X Factor contest. Kat had thought nothing could be as excruciating as the real thing. She was wrong.

She had spoken to the council about the Delaneys' housing situation, and had visited both Shardonnay and her sister Charisma, two doors down. She dreaded telling Rosie that the two girls were housed exactly where they had wanted to be, near each other and as far away from their mum as possible, and were delighted with their new homes.

'Don't tell her,' Shardonnay had pleaded. 'She'll go ape-shit!'

She had also fitted in visits to fourteen people who remembered when the estate had its own home beat officer and were happy to gossip without Kat having to explain. Unfortunately, some listed as original residents had moved on to the other side of the borough, the other side of the river, the other side of the world, or simply the other side.

Jeff Rampart was remembered as a good copper, fair and honest, quiet and friendly, popular with children, animals and old ladies, who enjoyed a drink with his mates both male and female, and did his job well. None of it got her any further forward; she still had nothing substantial and she was fast running out of ideas how to continue obtaining information without alerting suspicion. If the skeleton was Mel's dad, where was the motive?

Rampart would not have been killed for money: he had only his police wage to live on, and very little in the bank. He didn't own a house. He biked around the estate, and shared a car with his mother. Sex did not appear to be an issue. Kat's enquiries had failed to unearth any particular girlfriends although a number of people said he'd led an active social life since his wife ran off.

There was no ransom note to indicate a kidnap. Humble beat bobbies were seldom deemed worth the effort. Unless he was dead or amnesiac or wandering homeless, national insurance, employment records, medical care, cash withdrawals and accommodation would be on record somewhere. If he had done a runner and was living under a false identity his papers and records might be harder to find. Ruling out the last possibility, what remained? Revenge? For what? The miscellany of petty criminals he had helped put away appeared to bear no grudge. Kat had spoken to one woman he'd arrested for ten year's unpaid TV licence fines, who sang his praises.

'It was a laugh,' she told Kat. 'They put me in an open prison in a big Tudor manor house down Maidstone. Thought I was there for a month. Then I got released for good behaviour two weeks early. It was the best fortnight of me life, cheaper than Benidorm, no kids hanging around me neck all day. I made some real friends, too. They put me on a training course for numeracy and business, and got me an office job after I got out. I still keep in touch, you know, cards at Christmas and birthdays, sort of thing. I wouldn't have missed it for the world.'

The drinking crowd agreed he had been in the Stargazer on the night in question. It had been rowdy and cheerful and without upset. Nobody saw him after he left to go home.

Kat put more flip-chart paper on the kitchen wall alongside her regeneration chart, and followed that with a town planning blueprint of the original estate, although she doubted that would throw up any clues. She added names to the list of people she'd spoken to, highlighting those she still had to see. After each name she made a note of what, if anything, she had learned, and gazed out of the window, thinking.

She failed to get inspiration from the rusted engine parts that had appeared on her deck overnight. The boys had taken Winnie fishing. It was a relief not to have him tapping on the window to be let in or hogging the TV remote. Two nights ago she'd caught him watching an adult movie. In a new take on the infinite monkey theorem of typing at random and over time producing Hamlet, Winnie in his wisdom had successfully keyed in unlimited free access to an adult Pay Per View sex channel and put it on Favourites. Kat waited until he was out before doctoring the remote and activating the parental controls.

She hadn't spoken to Cosmo King, or to Rosie's second husband, Trevor Picket. She circled their names and in a creative frenzy followed it with question marks against a number of others. She stared at her work. It wasn't terrible impressive, merely a series of lists.

If Jeff Rampart was as popular and ordinary as claimed, if he had no enemies, hadn't eloped to Gretna with a girl, not cracked under the strain of walking the beat and done a runner, not been abducted by aliens via a rift in the space time continuum, where was he? She ruled out spontaneous combustion and that old fall-back the abracadabra thunderclap with accompanying magic puff of smoke. All that remained was the dead-in-a-ditch option. More than ever she was convinced Mel was right in putting her money on the skeleton being that of her father.

However, it did not answer the question of how he had ended up there. What was she missing? She checked the names on her pad once more. Picking up a pen she crossed out each name in turn until she was left with Cosmo King, Trevor Picket, and the missing Delaney brother. They'd been at school with Rampart. Rosie Delaney ditto. Kat added her to the page, drew a circle around it and added a big question mark.

Sooner or later she'd have to give Rosie the bad news about her housing expectations. She wondered how well the woman remembered Jeff Rampart. She checked her watch. Half one. They would have finished their Sunday roast by now. Best get it out of the way.

CHAPTER 23

Ten years earlier, artist's drawings for the multi-million-Euro makeover of the Sir Patrick Moore Estate had shown happy multi-ethnic groups strolling in Mediterranean sunshine along tree-lined avenues decked with hanging baskets. Such optimistic flights of fancy were only to be expected of architects, but on such a balmy afternoon, Kat could see what they'd been aiming for.

In Centauri Close, flat-roofed bunker blocks of flats had been demolished and replaced by three pretty terraces of cottage-style houses, with bright red-tiled roofs and pitched gables. Kat liked that they each had different coloured front doors.

Rosie Delaney lived at the top of the Alpha cul-de-sac of two-bedroom houses, each with its own front garden, matching car space and green railings. Small porches provided cover for wheelie bins and skateboards. Engerland flags, some in their enthusiasm reaching the ground, were strung from upstairs windows. There was an eclectic mix of real and faux burglar alarms, hollow and useless or cheap enough to be triggered by a bird landing on the windowsill.

One of the many houses sporting a red and white flag draped out of a first-floor window, number 20 was identical to number 22 to its right and number 18 to its left. It was also identical to numbers 15,17, 19 and 21 opposite, except that in place of a tiny lawn, it had colourful crazy paving from granite off-cuts salvaged from work by Rosie's partner. She also had a string of blue rope lights framing the bright pink front door which was almost hidden by a scruffy Volvo Estate with a rusted roof. Lack of a wheel, overflowing ashtrays and a mountain of empty beer cans on the back seat implied it did not spend much time on the road.

It did not seem to be family-around-the-table-for-Sunday-roast at number twenty. Through the wide picture window Kat could see Rosie

Delaney and two men. One, paunchy, middle-aged, languished on the rococo sofa in a sleeveless tee-shirt that left his belly button displayed above baggy jeans that had settled well below politeness. The other, whom Kat assumed was Karen's boyfriend Lee, was hunched in front of a plasma TV with a blank screen and minus its back panel. Decked out in a football strip and baggy jeans, he didn't look too well. He'd made a stab at maturity with a goatee, in the sparseness of which one hand was making a desultory attempt at grooming while he stared morosely at the TV. From the air of deep mourning in the room it wasn't necessary to have a psychic reading to know that the television, the cause of their gloom, was not going to come back from the dead in the near future.

'Should'a phoned. I would'a put a face on.'

Last seen, Rosie had been wearing half the cosmetics counter at Boots. Today she had not progressed beyond eyeliner, and had a bag of carrots on her head. Hugging an open tube of Pringles and a wine glass, she sucked on a cigarette which was covering her fluffy mules in ash dandruff. Kat had a nicotine rush from standing in the doorway.

There was a shout from the front room to close the effin' door and stop letting the effin' draught in.

'Miserable sod,' Rosie muttered. 'Come in, don't let the heat out.'

Kat thought it possible that through the smoke haze they might not have been aware that outside it was about as warm and bright as it gets in early May. Rosie's face puckered as she sucked hard and tried to keep smoke from getting in her eyes. The cigarette wobbled precariously when she spoke and clouds billowed from her nostrils. Single file, the two women squeezed past the bicycle in the hall. Close to, Kat saw the bag of carrots was only orange foam rollers under a red hairnet.

'She here for the rent arrears?' called the voice from the front room.

Rosie popped her head around the door and glared. 'No, bollock brain, it's about me transfer. Put yer head back on straight.'

They weren't anything like the Waltons.

'This is Colin, my partner,' Rosie said by way of explanation.

Kat reached forward to shake hands. The lump on the sofa coughed, giving her a demonstration of ferociously bad breath.

The place was filled with religious artefacts, saving the bother of going to church. Saintly table lamps rested beside saintly pictures and statuettes. Wall plates depicted hippy saints with birds, martyrs pierced with arrows, Christian warriors on and off horses. Kat expected the tea towels to be Shrouds of Turin, but they were plain, old-fashioned red and white stripes, hung to dry on the oven door.

'It's doing my head in,' Rosie grumbled. 'The telly's stopped working. Keeps changing channel all by itself. Next door's the same. Clear that stuff off, will you, dear. Wanna Pringle? I only have them for the coupons, so I can win a plasma TV.' She thrust the tube at Kat. Her cigarette wobbled and shed more ash.

'Er, no thanks.' Kat wouldn't have minded a cup of tea, but with the remains of last night's takeaway littering the work top and a sink full of crockery? No chance. She moved the ironing from a chair onto the table.

'Would you like me to close your fridge door?' she asked.

'No, leave it, dear. Lee and Karen had a row last night,' Rosie said, lowering her voice. 'Six cans of Stella and he turns into the Hulk, fights anyone not in a wheelchair.'

Lee, it appeared, was jobless and, as a consequence, depressed. Slung out by Karen, he had crawled home to his mother's in the early hours determined on suicide by gas oven, unaware his mum's new house was all electric.

'Daft bugger stuck his head in the fridge instead, and threw up over the Sunday chicken. We're going down the Harvester later for an all-you-can-eat buffet,' Rosie mumbled through the crunch of Pringles. She dragged on her Marlborough Light and blasted smoke through her nostrils. 'But sod him. What about my transfer?' The cigarette wobbled. Live ash landed on the kitchen floor like a stranded ladybird.

'Tread on that for us, will you?'

Kat stamped on the still-glowing ember. It had already scorched a symmetrical black hole in the pale laminate floor.

'I'm afraid that whatever way we look at it, a transfer nearer your daughters isn't possible,' Kat said. 'You're entitled to a maximum of two bedrooms. The girls' road only has three-bedroom houses.'

'But for regeneration moves, we're entitled to one bedroom over what we need. The second bedroom's for Lee. So we qualify for three.'

'Lee isn't a dependent. The council knows he lives at Karen's'. They're expecting to be rehoused as a family,' Kat explained.

'I dunno what to do now. I can't ask the councillors,' she said.

'Why is that?'

'I used to be married to Trev, he's Councillor Picket now, calls himself Trevor. We're not on speaking terms. First, I was married to Cosmo but we divorced when Shardonnay was ten and Charisma was six. Then I married Trev, and we had Lee. Once Trev got on the council, he started calling himself Trevor. He got too full of himself, just because he's the leader of the opposition party, with only two in it, which doesn't count for much around here. I didn't take up with Colin Cholmondeley – she had pronounced it Chumley – till much later, after my second divorce.

'Ah, right,' Kat replied. 'If you don't want to ask Councillor Picket for help, how about asking Mel Dickson, or the lady councillor from the other party?

'That councillor's too snotty-nosed for me, and if I told Mel Dickson, it'd get back to the grandmother. Joan Rampart and me, we've never got on, not since me and Jeff was an item after his wife scarpered. I wasn't married in them days. Joan never liked me, evil old witch.'

'You knew the Ramparts, then?' Kat asked.

'Yeah, but I was much younger than him. Hardly out of my teens.'

And I was born yesterday, Kat thought. Were that the case, it would make Rosie a child bride and teenaged mother.

'I heard that Mr Rampart disappeared leaving the two children with his mother,' Kat said, feigning the ignorance of an incomer. 'Why do you think that was?'

'Well, nobody knows, dear,' Rosie said. 'I remember, it was Easter, boiling hot. Bit like last week. The pub was packed. This is way before the community centre was built. Jeff and me was going out together that night; and I was all dolled up.'

Kat smiled politely. It was hard to imagine a younger Rosie; she may have been better looking in those days. Presumably she had not gone for today's underdone waffle look in an off-white candlewick robe with ash marks which was a few buttons short, and emphasised that she was considerably past her sell-by.

'There I was, all tarted up, and at the last minute I got called in to help out at the pub cos there's a rush on. Jeff came in, and all the old crowd: my brothers and some friends from West Ham and Wapping, and Cosmo, Trev, and Bernie and their mates. They drank themselves silly, seeing as it was Easter. The men who'd got work were subbing any who were on the dole. In the end half of them were so pissed they couldn't go home. Some just curled up on the banquettes. We had a hell of a job next day, clearing up.'

'Did Jeff spend the night there, too?' Kat asked.

'Now I come to think of it, no, he didn't,' the woman said. 'What happened?' she said. 'Let's see. I called last orders, then what? Yeah, I remember. One of the Wapping mob was sick on him. Jeff said not to worry, and he went off to the gents. I never saw him after that.'

'What do you think might have happened to him?'

'I can't imagine. I'd sunk a few myself by closing time. I wondered if he'd gone off in a huff because I'd been taking drinks from the Wapping mob,' she said. 'Wait, though. There was one thing.' She munched some crisps. Kat waited.

'When we was locking up, someone found his jacket in the gents. It was covered in sick. Pam, the bar manager, she had a stronger stomach than me, so she empties the pockets and leaves the coat in a carrier bag for him to collect and she drops the other stuff off at his house on her way home. Couple of days later we hear he's done a runner.'

'A couple of days?' Kat asked.

'Well, I was annoyed with him cos he was meant to be taking me home after work but he didn't show up. It might have been two days. I can't be sure after all this time. Hang on. Easter wasn't it? We must have heard he was missing on the Saturday; nobody ever went out anywhere on Good Friday in those days. It must've been the Saturday or Sunday. They never did find him? Lovely bloke, he was, too.'

'This bar manager, Pam, the one who took his belongings home,' Kat said. 'Do you know how to contact her?'

'Pam? Oh, shame, that: she was on that ferry that went down,' she said. 'You're too young. It was over twenty years ago. Car ferry, in the channel. They didn't close the loading doors properly and it tipped over faster than the Titanic, right there in the harbour. Hundreds drowned.'

'How awful. What about her family?' Kat asked.

'None left, now. Her mum died years ago. I never knew her dad.' Rosie dug inside her Pringles tube, seeming surprised to find it empty. 'I swear they put less in the packet these days. You used to be able to –'

Kat never found out what you used to be able to do. Raised voices from the living room did not suggest male bonding.

'Effin' 'ell, Rosie, stop nattering, and get in here.' Colin bobbed up through the serving hatch like a Punch and Judy man. Rosie squawked, sending Pringles into orbit. Colin disappeared from the hatch, reappearing seconds later in the kitchen, accompanied by a popping bubble wrap sound as he waded through Pringles.

'Lee, the barmy sod, he's on the roof; says he's gonna jump.'

CHAPTER 24

Colin led the charge upstairs to where trainer prints on the wall of the bathroom, and the medicine cabinet hanging askew, mapped Lee's progress.

Rosie followed, gasping for air through her Pringles.

'The roof won't hold him,' Colin prophesied, ignoring her predicament. 'Someone'll have to dial 999, or go up there after him.'

Kat was of the view that by the time the emergency services arrived it would be too late to do anything more than scrape Lee off the pavement, but didn't want to say so. Dozy Rosie was no more in any condition to go up after her son than was Colin, had either of the overweight pair been able to get through the skylight.

Where are the superheroes when they're needed? If this was a film, Kat would be Sandra Bullock driving a busload to safety, Michael Caine coming up with a brainwave to rescue the bullion before it slipped over the edge, or Flash Gordon saving the earth in fourteen hours. Yeah, dream on. In real life, she who hesitates is more likely to survive. However, the idiot could kill himself while they waited for the fire brigade. Waiting wasn't an option.

'Shit. Shit. Shit,' she muttered. 'Where do you keep your ladder?'

'Ain't never needed one,' said Colin. 'That's the council's job.'

That figured.

'I don't think we can afford to hang about waiting for the emergency services,' Kat said, hoping to be contradicted.

'You could always take the safety rail off the bunk beds, Col,' Rosie said. 'I had to whack Shardonnay's kids for using it as a climbing frame in the garden last week.'

There was an inevitability about it. Colin said he supposed he'd better show her where the rails were, leaving his other half to keep an eye on

Lee. Cigarette in mouth, he went ahead of Kat with all the vigour of a retreat from Moscow.

Given that Lee was not meant to be living with his parents any longer, Kat was surprised to find his room a slum. The armchair under the window was acting as an overflow for his chest of drawers. One wall was peppered with Blu-tack where he'd taken down posters. The bookcase had insufficient space for the DVDs, hair gels, and soccer paraphernalia. A mountain of socks had taken up residence on the floor. Lee's bed was the bottom half of a pair of bunks with the child-safety rails on the upper visible beneath a pile of clothes.

'Lee? You comin' down off that roof?' Rosie craned her neck through the skylight, giving a running commentary. 'He's standing there. He's moving across. He's going to sit down. No. He's standing there. Come on, Lee.'

Lee ignored her.

'Stop messin' about or I'll kick yer arse,' said Colin.

Definitely not the Waltons: this pair was something else altogether. Kat wedged the impromptu ladder in the bath, with a towel to stop it slipping, tucked her emergency cigarettes, lighter and mobile into her cleavage, hitched up her skirt and headed for the summit.

Her stomach gave a lurch when she poked her head through the skylight and spotted Lee perched on the shallow pitched roof. Her ankles were tingling before she'd even got out there. Ashton's chat-up at the civic photo-call had taken her mind off the scariness of that other rooftop two weeks earlier. She shouldn't have snubbed him. He was most likely somewhere on the M1 tooling back to the sticks after his sister's wedding. Just as well.

'I'll bloody kill myself properly this time.' Lee wiped a sleeve across his face and Kat brought her mind back to the situation before her.

She had often found herself in weird situations not of her choosing, but she'd never done anything this reckless. Negotiating skills were part of her job In theory, as long as they're talking they're not jumping. She crossed her fingers and hoped Lee had read the same training manual.

'Hello, Lee, how are you doing?' Pathetic. She was getting too old to lark about at altitude. Her mouth was dry. 'Mind if I join you?' she said, hoping he'd tell her to go away and mind her own business.

'What for?' He was talking. A good sign. Wasn't it?

'To see if you're okay. Can I come up?' she said, and waited while he gave her suggestion some thought.

'I don't care,' he said after a while. 'Not too near, or I'll jump.'

Half in, half out, she struggled to get through the skylight onto the roof where he was shuffling nearer the edge. The pitch was shallow, but nonetheless steep enough to do damage if she went headlong. Squeezing her backside through, she sat on the frame with her legs dangling inside the bathroom, and paused for thought.

Someone ought to have dialled 999 instead of making her go through all this palaver. She wondered if the dozy pair downstairs had stopped panicking and managed to get themselves sufficiently together to have called the fire brigade.

'Fancy a can of cola?' she asked, inspired.

'No. Wouldn't mind a Stella,' Lee said. 'Has Colin got the football back on, yet?'

'Not yet,' she said. Through the skylight she mimed drinking. 'Two, no alcohol, fast.' Two cans of Fanta were thrust upwards.

'Here, have this.' Kat held one aloft. 'Want to chat about it?'

'No, the only thing I wanna do is watch football,' he said, which was a pity because everything Kat knew about the game you could stick on the head of a pin and still have room to let.

She felt a tile slip when she shifted her backside up against the window frame for support. Lee spun around and almost lost his footing.

'You'll have to come closer to get this.' She held the can aloft.

'Yeah, all right.' Lee sat down and shunted in her direction.

The sun slipped behind a cloud making her wish she'd worn something more substantial than a sundress.

'You can come nearer if you have to, but don't try anything,' he said, stretching his arm for the drink.

She handed him one of the cans and heaved the rest of her onto the roof where she lay panting, grateful she hadn't dislocated her collarbone squeezing through the skylight. She wiped slippery hands on the skirt of her dress, surprised not to see blood. Micro-wobble-board fitness sandals were a bit of a liability on a roof. She slipped them off and squatted on the tiles before edging out, and tried not to look down.

Across the field, at the concrete footings for the new sports pavilion, a bunch of navvies paid no heed to the drama on the roof, and sat smoking around a cement mixer, their heads following the drum.

'Did they send you up here?' Lee asked, with a jerk of his head towards the skylight.

Kat glanced down to where Colin and Rosie stood with their mouths agape like gigantic baby birds waiting to be fed. She began to edge closer to Lee.

'Oi!' His yell almost dislodged her. 'You can bloomin' stop there!' He scuttled towards the edge.

Kat jerked back, leaving her sandals to bump across the tiles and disappear over the side. She wasn't having much luck with shoes lately. She'd be next if she didn't look out. She grabbed at an air vent and broke her last decent fingernail.

'I shall jump if they stay there, watching,' whined Lee.

'You don't want to jump, Lee,' she said. tempted, if he carried on like this to do everyone a favour and put him out of his misery. 'You're a bit off colour right now, that's all. Whatever is wrong can be fixed. You can always change things. It'll all be different tomorrow.' Yuck! Any more Hallmark moments like that and she'd be jumping with him.

'It just all gets on top of you,' he moaned. 'It's always the same.'

'I'm sorry to hear that. Jumping won't change anything for the better.'

Actually, it would, for her, because she could then go home to the evening she'd planned for herself – Rioja, takeaway, Winnie out with the boys, Thelma and Louise on the Movie Channel, early night, and raring to start work first thing Monday morning.

'If we keep shouting at each other like this, both of us will fall off.'

'All right, then. You can come over.'

Kat began to inch across the sloping roof on her backside, skirt hitched up like Widow Twanky. She was almost there when Lee lost his grip and they began sliding towards the edge.

CHAPTER 25

The chorus of shrieks that rose from below almost had them both off, and drowned the background of food van jingles and emergency sirens. At the crucial moment, Kat hooked her fingers under a tile. It held.

She waited for her pulse to settle before peering cautiously over the edge. They'd drawn quite a crowd. Krishna Ices, not missing an opportunity, was trading briskly. A burger van had set up alongside. The neighbours, keeping one eye on the kids and the other on the unfolding drama, were heaving Rosie's Volvo into the road. Others had hauled a children's trampoline from a back garden in Beta Centauri Close onto the cleared space. Winnie, home from his morning fishing and recovered from his ordeal at the vet's, had hitched a ride. He'd been to Kat's laundry basket again: even from that distance the grey thing he wore on his head was recognisably her rattiest bra. His lips were drawn back in a gruesome sepia-toothed smile. He was enjoying himself. Eyes wide and bright, he bounced up and down, avoiding the forest of limbs. The trampoline could become a lot more crowded if Lee or Kat took a dive.

Kat had not been fast enough to avoid Lee's second downward hurtle. As he'd grabbed her leg one of the thin shoulder straps on her dress snapped. Entertaining everyone with a striptease was the last thing she needed. With her free hand she looped the shoulder straps together, and wedged her cigarettes and mobile more firmly into her cleavage. Now that he'd got himself attached to her leg, how was she going to get off the roof without breaking her neck?

She could shake him off, but he'd plummet faster than share prices, and she'd be the bad guy. She could let him hang on, or do nothing until they both plunged earthwards or he dislocated her leg, in which case opinion would be divided. On the other hand, she could try to yank him back up. Since it would save their bacon and she'd end up the good guy after all, it was not much of a decision. Hooking one arm around the heating vent, she grabbed his tee-shirt.

'Come on, slow, back to me,' she said. This was the hard bit.

Grunting and puffing and muttering a string of obscenities, Lee hauled himself up between her legs to lie alongside her like an exhausted lover. Not elegant. She wasn't even sure it was legal in public, but they were both still alive, still on the roof, and still in one piece. Just.

'I'm gasping for a smoke,' Lee said. 'Got any fags?'

'What? Oh, yes, hang on.' Careful not to lose what purchase she had, she took her time dipping into her cleavage, attempting to hide her shaking hands as she recovered her cigarettes and her equilibrium. ***Smoking can seriously endanger your life and the lives of those around you***, proclaimed the big black letters. Not as fast as a hike off a pitched roof and a hard landing on a bunch of gawpers.

'Eh? Poof cigarettes? That all you got?' he protested, horrified. Lee was his mother's son: no question.

'So they're menthol,' Kat retorted. 'You either want one or you don't. Suit yourself.'

Presented with Hobson's Choice, Lee reached for the pack. Kat took one for herself, drawing several rapid breaths to keep it lit. She coughed as the four-months-stale toothpaste-flavoured tobacco filled her mouth and lungs. Another New Year resolution bites the dust. The smoke filtered out inelegantly through her nostrils. She'd almost forgotten the drill, but if being kippered kept her mind off their predicament, she'd keep him company, puff for puff, for now. As the lady said, tomorrow is another day. Lee shunted closer, drawing on the cigarette, menthol notwithstanding. So far so good. They sat a couple of feet apart, side by side, puffing, and watching an Airbus heading into Heathrow. It was getting near the holiday season. Busy time. Lee rocked back and forth. It was hypnotic. The sun had turned his fair skin pink. They both drew in tobacco, coughed in unison and went back to staring into space. Lee had smoked his way through his cigarette before he said anything further.

'You know Karen, don't you?' he said 'Works in the housing office. You seen our kid, Karlee, yeah? I can't even afford to feed her. Karen does it all. Sod it, give us another fag,' he demanded, reaching out.

Kat discarded her half smoked cigarette and bum-scuttled closer. As they lit up again she saw they were too near the edge. One small slip for mankind. The second cigarette tasted as stale as the first. Lee flicked ash over the side, and scrambled to his feet, perilously near the edge.

'Wait!' Kat yelled, her heart jack-hammering.

Her skirt was rucked up, her top was scarcely holding up under the strain, her shoes had gone for a Burton, and she was perched on the edge of a roof with a cigarette in one hand and a half-empty drinks can in the other like a protestor staging a prison roof sit-in. Half standing, trying to keep her balance, she tried hard not to be terrified.

On the ground, the cluster of neighbours and passersby had been augmented by two squad cars and the long-awaited fire engine. There seemed to be an argument in progress between the firemen and Rosie's neighbours over the trampoline. A voice bellowed that the noise was distracting the pair on the roof and could cause them to fall off. They all shut up at once.

A ring tone shattered the silence; Kat and Lee both jumped and lunged for their mobiles.

'Fuck! Mine's dead.' Lee flung his down in disgust. Kat watched, fascinated, as it went the same way as her footwear.

Caller ID showed Jack Ashton. A hell of a time to to say goodbye.

'Call you back,' she yelled into her mobile.

'No, you won't.' She heard Ashton in stereo. 'What are you up to?'

'Can't talk now, got a bit of an emergency here.'

'I can see that,' he said. 'More to the point, what the hell are you doing up there?'

He sounded tense. Not as tense as Kat, however, peering over the edge for a birds-eye view. There he was below, holding a mobile phone to his head as if he was about to blow his brains out.

'What am I doing? I'm practising to be a stork,' she snapped, disguising fear with witty repartee. Trust him to turn up to see her make a pratt of herself. After yesterday's wedding he should by rights have been heading back to the sticks. Kat found she was pleased that was not the case, but she could have done without him in the audience.

'Lee has a problem; we're having a chat about it.'

Lee said 'What the fuck's that thing for?'

A cherry picker was winding along the cul-de-sac towards them.

'Jack, the mobile crane's making Lee nervous.'

From roof height, Ashton and Mel both seemed shorter. The mayor had gone for a blue outfit today, with matching streaks in her upswept hair. The big biker, aka vicar, was there on what Kat at first took to be a quad bike. When she focussed in on him, she realised he must have been mowing his lawn when all this took off and had swung out onto the road on his machine. Karen and Shardonnay had arrived for their regular Sunday afternoon family get-together. Karen struggled to hang onto a large dog in one direction with her ankle hooked around a buggy wheel in the other. Shardonnay's big posh pram was bursting with kids fitted in as tight as trick cyclists on top of each other. Kat could see Barry down there. Cosmo King, too, and a group outing in wheelchairs from the dementia unit. Kat waved. Ashton raised a hand in acknowledgement.

'Okay, no cherry picker. We're sending up a fireman on a ladder to bring you both down.'

'No, wait.' Kat waved her arms at him with great vigour and almost unbalanced. Mel and Barry shrieked in girlish harmony. The concrete-mixer men whistled and cat-called.

'Sit still, for Christ's sake!' Ashton yelled. He hadn't needed his phone for that.

Kat, wedged against the heating vent, worked on her sang froid.

'Any chance of you coming in under your own steam sometime soon?' Ashton asked.

'Shouldn't think so,' she said. Her mobile pipped to let her know she was running low.

'Let the professionals take over. You shouldn't be up there at all.'

'You're repeating yourself, Jack,' she said. 'Don't get in a twist. We're fine. For a bit.' Beside her Lee grunted assent.

'Don't move any more than you can help,' Ashton said, craning his head. 'And for God's sake, hang on to something. What?' He turned aside. 'Mel wants a word.'

'Hi, you're a glutton for punishment,' Mel said. 'Listen, Karen says Lee's been in a mood all week. Do you want her to talk some sense into him? Apart from that, is there anything we can do at this end?'

'Not sure what you *can* do, but keep the phone on. I'll do the same but my battery's low. Stay in touch,' she said. Ashton and Mel went into a huddle with Karen and a man in a yellow hard hat.

'Karen's down there,' she told Lee. 'Do you want to talk to her, or shall we just go down? It's parky up here, now the sun's gone in.'

'There's nothing to go down for. Karen's dumping me if I don't get work soon. The only place we got to live is with her mum or mine. Ain't got no money. TV don't work,' he said 'Call that a life? Hello, Lee, got a problem? Hello God, how're you doin'? Time, is it? Yeah, sorry, Lee, no penalty shots in this game, it's all over, ended, finished, final whistle's gone, ta-ra. Rest in Peace. Lee lived here, died here, put up a plaque.'

'Stop it,' Kat said. 'Karen won't dump you. It's hard on her, living with her parents. She was just fed up. You'll get a flat, soon. They're building as fast as – Where are you off to now?'

Lee began to slide once more. But his luck had not entirely run out. He managed to wedge a foot into the guttering and come to a halt. She heard a series of frantic Morse code taps. It was Ashton.

'Kat, good, you okay? Take it slowly,' he soothed. 'We can hear you loud and clear. Karen's got a new house allocated, but it's not built yet. She says she's serious about him getting his finger out and finding a job. If he can do that before she's rehoused, he can move in with her and Karlee as soon as the new place is ready.'

'Get a job? Fuck that for a game of soldiers,' Lee sneered. 'Easier said. I got as much chance down the Jobcentre as winning the lottery. No use going down there on the off. Last so-called job they gave me was a joke. They had me scraping dog muck off the grass for a tenner a day. That's not my idea of work. Sod that.'

The Morse tap-tapping started up again.

'Yes, Jack?'

'No, miss, it's Paul McQueen.' It was the hard-hat man. 'I'm the site manager. I've been watching that lad jigging up and down faster than a fiddler's elbow; reckon he might be okay on the scaffolding. Tell him, if he's serious about wanting a job, he can start tomorrow morning. All he has to do is turn up on time each day and behave hisself. Six months work guaranteed if he's any good. With an option for two years on another site after we finish here. He's going to have to get down here fast, before we find someone else, though, cos I'm not messin' about.'

Kat turned to Lee. 'Did you hear that?'

'Yeah, most of it,' he moaned.

'Oh, for Heaven's sake, Lee, jump if you're going to.'

'What?' Lee gasped. 'You're meant to be talking me out of it.'

'Not any more,' she said. 'I'm getting bored. We've been squatting up here like two old lags on a sit-in and the sun's gone in and I'm getting chilly. You could have chosen somewhere better to jump from, while you were at it.'

'Somewhere better?'

'Look at us. Let's face it, this is hardly the Empire State Building. I mean, two-and-a-half storeys? That's not going to kill you. You're going to look a real plank when you end up in a wheelchair through your own fault. Anyone with any sense would have jumped weeks ago, when the council still had some decent high-rises left. It's a bit late now, when it's all been demolished.'

Lee hugged his knees under his chin, frowning awhile.

'Those poofy fags aren't bad,' he conceded. 'Give us another one.'

They lit up and stared out over the park. Kat's stomach gurgled.

'I could murder a pizza,' she said.

'Yeah, me too, but we ain't gonna get Meals on Wheels up here.'

Tap-tap-tap. Ashton. He raised a hand. She waved back. The crowd waved enthusiastically. Kat waved more vigorously.

'Stop waving to the audience, woman! You're not on *Strictly*,' he said. 'You'll go over the edge. You shouldn't be climbing around up there at all. Don't make things worse.'

'You're repeating yourself. I'm not climbing. I'm sitting. Lee's hungry. Says he fancies a pizza.'

'Pizza? What the–? All right, if it'll get you down any quicker I suppose I could call the takeaway and get them to deliver.'

'Pizza, salami, cheese, olives, anchovies?' said Kat.

'Four cheeses. I don't eat olives,' grumbled Lee.

'Olives on one half,' Kat said.

'Salami, four cheeses, anchovies, no olives on one half,' Ashton said. 'Anything else?'

'I want ricotta, gorgonzola, parmesan, double mozzarella,' Lee said.

'That's salami, four cheeses with extra mozzarella, half olives, anchovies: okay,' confirmed Ashton.

'Anchovies make me puke,' threatened Lee.

'I'll scrape them onto my side, all right?' Kat said, hunger rendering her ratty. 'We'll be here all night at this rate.'

'I don't want to be fobbed off with my sister's leftovers from the bar, either,' Lee shouted over the side of the roof.

'You watch your mouth,' shouted Shardonnay.

'They're ordering from the takeaway,' Kat said.

'As long as they do,' Lee grumbled.

'You'll have to come down before it gets here,' suggested Ashton. 'Or this crowd will have it off you.'

It was the two-stroke putter of the pizza scooter that brought Lee down, although Kat preferred to think it was her negotiating and people skills that did it. Lee lobbed another cigarette end over the side and made to follow her back towards the skylight. She stopped herself reaching to help. According to the negotiator's manual, *Dealing with Alienation and Fear of Failure in the Young,* this is the time when jumpers go, taking you with them. She put one hand on the window frame to anchor herself, before they climbed back into the bathroom. Lee made a lunge that sent her pulse rocketing. She forced herself to remain calm. She was cold now the sun was going, and she was fantasising about the pizza awaiting them two-and-a-half floors below. She'd broken her New Year resolution after four months, and now stank of stale tobacco.

'Promise you won't laugh?' Lee said, chewing his lip and staring at the skylight.

'Yeah?' she sighed. 'What's wrong now?'

'I'm claustrophobic; what if I get stuck?'

'Didn't bother you coming up here,' Kat said. Grabbing him by the waist of his jeans, she shoved him without finesse through the skylight and into the bosom of his family. The neighbours keeping vigil at the bathroom door were treated to a close-up of Lee's Wile E Coyote tattoo peeking over his Bart Simpson jockeys. Kat hauled her skirt back from half-mast and checked her top was decent.

'Thanks. You're all right,' Lee called back up to her as he struggled out of the bath, hoisting up his jeans. 'I could kill a pizza. Where is it, then? You coming, girl?'

'Yes, I'm right behind you. You carry on. I'll manage,' she said, easing herself down into the bath. She wondered if they had anything in their bathroom she could use to get rid of the taste of bile and tobacco before she got stuck in to the pizza that awaited.

CHAPTER 26

Kat propped herself against Rosie Delaney's Hot Pink High Gloss acrylic front door, and tried to stop shaking.

Dozy Rosie and her partner had retired to their sofa with their cigarettes and their Pringles.

Lee, offered the choice between a trip under sedation with the paramedics to the mental health unit or a fast ride in the back seat of a patrol car to a caution at the police station, opted for a bollocking at the nick. He'd taken possession of the pizza and Kat's last packet of cigarettes which was a tad unfortunate from her point of view because she was starving. On the other hand, doing without the pizza was just as well: after the rooftop tobacco-fest she could have harvested her tongue for cork insoles. She could chew on that.

The adrenaline pumping through her body hadn't had time to return to wherever it went after such crises. She pried herself from the doorframe and started shakily down the path. Before she'd taken more than a couple of steps Ashton hurdled the garden gate.

She hitched up her top and made an effort to be sociable.

'How did your sister's wedding go?' That sounded like lesson one in the etiquette book: how to initiate a cocktail party conversation.

'Forget the wedding,' Ashton said. 'You scared the life out of me. What in Heaven's name were you thinking of, up there?' His freckles seemed considerably darker in a face drained of colour. 'You could have broken your blasted neck. Having a monkey for a lodger doesn't make you Jane of the Jungle.'

'Winnie's not a monkey. He's a chimp,' Kat corrected him.

'Be that as it may, you might have been killed.'

'I wasn't,' she retorted, fully on the defensive. 'I could be knocked over by a bus crossing the road. We each do what we must.'

'We *do not* do things which common sense tells us not to,' he replied. 'Come on, let's get you home. Can you make it on foot? It'll be quicker than fetching the car. Here are your flip-flops.'

'Thank you, I thought I'd lost them. But they're not flip-flops.' she said. They're fitness sandals, and they cost a fortune.'

He sighed. 'Yeah, well, whatever. Come on.'

The weight of his hand on her back was surprisingly comforting. Without further conversation, he propelled her back to her front door.

'Key?' he said.

Kat reached up to the lintel.

Ashton sighed.

'That's incredibly insecure. Have you no sense of self-preservation? You can't leave a key up there. That's the first place a burglar is going to look. You should nev –'

'Oh, for God's sake, I can't do this, I can't do that. Stop banging on,' she snapped through the lump obstructing her throat. Conscious of his closeness, she turned away and went into the flat.

Ashton grabbed her arm. When she lifted her hand to push him off he tightened his grip, kicking the front door closed.

Kat flinched as he reached towards her.

'Relax,' he said, tucking an errant strand of hair behind her ears. Now he'd got his colour back, she saw he'd caught some sun at his sister's wedding.

Mesmerised by one freckle darker than the rest on the corner of his upper lip, she reached up, without thinking. His mouth was softer than she expected. She could taste his toothpaste. His mouth was gentle and the kiss lingered. She was glad she'd taken the trouble to liberate Rosie Delaney's mouthwash before she'd bailed out. He stroked her hair back off her face, his hand tracing a delicate line on her cheek, her jaw, her throat. His hands slipped the single remaining strap from her shoulders.

'Jack, I don't think this is... Oh, what the heck,' she whispered.

They kissed again and began working at each other's clothes.

'Wait, hold on, I left my wallet in the car,' Ashton murmured, drawing back a little. 'It's parked miles down the road.'

'No problem. I'll send you the bill later,' she teased.

'No, Kat, I wasn't prepared for this.' He moved back a centimetre.

'Doesn't feel that way from where I'm standing,' she said.

'I don't suppose you've got any protection?,' he asked. 'This was only meant to be a flying visit on my way home.'

'Like condoms, you mean? No. I'm on the Pill,' she said.

‘I’d better go down to the car and get something,’ he said.

‘What if I go off the boil in the time it takes you to get dressed and go all the way down the road to the car and back?’ she asked.

‘I can run fast.’

She smiled. ‘How fast?

He groaned. ‘Sure you’re okay with this?’ he asked, offering her an escape route.

‘We can’t stop now,’ she pleaded, ignoring the letter box pressing against her backside. She tried to remember when she’d last shaved her legs and whether her toenails needed cutting.

At some stage during the evening they found their way to bed, and slept, which left her with a problem she’d never encountered before: What about when he awoke? She never brought anyone back to her flat, and always got home before dawn. Which meant she’d never turn into a pumpkin and could always bypass the awkwardness of any morning after. So far, it was still the middle of the night, but he was fast asleep in her bed – that was another first – and clearly wasn’t going anywhere.

Kat had no idea of the protocol. The good nuns had never covered this in etiquette class. If he’d left everything in the car, would he expect to borrow her toothbrush? Should she offer him first dibs at the shower? Breakfast? She hated the thought of having to navigate her way through embarrassing pauses over coffee and cornflakes in the enforced cosiness of her minuscule kitchen. There was no milk, let alone cornflakes.

One of her arms had gone to sleep. With great care she tried sliding inch by inch out of his clasp without waking him. Trying to defuse a live bomb might have been easier. She lifted his arm and burrowed away, replacing the arm before attempting to slither out of bed. Ashton growled and curled himself more tightly around her. She stilled as his mouth brushed the back of her neck, felt his lips form a smile against her skin. He was not as comatose as he’d have her believe.

‘It’s nowhere near dawn, yet. There’s no rush,’ he murmured, Kat's fidgeting having meant she could no longer pretend to be asleep, either.

‘You okay?’ he asked, nuzzling the back of her neck.

Okay? He was out of his mind. She was well okay.

‘Yes, thank you.’

What else could she say? It’d been a while. Her sex life had been non-existent over the past millennium. She shifted onto her back.

Lifting up on one elbow, Ashton squinted at her, his closeness leaving him out of focus. She felt her eyes cross.

‘You’re good,’ she said, referring to his skill at not going boss-eyed.

'Well, you know what they say about anything worth doing,' he said, choosing to misunderstand.

They lay grinning at each other. He trailed his finger along her collarbone, and began to inch downwards.

'What about getting to work?'

'I'm doing my best,' he said.

'That's not what I meant,' Kat laughed. 'You're supposed to have gone to the frozen North today.'

'No rush. I'll go in the morning.'

'It's morning already.'

'Nope, not daylight yet. I'm working up an appetite. I had a look in your fridge, earlier. There's nothing there that won't give us both E.coli.'

'Sorry about that. You might be able to pick up something on the motorway,' she murmured, regretting her empty cupboards.

'I could,' he said. 'Not until the morning, though. A sex god could starve in the meantime.'

'Sex god?'

'You were fairly loquacious, and most definitely unequivocal in your appreciation earlier,' he said. 'I assumed you were talking to me.'

'Don't be so smug. I only pretended to enjoy the sex so as not to hurt your feelings.'

'You are too, too kind.' He kissed her fingers.

'There's nothing wrong with your ego, is there?'

'Nope,' he drawled. 'Humility is not one of my faults. Now, since there's nothing to eat, we'll have to think of something else to take our mind off night starvation.'

In a corner of her mind, she heard a car drive past, changing gear as it struggled to navigate the obstacle course of builders' rubble. Lal's intruder alarm was going. That was the second time this week. A determined scrabbling from the kitchen suggested the pet flap was under attack. Buzz off, Winnie. Grown-up time.

CHAPTER 27

Ashton drew the line at two-day-old Thai takeaway, suggesting she fed it to Winnie or, better yet, sling it in the bin. She'd missed out on Lee's pizza the previous evening. It was the middle of the night, but a 24-hour pizza shop said they'd deliver. Kat was too hungry to attempt any cracks about free-range anchovies or organic olives. Luckily her wine rack was better stocked than her fridge.

It was daylight, although the sun had not finished rising, when Kat awoke covered in nothing but a smile. She was surprised to find that aside from her brief panic about the morning-after scenario, it had never occurred to her to worry about Ashton's reaction to her, or hers to him. This feeling was something she wasn't sure she recognised. She told herself not to be so gormless, making an issue of it purely because she couldn't recollect the last time she'd had sex. And never sex *that* good. Spreadeagled on her front, she stretched, sunk her face into the pillow and let the the pigeons on her windowsill finish their morning racket.

Pizza crumbs littered the duvet. Her teeth were grungy. She was stiff in muscles seldom used, aching in places that had never seen the light of day. She needed a bath. Catching the sound of the radio and the aroma of fresh coffee she opted for a shower, ignoring the trail of discarded clothing stretching to the front door. Her pants were dangling from the light fitting. At floor level, Winnie scooted around on all fours, playing tiddlywinks with Ashton's shirt buttons and a cereal bowl.

She staggered into the shower to be pummelled by the hot water until she could stand upright, unaided. Half-way presentable, she headed for the kitchen. Ashton was looking out of the window with his back to her, drinking coffee and listening to the radio. His hair was damp.

'I'm sorry about the bare larder,' she said, her eyes glazing over as he straightened up and stretched, showing skin between shirt and jeans.

'You can't drive that distance on coffee.' She stifled an urge to sew the buttons back on, make fresh orange juice and a breakfast of lightly-boiled eggs. Or better yet, suggest they went back to bed. Not necessarily in that order. That she didn't wasn't down to strong moral fibre. It was more that she didn't possess a sewing kit, there were no eggs or fresh oranges, there was an ape in her hall and Ashton, with or without shirt buttons, should have left for the long drive home hours ago. He'd already brewed coffee. He'd also fixed enough ketchup soldiers to feed the three of them. She downed hers, going for a land speed record.

'I'm not sure I'll ever get the hang of this competitive eating thing,' Ashton said, taking a little longer than Kat but not as long as Winnie, who'd offered up Ashton's buttons in exchange for ketchup soldiers.

'You have to start young,' she said through a mouthful of ketchup toast. 'Lesson one: you don't stop to talk.

Aching and fuzzy-brained, she was determined not to be pole-axed by one night of unbridled, satisfying, energetic sex. Not bothered with equality issues, she walked with him to his car outside the leisure centre. Winnie wandered off in search of a breakfast more substantial. Nothing was open yet. It was still too early for anyone to be up and about.

'I'll be back,' he said, his lips brushing against hers. 'Don't stay out in the street too long in your underwear.' Grinning, he slid into his car.

'Oops.' She hurried back to her flat, leaving Ashton to make the most of the view. Inside, she leant against the wall. 'Wow!' Passing the mirror she caught her soppy grin and decided she'd work at home. If she could stop simpering long enough to get dressed.

She was too wired to concentrate, and ached in all the good places. Good sex beat the gym. She was hungry again. The fridge was pretty empty. She gave the three-day-old deep-fried Thai chilli squid a quick zap in the microwave to kill off the worst of the germs. It tasted all right, despite Ashton's earlier admonitions to sling it in the bin. Waste not, and so forth. Besides, she needed carbs to be able to line dance with the pensioners. She had almost polished off the squid when Ashton rang.

'Hi,' she said, unable to stop her mouth curving upwards as she listened to their synchronised breathing.

Ashton cleared his throat.

'How are you?' He sounded self-conscious, which surprised her.

'Fine, thanks,' she said. 'Well, no, I'm knackered. I don't know about you, but I'm not sure I'm going to be able to walk straight again.'

Ashton's laugh over 240 miles was spontaneous. He said he had arrived home in record time with the aid of a detachable police emergency strobe light and a disregard for the national speed limit. Police perks, he called it.

'Illegal and dangerous,' Kat scolded.

'Not with a flashing blue light. I was on official business,' Ashton protested. 'I had to get back here to prepare a forensic report for court.'

'And that makes it official? Hmm. Dubious,' she said.

'Done, now. So, what are you up to today? No more roof dramas, I trust.' The faint tinkle of ice as he spoke conjured up a picture of long cold drinks in heavy glasses, and all she could manage was re-heated chilli squid and limp chips in a plastic microwave tray.

'No, I'm staying at ground level today. Right now, I'm getting ready to go out,' she replied.

'Work or pleasure?'

'Working lunch.' she said, suspecting that line-dancing class with a bunch of geriatrics high on anticoagulant and heart pills wouldn't contribute much to the conversation.

'Anyone I know?'

'Some sports people.' That was stretching things.

'Going anywhere special?'

'There's a new restaurant, Amazing Grapes,' she said. 'It has a wine list big enough to watch football on.'

She hadn't precisely claimed to be lunching at this wondrous place. She wouldn't lie, just allow him to draw what conclusions he wished.

Not holding you up, am I?'

'Not at all. I was wondering what to wear.' She glanced at the goo that had found its way onto the leggings she had put on to line dance with the OAPs. A tunic would cover the stain, no problem. Her stomach griped, raising a doubt about the wisdom of scoffing three-day-old food so rapidly. She told herself an hour of exercise would sort that out.

'What have you got? Run it past me.' Ice tinkled. 'In case you're wondering, what you hear in my glass is Vitamin C. Energy drink. I'm recuperating.'

'Really?' she said. Last she'd heard, there were no vitamins in whisky. Nor protein, carbohydrate or healthy fibre.

Sitting there in her scruffy leggings she thought about what to say she'd wear to her imaginary business lunch. Shouldn't take long to choose between jeans, cargoes, one posh frock, a sun dress temporarily minus its straps, a couple of skirts, and half a dozen tops and tees.

'I'd only got as far as thinking about underwear when you rang,' she said, scraping a bit of soggy tempura off her leggings.

'What do you think? I think I'll wear a skirt, not jeans. But a skirt has to have real shoes. I'll get blisters unless I wear something to stop the leather rubbing. All I've got is hiking socks, winter tights, or hold-ups.

The line went quiet.

'Hello, Broadsword calling Danny Boy. Hello? Are you receiving me? she asked.

'Hold-ups,' Ashton finally said. 'What's holdups?'

'Stockings.'

'Tights, you mean.'

'No. Stockings.'

'Stockings. Proper stockings?' So predictable, men and stockings.

'Proper stockings.'

'I though you all wore tights or went bare' he said. 'So to speak.'

'Hmm, pas moi,' she replied. 'Unless it's deepest winter. Trouble with hold-ups is they're meant to stay up by themselves but never do.' She detached a flake of squid super-glued to her left knee.

'Stay up by themselves?

'Yes, they have a strip of clingy stuff at the top,' she said. 'But I must have the wrong-shaped legs or something, cos they always end up sliding down my thighs.' She could have gone on to say that left to their own devices they invariably bagged around her ankles like leg warmers, but that wasn't the ambiance she was aiming for.

'Then how do you keep them up?' he asked. sounding a tad breathy.

'I've a suspender belt somewhere.'

'Suspender belt?' At this rate, they'd be hauling him into Casualty for defibrillation. 'Don't let me slow you down,' he stuttered. 'I wouldn't wish to make you late for your lunch. You carry on.'

'Hang on.' She opened and shut a few drawers, inserting some B-movie sound effects into the game.

'How's it going?' he asked, as she approached the finale.

'Well. the only suspender belt I can find is a little black lacy thing. Not sure it's up to the job, though,' she said, slamming a drawer shut. She heard him whimper. 'I'm sure I had matching pants somewhere. Lord knows where they are.' She paused. 'I may have to go without.'

There was a clatter followed by a burst of static. They must have been having freak weather up North.

'You're breaking up. Is it raining where you are?'

'Er, yes. I mean no. Up here? Where am I? Newcastle. There's no static. The weather's lovely,' he said. 'My phone slipped. I'm covered in ice cubs and soaked in sco – I mean in vitamin C.'

'Oh, dear,' she sympathised. 'Still, as long as you haven't broken anything. Someone at the door. Must go. Talk later. Bye.'

She was amused to think of the trouble he'd have for the remainder of the afternoon, with 'vitamin C' on his clothes, trying to work after the image he'd conjured up in his mind. That would keep his morale up. As it were. His day would be a darned sight livelier than hers.

Kat's amusement was short-lived. Jigging around with the OAPs should have been fun. The warm-up had gone well. When they began jumping about in earnest, she was in trouble. She became short of breath, then nauseous, convinced she was going down with bird flu. The Bugle had reported three new cases in Bickeridge the previous week.

After another fifteen minutes, her limbs ached and her head throbbed out of time with the beat. It can't have been the twisting and stamping so soon after lunch. She wasn't that unfit. But they had been doing a great deal of hand clapping and toe and heel manoeuvres to the side and back, side and back, side and front. Burning acid rolled up her throat with each bend and sway and stomp. She had the beginnings of a classic migraine aura, shark's teeth fighting for space with the glitter ball catching the light and going round in the ceiling.

Kat was no match for the lively bunch in their plaid shirts and fringed outfits who had strutted their stuff in *Seven Brides for Seven Brothers* at the Sally Army OAP lunch club last Christmas while the rest of the borough had to put up with Aladdin and the Crankies.

Acclimatized by the institutional meals of her childhood, her digestive system could have doubled as the dustbin of the western world. She'd never had so much as a hint of indigestion in her life. Now her stomach heaved and swayed in contra motion to the dance, leaving her in no doubt. This wasn't post-coital lethargy. Breaking ranks, she dashed for the cloakroom as a tidal wave swept through her intestines. Ashton had been right about that squid.

Leaving them clapping and stomping to Boot Scootin' Boogie, she tottered home via the pharmacy.

'Don't bother to wrap it,' she said.

Mr Patel watched her gulp down half a bottle of magnesia before his wife had finished ringing it up on the till.

Kat felt hot and cold flushes chasing through her, and suspected she was close to dying.

At home, she sat on the lavatory and held a wet flannel to her forehead. The first Imodium tablet came back up. It was still whole. She took another. When that also reappeared, alongside today's lunch and last night's pizza, she changed her strategy. Armed with a bottle of mineral water and a thermos of black tea, she headed for bed. Codeine, Magnesia, Imodium: if that failed, she had a bucket.

One way or another, the squid made repeat appearances at regular intervals throughout the afternoon and evening. Later, between visits to the bathroom, she sat on the edge of her bed groaning, with her head hovering over the bucket between her knees, and guzzled Imodium and Codeine washed down with black tea. Tannin should do the trick.

Meanwhile, outside, a million birds slept, cats fought and hunted through rubbish bins, hedgehogs failed to make it across main roads, and urban foxes got into hutches in the new back gardens and killed off the estate's pet rabbits.

For Kat, sleep wasn't an option. Her skin was clammy, her eyes red-rimmed, her insides griped. Returning from the bathroom for the umpteenth time, she checked her bedside clock: 3 am. Next time she checked it was three thirty, then four, four thirty. Someone must have super-glued the minute hand. Each time she made a controlled stagger for the bathroom, she moaned at herself in the mirror. Finally, on one trip, she draped a towel over the glass so she wouldn't have to look. There was a constant fiery, burning taste high in her throat and she couldn't stop shivering. She took long, careful breaths to cope with the waves of dizziness that washed over her at regular intervals. When she wasn't staggering to and from the bathroom or trying to hold down cold, black tea, she curled into a ball and prayed for deliverance.

CHAPTER 28

It was two days, maybe three, she wasn't sure, before she was able to struggle back into the land of the living. She had turned her mobile off so people would think she was in meetings, on the road, or working in a no-phone zone. Ashton, tied up in court, texted her. Not wanting to bother him with her problems, however, she kept her replies broad and brief.

By day three, or it may have been four, she was sufficiently compos mentis to consider the implications of sicking up everything. At the pharmacy, her stomach still griping, she picked up painkillers as well as a Morning After pill. Mrs Patel had to be persuaded an ambulance was not required.

By mid-afternoon Kat had improved enough to be confident of being able to join Mel for a spot of lurking the next day at the Maurice Mickelwhite. The mayor had been away on a course and they'd had no reason to be in touch during the past week. Just as well Mel would be bringing coffee, as she doubted her ability to remain alert during the exercise, given her present weakened state. Although it wasn't strictly necessary to have a car, it made sense, both for comfort and for cover. She would drive around the block and park beside the building as instructed, where she would be camouflaged by two abandoned cars and the big metal dustbins. She could only hope that she didn't get pulled over for noise pollution en route; she'd had no time to replace the muffler which had parted company with her tail pipe on the westbound carriageway of the M25 a week earlier. But she had been on a motorway and the sign had said 'Hard shoulder not in use'. Otherwise, she could have retrieved the pieces.

She was not as much back on form as she had hoped when, still preoccupied with the state of her insides, she stalled three times after starting because she'd left the handbrake on. The fuel gauge showed empty, which meant that even the smallest journey tonight might mean she would not make it to the garage next time she needed to use the car. Fearful she would run out of petrol en route she started on a mad dash for the petrol station, before commonsense clicked in. She slowed down, driving to conserve petrol. Lucky it was downhill all the way.

The garage was busy. She had to drag the hose across the bonnet to get the nozzle in far enough to avoid splashing. Watching the litres chug in, it occurred to her that she might have sprung a leak. It had never taken this long to fill. Petrol prices were up again. The Mini's gas tank can't have been much bigger than a can of emulsion, but it was still forty quid a pop. It would have been cheaper to buy caviar. Finally, tank replenished, she kangaroo-hopped out of the garage.

The car was giving off a frisky Le Mans racing growl. After all that racket, she might have to give up the undercover idea. With no moon, no street lamps and doused headlights, parking took a considerable amount of noise and effort before she was tucked in on the dark side of the overflowing giant bins. She didn't want to get too close to two dumped cars that were still in the process of cannibalisation. Surprisingly, no-one had set them ablaze. Yet.

The place was deserted. The secondary lights, set into waist-high bollards, had shorted again. The Moor's free-range mongrels and pit bulls masquerading as Staffordshires were the right size for peeing on the electrics. The only illumination was a light in the cab of a bus with its back open, at the stand.

On Kat's right, the remains of a once-manicured shrubbery fought for space with the broken bench which seemed to exist solely as a recycling depot for food containers and used condoms.

Having escaped detection despite the exhaust noise, Kat hoped her luck continued and she stayed invisible. Still no sign of Mel, or coffee.

Turning off her mobile she clambered out for a recce. A short burst of rain earlier had left the path slippery. The night was a sauna. The old wooden bus shelter on the triangle of brown grass which the locals had nicknamed the Cokey Corral was empty, with no sign yet of the army of canines slung out with monotonous regularity each night for their final poop 'n' prowl. Kat heard laughter and the slam of a car door, followed by the unmistakeable diesel growl of a London black cab.

There were no lights anywhere in the community centre. Maurice Mickelwhite meets Marie Celeste. Most nights, after all else had gone quiet, you could hear the blip of the intruder alarm, and from outside the kitchen door you could often hear the hum of the refrigeration unit. She could hear nothing. They'd either forgotten to set the switches, or battened down the hatches for a lock-in.

She returned to the car. Still no sign of Mel or coffee. Crouching low, she snuggled under the Afghan crochet blanket she'd liberated from the children's home. The hand-made blanket had once been intended for the Catholic missions. A pre-teen Kat had claimed it for herself, having concluded that the world's afflicted were escaping the yoke of poverty and oppression by coming to work in Western Europe, and were probably earning enough to buy their own creature comforts. She had persuaded the good nuns that expectations amongst indigent pagans went a little higher nowadays than bright blankets crocheted by sticky-fingered schoolgirls. Now, in the comfort of her blanket, and packed to the gunnels with painkiller, she closed her eyes and waited.

She can't have dozed for long. Awakened by the rocking of the car, she reached for the door handle, eager for Mel's coffee. There were whispers and giggles nearby but she saw nobody in the darkness beyond the meagre overspill from the bus light. With great caution she hoisted her body up in the seat and checked from side to side. Nothing.

The car rocked violently, as if someone outside was shaking the vehicle. They weren't. It was someone in the car with her, unaware that she was curled up in the front. Unsure what to do, she burrowed deeper into the blanket, held her breath and put her trust in the suspension.

The crochet Afghan had seen service as a dog blanket for a short period when she had flat-shared with a fellow student who brought strays home. Despite ten years of use and irregular washing, there were still doggy deposits embedded in the blanket. Kat's sinuses were fizzing. She was unable to stop one of her killer sneezes hitting the airwaves.

There was a scream sharp enough to cut her a sun roof. The car jerked, and Kat was shunted onto the floor, banging her knee on the clutch on the way down. Unwrapping her cheek from the gear stick, she twisted her head to see a shape rocket out of the car and hit the ground on the run, shrieking. The woman was wearing a glittery top, a poppy red thong around one ankle, and a Road Runner tattoo on one buttock. Then a second tattooed backside appeared in the rear mirror and Wile E Coyote popped out of the car, head first. A couple with co-ordinating tats. Swearing in language so florid it may have been a foreign dialect, the luckless Lee, recognisable by his tattoo and clearly recovered from his recent flirtation with death on the roof, was clutching a pile of clothes. On the move, he tried to hoist up his pants and cover his predicament. It occurred to Kat that he seemed to spend a great deal of time with his kecks at half-mast. There was another colourful string of curses as he stumbled and dropped clothes into a puddle of something that might have been rainwater. Given the location, it could have been anything. The car rocked as he steadied himself against the roof.

Adrenaline fuelled, Kat shed the Afghan and slithered upright in the driving seat. Crunching into first, she screeched out. Her last view of Lee was his Wile E Coyote bum half into his Y-fronts in her driving mirror. The rest of him was concentrated on recovering the clothes, which her rapid getaway had catapulted off the car roof into the road. Lee was on a curfew, meant to be at home watching telly, not playing Romeo behind the Maurice Mickelwhite with his kit off and his hopes up.

Kat was no longer concerned with driving quietly or carefully. She put her foot down so hard on the pedal, it was a marvel she didn't get friction burns on the sole of her foot from the tarmac.

As the car screeched out onto Warp Drive, her tyres clipped the kerb and took out the post box and two gateposts. Never mind. Nobody sent letters these days. Not even before the recent snail incident had made licking stamps a health and safety hazard on the estate. The gateposts were scheduled to come down soon, in any case.

Apart from the bang when she sideswiped the post box. she hadn't felt any further bumps. Given it was too late at night for people to be out and about, she assumed she hadn't run over anyone or their cat. She flexed the muscles on her backside in rotation to veer left and then right to spin her back wheels out of the flowerbed and back onto the road, avoiding by a narrow margin sideswiping a white van and a gas-guzzler half as wide as the road, which was taking up two parking spaces.

The street lighting was better out on Warp Drive. She had a grandstand view of the streaker holding her breasts as she ran to stop them bouncing, baying at the moon like a banshee. Kat slowed down.

'Hey!' With the window open she realised shrieking was laughter.

Halting in mid howl the girl dodged behind a glossy evergreen.

'OW,' she yelped. 'Flamin' Norah.'

Kat flinched in sympathy as she drew alongside and saw Karen had plunged bare-arsed into a pyracanthus shrub, part of the expensive new landscaping. Kat remembered the nuns had called it The Good Lord's own barbed wire.

'Karen?' she called, leaning out of the window. 'Here, take this. You can't stay in those bushes all night. Lee's dropped your kit in a puddle. I reckon I've done enough for one evening. Nighty-night.' She dropped the Afghan out as she passed.

Back home, when she switched on her mobile there were four missed calls, and a text from Mel to explain why she wouldn't be able to turn up. Too late to think about that now. Kat went to bed.

Even though she was still suffering the after effects of her tummy bug, she found the Karen and Lee episode funny. However, if they were down to conducting their relationship in the back of parked cars, hers specifically, chasing up their housing must become her priority.

Come the dawn, she found a message from Barry on her hall floor. She had walked over the mauve envelope last night without noticing. It was a clipping from the hatches, matches and dispatches in the local rag, announcing the forthcoming funeral of one Francis Fostock,. The late Mr Fostock had, it seemed, shuffled off his mortal coil at his home in Bickeridge Oaks only days before. There was a Frank Fostock on Barry's list of people to be questioned. Bang went that idea, unless Barry was expecting him to rise from the dead. Lazarus did it in four days, but then again, he'd had help. Another one bites the dust, Kat thought. The funeral was to be in two days time. Friends and flowers welcome, it said. Barry had written in his best copperplate on the side, in green ink:

'Dear Holmes, Jungle drums say this guy was so crooked they'll have to corkscrew him into the ground. Let's you and me go detecting. Dress optional. Watson'.

CHAPTER 29

When Kat had been in the children's home, the nuns' open casket funerals were a popular, albeit infrequent, highlight. They'd had a couple each year. Which meant no lessons that day. The children processed around the bier, hands steepled in prayer, admiring the undertaker's art that had left the aged nun so wrinkle free. Such perambulations were followed by an old-fashioned sung requiem Mass, priests in purple, black-draped statues, plainsong, everyone in their Sunday best, high on incense, clutching penny candles, and the slow walk to the graveside.

Kat thought it a pity you had to go to church for such an excellent show, all for free, too. A penny candle wasn't going to break anyone's bank. Childishly self-absorbed, they had looked forward to the funerals, which meant visitors, and lemonade with iced buns for tea, largely to demonstrate how well the poor motherless orphans were being looked after by the good Sisters. In truth, there was little wrong with the children's daily diet, but the nuns liked to make a good impression.

When she left the home, having no family meant no more funerals. It wouldn't be polite to gate-crash every wake in town. As a consequence she had lost touch with the protocol of death. Barry had said dress optional, but she'd seen enough movies to know black was still de rigueur. In any case, it was nice to get dolled up for special occasions.

The Oxfam shop had black skirts. She also found a short boucle jacket from which, when she arrived home, she removed the buttons and got rid of the clunky collar. Barry said that with lilac braid added to the jacket it could pass for a classic Chanel, as long as nobody examined it too closely. She fished out a Lenten mauve tank top, covered the scuff marks on the heels of her Mary Janes with magic marker and tied her hair back. She topped off the outfit with almost-sheer charcoal stockings: guaranteed to take any outfit up a notch.

Barry, on the other hand, made no concessions. He was tarted up for Judgement Day in a well-cut black suit with a waisted jacket in unrelieved black. Despite his lack of inches, he wore his clothes well. Must be a gay thing, she decided.

'What do you think?' he asked, doing a Fred Astaire twirl around her living room. Envious of his talent with clothes, she was tempted to comment that all that was missing was the big hat that Winnie had commandeered earlier, and a pair of castanets.

'Very snazzy. Very funereal,' Kat said.

'Have to enter into the part,' said Barry. 'The black shirt and tie lend a certain ambiance, don't you think? What? Don't laugh, they'll think we're Mormons.'

'I don't think there's any chance they'll take us for Mormons,' she said. 'This crowd would be more at home with the Sopranos.'

Winnie had started out wearing Barry's black Borsalino. It came down over his eyes, and would have looked better on a non-ape. In Winnie's case, dressing the part didn't do him any good, because they left him at home, still in Barry's best hat, with the television and a bag of broken Hobnobs from Poundstretchers.

Lengthy requiem mass over, they joined the crowd of dark-garbed mourners for the slow parade to the cemetery. The procession, in its ostentatious display of wealth, was as kitsch as any royal funeral could ever be. Four black-plumed horses drew the gleaming carriage carrying the ornate ebony and brass coffin. Leading the mourners was a mint condition classic black limo with a privacy screen and tinted windows, and a chauffeur looking ready to peel off to a drive-by shooting.

'Don't stare,' murmured Barry. 'I don't want us having to do a disappearing act as a pair of transvestite jazz musicians.'

Frank Fostock junior had flown in from Tenerife to lead his father's funeral procession the half mile from the family home in Bickeridge Oaks to Saint Frigilaria's at Bickeridge Heath for the sung requiem mass. Monsignor Seamus Moriarty, a nephew of the deceased, had flown in from Rome, the Vatican no less, to officiate. Traffic in the suburb had come to a stop as the New Orleans Stompers, with 'Cheeks' Costello on clarinet giving a fine rendition of Muskrat Ramble, fell in behind the flashy limo, followed at a respectful distance by a cortege of gleaming black Daimlers, their roofs smothered in floral tributes. All had, it seemed, loved Frankie, if the messages picked out in red carnations were anything to go by. The florists had had a good day, too. Those not armed to the teeth with wreaths carried lighted candles. It was the ultimate East

End send off, with a real pearly king and queen, who'd travelled over from Peckham.

'Haven't seen any chimney sweeps yet,' Kat said, disappointed despite all the other trappings.

'That's weddings,' Barry tutted. 'Not funerals.'

'Would've been nice, though,' she whispered as they lowered the ornate coffin. 'Isn't this the guy they interviewed last week?'

'Mai oui, la même chose. I hear he was Cosmo King's father-in-law once upon a time. No, I tell a lie: if the living corpse talking to the TV people is dozy Rosie's dad, then *he's* King's ex-father-in-law. Which means the late Mr Fostock was King's uncle and therefore Shardonnay's great-uncle. Which makes her the granddaughter of the smarmy guy up front with the car.'

'Stop. You're making me dizzy. King must have more relatives than the Godfather,' Kat said.

He of the sinister limo, Edward known as Ted Delaney, whom the police for undisclosed reasons of their own had nicknamed Teflon, had once been a big man. Sallow and sombre of face, and shrunk by age to under six foot, he had more than a dab of Grecian 2000 in his thinning collar-length locks. The once-broken nose and tight lips gave him a cruel face. His two sons, with over-worked chests like wardrobes, dumb muscle in dark glasses and Bluetooth attachments, stayed tight behind, ramrod straight, watchful. The Botoxed widow Fostock walked with Delaney, looking like a goldfish being shepherded by a shark.

'Frankie's family's asked me to say a few words,' said Delaney, addressing the cameras. 'This is a sad day. I'll miss Frankie. We were almost family. People think we didn't get on, and we might have had our ups and downs, but we was younger and didn't know better, then. All that naughty-boy stuff got sorted. Frankie was a real pillar of the community. He was a good father to his son, Frank Junior, and a fine husband to Michelle-Gawd-rest-her-soul. He was a very fortunate man, because in the twilight of his days he found himself a new wife, the lovely Madison, although I'm sorry to say they weren't destined to be together for long.'

The brave widow Fostock dabbed Delaney's borrowed handkerchief over her Botox and smiled through her tears.

'Frank junior has been abroad for a while, but he's flown in to be here today to say goodbye and bon voyage to his dear old dad.' Delaney made a half turn. 'Son, I'm sure I speak for us all when I say Frankie, your old dad, and our dear old pal, will be much missed.'

The cameras zoomed in on Frank junior trying not to be seen behind a sorrowful Madison, who was making a meal of dabbing at her mascara.

Business over, the mourners were moving away from the grave. Kat was enjoying the ostentatious show of bad taste when Mel rang.

'You're on the telly,' screeched her friend, loud enough to be heard by the late lamented Frankie inside his box. 'How are you both doing? Spoken to anyone yet?'

'Shh,' Kat murmured. 'Bring it down a bit, will you?

'What?'

'It's a three-ring circus, but it's also a funeral,' Kat whispered. 'I can't yap on my mobile while they're still covering the coffin.'

'No, hang on. I'll talk quieter,' Mel said. 'They're showing it live. It's major creepy; all dark glasses and sharp suits.'

'Did you want anything in particular, Mel, or were you ringing for a fashion chat?'

'Grumpy,' Mel replied. 'Listen: when you talk to people, see what you can find out about the missing *Bernie* Delaney. Gran says Bernie, dad, Trevor Picket and Cosmo King were all mates at school.'

'Hang on.'

Kat didn't want to miss anything. Delaney senior had paid his respects at the grave and was cutting a swathe to his car, where the engine had been kept running. There was a collective bowing and scraping that lent his progress the drama of a papal audience. Delaney turned to the crowd.

'Now, you can't say Ted Delaney doesn't do things proper,' he said. 'Frankie's gone, least I can do is offer my hospitality to you all on behalf of Frank junior, and Frankie's lovely widow.' He patted her on the backside before he remembered where he was and moved up to her arm. 'You're all welcome back at my place to participate in some humble refreshment. Come on, now, don't be strangers.' Waving his hand in priestly blessing, he included the entire assembled company in his generosity. before handing Madison, the glamorous goldfish, into his shiny motor. Frank junior, overcome by grief, followed his stepmother behind the tinted windows.

'You heard the man,' said Barry. 'It's party time.'

'See if you can cadge us a lift while I finish this call.' Kat waited until he had strolled off to the overspill car park. They were using the wasteland behind the church, for which planning permission had been refused ever since a rare bat colony had taken up residence there.

'Kat? This missing Bernie, brother of the skinny spiv. Don't forget.'

'Delaney's offered hospitality,' Kat said. 'We're going to mingle.'

'Did you know Fostock was interviewed before he died?'

'Yes. Jack told me. They obviously thought he knew something.'

'I'd say so,' said Mel. 'What else from Jack the Lad?'

'He's away, working. We're communicating by text and e-mail,' Kat said. 'Listen, what if the skeleton is nothing to do with your dad and we're going round asking questions for nothing?

'I'd thought of that,' Mel replied. 'What d'you think? Gut reaction.'

'It's up for grabs. Maybe Fostock and/or one or more of the Delaney clan were involved in your dad's disappearance,' said Kat. 'Maybe not.'

'It's all ifs and buts,' Mel said, sounding glum. 'We've got more red herrings than Billingsgate fish market.'

'Mel, there could be any number of reasons why they were interviewing Fostock. They did say they were following up other leads.'

'You think I'm obsessing?'

'Well, if it's not your father you'll be upset cos you're back at square one. It may not even be this missing brother, Or Bernie, either.'

'Don't make it complicated. Are you going to chase it up with the lovely inspector?' Mel asked.

'Probably.'

'How is he, by the way?'

'Fine, far as I know. I've been off the radar with this tummy bug,' Kat said. 'If you'd turned up as planned the other night, we might have passed a few happy hours exchanging gossip.'

'Your phone was off,' Mel retorted. 'I've been tied up.'

'Of course my phone was off. I was on a stakeout. Couldn't have it burst into song at the wrong moment. I may bring you up to date when I see you. On the other hand, I may not.'

'You're a pal. Talk to you later, Kat. Take care.'

If the police investigation had uncovered anything new Ashton would have texted her. She and Barry would have to snoop around at the wake.

CHAPTER 30

Delaney, aka Teflon Ted, was an excellent host: Kat stuffed herself with dainty smoked salmon sandwiches with the crusts off and wandered around, listening to mourners reminisce about old times.

When she introduced herself as a friend attending on behalf of the mayor, mentioning Mel's maiden name, the floodgates opened. Not all the stories were new: she heard again how Jeff Rampart's thick-as-treacle wife had run off, that Bernie Delaney had also disappeared around that time, and that Rosie had worked at the Stargazer pub until it burnt down. Some may not have known Rampart well, but many recalled him attending domestic callouts or breaking up fights at chucking-out time. Some mentioned Pam the barmaid and the ferry disaster.

A woman wearing a little black cocktail hat with a tiny veil said Jeff Rampart had in a quiet way been one for the ladies once his wife left. In the hushed tones of the born gossip, she said she'd heard he might have got a girl in trouble and done a runner.

They were offered a lift home by Sylvia and Sid, a pair who had escaped from the Moor to a mock-Tudor barn in a gated enclave at Bickeridge Heights. The couple remembered Jeff Rampart.

'A good copper, wasn't he, Syl? Specially with kids, as I recall,' Sid the husband said. 'Had a lad of his own: Billy, poor little beggar, got brain-damaged in a hit and run. They never found who did it. His dad bought him a lizard, or a newt, something like that, cos he couldn't play with the kids much any more. Kid loved that lizard.'

'Salamander,' his wife corrected him.

'Yeah, same difference. Funny kid, spent hours walking around in the dark, getting insects for it to eat.'

'Then he disappeared, I hear,' said Barry, fishing.

'The kid disappeared?'

'No,' his wife broke in. 'The copper. The kid's dad.'

'Oh? I didn't hear that, love.'

'It's what I was told.' Sylvia shook her head. 'We'd moved by then, only lived on the estate less than a year, didn't we? They were still building it when my dad died and left us his place in Lanzarote.'

'They had a pub there when the estate first got built,' Sid said. 'The Stargazer. D'you remember? The manager kept a loaded gun under the counter and a German shepherd on the roof.'

'Didn't do him any good, though, cos it burnt down the week after they opened the community centre,' his wife added.

'Yeah,' he said. 'We'd already moved by then. Lived in Lanzarote twenty years. Only came back for the NHS.'

They dropped Kat and Barry off on the edge of the Moor. Sid, the husband, said he'd heard the copper had done some drinking after the double whammy of first the kid's accident and then the wife walking out. Kat didn't know how that fitted into the equation but was sure it would slot into place, given time.

While Kat and Barry were at the funeral, the Post Office had been to dispose of the snails. A wasted journey. because the post box had been seen off by Kat's driving skills the day before.

'The post office people were here for ages, trying to fix it. In the end they took it away,' Karen said, leaning in the doorway connecting the two offices. She had recovered from her amorous misadventure, and showed no sign of embarrassment.

'I loved those black funeral horses and the flowers and the pearly king and queen and that jazz band,' she continued.

'It was impressive,' Kat said.

'Dead common, though,' pouted Shardonnay. She was entitled. It was her family, she could say what she liked. 'I'm embarrassed.' She swung her head round; the nasal ironmongery rattled.

Kat winced. Shardonnay noticed.

'Yeah, makes a racket. I know,' she said. 'I started by having my eyebrows pierced when I was twelve, to piss off my dad. I used to pretend I'd been swapped in the hospital and I didn't belong to his family. I mean, what a collection. Take my mum, for instance. No, don't.

Kat wasn't going to comment on Cosmo's cockney capers and predilection for vodka and cigarillos, nor her mother's Pringle fixation.

'It's not just Delaneys, either; it's the Fostocks, too. We're all related. They're weird, the lot of them. For instance, my mum's wedding, yeah? Her dad banned cameras so no-one could take photos.'

'Why was that?' Kat asked.

'Go on, Shaz, tell her,' said Karen.

'Yeah, well, they had a shunt on her hen night. Come the wedding, there she is, a mile out in front with me, and her foot in plaster because she's cracked it and broken three toes. Pam, the one that died on the ferry later, she's matron of honour, with a big black eye. One bridesmaid's on crutches, another's wearing her arm in a sling, and the other one's in a neck brace with whiplash.'

'You're putting me on,' Kat accused.

'No, straight up. There's more,' said Shardonnay. Karen was laughing. 'The night before the wedding, my dad has a fight and ends up with a bandage on his head and suspected concussion. His best mate has three broken fingers and can't open the greetings telegrams,' Shardonnay said. 'Nobody dares laugh, cos there's the bride's father, granddad Ted, all done up, and a face like a duck's backside. He says nobody's taking any pictures or he'll be a laughing stock.' She gave a great guffaw that set them all off.

'Lee says, with his luck, the skeleton will turn out to be one of his mum's dodgy relatives,' said Karen when they'd finished laughing.

'Yeah, whatever,' said Shardonnay. 'Listen, I'm going into town, if you want anything.'

'No, ta. I'm all right. Apart from the stench in here,' Karen muttered, and picked up a perished rubber World War Two Mickey Mouse gas mask that didn't look as if it would be much help. The smell which Rosie Delaney had first noticed on her visit to Kat's surgery was by now unbearable. Karen picked up an aerosol in each hand and began shooting with both barrels. Kat backed into her cubbyhole and put Tiger Balm up her nose. It had worked for dissecting frogs in the school lab.

'Any chance of making this door airtight?' she called. 'The pong's coming from your side. What is it, anyway?'

'No idea,' said Karen, binning an empty aerosol. 'Trevor Picket was in earlier and said someone needed stronger deodorant. Cheeky sod.'

The source of the smell was a mystery. There was nowhere for anything – animal, vegetable or mineral – to hide. The reception area decor was minimalist: no carpets, crannies or cupboards. Opaque glass doors opened onto tiny interview rooms each containing its own table, telephone, computer, metal chairs, and alarm. Leading off was a tiny WC with a hand basin. Again, no shelves or cupboards. You couldn't swing a cat in the kitchen. Worktop, fridge, kettle, microwave, cutlery tray, one shelf for crockery, jars and tins. There were no cabinets, drawers or cupboards into which anything could crawl and die. The floor was concrete. The place was all-electric, no chance of a gas leak. Smokers used Kat's cubbyhole or sheltered beside the dustbins. The truly desperate sat on the broken bench in the aptly nicknamed Cokey Corral bus shelter beside the dog poop bins overflowing with empty beer cans, used condoms and discarded syringes.

'We've hunted all over,' Karen said. 'It's a mystery.'

'What about the door mat?' Kat asked, but the coir health hazard was so worn you'd see a matchstick under it.

'Somebody could've spilled something and it's dried and we haven't found it yet. I crawled around, sniffing everything.' Karen made a moue of distaste. 'Nothing. I'd ask the caretakers, if I could find one.'

'How about something from outside?' Kat moved a mug of cold tea to sift through a drift of post-its. 'Blimey, what's all this?'

'Relax. It's not as bad as it seems,' Karen said, shuffling papers.

'Glad to hear it.'

'This used to be the junk room. Most of it's not yours.'

'How can I tell?' Kat didn't fancy ploughing through that lot.

'I'll sort it out for you,' Karen offered. 'You go and do what you have to, and I'll shrink it down by the time you get back. I've listed the movers in the final two tranches.' She jabbed a purple talon at a folder. 'Some of the older ones are staying here, with relatives, so we needn't worry about them. They'll get compensation. I've marked the ones who're off to Magaluf. They're the last, so we can get all the flats pulled down as soon as they leave. Apart from that, how are you getting on?'

'Fine, thanks,' Kat replied, glancing through her to-do list.

'There's lots happening,' said Karen, keen to promote the estate's infinite variety. 'You done anything about that monkey, yet?

'No, I'm stuck with him. The Asbo kids are helping out,' Kat said. 'I'm surprised Animal Welfare didn't cart him off years ago.'

'Environmental Health didn't know anything about Winnie for ages,' she said. 'By the time they did, his owner was so frail that nobody had the heart to separate them. By the time the old lady went into a home, she'd had him ten years, housetrained him, taught him not to drink out of the toilet. If he'd been a parrot she'd have had him talking.'

'I took him to the RSPCA but I was conned into bringing him home. I thought that as long as those three lads are around, they might as well entertain the creature.'

'They were hanging about yesterday with skateboards. The monkey, too,' Karen said. 'You not a pet person, then?'

'Not really,' Kat said. 'I had a mouse once but the cat ate it. So I don't have pets any more. They either escape or die. Speaking of death, I'm off to steam out the tail-end of this food poisoning at the gym. After that I'll do the rounds, then I'll work at home. I'll keep my phone on.'

'Tell us if you hear anything about the police investigation from that copper,' Karen said. 'We were hoping for feedback from the support team but they've stopped coming in because of the stink. I'm lucky I'm on three half days and not stuck here all the time.'

'I'll leave you to it,' said Kat, heading off.

'Yeah,' said Karen. 'Hey, if you're going to be out for the rest of the day, can I use your office? It's not as smelly as mine.'

'Feel free.'

Mickey Mouse mask back in place, Karen shot off to collect her work. Kat could access work files from her laptop.

'I shall be here alone,' Karen said, coming back. 'I can't get Lee to keep me company; he's started his job. People were buying us drinks to celebrate, which is how we ended up hammered the other night,' she grinned. 'Sorry about that. I'm not sure I ever want to see another Bacardi Mojito. Listen, Kat, you don't think the smell might, well, it's like, I mean, it might be another, you know?' Her voice tailed off.

'What?' Kat finished loading her bag with its hundredweight of bric a brac and looked up.

'Well, I was thinking,' said Karen. 'What with finding the other one, the body, skeleton, thing, you know. The caretakers were saying they want the union rep to get the office closed and tell health and safety they think there might be another body under the floor.'

CHAPTER 31

Mel had left a message that she and Barry would be at the Busted Duck that evening, if Kat was up to it. She was.

The Duck had been artfully reconstructed with dark booths and private snugs. Popular with journalists, police and councillors, it was remarkably free of both drugs and noisy groups. It had a reputation as the best place for buying and selling information in South London. It also had a decent wine cellar.

The old cliché about clouds having silver linings might be true. There had been an up side to Kat's unfortunate squid episode. Clothes which previously were tight now fit. Revelling in her new slimness, she'd treated herself to a new pair of skinny stretch jeans and an embroidered multicoloured ethnic top. She'd also celebrated her return to rude health by getting her hair styled. She thought they might have sussed that she was unaccustomed to visiting hair salons.

Mel, aware she'd be recognised in the popular watering hole, was in a bat-winged voile dress in a ladylike shade of bog-roll pink. Barry, who planned to go on to meet his mates later, was done up to at least the sevens in matador-tight black pants, collar up on his Ralph Lauren shirt. He'd gelled his hair into spikes, half of which were in rainbow stripes, which, unless they were temporary, meant he was in for some stick at work the next day.

'It's quieter than I expected,' Kat said, taking in the dark wood and well-worn leather gentlemen's club ambience. 'I thought it would be full of tabloid journos and bent coppers exchanging secrets for cash.'

'They're all out on the towpath. It's a warm evening,' Mel said. 'We can join the crowd if you want.'

'No, we're settled, now; let's stay in,' said Barry. 'They can be a bit noisy. You two can toddle outside when I buzz off.'

'How're things in Glocca Morra, then?' Mel asked, sipping her drink. 'For someone laid low with food poisoning all last week you seem extraordinarily perky. Life taken a turn for the better?'

'Oh, you know, same old, same old. I always bounce back,' Kat smirked, leaning back into the hard-buttoned upholstery.

'Seen anything of PC Plod lately?' Barry asked archly.

'No, not this week,' Kat replied, adding, a little too quickly: 'What's that pink gunk in your hair? Not permanent, is it?'

'That was a suspiciously quick change of subject.' Mel pursed her mouth. If I didn't know you any better, I'd hazard a guess at the cause.'

'Such a smug face, too,' said Barry. 'Satisfied, smirky.'

Kat's face flared.

'Looks like somebody's scored,' said Barry.

Mel choked on her drink and coughed up cashews.

'Yep, she has. Tickle my toes with a feather and call me Mabel. I do believe she's had her wicked way with PC Plod,' Barry carolled, clapping his hands, delighted.

The barman glared at the noise in the corner. They ignored him.

'Blimey, Kat, that was fast,' said Mel. 'Bully for you.'

'I could almost fancy him myself,' Barry added. 'Nice bum.'

'Shhh, Barry.' Kat slapped his hand. 'Don't be crude.'

'Mates are allowed crude.' He leaned his elbows on the table. 'Oh, bollocks,' he wailed, ungluing his shirt from the table.

'Barry, stop fidgeting,' Mel snapped. 'Stick washing-up liquid on it when you get home. Here's me thinking you were laid low.'

'Whereas,' interrupted Barry. 'She was getting laid. Tell all.'

'There's nothing to tell,' Kat protested. I wouldn't tell you in here, anyway, and in any case, I never discuss my sex life.'

'Lucky you have one to discuss. We don't need graphic detail, give us a summary,' Mel pleaded. 'Please.'

'Was it sweet and romantic with soft music in the moonlight or hot, steamy animal passion, and knickers on the picture rail?' asked Barry, who'd given up fussing over the goo on his shirt.

'You can't ask things like that.' Kat was embarrassed.

'Oh, we are coy. Look, Baz, she's gone beetroot. Now, that's interesting,' Mel said. 'And she's the one who was insisting she could go for months, years even, without sex.'

'I never said years,' Kat said. 'The last time wasn't that long ago.'

'Not if you're counting in leap years,' said Mel, laughing.

'Was it a hit and run, or did he spend the whole night?' asked Barry.

'Barry, you are incorrigible. Hereby ends all conversation on the subject,' Kat said, taking a healthy swig of Rioja and giving her attention to the decor.

'Well, well, well,' Mel said, impressed. 'What was it you said last week? *I avoid any contact with the official processes of the law and in return they treat me like the original invisible woman, blah-di-blah, I never go out with coppers*, and what was the other one? Oh yes, there was the bit that began with *policemen are not my type*.'

'Fiddle-di-dee on type,' Barry said. 'No reason why she can't just kick his tyres and do a test drive. She doesn't have to keep him.'

'I can't believe you said that,' Kat said.

'Lawzy, Mizz Scarlett,' Barry said, all innocence. 'What am I like?'

This sent them into a burst of laughter, shooting crisps into the air. The barman jabbed his ice pick noisily up and down in his ice bucket, looking as if he'd like to use it on the trio of harpies shrieking in the corner and upsetting the ambience of his watering hole.

'Maybe I should rephrase that.' Barry dabbed his eyes theatrically with a turquoise paisley silk super-kingsize hanky.

'Don't bother,' Kat growled, checking for stray crisps.

'I don't want to rain on your parade,' said Mel. 'However, I heard that the girls have to take numbered tickets for Inspector Jack-the-Lad.'

'Sour grapes,' Kat said.

'Mel, nobody learns to play the piano without practising,' Barry chipped in. 'Don't take any notice of her, Petal.'

Short-term affairs with no strings suited Kat. Mel had been right. She could go a long time without. Going for the cocky, self-absorbed type inevitably led to short, no-hassle encounters that ended before a relationship could begin or the dry rot of boredom set in. None of the men she dated were around long before being dumped. Ashton's relationship record didn't matter. It was intended to be fun. She nibbled on cashews, determined now she'd lost a kilo or two not to stuff herself with calories, but self-denial was proving tough work.

'So, tell us, and then we'll leave it alone. Marks out of ten.' Mel lowered her voice although there was nobody within earshot.

'Hang on.' Barry rose and peered over the panelled partition into the adjoining snugs. 'All clear,' he announced, sitting back down again.

'I don't care if we're the last two left on earth. I'm saying nothing. A lady never tells.'

'When were you ever a lady?' laughed Mel. 'I'm not asking you to tell us private stuff, just marks out of ten.'

Kat choked on her drink. 'Talk about a dog with a bone. You politicians never give up, do you.'

'Asking for marks isn't too much to ask for,' Barry remonstrated. 'Mel, the poor girl, she doesn't get out much these days, apart from doing the mayor's stuff. Me neither, at the moment. My love life has taken a dive lately.'

'You're such frauds,' Kat laughed. 'Okay, out of ten? Hmm.'

'Don't keep us in suspense.' Mel stopped drinking. 'Come on, I won't raise the subject again. Tell us thirty seconds' worth and then we'll leave you alone. Promise.'

'Thirty seconds? I dunno, I'd say,...'

'Yes?' the other two chorused.

'Bearing in mind that my grading system might be a bit off, seeing how according to Mel I don't have sex more than once every leap year, I'd say he was oh, let's see. Out of ten?'

'Yes?'

'I'd say he was, oh, I dunno. Let's think.' Kat took a sip of her wine.

'Stop prolonging the agony,' pleaded Barry.

'I can't stand the suspense,' Mel whined.

'Thirty seconds, then we talk about something else. Okay, marks out of ten. How about twenty?'

'You're kidd...'

'Then twenty,...'

'Oh my!'

'..then nineteen.'

'How did – '

'Time penalty.'

'That's a bit – '

'Naw, referee's decision is final.'

Mel's robust shriek could have scraped paint off walls. A couple in the corner lowered their eyes and put on the polite frozen smiles with which the middle-class English deal with threatening behaviour. The barman kept a fearful eye on them, as if he expected them to pole dance naked on the tables at any moment.

'Don't get too excited. He went back to the sticks first thing next morning and we've both been busy, apart from the odd text. I don't suppose he'll last long.'

'That's it, you hedge your bets,' suggested Barry.

'What's wrong with the old self image?' Mel asked, sipping her drink. 'You think he's staying around just for the sex?'

'Bugger self image. But the sex is certainly worth staying for,' Kat grinned lasciviously.

'Did you share a toothbrush and make polite conversation over coffee and coco pops at breakfast?' Barry asked.

'Coco pops? Kid's stuff? That'd put me right off him,' said Mel. 'I like my blokes to have hair on their chest.'

'Yeah, the last one was called Lassie,' Barry chortled.

'You are both disgraceful,' Kat laughed. 'No coco pops. I don't do cereal. The cupboard was bare. We rang for a pizza in the middle of the night and ate it with a nice Chianti. Okay, not Chianti. It was a middling Rioja from Tesco.'

'Blimey,' breathed Mel. 'How did you persuade the pizza people to deliver to the estate at night?'

'Jack told them he was guarding a police witness and couldn't leave the safe house. They couldn't get to us fast enough.'

'I must try that one,' said Mel.

'One thing I will tell you, though, and I'm still trying to work out how it happened: I let him stay all night. I have absolutely no idea why. That's a first, for me,' Kat admitted, adding, 'He made ketchup soldiers before he left. There wasn't any Marmite.'

'Sounds all right to me,' Mel said.

'A chap after my own heart,' said Barry. 'Don't waste him.'

'This time next month I'll have gone off him, and he me.'

'Yeah? And pigs might!' Mel snorted, taking another slug of multicoloured hooch and twirling her cocktail umbrella. The barman must have had a sense of humour after all; he'd given her a cocktail brolly which colour co-ordinated with her outfit.

'Time to talk about something else,' Kat said.

'Okay,' Mel said. 'You said your love life's taken a dive, Baz.'

'I am, as they say in the theatre, resting,' Barry sighed.

'What happened to Terry?'

'Silly cow decamped with a German sous chef from Dusseldorf called Erich. Not before time, either. Since he came back from Tibet he's driven me nuts. I didn't mind him sitting around chanting om-diddle-om-pom for hours on end. I didn't mind the singing bowls, the joss sticks and floating blossoms, or the prayer flags draped around the flat, but he kept giving stuff away. The last straw, he donated my George Foreman fat free grill to a pair of Jehovah's because he thought they might have dangerously high cholesterol. The mind boggles at what he might have given away next if he hadn't met Erich the Kraut and been whisked away. We are so over. Whatever did I see in him? I'll be flying solo for a while. That leaves you the only one with a sex life, Petal. So we'll be relying on you.'

'What about me?' demanded Mel.

'You're too busy poncing around being the mayor to go on the hunt for a replacement husband.'

'That reminds me: I promised to tell you about my trips up the aisle,' Mel said. 'After I got shot of Ray slime bag Dickson I married Randy Raoul. I met him in Buenos Aires when I was backpacking. He was mega rich, beautiful manners, generous, as they say, to a fault. Sexy with it. However, where other people have mood swings, he had gender swings. Couldn't make up his mind whether he was Raoul or Raquel.'

'She still won't give me his address,' Barry pouted.

'Not your type, Baz,' Mel said.

'Tell her about the others,' said Barry.

'Yeah, why not.' Mel's laugh rattled the optics and scared the couple in the corner into leaving. 'Next came Giorgio Geroulianides, my Greek. I didn't bother changing my name that time. He was a stage actor, big in Greece, bit on the short side, sexy in a Greek tragedy way. Turned out to be as libidinous as a recycled rice pudding, didn't know the difference between a uterus and a U-bend. To add insult to injury, he stashed all his worldly goods and as much of mine as he could lay hands on in some sleazy tax evasion scheme in Germany and I didn't get a bean out of him when we parted company.'

'Gosh, Mel, you certainly pick some weirdos,' said Kat, when they had stopped laughing.

'I haven't told you about the best one yet, number four, Con.'

'You're having me on. Why haven't I heard all this before?'

'We've never sat dishing the dirt before,' Mel said.

'Mel's an old-fashioned serial romantic,' Barry said. 'Like Elizabeth Taylor. Remember her? She was married eight times. She said she felt obliged to marry any man she slept with.'

'Trouble with that is the risk of ending up with someone you could spend half your life trying to get rid of,' warned Mel. 'Luckily, mine were as keen to get rid of me as I was of them.'

'You're terrible,' said Kat. 'This is all new to me.'

'You ought to make time for girly gossip now and then,' Mel said.

'Gotta keep working,' Kat said ruefully. 'Or I'd starve.'

'I doubt it,' Mel said tartly. 'Anyway, number four, Francis Xavier O'Connor, big Irish mercenary I met in Morocco. Answered to Con.'

'I once had a very disappointing holiday in Tunisia,' Barry broke in. 'It was during Ramadan, when you can't get a bite to eat before sunset, or a drink at any time.'

'Not unless you're booked into an international five-star at a thousand a night,' Kat said.

'Spot on. Nail on head and all that jazz,' said Barry.

'Yeah, well,' said Mel. 'There I was, starving to death and gasping like a flounder when Con hoves into view, or is it heaves? Anyway, there he is, the size of a Russian tank, carts me off to an underground bar in town and stuffs me with food and booze. He was between wars; I was between husbands. We joined forces on a gigantic pub crawl across the teetotal wasteland that is North Africa. We had the time of our lives: we ought to, considering how much effort went into it. By the end, I could have written a doctoral thesis on fluid dynamics. Fluid, oh, never mind.' Mel wiped her eyes, delighted with her own joke. 'Anyhow, we'd drunk our way through all these miserable, dry countries along the coast and ended up legless in Jordan, in a plastic Paddy pub hidden behind some embassy or other in Amman. Long and the short, we promised to honour and obey, and signed on the dotted.'

'I know,' said Kat. 'Then you found out he'd got a wife and six kids at home.'

'Nope,' Mel said. 'Nothing like that. When the novelty and the booze wore off, we discovered it wasn't a register office. All we'd signed was a UK visa application. We kissed each other on all four cheeks, and went our separate ways.'

'You're exaggerating,' Kat said.

'God's truth.' Mel feigned hurt. 'I lie not. Con was my last. Since then, I've been busy being mayor. Maybe I could take lessons from the inspector on refining my pulling technique.'

'The lovely inspector can put me in handcuffs any day of the week,' said Barry. 'I'd come quietly.'

'Barry, as I said earlier, you're being crude,' Kat said, trying for dignified, but ending up sounding school-marmish.

'Yes, Barry, shut up;' said Mel. She turned to Kat. 'Maybe I can have him off you when you're finished?'

'Not if I get there before you, ducky,' said Barry, and with ear-splitting whoops and shrieks they were off again.

The lugubrious barman must have suspected they'd smuggled in something to add to their drinks. It took awhile before they'd spluttered to a halt, bubbling with occasional bursts, like Icelandic geysers.

'If either of you lays a finger anywhere near the lovely inspector before I've done with him, you'll be sleeping with the fishes, and he'll be confined to a wheelchair, minus his gonads,' Kat warned.

Off they went again like a bunch of schoolgirls unable to stop giggling in church.

'Stop it; we'll get slung out.' Kat slipped off her shoes and curled up on the sagging upholstery, almost hidden by the sides.

'Is that really the time?' asked Barry. 'I'm going to love you and leave you. Gonna go dish the dirt with the boys.'

'If I get another round, think the barman might perk up?' said Mel.

They left Kat checking her clothing to see if the earlier explosion of crisps might have left a lasting impression. By the time she'd finished, Mel was on her way back.

Trailing behind her was Jack Ashton, loaded up like a Sherpa heading up to base camp.

CHAPTER 32

Ashton seemed cheerful despite having turned up in time to get lumbered with paying for the round of drinks. He can't have been in court that day; he was in jeans and a lavender pull-on that matched his eyes, emphasising the colour of his hair. Once again he wore loafers, sans socks. He had been carrying a lightweight jacket which he'd tossed over his shoulder, freeing up both hands to carry the drinks.

'Hello.' Kat moved Mel's handbag off a chair next to her. Ashton slid a tankard-sized wine glass in front of her and nodded his head towards the sofa where she was sitting.

'Budge up.'

As he settled beside her, Kat felt a nip in the base of her stomach and hoped she was not in for a rerun of the killer squid episode. She took an over-enthusiastic swallow of her drink, knocking back half the glass in an attempt to get her voice to work without squeaking. It was her second glass of the evening. Ashton, on his first beer, must have thought she was alcohol dependent and wonder what he might have got himself into. She took a second, more delicate, sip to prove that she could behave properly when she wanted.

'Well, Inspector,' Mel said, not missing a thing, and getting a big kick out of all the undercurrents. 'Last I heard, you'd gone back to the boonies. What brings you back down here now your sister's got herself safely hitched?'

'I had a meeting at Scotland Yard earlier,' he said, ignoring the crack about the boonies.

'Bit of luck, finding us here,' Mel said. 'We turned our mobiles off to escape the Moor for a quiet drink.'

'Half the nick's out on the towpath tonight. You were recognised.'

'We'll be sure to be in disguise next time,' said Mel.

Kat concentrated on the cashews Ashton had brought with the drinks. It was hard work, trying to cut down on snacking. She told herself the cashews would do instead of supper, save cooking.

'How's it going?' he asked. 'Any more excitements, incidents or accidents? Tummy okay? I warned you about that takeaway.'

'We all make mistakes,' she replied.

'It's been quiet down here. We've had no new bodies, dead pigeons, burglaries, or barmy teenagers on roofs to deal with,' Mel said, licking her finger to pick up the last crumbs from the crisp packet.

'Good. I gather you were at the funeral. I assume you kept out of trouble, since you're neither hospitalised nor in the nick.'

'Hey, things happen to me; doesn't make it my fault,' Kat said.

'No, of course not, but you do bring a certain something to the table, wouldn't you say?' He eyed her over his beer.

'Charisma, it's called,' she replied, picking a raisin from the cashews.

'Is that what it is?' he said, busy with examining the froth on his beer, smiling a little.

'Shardonnay's sister's called Charisma,' Mel said. 'God knows where Dozy Rosie gets her kids' names.

'Charisma, Shardonnay? Essex, eat your heart out,' laughed Ashton.

Kat had found a rogue raisin among her one hundred per cent neat cashews. She wondered if they'd give her a compensatory free packet if she complained to the misery guts behind the bar. Two packs if she quoted the Trade Descriptions Act at him.

Ashton shifted a little to get more room. This seemed to require running his arm along the back of the sofa. His hand came to rest ever so casually at the back of her neck. She tensed. Mel smirked. Ashton, opened his mouth to say something, but changed his mind.

'Cheers.' He raised his beer and took a long swallow.

They shuffled crisps and nuts for a while, and admired the brassware on the walls.

'Tell me something,' said Ashton, after a bout of silent meditation. 'The Patrick Moore Estate – I'm guessing here, from some of the street names, there might have been some attempt at an astronomy or space theme. But how did names like Julie Andrews, Glenda Jackson, Alec Guinness, and the other one, Maurice Mickelwhite, how did they get in there? Am I missing something important?'

'I'd let you work it out for yourself but we'd be here all night. It's the daftest story. Nobody could dream it up if they tried,' Mel said. She took a polite sip, careful not to disturb either of her little umbrellas.

'Don't bank on it,' said Ashton. 'Policemen get told all sorts of tales by all sorts of people about all sorts of situations.'

'Try this, then,' Mel said. 'Back in the seventies, the estate was being built as a joint project by Bickeridge council on one side of a new road and the Greater London Council on the other. Space exploration and astronomy were all the rage at that time. The Bickeridge architect was a Sky at Night fan, hence the name of the estate. He wanted roads named after stars and planets and space exploration. Bickeridge Council produced a list, got it approved, and their road signs, including Warp Drive for the new road going through the estate, were duly installed.

However, the GLC got a bit behind. Ordnance Survey and the Post Office began demanding their list of street names, but nobody could find the paperwork because it was the summer holiday season, and half the GLC secretaries appeared to be away on holiday or maternity leave.'

'Tell him what happened next,' Kat said.

'The Post Office got impatient, said they wanted a list of stars by close of play the following day or else. Some minion at the GLC panicked and just copied names from the West End cinema listings in that week's Time Out. The post office approved the stars' names and the GLC roads got their signs. By the time everyone was back from their hols and realised what had happened, it was too late to do anything. The signs were up. The tenants had got their new homes and weren't bothered what the streets were called.'

Last time Kat had heard the story, it had been a sacked planning officer with a grudge and a twisted sense of humour who'd drawn up the GLC list. It was still a good tale.

'That explains Julie Andrews and co, but why Maurice Mickelwhite?'

'Ah, that was another cock-up. Someone had heard that Michael Caine preferred using his real name for everything except work.'

In the ensuing hilarity, Kat underestimated the amount in her glass and spilt some. The other two maintained a tactful silence when the stain on her blouse spread like she was breastfeeding neat Ribena. She decided it was time to skip to the loo.

Shifting red wine is never easy. The wall-dispenser had stain devil, amongst other things. It was a regular little pharmacy: indigestion tablets, tampons, breath-freshener, body spray, condoms. She might try a squirt of breath freshener. Ditto body spray. It'd make sense after all the crisps and nuts to have indigestion tablets for later. She had nothing smaller than a tenner. Change given, it said. She pressed the button under the picture of the stain remover.

Charles Darwin disappeared into the machine, and with the rapid ker-ching, ker-ching, ker-ching of a one-armed-bandit coughing up its jackpot, the contents of the condom drawer disgorged onto the floor. The change-giver was kaput and now the blooming things wouldn't go back into the machine. Ten quid's worth. It would take determination to get through that lot. And stamina. Carting them out to the barman to ask for her money back would be embarrassing. Dump them and she'd waste her tenner. If only she'd brought her bag into the loo, but she hadn't. The tote she carted wherever she went was on the seat beside Ashton. She could hardly pop out for it now. Another avenue closed.

She was on the Pill. What was she going to do with two dozen condoms, apart from filling them with water and attaching them to her clothing to use as emergency water rations? There wasn't much call for survivalist skills in South London. She stuffed the condoms down her jeans, and trusted to luck that she'd make it back to the sofa without Ashton or Mel noticing. She'd get a chance to transfer them later.

'Mel was telling me about the Fostock funeral,' Ashton said.

'Yes, amazing, wasn't it?' Kat said.

'I caught some of it on the News.' He licked froth off his lip. 'I imagine Frankie the Fixer will be a great loss.'

'Fixer?'

'He fixed things. We're not talking car repairs or Corgi installations, here. He was the person to go to if anything illegal wanted fixing. Anyone needed a clean car for a bank job, or wanted to dispose of a dodgy one, Frankie would fix it. He had storage arrangements, short or long term, for any weapons you couldn't afford to have discovered hanging around the old semi-detached. He was good with money, too. He could fix instant interest-free non-repayable cash loans to encourage amnesia in security guards or witnesses.'

'As creepy Ted Delaney said at the funeral, he will be well missed.'

'Speaking of the funeral,' said Mel. 'Kat and Barry have been talking to people there who knew my dad and we heard all the gossip, but I'm not sure we're further forward. Have you heard any more?'

As Barry had done, earlier that evening, Ashton glanced around to check for eavesdroppers. The place was empty. The rest of the punters were whooping it up on the towpath outside despite being restricted to the indignity of plastic glasses. Mel shunted her chair nearer so Ashton didn't have to raise his voice.

'The police aren't convinced the skeleton is your father, Mel,' he told her. 'They're inclined to think it might have been gang-related. The likeliest option is the missing Delaney, Bernie. Interviewing the Fostock clan stirred things up, as you can imagine, because within twenty-four hours Fostock senior had unaccountably shuffled off his mortal coil whilst taking a bath.'

'One could make jokes about going down the plughole,' Kat said.

'One won't, though,' Ashton said. 'Will one?'

'One won't.'

'The Delaneys think Fostock arranged Bernie's disappearance.'

'But who bumped off Fostock?' Kat asked.

'The surveillance team fouled up. We can't put any of the Delaneys near Fostock's place at the time Frank went to his reward.'

'Fouled up?' Kat asked.

'It had been raining heavily. Visibility was poor. They tailed Delaney's next-door neighbour by mistake.' Ashton admitted.

Mel snorted with laughter.

'Ted Delaney went quiet after the funeral. His two muscle-bound sons have disappeared off the face of the earth. None of the family is letting on there's anything going on. Everyone's clammed up.'

'I don't suppose Dozy Rosie's going to grass up her own father,' Mel said. 'Shardonnay likes to put as much space as possible between herself and the family, so if she knows anything she's a better bet for information. However, it's a big extended family and its easy to lose track. Working out the relationships is like unravelling string.'

'Legend has it that over the years the body parts of both families have been distributed over a variety of building sites in London and the home counties,' said Ashton. 'It's too long ago and too large an area to do much about it. '

'There were plenty of opportunities in the sixties and seventies, with all that building and redevelopment that went on,' Kat said.

'I'm convinced it's my dad. That wouldn't necessarily stop it being gang related,' Mel said, putting her glass down. 'Kat, tell him what we have so far.'

'Rosie had a date with Mel's dad,' Kat said. 'But it went pear-shaped when she had to work. Mel's dad went out with his mates instead, same pub where Rosie worked part-time. Things went well until they called last orders, when someone was sick over him. He disappeared into the gents to clean up, and she never saw him again. They found his jacket later in the toilet, with his belongings in the pockets. The bar manager, Pam, said she'd leave the contents at his place on her way home.'

'Gran didn't mention any of that,' Mel said.

'If the barmaid never got around to giving it to her, your gran wouldn't have known about it. Learning about the jacket doesn't prove much except that it places your father at the pub on the night in question. You can't rule out anything,' Ashton replied. 'However, he was shorter than our skeleton. Apart from injuries consistent with a fall, there's nothing that indicates a gang killing. They usually burn or torture before chopping bits off. They like to spread remains over more than one site. Fostock dying naturally in his Victorian roll-top is hard to believe. He might have been helped on his way by somebody thinking it's Bernie's skeleton and that it had been put there by the Fostocks.'

'Fostock was elderly, maybe he really did slip in the bath,' suggested Mel. 'A genuine accident.'

'He never used that bath,' Ashton said. 'He had a walk-in, for his arthritis. His bath was hidden in a closet.' Ashton eyed the empty glasses, and rose. 'Another?'

Kat watched him saunter off for replenishments. Mel folded her arms and leaned back in her chair.

'What?' Kat's face reddened.

'It's amusing, just watching you two. He's smitten,' Mel told her. 'If I wasn't here he'd be all over you. You're both lit up like Christmas.'

'You exaggerate,' Kat protested. 'It's only a sex thing. I'm not getting into anything serious.'

'Could've fooled me,' Mel said.

'You've been reading Mills and Boon again,' Kat said.

'I'm happy to be proved wrong,' Mel said. 'Especially if I can have the sexy inspector when you dump him.'

Kat watched the current object of her libidinous musings chatting to a barman slightly less lugubrious now a calming influence had arrived. Barry was right: Ashton did have a nice bum. Must be all that running.

'Oi, concentrate. What do you think?' Mel asked.

'What? Oh, your father? You really are sure it's him?'

'Well, yes, I am. But let's try to fill in some missing links, and see if it gets us any further forward,' Mel replied.

'We need to find out there he went when he left the pub that night. Another thing - what happened to the stuff in his jacket if it wasn't left with your gran? The last we hear of your dad, his jacket is still at the pub where he left it, and the contents of his pockets are winging their way to him via Pam, the late barmaid except that they don't get passed on. Thirty-odd years later a mystery skeleton coincidentally minus possessions appears. Cosmo's idea about the gang stuff is a red herring.'

Kat turned her attention to the bundle of unwanted condoms that were taking up room in her back pocket and was about to move them into her handbag when she saw Ashton coming back with the next round of drinks. She couldn't make the transfer now. He'd see, and he'd probably come to the conclusion that she was as thick as a brick.

'There you go, girls,' he said, settling in so close beside her that she became worried he might notice the outcrop of rubber goods on her back pocket where she'd stashed her unwanted purchase.

She tried not to fidget. Mel winked and took a large swig of her multicoloured cocktail. Going up in the world: the barman had given her three umbrellas this time, as well as a cherry.

'Right,' Ashton began. 'Let's see what we have so far, positive and negative. Positive: Jeff disappears thirty years ago, the same week the foundations were sunk. Another positive: the Easter weekend that year was one of the hottest on record and would have speeded decomposition, leaving us with the skeleton. So we can probably assume that whoever it is, they went into that hole over the Easter weekend. Yet another positive: the skeleton is without ID or belongings and we know Jeff mislaid his jacket and its contents.' He was ticking off each point with his fingers. 'Now, negative: there are no dental records. Any that weren't computerised were destroyed when the practice changed hands.' He took a sip of his beer.

'We need to take this a step further. Time we spoke to your grandmother, Mel. I'll give you my number. Can I leave you to arrange it? You might like to be there when I talk to her.' His mobile rang.

'Do you mind if I take this? Work.'

Moving away, he slipped effortlessly into business mode. No more lounging and laid back, he was the professional: ramrod straight, expressionless, speaking shortly between long periods of listening.

'Nice legs,' said Mel.

'Behave, Mel, you're sex mad.'

'A girl has to have a hobby.' Mel grinned salaciously. 'I wasn't going to mention it, but when he frog-marched you home the other day after your rooftop heroics, the community support team were offering odds on whether he was going to give you a bollocking or a seeing to.'

'What?'

'You heard. That open-mouthed gape doesn't suit you, by the way.'

'Next, you'll tell me the whole estate is in on it,' Kat said. 'I think I need another packet of nuts.' She got up and headed for the bar.

Mel was sniggering into her cocktail when Kat returned.

'You did the sexy strut so well,' she said. 'But I'm afraid it was all wasted. He's on his phone still, facing the wrong way. When he comes back I'll make myself scarce, leave you to it, if you like.'

'Thanks, Mel,' she replied. 'I owe you one.'

'Yeah, you do. A detailed description of Ashton in bed would do,'

'Get one of your own.' Kat slapped Mel's wrist. 'Shh. He's coming.'

They straightened and smiled at Ashton as if butter wouldn't melt.

'Sorry, girls, I'm going to have to move it. Duty calls.' He leant to retrieve his jacket, the hairs on his arm brushing against Kat's bare shoulder. It gave her an electric charge that almost jolted her out of her seat. She managed to get her glass back on the table without mishap.

'Drink up.' He drained his beer. 'I'll give you both a lift home. They've started playing with their breathalysers outside on the towpath.'

He dropped Mel first and came back to Kat's for coffee, amongst other things. He wasn't in such a hurry to leave after Kat dislodged the contents of her pockets while getting out of the car.

'Be a shame to waste them,' he said, reading the different labels.

Kat was impressed by Rise 'n' Shine Glow in the Dark, and said so.

'My pleasure,' said Ashton. 'Let's see what else we've got here.'

CHAPTER 33

Ashton knew that with everyone having to juggle dates it was inevitable that when he was granted an audience with Mel's granny, Kat would most likely be tied up with developers. There would be no chance to meet up over dinner, either, as it was the night of the residents' meeting to discuss Majorca. It seemed their schedules were destined never to coincide sufficiently for them to go to a film, have dinner together, or get to know each other.

He picked up Mel at the council offices on the way. Joan Rampart and Kat lived at opposite arms of the same E-shaped block, but with enough distance between to be considered separately. Mrs Rampart's neighbours included Karen and the baby, who were living with her parents while waiting to be housed, and Cosmo King. Judging by the televisions raging at full volume along the corridor, the majority of the remaining neighbours were elderly, or hearing impaired, or both.

Mrs Rampart's front door was covered in stickers. Given the quantity of flaking door paint in the block, Ashton was surprised there were no notices to warn of lead poisoning. As they reached her door with its *Beware Fierce Dog* picture cut from a rabies poster, there was a loud explosion and automatic gunfire from inside. Mel's knock set off a savage barking and snarling.

'If it's Jehovah's or Morons, you can buzz off.'

'Gran. It's Mel.'

'Who?'

The TV battle cut out in mid scream but the barking continued.

'It's Mel, I've got Inspector Ashton with me. Undo the chain and let us in.' As Mel rattled the letter box, the heat that belted out was enough to barbecue chicken. 'Turn the dog off. It's giving us all a headache.'

The electronic barking stopped.

'Stand in front of the spy hole so I can see you.'

There was a glass eye set in the door, well below five feet in old money. Ashton and Mel stood back and leaned over like giraffes at a water hole. There was a lengthy symphony of muttering and the withdrawing of multiple bolts.

The old lady was no pushover for the doorstep con-merchants. She took her time squinting through the door chain to check they weren't after her savings, which, Ashton thought, she most likely kept under the bed or in a faux electric wall socket. He had had lost count of the old people he'd met who kept their valuables in an old *I Can't Believe It's Not Butter* tub in the fridge.

'Don't let the cold in,' she said, taking possession of the boxed cream cake he had stopped off to buy on the way. Inside, the flat smelled of beef burger and air freshener.

Mrs Rampart's daisy-pattern hem reached her ankles, not so much by design as from a lack of inches brought on by osteoporosis and old age. Minus her big hat and handbag she was simply another frail old lady. He glanced at the TV, which had been paused on a gory shot of a girl going through a car windscreen. Maybe the old girls wasn't so frail. Gift notwithstanding, it didn't stop her saying what came into her head as they made themselves comfortable.

'I haven't seen hair that colour before. Is it real?'

'Gran,' Mel scolded. 'You can't say things like that to people.'

'Yes, I can. At my age, I say what I like,' the old lady replied smugly.

'Er, yes, the colour's real,' Ashton replied, not in the least put out.

'They say redheads have a terrible temper. You got a temper?'

'I don't think so. In a family of redheads, temper doesn't get you far.'

'No, don't suppose it does. Get yourself comfy. You can call me Joan. Or you can call me Mrs Rampart. Either'll do,' she said. 'Mel, put the kettle on, girl. There's scones in the kitchen. I'll hang onto the cake.'

She took a while to get comfortable, commanding Ashton's attention in rearranging cushions and footstool to her instructions. He congratulated her on the commemorative royal wall plates, which seemed to please her. Assuring her that her scones were better than the shop bought variety, he asked if he could have the recipe for his mum. If it wasn't too much trouble.

'No wife, then, or doesn't she cook?' queried the old girl. 'You're old enough to be married. Not one of them gay rainbows, are you?'

'Er, no, I'm divorced.'

'That's all right, then. Any kids?'

Mel mimed a cringing apology behind her grandmother's back.

'Not exactly, no.'

'Not exactly? What's that mean?' she probed.

He explained his ex-wife now lived in New Zealand.

'New Zealand, it's not the sort of place you can hop on the bus to see the boy.' Joan Rampart sympathised 'There's plenty from here that hops it with their kids, but they mostly only get as far as New Malden.'

'It was good of you to see me, Mrs Rampart,' he said, more used to doing the asking rather than answering questions, and wanting to get to the nitty gritty. 'Tell me if it gets too much for you, and we'll stop.'

'Thank you, dear. Ain't you got lovely manners? Don't suppose you're in the market for another wife, are you? Mel's free. Why don't you grab him, girl? Time you gave it another go. None of us is getting any younger.'

'Gran, behave yourself,' Mel sighed, rolling her eyes.

Laughing, the old girl tucked into her scone. She was taking so long on each bite that Ashton wondered if she might have been counting the raisins with her teeth.

He glanced around. Mel had told him earlier that her grandmother was waiting to move house but there was no sign of upheaval or preparations. An empty burger box and an open DVD case were minor deviations from the general tidiness. The flat was spotless, the sideboard polished to display china ornaments on mirrored shelves: Germanic angels and chubby children in smocks, with their toes turned in. A rack of DVDs was lined up with military precision, in alphabetical order. Tilting his head, he saw Singin' in the Rain alongside Reservoir Dogs, Pulp Fiction, Die Hard. He'd been right: she wasn't so frail.

The old lady finished her scone and gave a polite burp behind her hand before taking a dainty sip of tea.

'My gran swore by a Guinness a day, but with my waterworks I can't take too much liquid, though I still enjoy a nice malt whisky in my tea when I can.' She eyed Ashton, on the off-chance but nothing was forthcoming. 'Times change, eh,' she sighed. 'Pour us another cup.'

Mel obliged.

'Time was, you'd leave doors and windows open and not get robbed,' she mused. 'Kids played outside without getting interfered with or kidnapped. It's not like that today.'

Mel began to fidget, eliciting a baleful glare from her grandmother.

Ashton remained silent, although he knew that while they might have left their doors open and let their kids play in the street, people did break in, and rape and pillage and rob, and abuse their children. The difference was that in those halcyon days you kept quiet about it, worried what the neighbours might think. Neither did they have the benefit of TV and the tabloids broadcasting in minute detail to all parts of the globe within moments. The old lady's selective memory ignored any mention of Billy's hit and run accident. So much for playing safely.

'No plastic 85-inch digit tellies that you have to sit in the garden to watch, then,' she mourned. 'We're living in a foreign country, now.'

Ashton guessed Mel's responsibilities as the borough's mayor must leave the old lady alone a lot. Now she had visitors she was clearly going to make the most of them. He gave her his complete attention as she recalled a fairytale past of spontaneous street parties where ageing matriarchs danced with their skirts up, imitating the queen mum doing the hokey cokey.

The room was warm. He made an effort to stop his eyes from glazing over when she went into a litany of praise for the golden days of Timothy Whites and Mac Fisheries, Cy Grant's guitar on the BBC each night, coal fires, friendly rag and bone men, and nice young rent collectors who called each week and always stopped for a chat. According to her, in those days the tailors were all Jewish, laundries Chinese, and Irish navvies wept beery tears as they sang the Black Velvet Band in the pub.

'Gran, the inspector can't stay long,' Mel said, trying to divert the old girl's stream of consciousness. 'Are you up to answering a few questions about when my dad went missing?'

He guessed he wouldn't have to go too softly, softly with his questioning. Not with that collection of DVDs.

'You carry on, son. I don't mind talking about poor old Jeff, Gawd rest 'im. It's all so long ago now.'

'Thank you, Mrs Rampart. Say when you want to stop.'

Stop? She was in her element: home-made scones, chocolate cake to follow, captive audience, the undivided attention of a presentable and polite young man.

'We're still trying to identify the body. Mel seems to think it might be her father, although we've been unable to discover if that is the case. You may be able to help us. Am I correct in saying that your son, Jeff, disappeared thirty years ago?'

'Thirty two, dear. Vanished off the face of the Earth.'

'What did you think had happened to him?'

'Well, let's think,' she said, resting her forehead on her fingers, rubbing it a little and leaving patches of red across the skin. 'At first, when he didn't come home that night. I wasn't too worried. Maybe he'd found himself a new girlfriend. I thought it was a bit odd that he never contacted us to see how the kiddies were. By the next evening, when we hadn't heard a dicky bird all day, I started worrying. I left the kids with the next-door neighbour and went down the Stargazer to see if anyone knew where he was. There was hardly anyone there, it was still early. Rose Delaney was on bar duty. She had her eye on him in those days. I ask you, a Delaney with a copper? I never spoke to her. Someone said he'd been in the night before but left before closing time.'

'You must have been worried by then.'

'Not too worried. He was a grown-up. He could fend for himself. I knew there hadn't been an accident. Someone from the nick would have been round. I gave it until next morning, Saturday, then I rang them.'

'I understand his wife left just after Mel was born, and that his son had been disabled by an accident a few months before that. Is there any possibility that he'd had enough? Went off with a girlfriend, perhaps.'

She frowned. 'No, that's not like Jeff. He wouldn't leave without saying. He was a very proper sort of person, if you know what I mean. Always did things right.'

'Had he fallen out with anyone? Upset anybody who might have wanted to harm him? What about enemies?' From the reaction, he might as well have switched to speaking Chinese.

'What? People after him, you mean?'

'That sort of thing.'

'No, nothing like that. I rang the station. They went all over, asking people, tried the hospitals. After a bit they said I should get on with my life and not expect him back and they'd get the kids taken into care, but I said no, I'd keep them with me, cos you never know, he might've turned up. Do you think this skelington is him, then?'

'It's possible,' Ashton said gently. 'They're still doing tests but they're a bit short on DNA. They can't locate any dental records.'

'You won't get anywhere there,' said the old lady. 'They slung the files out. The new dentist had a computer.'

'Ah, that's a pity,' Ashton said.

She tapped his knee. 'You know, I had to wait over a year for a hip replacement. Here, would you believe I'm eighty-eight?'

'And I can see you're in excellent shape, Mrs Rampart,' he replied.

'Thank you, dear. Now where were we?'

'Your son Jeff had gone missing. What did you think when they told you they had stopped looking for him?'

'I knew Jeff was dead,' she said. 'Felt it in my bones. He had no reason to do a runner. I thought he might have been on undercover work, like that dogs film.' She glanced at her DVD collection for inspiration. 'The one where the job goes wrong and they find out he's an undercover cop and his gangster friend kills him.'

'Er, I don't think so.' Ashton had come across stranger things than geriatric Tarantino fans.

Mel shrugged and made a face across the room.

'Your son was a uniformed beat officer,' he said. 'I don't think he would have been working undercover. What about problems at home or at work? Was he worried about anything?'

'No, well, no more than the rest of us.' She glanced over at Mel. 'Give us another cuppa, darlin' and fetch the rest of the scones. Today's Whopper wasn't as big as yesterday's. Have a word with the Meals people, will you, Mel?' Mel went off to get the scones.

'Where was I,' the old lady said. 'Oh, yes, worried, you said. Well, he was always worried about Billy. It was hard on him, even before Dolly, the kids' mother, did a runner. She couldn't cope. Her lift didn't reach all floors. Dopey Doll, the neighbours called her. She was so gormless, she thought Pearl Harbour was a black jazz singer.' Laughing, she wiped her eyes. 'Good thing she ran off with that cinema bloke. She'd never have managed with two kids. Sorry, Mel. I tell it like it is.'

'That's all right, Gran. Tell Mr Ashton about Billy.'

'Poor little blighter was on his trike in the cul-de-sac and this driver reversed in, real fast, went over him, then shot off like a demon. They never found out who did it. The lad's not all there, now. There's a name for it, they did tell us but I can't remember. The police fixed up a special boarding school for him. Miles away, it was. He was home for Easter when Jeff disappeared; he was upset. Kept saying 'Daddy gone, bye-bye,' day in, day out. Drove us barmy. The only person who could calm him was that skinny little squirt Cosmo King. Met him, have you? I must say he came up trumps for Billy in them days. Next thing we hear, Billy's salamander ups and dies cos he's forgotten to feed it. He and his dad used to go out and find slugs and things. Jeff had it given to him by some politician bloke.'

'Where is Billy now?' he asked.

'When he got too old for the school they moved him into a sheltered home down the road, in Lower Bickeridge. We were very lucky there. It was either that or the loony bin.'

'They're not called loony bins any more, Gran,' chided Mel.

'It might help if we could talk to your son's friends from those days. His drinking pals, football mates, girlfriends, neighbours. Mel's helped us with some names,' Ashton said, handing over Kat's compilation from Mel and Barry's efforts a week earlier. 'Are there any others you can think of that might have been missed?'

The old lady examined the list for a while, her eyes darting across the page, clearly not needing spectacles even at eighty-eight.

'No, I think you've got them all. You've included Rose Delaney, I notice. She tried to get her claws into him. Then, soon as he disappeared, she and Cosmo King galloped down the aisle with him faster than Red Rum. Nobody was surprised when that didn't last long. Half the names in my address book are gone now or moved away. It's a long time. If you find this skeleton is Jeff, I'd like to give him a proper send-off at last.' She put her empty cup on the tray. 'Yes, a funeral would be nice. I think I'm ready for a rest. Me eyes are tired.' She dabbed what might have been a tear. 'Give us a hand, son.'

Leaning on Ashton she hauled herself from the chair and headed for the bedroom, accepting his thanks for her time with a gracious nod. She was still clutching the cake he'd brought. It was unopened.

Ashton was checking his watch when Mel came back from her grandmother's bedroom.

'It's getting late.' He picked up his jacket from the back of the armchair. 'I won't hang about. You've got a meeting at the town hall. I go that way; I can drop you.'

They walked to his car, which he had parked in his customary spot a short way down the road in the full glare of a new street lamp outside the leisure centre. He was not yet confident of parking his pride and joy on the older parts of the estate. However, after having discovered from police gossip that Meccano Mickey and his mates had been awarded their anti-social behaviour orders for nothing more threatening than a surfeit of what a generation earlier would have been no more than boyish high spirits, he had parlayed a deal with the Asbo trio who with Winnie in tow were honing their entrepreneurial skills by establishing a fully comprehensive vehicle protection scheme on the estate.

'Residents' meetings are not my thing,' he said, dropping Mel off amongst the crowd at the town hall. 'I need to finish off some work. Tell Kat I'll be in touch.'

CHAPTER 34

It had been standing room only at the residents' meeting. Kat had taken the precaution of distributing a leaflet to tenants beforehand, explaining the pros and cons of the Magaluf exercise. The leaflet also explained that her original plan for a four week low-season turnaround had grown into a five, possibly six week stay but that it would be at a four-star spa hotel, full board, all found, at the council's expense. The longer period would clear the decks – literally – for demolition and rebuilding to take place at a rate of knots. Once residents had had confirmation that all their expenses for both the holiday and the subsequent house-moving exercise would be covered, and that they would without exception be able on their return home to walk straight into their new homes where their removal vans would be lined up outside awaiting for their instructions, everyone was in favour.

Kat's good humour changed when she returned home to find the garage area below her flat strewn with bits of burnt Mini Traveller. Of Ashton, or his Merc, there was no sign, which indicated that he was still working or out and about with his camera and that his car was as a consequence out of harm's way. There were signs that the fire brigade or the police or both, had been and gone. The Moor had a history of spontaneous combustion, vehicles and garages alike. The forces of law and order always turned up, if they had nothing better to do. Ditto a fire engine or two. They'd go through the same old rigmarole, everyone would have an ice cream from the van that always seemed to follow in the wake of the emergency vehicles, and then they'd all buzz off home.

'Kids, probably,' Kat said, telling Ashton about it when he phoned to ask how the meeting had gone.

'Maybe,' he frowned. 'I don't like the idea of you staying here on your own. What happens if you upset someone with your amateur sleuthing? Promise you'll be careful while I'm away.' After the success with his demolition pictures, Ashton was busy building up a portfolio.

Kat thought it was nice though unnecessary of him to bother about her safety. However, she wasn't going to argue. She was used to cars spontaneously combusting in dark corners on council estates. Nothing new there. The Mini had been well past its sell-by, and no great loss. However, she was now without wheels. What would she use for the carnival parade the following weekend?

'No problem. I'll borrow Liam's Land Rover,' Ashton reassured her. 'One proviso: I do the driving.'

She could hardly argue. He was, after all, doing her a favour.

Anyone on the estate not shopping for holiday kit was gearing up for the carnival. Meanwhile, Curly, Chemo and Meccano Mickey were refining Winnie's skateboarding technique. The foursome were avoiding trouble, and so far nobody had grassed them up on their vehicle protection scheme.

Mel was squeezing in as many mayoral meetings and visits as she could now her year of office was drawing to a close. The big biker – he who had turned out to be the local vicar – had roared off on his bike to a seminar, or it might have been a seminary, and wouldn't be back until the week of the carnival.

Kat worked at home that week, out of range of the disgusting smell at the housing office. Karen had grown paranoid about the possibility of another body turning up, and had nagged the police, who trotted round with overalls, detector kits and a dog, and insisted that the unsavoury pong, whatever it was, did not emanate from remains, human or otherwise, that might be buried or otherwise hidden in the building. Despite their reassurances, Karen and the housing team, unable to bear the stench any longer, marched out in protest, swathed in face masks.

An hour afterwards the council's health and safety team arrived in full chemical hazard kit making everyone think the TV company were filming on the estate again until a council officer ran '*working for your health and safety, do not cross*' red and white plastic tape across the housing office steps.

Residents went to fetch folding chairs and bottled drinks, so they could watch in comfort. They were not disappointed when half a dozen council workers kitted up as deep-sea divers in Perspex bubble headgear and breathing apparatus trooped out of a van with a Hazchem logo on the side and disappeared into the estate office. Their back-up team remained outside, isolated from the spectators with an outer circle of red and white plastic tape to form a secondary barrier, behind which they settled around a yellow chemicals drum to play poker.

The Bickeridge Bugle, fortuitously forewarned, was there to record everything for posterity. Nobody had any idea what was happening inside the building. More residents turned up to gawp. By dusk it had begun to resemble a vigil for trapped coal miners. As darkness fell, the safety officer said they only got paid overtime for emergencies, so they might as well go home and begin again next morning.

Activity resumed at half seven the following day. Spectators and folding chairs were already back in position when they arrived. One woman had left her towel on a chair overnight but found both towel and chair had disappeared. Some wag suggested it may have been transported by Germans to the nearest swimming pool.

As the morning progressed, it was clear that day two was going to be less exciting than day one. The watchers were becoming restive and muttering about going home for lunch when there was a loud whoop from inside the building. Outside, OAPs with wartime memories hit the deck and covered their heads. However, it seemed the wild whoop was a false alarm. There followed a profound silence. Time dragged.

When the door finally opened, over an hour and a half later, spectators craned to see what was going on. The poker game, which had been resumed in the lee of the council's health and safety van, came to a halt while someone spoke on a walkie-talkie. Minutes later, the B team dropped their cards, loaded up with pressure sprays attached to drums slung on their backs like rucksacks and plodded into the building to join their colleagues.

By now it was lunch time. Stomachs may have been rattling against ribs but nobody dared go home now for fear they'd miss the denouement. For another hour they were treated to comings and goings amidst a symphony of whirring and whooshing from inside the building.

Kat was itching to see how it would be resolved. She decided to remain with the little band of watchers a while longer. While she used the time to send and read text messages, she half listened to the tenants speculating about leaking mustard gas canisters from the war, dead animals down the toilet, and scary insects' nests boring into the solid concrete walls: they were making it up as they went along.

The technicians reappeared, loaded their equipment into the council vans and sped off. Kat won the communal dash to the estate office, which they found scrubbed up cleaner than an operating theatre.

'You'll never believe what happened,' Karen said.

'What?'

'Someone had put rotted prawns in all those little light fittings above the councillors' portraits.'

Kat remembered the tricky trio tucking into their Thai takeaway a week ago but didn't say a word. The smell had gone, its cause removed. The brass light fittings had been taken away with the councillors' portraits. The wall, for three decades graced by political mug shots, was empty. Kat was not alone in thinking it a blessed relief.

'They've taken the pictures and stuff off to clean. I wish they'd remove them altogether,' sighed Karen.

'Why not suggest they let you keep the walls clear to avoid similar problems in future?' asked Kat, setting a precedent and probably earning the gratitude of future generations.

Fun and games over, everyone returned to where they should be. In most cases this was back to preparations for the carnival. In addition to the street parade, there were to be displays on the big field and a fly-past by Red Arrows. Heats for the carnival princess, talent contest and the Scrabble championship were in full swing.

None of this left much time for Kat's sleuthing skills to get an airing. The unidentified skeleton continued to be a mystery, although on the chance that it might be Jeff Rampart the police had finally got around to taking DNA from Mel and were awaiting the results. The news that it might be the mayor's father had been kept surprisingly quiet.

Using the pretext of learning more about the history of the Moor estate, Kat had spoken to a number of people. Of the many who had known Jeff Rampart in those days, few claimed they had been close, often citing his job as the cause.

Unrelated to the mystery, DNA had become the latest fad on the estate after a seemingly endless series of paternity squabbles on daytime TV. Shardonnay, stubbornly convinced she'd been swapped at birth, had sent off her DNA and that of Cosmo.

'I'd run around the estate naked if it meant that moron wasn't my dad,' she told Kat and Karen. 'I mean, I don't need to be the daughter of somebody famous; anybody will do, so long as it's not him.'

'You never know your luck. You could be the secret love-child of the world's richest man,' Kat joked

'Dream on,' said Mel.

Kat meanwhile booked the hall in the leisure centre for the Scrabble heats. There was an anxious moment when she learned it would clash with the count for the Magaluf ballot. In the end, she agreed to a shift system on the understanding that the council wouldn't turn up and expect to start moving the furniture around or begin counting the ballot until the Scrabble was done and dusted.

The day had gone well. The Scrabble quarterfinals had ended in plenty of time for the half-five handover and the election team had kept its promise not to jump the gun by turning up too early. With the three local councillors each belonging to a different party, it made sense for all three, despite or because of their different political loyalties, to scrutinise the piles of Yeses and Noes waiting to be counted on a central island of trestle tables. The result wasn't expected for two hours after the opening of the last box.

Bickeridge would be the first local council to send council tenants abroad to save money. Magaluf was about to go down in history as the preferred local authority option to B&B. It could set a precedent, a fact much trumpeted in the right-wing press. The story had captured the attention of more than just the local rags, and there were enough cameras whirring for a royal wedding.

The tenants were on their best behaviour, a state of affairs which Kat hoped would continue. The last thing she wanted was for something with her imprint on it to go adrift.

Since the pigeon fracas, the press had been staking out Bickeridge, letting it be known that newsworthy leaks coming in their direction would be rewarded. The leader of the council had discreetly diverted the council's contingency fund into daily bugging scans of all town hall washrooms. Councillors, believing themselves sufficiently important to merit electronic eavesdropping, dusted off their land lines, mothballed their mobiles and began talking to each other instead of via email. Kat was relieved the media hadn't caught Lee's rooftop escapade, but she wasn't holding her breath. Unless war broke out or there was another sex scandal to divert the nation, she was bound to turn up sooner or later in headlines a foot deep.

Mel had barely given the signal to begin counting the ballot when Kat noticed the ticking Tesco bag-for-life under a stack of chairs in a corner. Despite her training, she was reluctant to abandon ship and risk a repeat of the committee's knee-jerk reaction the night the car alarms went off. People panic if they expect to be blown apart any second.

Of Ashton, who had been photographing the Scrabble earlier, there was no sign. It didn't take a mastermind to guess he'd be in the cafeteria.

Mel calmly announced a technical hitch and made for the exit accompanied by a clutch of hangers-on.

Kat dialled 999 on her mobile. That done, she prepared to broadcast a low-key message to leave the hall, but the microphone was dead. She gave it a hefty whack. It emitted a howl like a newborn baby.

The sound engineer, who had expected to spend the evening in the bar once he had set up the equipment, swung around in his chair so awkwardly that he gave himself whiplash. With no time for politeness or sympathy for his plight, Kat manhandled him out of the way to reach the console, while both he and his microphone wailed in unison.

People thought the results were about to be announced unexpectedly early and got quite animated.

The outside broadcast crew had relaxed after the BBC had done their customary projections of population and turnout broken down by age and sex and announced that this would be the first counting of a ballot where they didn't expect to have to wait longer than it would take to rebuild the Queen Mary. Now it seemed they might be wrong. The producer swallowed his toasted fried egg sandwich in one and shot out of the cafeteria without paying. Outside, the cameraman sighed, docked his spliff behind his head-phones, jammed an eye into his viewfinder and went back into the hall to find something worth filming.

Kat imagined the ticking was becoming louder but suspected it would prove to be nothing more dangerous than a forgotten Scrabble timer. She nonetheless moved closer to the exit.

She swung around as her radar sensed the moment Ashton sauntered in from the back of the hall, seemingly unaware of pressing danger. A young constable waylaid him, looking worried. At the exits, uniformed police trainees were doing a poor job of hiding their excitement. For some it was their first suspicious package. Some people with a death wish tried to come back into the hall.

At the exit, Mel was doing an impromptu sign language with her fingers towards the ticking Tesco bag, uncertain whether to go forward or back. Ashton, with the constable in tow, picked up the microphone, calmly announced an emergency and ordered everybody out.

'This is not a drill,' he boomed. 'I repeat. This is not a drill.'

A small group not wanting to miss anything surrounded the mayor, seeming confident that so long as police remained in the hall, nobody could be in any danger.

In her peripheral vision Kat saw two polling clerks huddled over a table containing ballot papers. She glared, thinking it might have crossed their minds that this was an opportunity to do a spot of vote rigging. Red faced, they stopped what they'd been doing, and strolled out of the room.

Sirens broke through the hubbub: ambulance, police, fire, at least two engines from the sound of it, and a different ice cream van. Unless Krishna Ices had dropped Greensleeves for the wishy-washy fish tank tune that they keep using in everything from TV ads to full feature films.

A constable was un-clogging the exit and ushering a line of people to safety. Kat held the door open and tried to look like a fire marshal who'd come out without the official red hat. Ashton was semaphoring across the room to attract the attention of the constable and was having as much success as he would have had be been trying to hail a taxi in the rain. She was about to take pity on him when the constable gave a thumbs up sign.

'Bomb disposal's just arrived, sir' he yelled, causing a stampede.

CHAPTER 35

The B word ricocheted around the room faster than bird flu in a turkey farm at Christmas.

From upstairs meetings and evening classes, and from basement gyms and fitness studios, the building was evacuated in orderly lines. Everyone was remarkably co-operative. Nobody was contemplating hanging about, not with the possibility of a bomb somewhere on the premises.

Sky News grabbed their pints and bolted out of the bar. The politicians weren't far behind, and were showing more activity than they had managed to demonstrate during their entire term of political office. Anyone who had at first lagged behind hoping to film the proceedings on their mobile and put it out on You Tube suddenly decided they couldn't wait to get out of the room fast enough.

Emergency strobes had turned the car park into Sunset Strip. In the bus lay-by, three food vans jostled for space. Bickeridge Young Socialists, ejected from their AGM in the cafeteria, downed cans of shandy and heckled some Conservative Widows Club ladies, one of whom calmly produced a Tupperware container of sausage rolls and offered them round, ignoring the scruffs on their left. A pair of Greens, who seldom turned out for anything less than whales or wind farms, chained their tandem to the nearest litter bin and sought out the head of housing to ask why the council weren't putting tenants in mobile homes on the coast rather than mucking up the ozone layer with a plane to some holiday resort in Majorca.

As she passed the Sky News team barricaded in their van and hemmed in by motorbikes Kat heard the cameraman rehearsing reasons why in his crew's Gadarene rush to exit the building with their pints intact, they appeared to have left their humongously expensive camera equipment behind to be blown to kingdom come.

Winnie and the boys, as wasps to jam, had shown up at the first hint of chaos and were throwing half-hearted insults in the direction of a skinny hippy weaving along the road with the gentle gaze of someone who knew the answers were blowing in the wind. He failed to hear their taunts over whatever was pounding through earphones under his tea-cosy hat. Nor was he fazed that one of his would-be torturers was an ape in concrete-pulverising Docs, with a net tutu hoisted up to his armpits.

The crowd soon spread onto the park, where Barry was organising the older children into building a bonfire from broken furniture. Winnie and the boys soon got bored with their hippy baiting and produced a box of paper for burning. Chemo offered up a Dr Pepper bottle of paraffin to get the bonfire going. The younger children, high on additives and junk food, were over-excited, running around hitting each other. Grown-ups ignored the racket and pretended none of the kids belonged to them.

'Good, eh?' said Karen. 'Until that bomb turned up, this was about as exciting as opening an umbrella.'

An additional fire crew turned up unexpectedly after losing themselves amongst the gas company's road diversions on their way home from a warehouse fire in Croydon. After a quick check that their professional services were surplus to requirements they radioed their position back to base, blaming their SatNav, and joined the line of dancers snaking its way around the bonfire.

Amidst showers of sparks and shrieks of laughter, revellers flapped at singed clothing like demented penguins having a great night out. The council's health and safety officer, turfed out by the bomb experts, joined the conga line.

Ashton was trying to get some life out of the loudhailer when a bomb squad officer holding his Perspex headgear as if offering the head of John the Baptist came out chatting and laughing with a uniformed inspector. The uniform grabbed the loudhailer and banged it hard against a lamp post. There was an eruption of static.

'Ladies and gents, your attention, please.'

The conga continued uninterrupted, albeit without the attendant shrieks of delight.

'Madam Mayor, councillors, ladies and gentlemen,' the uniform began. 'The suspicious package has been safely neutralised. The building has been searched for further devices, and it is safe for you to return to the hall. I am advised that the ballot is ready to be counted. Thank you.' He handed the loudhailer back to Ashton, who stuck it under his arm and headed towards his car.

Kat sauntered over. Not too fast. She'd give him time to get there. He was leaning against his car door, arms crossed, jacket slung over his shoulder in what Kat could only describe as a pose.

'Here's one emergency you can't put down to me,' she said, pre-empting any witty comment.

'Not entirely. I expect something to happen when you're around.'

Kat was tempted to make some pithy repartee or put down. On second thoughts, life was too short.

'After all that, what was in the bag?' she asked.

'You'll never guess.'

'A Scrabble timer that turned itself on?' That was logical.

'No,' he said, enjoying the moment. 'It was a gift-wrapped vibrator from the scary new shop the local *Mothers Against Sex* have been campaigning against.'

'Oops,' Kat laughed. 'Red faces or what?'

'That's what happens when the shop puts the batteries in before gift-wrapping it. No receipt in the bag, and I doubt anybody's going to own up. Even if they did, they won't get it back from the bomb squad.'

'They're not going to blow it up?'

'No,' Ashton replied. 'They're taking it in as material evidence. Meanwhile, someone's drawn up a roster.'

'A roster?' The penny dropped. Kat grimaced. 'Oh, gross!'

'Two of the councillors saw the boys messing around at the back of the hall earlier and reckon it was one of their hoaxes,' he said.

'If they thought it was a hoax why were those two heroic representatives of the people first out of the hall once you'd you called an emergency,' Kat said. 'Never mind, it jazzed up the evening.'

'Except for the unlucky birthday boy. Or girl.'

'The media is going to have a another field day, coming so soon after those damn pigeons.'

'Relax,' he said. 'You worry too much. Look, it's not late. Neither of us has eaten properly all day. How about dinner? I'm down in Basingstoke tomorrow, so I don't have to rush off. There's a new restaurant across the river that's had good reviews. We'll have a romantic meal in a room big enough to talk without sharing our lives with the next table.'

He was offering her four stars, tassels on the menus and Bach in the background. Didn't necessarily mean the food was any good. But he'd said romantic. And she was starving.

'Have we time to go back to my flat, so I can change?'

When the votes were counted, it was no surprise that so many were in favour of a freebie in Magaluf. Strangely the turnout wasn't as high as anticipated, and there were rumours about missing votes. A search failed to find any mislaid boxes or bundles. The Asbo three, minus their simian D'Artagnan, joined the search but quickly grew bored and said they had to go and plan their Macbeth costumes for the carnival fancy dress.

Kat didn't have much in her wardrobe that was suitable for fine dining. Back home, showered and perfumed, she opted for her perked-up posh frock. It was the sort of dress that felt good with proper stockings. And she actually did have a suspender belt that matched her underwear.

Which was when Ashton decided that he wasn't in the mood for a restaurant after all.

CHAPTER 36

Two weeks later than planned, Kat and Mel met for their surveillance outside the Maurice Mickelwhite. In the pitch dark space between the two giant bins Mel's inability to keep still was getting on Kat's nerves.

Instead of hunkering down in the comparative comfort of the Mini, as planned, with coffee and sandwiches, they were reduced to lurking in the shadow of the bins. They were without transport since Mel had sold her car once her licence had been impounded by the DVLA, Kat's had gone up in flames, and the mayoral limo was out of the question.

What was to have been a quiet Friday-night's simple surveillance, staking out the community centre, seemed to be growing into a spot of breaking and entering. Could a mayor be arrested for breaking into what was technically their own property?

Kat was dubious of finding an explanation for the bar deficit. It was theoretical, anyway, as the new centre would not be applying for a licence and hence the loss would not be repeated.

It went without saying that the place had to be clear before they did their burglarising. Mel had checked her watch more times than Kat could be bothered to count. She was doing it again. With Pavlovian promptness, Kat glanced at hers, and saw eight minutes had elapsed since they had last checked. She marvelled at the ability of time to stretch itself. More sighs. More fidgets. Sensible people were at home and tucked up in bed hours ago.

'I'm tired of whispering,' Mel emoted, forgetting that she wasn't in the council chamber. Unfortunately, Mel was one of those people who are incapable of maintaining a conversation at anything less than full blast, whatever the circumstances.

'Shh. Someone'll hear. We could end up in the nick. How embarrassing can that be: you the Mayor, me a trusted advisor!'

'We're not going to get caught,' Mel said. 'Nobody's going to see us. Just as well they've emptied all the other flats at your end of the block. In the old days we'd have been spotted by any number of sleepless geriatrics peering through the curtains.'

'We could have borrowed Shardonnay's wheels to sit in,' Kat said.

'What? Shitty Shitty Bang Bang? She'd only have wanted to know why,' Mel pointed out. 'You don't seem to be affected by the cold. I didn't know it would be so chilly.'

'I'd have thought your layers of fake tan would keep the cold out. You know, like the stuff channel swimmers put on.'

'Oh, ha, bleeding ha,' Mel said. 'We are full of beans.'

'Why do blondes with great skin like yours, all peaches and cream, pay a fortune to keep up an unnatural tan?'

'Cos a tan looks healthy,' Mel said. 'It's all right for you. You started off with a decent colour. I'm so pale I could get the lead in a Japanese Noh play. Plus, so-called peaches and cream goes blotchy in the sun.'

'My heart bleeds. I'm hungry,' Kat said, wiping her fingers after touching the bins. 'You could catch anything out here.'

'We could do this another time,' said Mel, lacking vigour.

'Too late, now. It'll keep our minds off other things.' Kat said. 'It's been a long, hard week.'

They leaned against the wall in companionable silence interrupted by the soft sound nearby of flapping plastic. 'You come to any decision about the lovely inspector yet?' asked Mel.

Kat nodded slowly. 'Well, he's still around. Anything longer than a fortnight risks becoming long term. Not sure I can handle that.'

'Ahh.'

There was a long silence.

'Want to hear something daft?' Kat asked.

'Anything to stop me keeling over from boredom,' said Mel.

'I've been doing weird stuff.'

'What sort of weird?' Mel asked eagerly. 'Kinky sex and stuff?'

'Not kinky. No,' Kat laughed. 'Last week I just happened to have a meeting up in the West End. When it finished, everything was still open for late night shopping. I found myself wandering in and out of shops, looking at clothes. Weird, or what? I never go shopping.'

'What's weird is *not* shopping,' said Mel, whose definition of a place of outstanding natural beauty was an all-weather shopping mall.

'They only need to put shops at the top of mountains and you'd win the Three Peaks Challenge,' said Kat.

'Now you mention it,' Mel said. 'D'you know, every weekend and school holidays when I was a kid, me and my mates used to disappear into the Oxford Street Triangle and spend dawn to dusk in the shops.

'Shopping's such a girl thing,' Kat said. 'The idea of linking arms and sailing round the shops doesn't do it for me. A quick in and out at the Co-op, clothes from Oxfam, everything else from e-bay, and I'm sorted.'

'Yeah, and it shows, if you'll pardon my frankness,' Mel said. 'You must do *some* proper food shopping. You can't live on takeaways.'

'I cooked a real live meal in the oven the other night. Table, not laps. Plates, knives, forks, the full works. You'll never guess how many tins I had to open.'

'See, you *can* do girl things, when you put your mind to it,' Mel explained. 'Next thing, you'll be getting a second-hand sewing machine and start making curtains and cushions.'

'A sewing what-sheen?'

'Don't pretend I'm talking some obscure aboriginal language,' Mel said. 'The sexy inspector must be tweaking the right knobs. As it were.'

'I'm not used to this sort of high octane relationship,' Kat said. 'It's not real-life stuff.'

'Oh, come on! There's nothing unreal about great sex,' Mel said. 'Maybe Jack Ashton could be the great passion of your life.'

'No such creature,' Kat answered, dryly. 'Neither of us wants anything long term. It's fun, though. Living two hundred miles apart and not seeing too much of each other is the right dynamic for a successful relationship.'

'Well, whatever it is, bully for you. Wait and see how it pans out. You're both busy with work now. Find some time for yourselves, once you're finished here. Why not take my villa in Spain, chill on the beach?'

'Ahh,' Kat sighed. 'I didn't know it was on a beach. I don't do beaches. I've got a bit of a hang-up about the seaside.'

'Really?' Mel asked, then, not afraid to rush in where angels might fear, she went on. 'So what put you off beaches? You nearly drowned?'

'Something like that,' Kat said. There was a silence as they peeped around the side of the building to see if anything was happening. In the pale glow of the one remaining bollard light, summer grass the colour of sun-bleached bones was patiently waiting for the first drop of rain to fall.

'Well, don't stop, now you've mentioned it. Tell us about this beach thing,' Mel suggested. 'It'll pass the time.'

'Oh, what the heck, May as well,' Kat said. 'You may wish you'd never asked.'

'I can't stand here doing nothing, waiting, ' Mel said. 'I'm ready to listen to anything.'

Long before that traumatic seaside trip, Kat had begun blocking out parts of her childhood and taking refuge in books. Books liberated from the school library had kept her company on the nights she went hungry to bed after being locked out when her mother's boyfriend came home. In the past, when asked, she always admitted to being brought up in care. Little more than that. Anything more only made people uncomfortable.

'What they say about boats having air pockets when they tip up is true,' she said. 'However, I'm getting ahead of myself. I'll begin at the beginning. Stop me when you've heard enough.'

'You carry on,' Mel replied. 'I'm agog.'

'I never knew my dad. He'd legged it before I was born. My mother had terrible taste in men. She'd get beaten up and be patched up in Accident and Emergency, the police would arrest the man, I'd go into care until she came home and found another one to beat her up, and off we'd go again. I was in and out of that care home so often they should have installed revolving doors.' Kat said.

'None of the men fancied having someone else's half-caste kid hanging around. I got fed Hula Hoops to make myself scarce.' She'd grown up hating Hula Hoops. 'When I was eight, she had a boyfriend in the army. He was never there long enough to beat her up. I still had to keep out of the way, but I hadn't had to go into care for a while. He was due home when she discovered she was pregnant, and said we'd have a girls' day out at the seaside, just the two of us, because she might be too busy afterwards. I'd never been on a train before. I sat with my nose glued to the window, imagining people in their houses being envious of us and wondering where we were rushing to. When we got there, I wanted to hire a pedalo for an hour, but my mum said we'd have a proper boat, and she hired us a dinghy for the whole afternoon.'

'Oh, no,' Mel wailed, unable to resist jumping the gun. 'Your mum drowned! So that's why you were taken into care.'

'Not quite.'

Alone, with her mother gone, Kat hung on in an air pocket under the boat, fearful of being eaten by something nasty with tentacles and teeth.

'Afterwards, when the hospital asked me who they should ask to fetch me, the only person I could think of was the lady in the sweet shop but I told them I thought she probably already had enough children of her own. Social services took me back to the kids' home, and there I stayed, little Orphan Annie, until they packed me off to university.'

'Gosh, that's awful,' Mel said. 'I was too young to remember my parents but losing your mum like that must be much worse.'

'You'd think. However, it ain't over until the fat lady sings, as they say. Four years later, a neighbour visited Germany and saw her, large as life, with a three year old. She'd married the soldier. She told the German police she remembered being in a boat and getting a whack on the head. However, they discovered that immediately before the seaside trip the soldier had offered to marry her but not if she brought me with her. Turned out that as soon as she received her Army travel voucher she deposited me in the drink, legged it for Germany,' Kat said. 'He assumed she'd put me in care or had me adopted.'

'Blimey O'Reilly! What happened to her in the end?'

'No idea. I was twelve when she resurfaced. They said I could visit her on remand. That's when I told them how she'd pushed me in.'

'Oh, blimey, what can I say,' Mel gasped. 'So she's still alive?'

'Who cares? Forget the psychiatrists who say battered children will love even the most cruel or neglectful parents, regardless. Not true

'Phew! Does Jack know this?' Mel asked.

'Good Lord, no. You're the only one I've told. Social services and the police made the right connections at the time, but I was too traumatised to be questioned. At first, I refused to eat, didn't utter a word for months. You know how stubborn I can be. Later, I made the nuns give me swimming lessons at the local baths so it wouldn't happen again. But I've never dared go anywhere near the sea, just in case. Apart from that, I recovered. I'm here.'

'Barry always says worse things happen at sea,' Mel said. 'Sorry, that was insensitive. Shouldn't have said that.'

'It's me who should be sorry,' Kat said. 'I've probably ruined your night out on the tiles.'

'Behind the dustbins, you mean.'

'Listen, this villa of yours,' said Kat. 'How close to the water is it? Maybe I can get around the problem by facing inland or something. I'm going to need a rest after all this. Non-stop twenty-four hours on call over three months can be wearing. I'm fitting in bed as and when I can.'

'Yes, I noticed,' Mel said, leering.

'I'm talking beauty sleep, here.'

'Yes, I believe you. Not.' Mel said. 'They'll all be off to Magaluf soon. Then you can settle down to do the paperwork without having to stop and deal with the tenants problems, except for the few days when you pop over there to finalise things with them before they move in.'

'Yeah,' Kat said, watching a mangy fox sniffing around the overflow of black sacks beside a square Euro-bin across the road. 'Meanwhile, we're stuck here, between two dustbins the size of grain silos.' She slouched against the wall. There was a long silence as they both contemplated the rubbish overflow. The fox crossed the road with a bundle in its jaws.

'Do you ever think what you'll be doing in ten, twenty years?' Mel asked. 'I don't see myself staying single all my life. Do you?'

'I'm one of those people best left on their own,' Kat said. 'I'm used to fending for myself. Even when I was surrounded by kids in the home I was never a team player. The good thing about flying solo is that you make up your own rules: eat what you fancy when the mood takes you, have baths at lunch time, watch any TV you want, no fighting over the remote or getting slagged off for recording over the Cup Final.'

'No-one to share the duvet, or make TV meals for,' Mel said. 'Room to yourself on holiday, for a single room supplement. No distractions, time to catch up on all that reading. I couldn't keep it up for long. Too much aloneness makes me melancholy.'

'Hmm,' sighed Kat, leaving another long silence.

'You know you're going to have to tell Jack some of this, don't you? It's not fair, leaving him out of it.' Mel peered into the darkness. 'Hang about. I think something's up.'

CHAPTER 37

Shardonnay and her partner came out of the Maurice Mickelwhite. Most surprisingly, for once they weren't squabbling. There were no lights. It looked as if the place might be empty at last.

'About time,' Kat muttered, glancing at her market-stall Omega. It wasn't going. No surprise there.

'Nearly one.' Mel said.

'You ever noticed how similar you and Shardonnay are?' Kat asked. 'Not related, are you?'

'Not as far as I know, but I see what you mean. We're both tall, fair skin, blue eyes. And under my expensive high lights and streaks, I've got the same sort of dirty blonde hair.' Mel said. 'In junior school, even though she was a year below me, we were a matching pair of angels in the Christmas play.'

'I was never angel material,' said Kat. 'Once I was a crocodile, trying to find the infant Moses ahead of Pharaoh's daughter. Talking of parent-child relationships, it's a funny old world, when you think of it: you're looking for your dad, Shardonnay'd like to get rid of hers, and I couldn't care less who or where mine is.'

'Karen told me Shaz has sent off her DNA to see if Cosmo by some stroke of good fortune might not be her dad after all.'

'Wishful thinking,' said Kat. 'Didn't Rosie Delaney go out with your dad for a while? She said they were an item.'

'More wishful thinking,' said Mel. 'I heard Rosie was desperate for a husband. Any husband. She got pregnant, caught Cosmo, divorced him, married Trevor Picket, divorced him, too, and ended up with thick-as-treacle Colin Chol-mon-de-ley,' Mel said, pronouncing the name as four distinct syllables. 'I hate hanging around doing nothing.'

'You want to go in now?'

'No, we need to make sure Barry's left,' Mel said.

'Where's Cosmo tonight?' Kat had no wish to bump into him.

'Told Shaz he was off to see her granddad.'

'He was very insistent I kept him up-to-date with the investigation.'

'Yeah, he likes to keep a finger in the pie,' Mel said. 'The place is pitch black. Do we know that Barry definitely went in this evening?'

'Yes, I checked.' It was eighteen minutes since the place had gone quiet. 'There's no sign of life. What do you think?'

'I'll take a dekko. You wait here.' Mel slipped round the side of the building and disappeared into the darkness.

Kat was ready to suggest they gave up and went home after she heard Mel fall over her second dustbin. Instead, she rang the Maurice Mickelwhite on quick dial and got Voicemail. Un-mayoral oaths and the hollow sound of aluminium cans rolling along the ground came out of the darkness as Mel's number eights stumbled over obstacles.

'No sign of anyone except that barmy monkey perched on the bus shelter picking nits,' she whispered. 'Half one: safe to go in by now.'

Mel would know the terrain, after her little trip; Kat let her lead. They moved out of the protection of the dustbins, and along the side of the Cokey Corral to the rear of the community centre, where Mel tried a window.

'No good, they're safety mesh. I'll try the back.' She tiptoed to the door. 'Damn. It's locked.'

'Have you got any hairpins?' Kat whispered.

'Oh, for goodness sake, it's a bit late to worry about your hairdo.'

'Duh.' Kat gave her a glare. 'I was going pick the lock.'

Holding a pencil torch between her teeth she worked on the back door. In films, locks were picked with indecent haste. After a quarter of an hour the battery had died and Kat, despite heroic patience, had got nowhere with the hairpin. Mel fiddled with the lavatory window, using each function of her North Korean army knife. Both women jumped when there was a sharp snap.

'Done it,' Mel almost cheered. 'Knew I'd find a use for the horse's hoof thingy one day. Give us some room.'

Abandoning the door, Kat tiptoed over. Mel was assaulting the open lavatory window, trying head and then feet first, going into contortions in her efforts to squeeze through a space not designed for a girl who had never understood the point of anorexia.

'Ow, talk about eyes, needles and camels,' Mel gasped. 'I think I may have dislocated my neck.'

Kat helped her wiggle backwards out of the window. Mel landed heavily.

'You try,' Mel said, rubbing her shoulder. 'You're smaller.'

Kat examined the window.

'My bum's not going through there, either, but I'll give it a go.'

'Pity they reset the door code. I knew what it was, a month ago,' Mel said, leaning against the door, wheezing.

'There's a key code?' At the window, Kat paused in her wriggling.

'Yeah, but Barry changes it each month.'

Kat eased backwards out of the lavatory window.

'We could try the brewer's hatch,' Mel said. She had torn her tee-shirt on a nail and collected cobwebs in her hair.

'Padlocked. I checked,' Kat said. 'We need Picket's bolt-cutters.'

They sat against the wall. And for their next trick? Winnie swung over from the top of the bus shelter to see if he was missing anything.

'Shoo, go home. Buzz off, go find the boys.' Kat flapped her hands.

Miming disappointment, he gave her a leery big air-kiss and turned his attention to the lavatory window. Even an ape could work out that both women were too broad-beamed to squeeze through the one window not wired to the security system.

'Don't even think about it,' said Kat.

Winnie gave her a V sign and disappeared into the lavatory.

'Barry'll get the shock of his life when he opens up tomorrow.'

'Mel, are you sure the old door code won't work?' Kat asked. 'One place I worked, they never bothered to think up more than two codes so they could alternate, one month on, one month off. Worth a try?'

Kat's lock-picking idea hadn't worked; Mel was inclined to ignore this further suggestion. However, nothing venture. She closed her eyes.

'You can't go to sleep here,' Kat said, ready to call it a day.

'Shh. I'm summoning up the code,' Mel said, in a trance.

'Okay, Mystic Mel, but don't take all night. I'm chilly.' Kat was losing interest in their not-so-excellent adventure.

Mel hummed tunelessly, poking at the key pad. Winnie popped out of the loo window, startling them. He raised a hairy arm and waggled Barry's keys in the air, lips wide in a toothy grin.

'Winnie, bless you,' Mel said, as they high fived. 'You beauty.'

'Should have sent him in sooner,' Kat said, begrudging time wasted with their backsides wedged in windows.

'Shouldn't have chased him off in the first place,' Mel said. 'Barry must've left his keys behind.'

'Barry may be a dab hand at whipping up a good Kahlúa,' Kat said. 'But he's pants when it comes to security.'

'Which makes it our good luck,' Mel replied.

The back door wasn't alarmed. They let themselves in. Winnie blew them a big raspberry, gave them a victory sign, and went into the bar. Soon they could hear him jiggling the coin tray on one of the two pinball machines.

'Barry's been burning joss sticks again.' Kat inhaled.

'Naw, it's more likely to be Shardonnay's overcooked risotto,' Mel said, sniffing. 'She was on kitchen duty earlier. You must have a good sense of smell. I don't get a whiff of anything.'

Careful not to bump into obstacles, they moved along the corridor, stepping around chairs left un-stacked after the talent show heats. Power cables for make-shift stage lighting, tied together with gaffer tape, trailed across the floor, to disappear behind the bar. Nothing moved but for an oscillating light on the pinball machine. Winnie, who had rapidly lost interest in the pinball machine, was in the kitchen picking over the contents of the fridge. And from the sound of it, finding them lacking.

The coast was clear. Through the open door of the tenants' committee office, Kat saw the outline of a computer on a desk that hugged one wall. Perching on a rotating chair, she rifled through the pile of letters and bills. Cosmo had left his computer on standby. She clicked the mouse to bring up the screen.

'Another one who's not exactly security conscious.'

'Shush. Just keep looking.'

'Won't do any harm to take a peek at his files.' Kat said as she continued searching. 'I can't open some of the email attachments.'

'It won't be on his PC.' Mel glanced over her shoulder. 'It'll be somewhere else, not filed under *Dodgy Deals and Backhanders*.'

They continued going through the desk and box files searching for they knew not what, exactly: a clue, anything.

'I can think of a hundred things more interesting than exploring Cosmo's drawers. I'm getting cramp.' Kat's eyes were gritty; she might have been buried in fine sand. 'What are we looking for, anyway?'

Mel said they'd recognise it when they found it.

'Shove over.' She shunted Kat off the seat, and sat down in front of the screen. 'We're running out of time. Where's that cash gone?'

Kat rotated Mel's arm to see her watch. They'd been there nearly two hours. They'd have to get out of there soon, before their luck ran out.

'What are we going to do?' said Mel, unwilling to leave.

'Easiest thing would be to put everything on a memory stick, but it didn't occur to me to bring one. Don't suppose you've got anything tucked into a pocket, have you?' Kat asked.

'If you two could just see yourselves!'

Mel swore and shut her hand in a drawer. Kat jumped, and almost fell off the swivel chair. They spun around, red-faced.

'You were getting warm, there, Mel. Right-hand drawer,' Barry said from the doorway. 'I never thought it could take anyone so long to get into this place, given the crap security. I had to give Winnie the keys in the end.'

'Gee, thanks,' Kat said with sarcasm.

'My heart's racing: you frightened the life out of us,' Mel scolded, on the defensive after being caught in the act. 'And now I suppose you're pissed off that we left you out of this.'

'Not at all. I could've saved you loadsa bother, but I was having fun listening to you two trying to get in. You had only to ask,' Barry replied. 'If you want to know where Cosmo's hidden a stash of cash, forget it. There are no biscuit tins filled with crisp tenners. There are no secret files, either. The deficit is a matter of simple book-keeping.'

'A deficit of over twenty-five grand has to be more than someone not being able to add up properly,' Kat said, across the desk.

'True, Petal,' he said. 'Here's how it works: I'll try not to sound like Mr Micawber. Expenditure per bottle, ten pounds. Estimated income per same, fifty pounds. Based on sales of two pounds per tot, a twenty-five shot bottle gives a forty pounds profit. Or not, in this case.'

'Why not?' asked Mel.

'Quick answer or the long one?'

'Simplest will do,' Mel said.

'Yes,' Kat nodded.

'Cosmo and the committee have carte blanche to help themselves to drinks, daytime, evenings, meetings, late night lock-ins. With the possible exception of the vicar, the entire committee's at it.'

'But not twenty-five grand's worth,' said Kat as she gave up trying to do the mental arithmetic.

'There's committee perks, too. The chairman, treasurer and minutes secretary often take home a bottle of gin when they leave at night. See how it adds up over forty-five, fifty weeks a year?'

'Why not stop them?' Kat asked.

'Custom and practice, Petal. They've always done it. I mentioned it, once, in the beginning, and was told the system was introduced to attract volunteers to run the community centre, and it would do more harm than good to stop the perks. It's not illegal, and I'm not the boss on that particular issue. The centre's run by the tenants' association.

'We're going to have to blow the gaff,' Mel said. 'Cosmo and his mates will have some explaining to do.'

'Won't get the money back, of course,' said Barry, stating the obvious. 'How's about I lock up and we tootle off to bed? I've already sent Winnie home. It's late. You can have a record of all the sums, the unexpurgated version, including my original projections and a log of all the freebies tomorrow.' Barry switched off King's computer and moved to the door. 'Need a lift, Mel?'

'I'm staying round the corner with my gran tonight, thanks all the same. It might be a good idea if one of us walks Kat through the alleyway at the back.'

'I'll do it. Ready when you are. Let's boldly go.' Barry closed the door and set the alarm.

Mel breathed in the night air, taking a couple of exploratory sniffs. 'I *can* smell something now. Have you been burning joss sticks?'

'Naw, I expect someone's been roasting dead animal parts on their barbie,' Barry said as he led them into the night. 'It's almost three. My beauty sleep beckons. Nothing depresses a chap more than wrinkles he can't pass off as laughter lines.'

They waited until they saw Mel turn the corner to her gran's place.

'I'll see you all the way to your front door, this time,' Barry said, following her up the steps to the walkway.

Big mistake. She ought to have let him do a recce first. The hall light seemed to have blown, otherwise she'd have seen what awaited them. With Barry still at the open front door, Kat had strolled half way along the darkened hallway before she heard someone coming towards them. She didn't think it was the chimpanzee this time.

CHAPTER 38

Kat shot back up the hall towards the front door. Feet pounded behind her. Barry wasn't as quick at getting out of the way as he might have been, given his football days, and she ran into him. His head hit the bin cupboard with a crack. Down he slammed onto the floor like a hundredweight of potatoes.

Sensing a blow coming from behind, Kat tried to shift sideways. It bounced off her head, clipped an ear, and landed heavily on her shoulder. Before she could turn aside her assailant caught a handful of hair and yanked her towards him. Swinging backwards with an elbow she managed to connect with the soft space under his ribs and heard the air whoosh out. She jabbed him again, but his fist rocked her back. A spasm of pain shot across her shoulders. She swung her legs up and back, aiming to catch her attacker in the groin. Her head was jerked backwards. She'd done self-defence classes, so she knew the drill: stomp on his instep, plough an elbow into his gut, shove a knee in his groin, and finish with a sharp punch to the jaw. She had come top of the class at the leisure centre with the rest of the girls. As she struggled against the tight grip that pinned her upright, the best she could manage now was a feeble kick that made contact with a bony shin before a leg hooked around hers, making her stumble over Barry's body, slumped across the front step.

There were two of them. The other, bigger one, hit Kat low and hard in a textbook tackle. The breath left her body with the jarring grunt of a desperate Wimbledon champion. Face first, her arms trapped at her sides, Kat went down so hard the carpet was pushed into her mouth, making it hard to breathe. She twisted around and attempted to kick her attacker. He was on top of her. She tried to get up but found he was too heavy. She endeavoured to push him off with another kick but he was too strong. She managed to half rise before a hand walloped her hard across the face, catching her ear. Her head buzzed angrily. White shards flashed across her eyesight as she was shoved against the wall. She hung there with her head pounding, lungs burning, and her face smarting. The din in her ears gradually separated into voices.

She had recognised Cosmo King both from the dodgy Cockney slang and the stinking camel-dung cigarillo overlaid with gin and extra strong mints.

'Stay there, dead quiet. I know how to use this and I will if I have to,' the other one said.

It was the smarmy mourner from the funeral. He of the kitsch stretch limo. Kat doubted that the gun in his hand had come from e-bay.

King grabbed her neck from behind, twisting her left arm up behind her back, and dragged her along the hall, into the bedroom while she tried once more to kick him in the groin. He forced her into a crouch towards the floor. Dragging her across the room on all fours, he pushed her onto a low wicker bedside chair where she sat down so abruptly it jarred her spine.

'Wha–?' She spat out pieces of carpet fluff and tried again. 'All right, I've guessed you're not burglars. What do you want?'

'Shut it,' demanded Delaney.

'Strewth, this place ain't half a dump,' said King. 'Would you Adam'n'Eve it?'

'Nobody dies from sleeping on an unmade bed,' Kat retorted. 'Like I said, what do you want?'

Ted Delaney was beside the window. He spoke without turning.

'Tie her to the chair, son.'

'Tie her?' King asked. 'I never got me knots badge in the Scouts.'

'Stick gaffer tape round her, then,' Delaney snapped. 'Give us her mobile. I don't want her gettin' on the dog to Old Bill.' He passed King a roll of white duct tape.

This was the second time Kat had come swanning home without first engaging her brain. It was also the second time she'd ended up in difficulties as a result. This pair made the earlier burglarious incursions by the delinquent Winnie seem piddling by comparison. The ape clearly agreed, because the coward had disappeared under the bed. Kat meekly handed her mobile over to be pulverised by one of Delaney's patent size twelves. So much for talk-as-you-go. There was no possibility of summoning help unless her SIM card had acquired the capacity to lead an independent existence as a homing device. And pigs might. She wished she'd had the foresight to get herself fixed up with the same

Blackberry with built-in GPS lone-worker 24-hour tracking system the council used for its staff.

The street had been deserted when she and Barry sailed in. Not surprising, given the hour. Any other time, the place would be teeming with static radio noise from patrol cars, even if they were only cruising for somewhere to put their feet up and have their cocoa. At three in the morning there was nobody around.

Where do policemen go at night, she wondered, You might as well ask where do flies go in winter, or why can't horses walk backwards, and if forty-two is the answer to the ultimate question of life, the universe, and everything, why did it need seven and a half million years of calculation by a giant supercomputer to work it out?

'Stay behind the bint, Cosmo.' Delaney lit up a cheroot, revealing his face as it sneered its way around the room. Gone three in the morning and he was in sunglasses. King, for once, was not.

'Gawd, will you take a gander at this place,' Cosmo said.

Now that Kat was pinned down by his minion, Delaney was sufficiently relaxed to lay his gun on the bed.

'Strewth,' he said. 'This furniture'd be more at home on a tip, if you don't mind my saying.

'I don't imagine you're here to offer a house makeover,' Kat replied

'You're right,' drawled Delaney. 'I thought we might have a little chat.' He waved a hand the size of dockers' lifting gear.

Kat felt her arm wrenched from behind.

'Ow! That hurt.'

'It's meant to.' King gave her arm another yank.

The pain made her nauseous. Any more and she would throw up over Delaney and his Italian designer double breasted. That'd show him.

'Beg your pardon. Don't think I introduced meself. Ted Delaney, businessman, enter-prenooer, and angel investor.'

Angel what?

'Why are you really here? What do you want?' It came out with more of a squeak than Kat would have wished.

King ignored her, leaving the talking to his boss.

'We don't answer questions. We ask,' Delaney said. 'What do you think I want?'

'I don't know. I'm not bloody psychic.'

'Got guts, ain't she, Cosmo?'

She'd gone wrong somewhere. This wasn't working out according to the script. What had happened to the scene where the villain goes into a detailed monologue about his own brilliance, claiming credit for unsolved crimes, thus giving the plucky heroine time to call in the cavalry, or to escape with one bound?

King hovered behind her, muttering.

'Uhn-uhn, no, Cosmo, don't be impatient, I'll tell you when,' said Delaney. 'So, Miss Curiosity-killed-the-Kat, that headache you had last time you had a break-in ain't nothin' to the one you'll have if you don't cooperate now. Cosmo's skinny, but he's all muscle. Docker's genes. Muscles of steel. He's rarin' to give you a good thumping.'

The top of Kat's scalp tingled.

'You behave yourself and you'll not be harmed,' Delaney smirked. 'Not if you answer my questions. Otherwise, different kettle.'

'I can't concentrate with this demented stick insect wrapped round my neck.' Kat glared at King.

'All right, Cosmo, let the crazy bitch go, but stay close.'

'You say so, guv.'

Kat had an insane desire to check King's wake for slime tracks. He would probably give Delaney's patent wing tips a quick lick if asked.

Delaney was making himself comfortable on her bed. She cringed at the prospect of having to sleep under that duvet again. The pressure on her neck and arm eased slightly. She rubbed her shoulder.

'You comfortable, there, girl?' Delaney asked without enthusiasm.

'Not particularly.'

'Tough. You'll live.' He leaned sideways against her headboard, with his back to the window, piggy eyes narrowed.

Averting her eyes, she caught the glint of a simian eye from the gloomy litter of dirty washing beneath the bed. It was the miserable, cowardly ape, keeping well out of sight.

'All right, little Miss Mastermind, you've got two minutes on your specialist subject. And Pass ain't an answer,' Delaney said. 'For starters, tell us who they say was in that hole. My brother Bernie, is it?'

'Bernie? How would I know?'

'Cos you're shagging that ginger copper,' he growled. 'You shouldn't blunder into things what's none of your business. What's Old Bill bin saying?'

'I have no idea. I don't get told police business.'

'That's not what I hear. Won't ask again.'

'She lacks a proper incentive,' snarled King, behind her. 'Shut up and do as you're told.'

'Tell us,' said Delaney. 'Or I'll let Cosmo do what he wants.

'Since Cosmo seems to have his finger in the community pie, why not ask him?' Kat asked. 'He was such a mate of your brother.' She had no idea what she was talking about, but it had Cosmo rattled.

'What's the silly cow on about?' Delaney asked.

'Nothin, guv. Now, Miss Mouthy, you asked for it.' His bony fist slammed into her head. She blacked out for a second. When she opened her eyes she saw Winnie had huddled further under the bed. She knew the moth-eaten fur ball must be frightened, from the soft raspberry from under the bed as the ape broke wind. His teeth were chattering louder than castanets. Her assailants must be deaf.

'Bloody Norah,' King exclaimed. 'Don't half pen an' ink in here.' He took a roll of gaffer tape from his pocket and tore off a length. Roughly jerking Kat back into the chair, he cuffed her across the head with the flat of his hand.

'I've been dyin' to give the mouthy cow a clout ever since she come 'ere,' he growled. 'There's lots more where that come from, and now I'm gonna –'

They were destined never to discover what it was that King was gonna. The blast of an explosion rocked the building, drowning out the details, and bringing all conversation to a halt.

CHAPTER 39

The explosion sounded like a gun going off. Dazed, Kat landed on her knees in a sea of glass, saved from serious damage by the fabric of her jeans. The force of the blast had blown in the bedroom window, showering the bed and its occupant.

If, as Barry had said at the Fostock funeral, Delaney had looked like death warmed up then, now at least he had an excuse. Except that warmed up was not exactly correct. He was pinned, wide-eyed, on his back across the middle of Kat's bed, skewered through the neck with a shard the size of a Jor-El memory crystal.

There was a demented howl, and Winnie rocketed from his hiding place under Kat's bed. He flew across the room, paws out, fixed bayonets. King screamed, pure Anglo Saxon without a trace of cocky Cockney humour, as the jibbering ape leapt on him and sunk its claws into his face.

Staggering upright, Kat pried the creature away from King. Skin came away. Oops, she thought. *Quel dommage*. Never mind, serve him right. Hugging Winnie close and murmuring calming noises, she edged over Barry's body and ran down the steps.

Outside, a big, crackling orange torch of fire lit up the sky. In an illusion caused by the heat the Maurice Mickelwhite shimmied like a belly dancer. Disoriented, Kat made her way across the road where a crowd was gathering outside the blazing community centre. On the other side of the building, the estate office windows had blown out, and with them, mangled purple plastic chairs.

There was a bang and the front doors shot across the car park. Kat rather hoped they would land on King's car.

'Where's the fire crew?' the vicar shouted into his mobile. His Rocky Balboa dressing gown with its colour co-ordinated paisley ascot over pale, bare legs was a striking choice of outfit to wear when out and about amongst one's parishioners. He jerked his head towards the burning building. 'Is anybody left in there?'

'No,... all... gone... home... ages... ago,' Kat gasped.

The residents' rep could kiss his brand-new office carpet goodbye. Even in the unlikely event that it had been salvaged before the building went up, Kat doubted they'd be keeping it stored safely for when he came out of jail. If he got that far, given the state of his face after Winnie's attack.

'Shall I call and tell Barry?' the vicar asked.

Last seen, Barry was out for the count on Kat's floor, but nobody was to know that. She was about to explain when another explosion took the roof off, rattling her fillings. Ears ringing, shrapnel scattered around her, knees wobbly, she sunk onto the grass clutching the trembling chimp. Head to head on the verge, they waited for the next explosion.

'Jesus, Kat, I should've guessed you'd be here,' Ashton said, looming above her in stereo. He must have been jolted awake from sleep. His overlong hair curled damply along his neck, the shadow on his chin was way beyond five o'clock. He was in running shoes and a disreputable tracksuit with a broken zip at the neck. The sleeves were pushed up. He, who had an uncanny knack of turning up when Kat was not looking exactly presentable, was definitely not at his best.

'Are you hurt? You probably ought not to move, but we need to get you somewhere safer.' He smoothed the hair out of her eyes, and felt around for injuries.

'What?' she asked, feeling groggy. Her knees ached.

'Where does it hurt? Can you hear me?'

Kat could not work out where the blood was coming from. Apart from the odd bruise and a few scratches, she wasn't injured, except where she had banged down onto her knees, and bruised knees were hardly injuries.

'Can you get up? Here, let go of the bloody animal.'

She tightened her grip and stared at the still smouldering building. Ashton stopped trying to prise them apart.

'All right, keep him. But up you come, slowly,' he said. 'You can't stay there. It's full of broken glass.' He hoisted her to her feet, slowly, wrapping an arm around her and Winnie.

'It's okay, I've got you,' he said.

The fire engines arrived. Two or four, who knows? Kat could see and hear double of everything: Ashton, bystanders, bells, whistles, sirens.

'Ice cream van not here yet?' she asked the paramedic. Krishna Ices was usually one of the first to arrive after the emergency services.

He eyed her warily, muttering something about concussion and humoured her by asking if she wanted a cone or a lolly.

She watched firemen leap on and off their engines and dart about, lugging hoses around in a search for the hydrant, which had been smothered by builders' rubble. People were shunted into a safe zone behind plastic tape. There seemed to be a great many paramedics.

'Right, Miss. Let's have a butchers at you,' said a pair of identical twins. She blinked, and one disappeared.

'No. It's okay, I'm fine,' she coughed through a lungful of smoke.

'I'll give you something to help you breathe properly.' He had a face mask with a tubed container to put on her face.

She cleared her throat. It hurt. 'No, I'll be okay in a second.'

'Can you take the animal off her, squire, and get her into the ambulance so we can lie her down and clean her up?'

'Not my blood,' she said, pushing the paramedics away. 'Cosmo's'.

'Cosmo's the monkey's name, is it? Okay, we'll take a look at Cosmo later. But for now, you must have oxygen. You've inhaled some smoke.' They were determined to minister to her.

'Take a puff. It'll do you good,' Ashton pleaded. 'Water?'

'No, I'm okay,' she repeated. 'I can manage. Don't need anything.'

'They want to give you the once-over.'

'No! No ambulance,' she said firmly. 'No hospital. No doctor. No nothing. I'm not hurt.' Kat was sure he didn't believe her. She sucked air, trying to think coherently and stop shaking.

'All right, no ambulance.' Ashton waved the paramedics away. 'Leave her with me for a while, I'll get her to see sense.' Turning to Kat he said 'Come on; let's get you up and find out what's hurting. Careful.'

'I'm all right. I don't need help.'

That clearly was untrue. His arm stayed around her, propelling her across the grass verge.

The firemen had finally located the hydrant. In moments the ground became churned up with heavy tyre grooves awash with filthy water. She noticed that two of the four engines were packing up their hoses and hatchets, having arrived too late to be of use.

At the edge of the ruin, a fireman in a yellow poncho was gloomily poking through the heap of waterlogged soupy ash and twisted, melted purple plastic chairs, all that was left of Maurice Mickelwhite.

'Might've saved it, if we'd been here in time,' he moaned.

Ashton guided Kat through the mess of water and mud, past the small crowd of spectators. She concentrated on getting one squelchy foot in front of the other without falling.

'Hang on,' she said, stopping dead. 'What about Barry?'

'They've gone to his place to fetch him. Don't worry about that. Let's get you home.' He turned in the direction of her flat.

'His place? No. He was with me. My flat,' she gasped. 'There's broken glass and dead bodies all over the shop. Barry's hurt. I had to leave him there. Couldn't move him, cos I had Winnie.'

'Stay.' Ashton changed direction and led Kat and her furry bundle to his car. 'Will you be all right for a while? Okay, sit tight until I get back. Understand? Don't go anywhere.'

'Where are you off to?' she asked, dragging in gulps of smoky air.

'Not far,' he said. 'Just stay here.'

Kat watched him talking to a couple of uniformed officers. They glanced over at her briefly before all three hurried off in the direction of her flat. When the bedroom light went on she could see most of the glass was gone from her window. A constable leaned out and beckoned to the paramedics who picked up the first aid pack and jogged over. It was stuffy in the car. She could hardly keep her eyes open and was barely conscious of the comings and goings.

Barry was wheeled out hooked up to an oxygen cylinder, so she knew he was still in the land of the living. The ambulance bell was ringing loud and clear as they raced off. What seemed like ages afterwards, another stretcher was brought out and placed in the second ambulance. No oxygen or bells this time. A third ambulance was still parked on the grass when Kat's eyes closed of their own volition.

The movement of Ashton settling into the driving seat woke her. True to his word, he had made sure they didn't cart her off to hospital. There had been no further attempts to question her. She didn't know if that, too, was Ashton's doing or if an educated guess had told them they wouldn't get much sense out of her until morning.

'You okay?' He aimed the car away from the estate.

'I think so. Where are we going?'

'Liam's old place. Your flat's a crime scene.'

She closed her eyes tiredly: she would have killed for a stiff drink. She had fled her flat without stopping to pick up anything. No bag. No clothes. No toothbrush. No Barry. She still felt guilty about that. She'd left a perfectly good bottle of Rioja open to breathe on the draining board, ready for when she got home. She wondered if Ashton would go back for it if she asked nicely. She was dizzy. Her glucose level had taken a dive. That Rioja would've fixed it.

'Have you got anything to eat?' she mumbled. She was always hungry these days. Must be all the rushing around

Ashton nodded towards the glove compartment, where she found a triple Bounty. The man was a treasure. She and Winnie chomped their way through bars one and two. There was a short interval while the pair of them were occupied sucking bits of coconut from between their teeth. Then Winnie dozed off, which left bar three for Kat. That gone, she slouched down in the seat and closed her eyes.

She must have slept. The car had stopped. There was only the slow ticking of the cooling engine. Ashton's head was touching the steering wheel. She was unable to tell whether he was asleep, dead, or in deep contemplation of the steering column. As she shifted in her seat he lifted his head and gazed out of the windscreen without speaking. They were parked outside an impressive Victorian pile, all deep gables, warm red bricks, big bay windows, triple front door, with a wide front porch. Without a word, he took the key from the ignition and climbed out, motioning her to stay put while he came around to open the door for her. She was still clutching Winnie.

'I can manage; I'm fine.' Being beaten up had left her tetchy. An invalid she was not.

The porch featured three front doors, craftily arranged to give an impression of a large house in single occupation. Liam Grant's flat took up the entire ground floor of the late Victorian building. The other two doors led to flats on each of the two upper floors.

A state of the art flat screen wall mounted digital TV dominated the living room and she could hardly miss the enormous satellite dish out the back for foreign channels.

'Let go of the damn monkey. We'll sort him out in the morning.' Ashton had produced a packet of wet wipes. When she did not respond he prised the animal out of her hands and put it on the floor of the small cloakroom, firmly closing the door.

'You've collected some bruises. I'll put stuff on it in a second. There's mud on your face.' He touched her cheek with his thumb, his other hand resting in the small of her back. 'I'll get you a drink.'

Kat brightened. 'A large scotch would do me nicely right now.'

Ashton shook his head. 'No alcohol. Not allowed.'

'In that case, no thanks.' Kat shook her head and found the headache was still there.

'How about a cup of tea?' he asked.

'No, I don't want anything.'

'Coffee?' He waited.

'No, thanks, I'll manage.'

He touched her face gently, soothing, stroking her skin.

'Jack, it's five in the morning. I'm knackered. I've got a headache.' She never thought she'd turn into the headachy type.

He clamped his mouth over hers, effectively shutting her up.

'Doctor's orders; I have to stay with you and keep you awake for an hour or so, to make sure you're not concussed.'

She was too tired to argue. Not all her neurons were firing properly. Maybe she did have concussion. It might be fun to see how much effort he was prepared to put into ensuring she stayed awake for the next couple of hours.

CHAPTER 40

Kat wasn't sure what she had expected of his brother-in-law's flat. Manly squalor with a phalanx of bottled sauces in the middle of the table and the recycling bin full of beer cans wouldn't have been far off. However, the place was so tidy it hurt.

Liam Grant's flat, or more appropriately, Liam and Lottie's flat, seen in daylight, was a long way removed from tacky bachelordom. They could have hired out the bedroom wardrobe as a Gap franchise. The open-plan living and dining room took up three-quarters of the ground floor of the impressive conversion. Light and airy, it had cushioned box seats fitted under deep sash windows in a large bay. The floor looked as if it was the original, polished through wear and care to a patina unconnected with the application of any sealant or instant shine. The sofa was an ocean of leather from whose depths only someone with the thigh muscles of a weightlifter would get out. Unlike Kat's flat, which could have been rented out to film companies as a location for a displaced persons' camp in the aftermath of an earthquake, the place was spotless, text-book tidy, ready for an upmarket magazine photo-shoot.

As she passed the kitchen door on her way to the shower she heard Ashton talking quietly: on his mobile or maybe he and Winnie were doing some male bonding over the cornflakes and fresh fruit.

The bathroom was an enormous tiled affair with all the works: shower, loo, bidet, washbasin, Jacuzzi – the lot. There was plenty of hot water which gushed out of multiple showerheads the size of meat plates in jets that could have stripped paint.

Kat's hair stank of bonfire. She closed her eyes against the blast of hot water, and stood there, trying to feel half-way to human. Groping for the shampoo, she shrieked as something slithered across her shoulder in a terrifying Psycho moment. Her eyes shot open.

Ashton stepped into the spray. He was fully clothed. 'I thought I'd help wash your hair, or scrub your back. Or something,' he said, massaging shampoo into the tangle. 'Mmm, smells much nicer than barbecued plastic.' It came out muffled by shampoo foam from her hair.

It was Friday. Saturday by now. They had the whole weekend. No rush. She felt a tug of lust as the arch of his body followed the movement of his arms as he reached to lather shampoo into her hair.

'You'll ruin your clothes,' she protested, without undue force.

'Is that bothering you? Hang in there a second.' Rubbing his feet against his legs, he worked his jeans off.

'That's not what I – '

'Drip-dry,' he said. He stopped massaging her hair and soaped his shirt. 'This was headed for the laundry, anyway.' He must be as crazy as a bucket of frogs, she thought.

'How often do you put your clothes through this little ritual?' she asked, unable to stop laughing.

'You may not appreciate the finer points of haute couture in men's fashion. The designers recommend it. If you don't do it regularly it invalidates the guarantee,' he said. 'The instructions are on the label. It's good for the fibres.'

'I don't believe you.'

He read the label on his shirt: 'Wear this garment while washing to protect its shape. See, that's what the picture of the two little hands means. For my next trick –' He waved a toothbrush and began to scrub his watch, holding it up for her to see. 'It's waterproof.'

He draped the watch over the soap holder. 'It'll tell the time even better after a clean. Where was I?' He moved the centre of operations to her back.

'I don't generally sing when I shower, but I can make an exception. Have you any special requests? How about some Wagner? I know: the Flying Dutchman. Lots of water in that. Fantastic ending. They drown.'

'Jack, you're barmy,' Kat laughed. 'Cary Grant and Audrey Hepburn did this in a film. You won't know it: it's not a bloke's film.'

'Oh, I dunno. And in any case, he was alone in the shower, as I recall. Audrey Hepburn never got in with him.' He shrugged off the last of his clothes.

'Hang on! Cary Grant kept his kit on,' Kat said. 'As I recall.'

'That's because the Americans are prudes, and he was nearly sixty and had a bit of a paunch,' replied Ashton, demonstrating his lack of paunch or prudishness.

'Alas, poor Audrey,' Kat lamented.

'Poor Cary.'

They stopped laughing.

'Let's give the Flying Dutchman a miss,' Ashton said. 'This next bit's going to be a bit tricky. You might want to hold on to something.'

Ashton had another shower a little later, solo this time, while Kat remained in bed and Winnie squatted on the gigantic leather sofa snacking on dry cornflakes from the packet and watching Pingu re-runs. Then Ashton and Winnie went out, leaving Kat dozing.

It was afternoon when Ashton returned alone. Kat was still in bed. She felt the mattress give.

'Mmm,' she drawled. 'You were gone for ages. I'm still not awake properly, yet.'

'I'll try not to disturb you,' he said, letting his hands roam.

'You won't take it personally if I doze off again, will you?'

'Of course not,' he replied. 'You go ahead and have a good rest. I'll just do what I have to. You don't need to wake up. I'll try not to disturb you. You won't even know I'm here.'

'I suppose I could try to stay awake for a couple of seconds,' she said.

'Hey, that's generous of you. I'm truly grateful. I won't take too much of your time. I know how boring you find this boy and girl stuff.'

They lay there, hip to hip, grinning at each other. Kat supposed there were worse ways to spend a weekend.

Later, Ashton zapped through the movie channels. Curled together on the IKEA faux fur tiger-skin – a real dead tiger would have been a touch naff, regardless of correctness, political or otherwise – they settled for Susan Sarandon and Geena Davis creating mayhem and tooling around in their 1966 Thunderbird convertible.

'That'll teach him,' Kat said with glee when the girls fired their pistols into the fuel truck.

'You're quite an anarchist at heart,' he said.

They were chomping through the remains of Lottie and Liam's wedding cake which had been in an airtight container in the fridge.

'Yup, I'll go along with that,' Kat said. 'How can you eat so much and get away with it? Don't say it's because you run every day. Exercise makes me hungry.' She envied his ability to not pack on the pounds.

'I have a good metabolism.'

'If you say so,' she said. 'I thought you were meant to be rushing back to this heavy case that's coming up at the Old Bailey. Shouldn't you be half-way up the motorway by now?'

'No, it's Saturday, remember,' he replied. 'I don't suppose you want to spend the entire weekend in a bath robe. I'll see if I can salvage any clothes from your flat later, if they let me in. Don't forget, the place is still a crime scene.'

'No, no, I can do it.' She cringed at the idea of him going through the dissolute tangle of tired bras, stressed knickers, and odd socks in her underwear drawer.

'I put yesterday's clothes in the machine to get rid of the aura of burnt plastic. Won't be dry for ages. There's nothing of Lottie's here that'll fit you apart from a hospital overall, and some flip flops that'll flip off. We'll try one of my tee-shirts. The neighbours will think I've brought Orphan Annie home for half term.'

'Where are the happy couple living now?'

'New house near my parents. They're letting this place out.'

They munched in companionable silence.

'I sometimes forget that normal people have normal families and like living near each other.'

'Normal? I suppose my family's normal. Ordinary, anyway. None of us have made a killing on the lottery, become a pop star, or married royalty. We don't fight or do dramas. My father's an ENT surgeon, my mother nurses part time. Lottie's a child psychologist. Liam and I were at school, then university, together. I have two older sisters. Sarah's married, no kids, runs a rural medical centre with her husband in Nepal. Helen's a flight purser, with an autistic five-year-old, Ben. My parents care for him when she's working. Grandparent in a residential home in Brighton. That's about it. How about you? No family, you said.'

'My father legged it before I was born, mother ditto eight years later. When she disappeared I was taken into care.' No need to go into sordid detail, despite Mel's advice to the contrary. 'With my suntan, we can assume my dad wasn't from these parts, so it's a safe bet that I'm not likely to bump into him in the near future. I must have relatives somewhere, I suppose, but I'm not bothered. Thirty-two years of silence is a good indicator of their indifference. The nuns at the home were the nearest I got to family, and most of them will have shuffled off their mortal coil by now. The kids came and went too quickly to make any lasting relationships. It's no big deal.'

'You can share my family.' He dropped a light kiss on her nose.

'Ta. Tell me about your divorce,' she said, but stopped when she saw his expression. 'No. Sorry, I shouldn't be so nosy.'

'It's all right. It's a long but not particularly edifying story.'

Ashton put on a too-big Moscow Ritz Carlton bath robe and went to stand by the French window looking into the back garden.

'From the moment an uncle gave me an old Leica when I was twelve, I'd daydreamed about becoming a famous photographer. I'd be fought over by magazine editors, headhunted by expedition leaders, travel the world picking up awards like fleas. My parents thought it was a fad that would run its course, and steered me into a degree in forensic and photographic science.'

'It's a long way from being a policeman,' Kat said.

'Yup. Best-laid plans. I blew it,' he said. 'Suddenly I'm about to be a father. Too late for a termination, she's pushing for a quick wedding, bang goes fame and fortune and I find a job with a decent income and guaranteed career path so as to support a mortgage, and later, maybe, private schooling and holidays in Tuscany. Meanwhile, she's stuck in a shoe-box flat, soaking nappies and sterilising bottles day and night. I worked police hours, never came home for meals. Her degree was wasted. The only time she got to use her brain was in negotiating terms with a babysitter for the few occasions we went out. We papered over the cracks and ambled along for four years, until she finally admitted Simon wasn't my son, after all, and she now wanted a divorce to marry the child's real father, a New Zealander we'd both known at university. So that was it: off she went, taking Simon with her. I haven't heard anything since. It took awhile to come to terms with that.

'What can I say, Jack? I am so sorry.'

'Yeah, life can suck.' Ashton leaned over to rummage for more cake. 'We learn from our mistakes. I won't be repeating that one.'

Neither was really watching Thelma and Louise frozen in time as they took off in their Thunderbird over the edge of the Grand Canyon. Sometimes you leave the television on to fill a space.

CHAPTER 41

'I should have known a barbecue wouldn't smell that way,' Kat said when Ashton told her how the fire had started.

Electricity cables in the skirting had overheated and lain smouldering for hours behind the shared plywood walls of the community centre and housing office. Once ignited, the fire had spread through the two buildings, a spectacular double act that certainly impressed. Krishna Ices, for once, had missed the show. The milkman, however, for whom half three was the middle of the day, benefited from the absence of the ice cream van and did a roaring trade in milk, orange, and *pain au chocolat*, which he was pioneering on the estate.

With luck the fire might have fizzled out had it not reached Karen's stash of aerosols, the Desert Fires, the Persian Glows and the rest, which caused things to escalate. Within minutes, the windows had blown out. Debris had shot across the road, heading like a ground-to-air missile straight for Kat's bedroom window. From the housing office the fire spread to the Community Centre, where Shardonnay's two Crème Brule blowtorches went up, followed by cleaning fluids, polishes, cooking oils. When the pressurised draught beer canisters under the bar reached bursting point they blew. Pink and purple plastic chairs and Formica tables were hurled across the car park into Warp Drive, signalling the end of the Maurice Mickelwhite Community Centre. They wouldn't be needing their liquor licence any longer.

The failure of the fire brigade to arrive in time was explained: they'd gone in circles after the estate's new layout had been made even more unfathomable by the gas company's having jumped the gun in putting out diversion signs ahead of digging up the roads the following Monday. By the time the first fire crews had navigated the maze of diversions there wasn't an awful lot left on which to play their hoses.

'Fires regularly begin this way,' Ashton told Kat. 'Particularly if you run heavy-duty arc lights from too-small circuits. By the way, I saw that rotund councillor strolling around the site with one of the housing officers this morning. Does he always carry bolt cutters?'

'What? Oh, yes. I'm told that in the days before we all had mobiles, he used to be a housing officer. One day he went to evict a family but they locked him in and boarded the place up. It was three days before they found him.' Kat laughed. 'Now he never goes out without his bolt cutters and a Bluetooth with a 24-hour guardian alarm.'

'You must meet as many lunatics in your job as I do in mine,' Ashton laughed. 'Your flat's going to be written off; they wouldn't even let me in to get your stuff, maybe later today. The housing director was there. He's decided it's bad enough to include in the next round of demolitions. I understand they're giving you a new place on Monday: the show flat, apparently, above the leisure centre.'

'Next door to Barry? That'll be handy,' Kat said. 'What did you do with Winnie? Is he okay?'

'He's fine,' he said. 'The kids have stashed him with a couple of duvets and a bunch of grapes in the boiler room at the back of the OAP club. The boiler's on for the old dears, so he'll be okay.'

'I asked the RSPCA to get rid of him,' Kat said. 'But some snotty kid shamed me into bringing him home again.'

'You don't hate the thing as much as you pretend. You were welded together last night, refused to let go of him.'

'Only because I had to get the darned creature to safety.'

'Yes|, well, Winnie's a hero,' he said. 'Cosmo King's in hospital under surveillance and will need plastic surgery. He may lose an eye. Meanwhile, he's being charged with assault.'

'It makes the bar deficit case seem piddling.'

'That's only for starters. From something King said when he was half conscious, the police have started to come around to the idea that Mel might have been right about the body being that of her father. They also suspect King might know more about it that he's letting on. Forensics have found a dent in the head which could have been caused by an accidental fall or from an attack with a rock.'

'Last night, Ted Delaney was under the impression that the skeleton was his brother Bernie.'

'He was behind the times,' said Ashton. 'Europol cleared that up. King may be telling the truth when he says he doesn't know the whereabouts of his old mate Bernie. But he knew exactly what happened, back then. Looks like our humble beat copper may have discovered the brother was skimming from Delaney's operations. Could be that Bernie was about to be nabbed, and big brother Ted was going to find out what he'd been up to. So the nosy copper had to go. Unfortunately, it seems they may have got rid of Rampart without first finding out if he'd told anyone. The suggestion is that Bernie may have panicked and done a runner to the Costa del Crime, to get away from his brother. Delaney's heavyweight sons are apparently combing Spain for their Uncle Bernie, as we speak. They're anxious for a word before the Spanish police find him and bang him up.'

'What a mess,' Kat said. 'And what about Barry?'

'He's fine, apart from smoke inhalation and concussion. They're keeping him in for observation. No visitors. Get dressed. I'll take you over to your flat to see if the fire officers have salvaged anything. We can stock up with food on the way back.'

She went out in one of Ashton's tees, which on her was the right length to pass as the next fashion trend in short hemlines. Lottie's flip-flops were two sizes too big, but they kept her feet off the ground. Just.

They needn't have bothered. Nothing salvageable remained in her flat. Any windows not broken by the first blast had gone for a Burton with the final explosion. The rooms were sooty, the bedroom littered with broken glass, out of bounds. Her bed was tied up in red and white plastic crime scene ribbon like a dysfunctional pass-the-parcel game. There was a strong sense of barbecue about the whole place.

She retrieved the Newton's Cradle of clicking metal balls and her laptop, both which had escaped damage, from the living room. Although if she wanted to keep her big chair it'd need substantially more than a bit of a dab with foam cleaner. On the way home to Liam's flat, Kat replenished her wardrobe at Asda and left Ashton to carry out a surgical strike on the grocery aisles.

CHAPTER 42

It had taken the parks department half the week to trail strings of fairy lights along the carnival parade route. Remembering how popular the bunting on the roof of Julie Andrews had been, Kat attached Buddhist prayer flags to the church cross. It gave it a decidedly Himalayan multi-faith touch.

Barry, discharged from hospital and under orders to take things easy, had been dipping and zipping around since dawn, getting on nerves. The two opposition councillors had turned up despite what each had separately termed pressing affairs of state. Picket had dressed up in honour of the occasion. His tweed cap would have gone well with gaiters and a brace of pheasant, but it did nothing for the striped blazer and the two-tone co-respondent shoes. The woman opposition councillor was in a flowered Jeff Banks outfit, the label so visible at the back of her neck that it had to have been done for effect.

'Hurry up, Petal,' panicked Barry on his mobile. 'Where are you?'

Two months from its inception, they had reached carnival day unscathed. More or less. The place teemed with fancy costumes and glitter. The downturn in the economy seemingly hadn't yet reached Bickeridge. Kat had roped in all the help she could. On the galvanised mesh fence around the builders' compound, which was all that remained of either Maurice Mickelwhite or Precinct 13, the infant school had hung a large bed-sheet banner with a painted *Carnivul Today* message. A pair of beefy PTA mums with butterfly tats and builders' bums were stretching a similar banner across the road outside the leisure centre. Their spelling showed no improvement on the children's.

'Up a bit, Stace,' yelled one, as a red double-decker bus trundled over the speed humps, almost taking the sheet with it. The police weren't closing the road to through traffic for another hour.

The PTA mums, all tats and tank tops, lit up and ambled off to find a ladder, leaving their sheet unsupported. The banner fluttered to the pavement, enveloping an elderly couple who had joined the crowd gathering to watch five caretakers who appeared to be giving the pavement an unaccustomed scour clean. The elderly couple fought their way out of the drifting sheet and did a U-turn into the health centre for stronger medication. Four more caretakers came out of the betting shop to join the first five. Nine caretakers. With nine brooms. It was a photo-opportunity too good to miss. History was being made.

Floats were trundling off in the direction of Bickeridge town hall. The sun sparkled off windscreens buffed to a crystal finish. A World War Two fire engine with a hand-operated ladder attached the second welcome banner high enough not to snag on passing double-deckers.

'I'm all sixes and sevens,' Barry, resplendent in the war paint and feathers of a Hollywood Indian chief, was agitated. 'They keep pinching each other's helpers and Jack's stuck on his own with the elephant.'

Someone had given Shardonnay's dog a peppermint green rinse and a pink bow. It didn't seem to bother the dog, nor the score or so pre-school mums and toddlers travelling with Barry and Shardonnay in an open-top thirties London bus. Barry's conductor's bandolier held pink and green cardboard bus tickets.

'Green for mum, pink for little treasure, dogs go free,' he explained. 'Actually, they all go free, but the kids like using the ticket machine.'

Ashton had claimed his brother-in-law's Land Rover could carry anything that Noah squeezed into the Ark and a lot of things which didn't. He hadn't baulked at the elephant.

'Where is Jack?' Kat asked.

'Behind the library. I think he might be a bit shy about his handiwork,' Barry said as he, Shardonnay and their busload disappeared along the road, decorated floats and cars chugging obediently behind.

On the grass strip outside the leisure centre stalls were being prepared. As well as bric-a-brac, jumble and DVDs there was sturdy garden furniture and bird tables, a pokerwork sign advertising it all as having been made by the Young Adults Special Needs Group. Next door, the Conservative Association's blue-draped stall was lining up novels and biographies by or about Tory politicians, centred on a pillar of volumes of Margaret Thatcher's Thoughts of Greatness.

An ageing couple in rimless glasses and Ban-the-Bomb badges were offering Che Guevara berets and posters. Lib-Dem ladies old enough to have known Lloyd George were displaying home-made cakes and jams.

A Friend of the Earth, according to his tee-shirt, clutched a bundle of leaflets about status dogs and examined the jams while he waited.

There was already an overwhelming aroma of fried onions and peanut sauce coming from three separate food stands. A large lady wearing a saffron silk sari which matched the paintwork of the Krishna Ices van was arguing over her pitch with the Sun City Ice Cream man. Kat's money was on the lady.

She rounded the corner at a gallop to find Ashton engrossed in the elephant. She had seen him only once since the night the Maurice Mickelwhite went up in flames. They still hadn't had their romantic dinner. Absorbed with attaching the elephant to the car, he had his back to her. She kept quite still, watching, and could tell from his body language the exact moment he sensed her there.

'What do you think? You can be truthful,' he said, kissing her on the nose before standing aside so she could admire his handiwork while his free hand did something slow and tingly on her neck. He was in baggy cords and a faded granddad shirt with bone buttons.

'What do I think? Not bad, for a barn raising,' Kat teased.

'Not me. I'm talking about the elephant.'

'Ah, she's very impressive, too,' Kat replied, eyeing the pink plastic blancmange Dumbo on the Land Rover roof.

Ashton tied the last elephant foot to a wing mirror. Done, he stretched out a hand. Kat was uncomfortable with public displays. Ashton noticed her hesitation.

'Relax. You look nice. You don't scrub up so bad, yourself.'

Kat was in the new stretch jeans she'd bought after her meagre wardrobe had been written off. With it she wore a loose, multicoloured ethnic tunic that wouldn't show the grime she'd have collected by the end of play.

'Hey, I'm at work. Behave. This is not a date.'

'I guessed that much,' he mumbled into her hair. 'But since it's the best deal I'm gonna get today, I'm making the most of it.'

'Behave nicely and you might get lucky. What are we going to do about the windscreen? I won't be able to see much of where I'm going.'

'No change there, then,' he returned, smartly stepping out of range in case she took a swipe. He must have rehearsed that one for days; Kat's driving skills were one of the seven wonders of the Moor estate.

'Shall we try it for size?' he asked, opening the passenger door.

Kat wriggled in under a pink elephant thigh onto the bump above the transmission between the two front seats.

'How much can you see,' Ashton asked.

There was less room than on the front passenger side, but the visibility was better through the thin letter-box opening that was all that remained now the elephant was in place. She assumed Ashton knew how much or how little windscreen it took to be legal.

'Seems fine from here,' she said, wishing she'd practiced a few times before trying to balance like Lawrence on his camel with one leg bent at an angle on the transmission.

'That'll hold it.' He tightened the string on the wing mirror. 'I'll rely on you to see where we're going. Oh, and if you have any ideas about having your wicked way with me in here, we're not alone.' He nodded towards a happy soul with more than a hint of institutional cooking about him who was sprawled across the back seat, hugging an electronic game. 'Meet Mel's brother. Say hello to Kat, Billy.'

'Hello, Kat,' intoned Billy. Kat recognised their passenger as the nervous young man from the Julie Andrews demolition party who had been so fascinated by the implosion.

'Mel's deputy's got flu so she's doing both jobs today,' Ashton said. 'She'll get here in time to judge the floats.''

'Hello, pleased to meet you.' Kat stuck a hand out.

His smile widened. 'Hello. Will you be my girlfriend? My friends will be jealous.' His speech was furry, in the manner sometimes used by the profoundly deaf. He grinned at her over the back of the front seat, as excited as a child.

'I can be your special girlfriend,' Kat said, 'Just for the carnival.' She caught a nod from Ashton who was checking if there was enough windscreen left to drive safely. Just about, but it would do.

'Little hand says it's time to rock and roll,' said Ashton, slipping into first and sprinting for the town hall, clearly keen to give his advanced driving skills an airing once they were off the estate. He didn't seem to mind spending his day off work chauffeuring a pink plastic elephant and a hefty young man with the IQ of a five year old.

It was uncanny. They raced down the deserted main road, an eerie vast emptiness, to the mustering area which by contrast was swarming. There were marchers and bands in uniforms and fancy dress, vehicles disguised as mushrooms, castles and space ships. Two body-stockinged Lady Godivas with identical yard-long tresses glared at each other. The one on the bike with a horse's head on the handlebars was ahead on points. Caribbean pirates, Batmen, Supermen and four ladies wearing Margaret Thatcher blue suits and Ronald Reagan face masks carrying cardboard sawn-offs milled about rattling their buckets and demanding hard cash for the mayor's charity. There was a constant hiss of walkie-talkie interference from police radios.

'Who's pinched Keanu's toggle?' shouted a scout leader with a long nose like a porpoise, and blew his whistle, while a sea cadet corps guarded their cardboard battleship against a wobbly fabric background of a cruel sea. A purple and green lorry of suffragettes pretended not to notice the acned comprehensive boys in their England colours. Doting grannies draped Neapolitan ice cream coloured net on a lorry-load of overweight carnival princesses wedged together to stop them rolling off their float. Next door, grim-faced football mums with wet hankies performed licky-spit on little faces. Barry waved and yoo-hooed at Billy and dished out pink bus tickets. It was getting on for half ten.

Billy glanced up briefly from his game to acknowledge Barry's greeting. 'I'm like Jonah in the whale, aren't I? This is my girlfriend.'

The two opposition councillors were in an open limo long enough to need a drummer to keep three banks of oarsmen in strict tempo. There was no sign of Mel in her mayoral regalia. This event on her own patch was to be the final appearance of her year in office. After the weekend, the chore would be handed over to her successor. Mel had told Kat that in preparation for his inauguration, Councillor Khan, the incoming Mayor, had politely requested the removal of all alcohol and coffee from the Members Room bar. It was going to be a dry year in local politics.

'When I get out of the car I'll need sun block,' Ashton said. 'You haven't any in that holdall you cart around with you, have you?'

'Or course I have,' Kat responded. 'Be prepared, *c'est moi.*'

'I won't be able to see much,' Ashton explained, fiddling with the dashboard controls. 'I'm relying on you to guide me.'

'I could drive and let you navigate,' Kat suggested whereupon Ashton fell about, jibbering at the idea of her being allowed to drive him.

'Can't see any sign of your guide dog, oops, sorry – parade marshal – who's meant to lead us,' he sniggered. Making a big song and dance about it, he squinted with streaming eyes through the letterbox-opening on the windscreen, wiping a hand across his eyes, and giving involuntary snorts of mirth.

Kat would get even. She had glue stick in her bag that looked almost identical to sun block.

'Parade marshal? How about the copper in front?

'Constable Singh?' Ashton beckoned to the turbaned community support constable standing beside his bike.

'Yes, sir.' The lad seemed unfazed to see a hairy arm appear between the front legs of an elephant.

'It's AJ, isn't it?'

'Yes, sir, Adjaiye Singh.'

'Are you meant to be leading us, AJ?'

'Yes, sir, ready when you are, sir.'

'Worked out the route in your head?'

'Yes, sir,' Singh answered proudly. 'Follow the cones and signs back to the Moor, wait for the mayor to judge the floats and fancy dress, then clear the road and disperse the vehicles around the park so people can see them properly. After that we open the road to all traffic.'

'Good,' said Ashton. 'Let's synchronise watches. I've got ten thirty-two, though I'm up for offers.'

'Ten twenty-nine, sir,' corrected Singh.

'Half ten, on the dot,' Kat replied, surprised to find her watch working again. 'I set it by the radio this morning.'

'Shall we settle for half ten, then? Yes? 'Okay, off you go.' Ashton released the hand brake.

Singh did something clever with his turban, knotting it into a swimming cap shape before jamming his helmet on top and hopping onto his motorbike. Kat glanced back to check the line-up. What little she could see of the elephant in the driving mirrors seemed a touch wobbly, but it had remained upright and was waving its trunk in the right direction. Behind them were three dozen pre-teen drum majorettes in short frocks, followed immediately by the brass band in their uniforms and epaulettes. Four be-medalled pensioners were wedged tightly into patio chairs jammed into the bucket of a JCB where they had a birds-eye view of a dozen or so nubile young ladies preparing to bounce up and down and twirl their tassels.

'Is it legal to haul geriatrics along the public highway in a digger bucket without yellow helmets or safety harness?' she said.

'Let them enjoy themselves,' said Ashton. He turned to Billy who was jigging up and down on the back suspension. 'All right? You want to start us off?'

The drum major hoisted his enormous mace. Billy, well versed in the green cross code, leaned out, looked left, looked right and looked left again and seemed satisfied.

'Go-go-go,' he shouted.

'I've always wanted to do that,' said Ashton, but their wagon master hadn't finished.

'Wagons ro...oll,' Billy sang, louder than a foghorn at sea.

It took the parade a couple of seconds to translate it into action.

Singh sat up straight on his bike, waiting, his long legs trailing the ground. He checked his helmet again. Then they saw him freeze.

'What're we waiting for,' Ashton called as the constable stayed put, mouth opening and closing like a fish. 'The second coming? Off you go.'

'Off we go, off we go, off we go,' went Billy from the back seat while the electronic games, left to its own devices, beeped in unison.

The Sikh constable flushed. 'Sir? You don't happen to have a map on you, do you, sir?'

CHAPTER 43

'Your luck's in. I never go anywhere without. Here you go; I'll have it back afterwards, if I may,' Kat said. She flourished the map which she had excavated from the junk in a handbag which could compete with the Tardis for capacity.

After two months on the Moor, where roads changed daily and diversion signs sprouted faster than winter broccoli, Sat Nav was useless. Kat travelled the estate on foot. Her annotated, hand-drawn map beat the timid efforts of the council, who tried to keep up by photocopying the daily changes and glue-sticking the results on top of the borough's definitive map, which must have been registered at about the time the first of the original residents moved onto the estate.

Singh clipped Kat's map onto the front of his motorbike between flashing beacon lights. Sitting bolt upright, he led them off: big pink elephant, ramrod-straight drum major hurling and twirling his five-foot gleaming chrome mace, Barbie drum majorettes skipping and swirling in his wake. Two brass bands were competing to out-blow and out-bang each other rather than relocate further apart before the parade got going. The garish, noisome convoy rolled out of the town hall car park and onto the public highway.

Diversion signs would keep the parade self-contained, and traffic at bay. Elderly ladies with baskets on wheels outside Sainsbury's waved. A young man fidgeting outside the driving test centre looked nervous enough to throw himself under the elephant as they went by. Past the police station with its twin blue lights, hanging baskets and wanted posters. It was too early for the charity shops: foxes had mauled the sacks of jumble deposited in their doorways. Parked outside the fire station was the shiny red and brass vintage engine that had been giving rides to the kids earlier. Entering into the spirit, its crew had donned period gear. In a sliver of wing mirror unhindered by elephant, Kat watched them tag on to the end of the procession.

'Are we there, yet?' Billy stopped playing his game and peered out as they passed their third deviation sign. 'Are we at my Gran's?'

'Soon,' Kat reassured him, and turned to Ashton. 'We should be near the old girl's place by now,' she whispered. 'I thought the plan was to approach from the front.'

'Don't worry. With street cones, a police outrider, a map, and you navigating, what could possibly go wrong?'

'We shouldn't have turned up Neptune Way.'

'It's probably only to avoid more road works,' Ashton said.

Kat wasn't convinced. Unforeseen changes were all very well but her mental geography told her that if they kept this up, some of the roads were going to be one way in the wrong direction. She stayed quiet when they passed more road closed signs and another deviation. She was in no doubt that they had gone the wrong way when they led the parade straight across Warp Drive, around a horseshoe and back out into the main road.

'Hurray!' shouted Billy, bouncing excitedly in the back. 'Flags.' Kneeling up on the seat and peeking through a hole in the elephant, he pointed back down the road where Kat could see a crowd of flag-waving spectators. She could also see the tail end of the parade going the other way across the far end of the street.

'Any more deviations and we'll end up doing the London to Brighton,' Ashton muttered.

'Why not flash the beanpole on the bike and get him to do a U-turn?' Kat suggested, ignoring the half-mile long undulating kite tail of noise and colour sweeping along behind them,

'We can't turn without a pile up,' warned Ashton. 'Not with all this lot coming up behind us.'

Kat moved an elephant foot to stick her head through the side window. There was colour and noise from pavement to pavement. A three-point-turn on the Thames in an oil tanker would be easier than attempting to change direction here.

'What do we do?'

'You're doing the navigating.'

'Try turning left here,' Kat said.

'Don't even think about it.' Ashton continued driving. They had reached an empty one-way street. Trouble was, it was the no entry end.

'In that case, where to, now?' said Kat

'Where are you?' A squawk fought its way through a burst of static on the car radio.

Ashton picked up the handset. 'Who's this?'

'Debbie Houston, duty officer at the station. There's a crowd waiting at the leisure centre.'

'Well, Houston, we have a problem,' Ashton muttered.

'Thought you might say something like that. Is that DI Ashton?'

'Yes. Hi, Debbie, there's been a slight hiccup. We haven't made it back to the estate yet. We seem to –'

'Yeah, it's okay, I'm tracking you on the screen now. You're way off. You must have turned too soon. You should have turned into Warp Drive. Looks like you went straight across the end of it.'

'No alternative,' explained Ashton. 'It was closed off with cones. There are a couple of diversions we weren't told about.'

'What's that?' the radio squawked. 'Hello? You still there?'

Ashton was squinting long-distance, his eyes creased with concentration. He gestured at the radio. Kat picked up the mike.

'Hello? This is Kat Shakespeare. I'm navigating.'

'Could've fooled me,' Ashton muttered. Kat was tempted to stick the radio up his nose.

'Hi, Cathy,' the radio voice said, getting it wrong, but this was no time to argue. 'There are no diversion signs there, not on our map or the one we were sent with the application form.'

'Christ on a bike,' Ashton muttered. 'That much is obvious. Tell us something we don't know.'

'Hang on a minute,' the radio trilled. They were left with static. Ashton continued driving, dead slow.

'Hello?' the radio again. 'The gas people are down to do the mains on Monday. They must've jumped the gun.'

'Oh, bollocks!' Kat yelped. 'What the f– '

'Bollocks'll do,' Ashton interrupted. 'Don't go for broke.' His eyes were fixed on the road.

The good nuns would have had the procession on its knees by now for a communal pester of the Heavenly multitude of whichever saints are meant to hold a watching brief on navigators, travellers and lost causes. Kat knew the drill; a convent education is never wasted. Unfortunately, it was doubtful if the crowd rumbling along behind them would go for it.

'I'm losing the will to live,' said Ashton, indulging in theatrics and banging his head on the steering wheel.

'Sir, do you need help on the ground?' Debbie was still on air.

'I'll get back to you on that one when I'm sane.' His head banging had given him a red mark across his forehead.

'Yes, sir. Get on the blower if you want us to send in the troops.'

The radio went silent.

They were doing under two miles an hour through an elite enclave of huge, architect designed houses originally planned around what was to have been a new golf club. However, a change of politics on the council had produced the Moor estate instead.

Kat recognised the road as the one where Sylvia and Sid, the Lanzarote couple lived. This invasion by the clamorous cavalcade now swinging along to the Muskrat Ramble would be a bit of a culture shock to residents hitherto insulated against encroachment by multiple security sensors and self-cleaning double-glazed leaded lights. Kat didn't have much sympathy: this particular residents' association had a history of petitioning the council for the installation of its own little Berlin Wall in an attempt to deter the Moor's riff raff from rat running past their Fifties-built double-fronted Tudorbethan desirable detached residences.

'Oooh, pretty flowers,' Billy sang out.

Kat had been too busy squinting at the house interiors to see the funeral motorcade that turned into the road ahead.

'My cup truly runneth over,' Ashton breathed, slowing to a respectful distance. 'More effing corpses!'

'Effing horses? Where?' sang out Billy.

Kat tried not to laugh.

Ashton cursed inaudibly and slowed even more.

From a small side road, a remarkably agile arrangement of branches and leaves swung across the road in front of them.

'Oi, miss?' It was Curly, Chemo on bikes, and Winnie, similarly covered in greenery, riding pillion on Mickey, in the rear, who had been allowed his wheelchair back for the day. There was a 'Heavy Plant Crossing' sign taped onto the back of the chair.

'They said they were going to dress up as characters from Macbeth,' said Kat.

'They are, loosely. At a guess, I'd say that's Birnam Wood, on the move,' suggested Inspector Clever Clogs.

'I don't recall any Triffids in Macbeth.'

The three boys were laughing so much they had trouble staying on their wheels.

'Hey, they're waiting up the estate, mate. You're barking up the wrong tree.' They laughed again.

'Cheeky devils aren't telling me anything I hadn't worked out for myself,' Ashton muttered darkly.

'We can show ya, if ya want.'

'If I sit here any longer I'm going to turn into a pillar of salt,' Kat said. 'My backside's gone numb.'

Ashton glanced at her in the mirror. 'Believe me, this is not a good moment to ask me to give it the kiss of life.'

'Worth a try, though,' Kat shrugged.

'Okay, boys,' said Ashton. 'Let's get us to Dunsinane, then.'

'Done what?'

'Never mind him,' said Kat. 'He reads too much. Do your worst, boys,' adding quietly, 'It can only get better, after this.'

The Birnam Wood quartet took up pole position, waiting for the funeral cortege to get out of sight before giving a theatrical forward signal and nosing the parade out into the main road.

Head up, back straight, the drum major carried the procession along behind him. The boys took turns to peer backwards through their foliage to check the parade wasn't lagging. The drum major had marched out of one of his boots along the way. Half booted, he marched and tossed his mace with much the same panache as before. Almost. The majorettes soldiered on despite succumbing to a little stagger here and there. The carnival princesses in the relative comfort of their float waved as instructed, but to disappointingly empty streets. The half-mile parade weaved along behind the pink elephant. With the boys moving road barriers and ignoring no entry signs it took only a few twists and turns to break out of the holding pattern.

Kat sat back as they passed the ruins of Julie Andrews, the crime scene and the epicentre of the great pigeon debacle two months earlier.

'Daddy's gone,' Billy said. 'Cosmo's got a shiny lorry,' he added.

Ashton glanced at her, one eyebrow raised.

'What set that off?' he muttered to Kat.

'Nobody's told him Cosmo's under guard at the hospital,' Kat said. She wriggled onto her knees and leaned over the back of the seat.

'Hey, Billy, were you hoping to ride in Cosmo's car today?'

'No.' Billy said. 'Cosmo let me ride in his new car. Not his lorry. Long time now.' He went back to his game and they continued in silence, aside from the constant electronic ping. 'Cosmo's Daddy's friend. And the other man,' Billy said.

'Who was that, then, Billy?' At least it gave them a break from the irritating electronic pings.

'Bernie,' he said. 'Daddy fell down. I told Cosmo and Bernie. They said he was asleep. Said I shouldn't be out at night, and not to tell.'

Ashton's foot slipped off the clutch. The car stalled.

'Sorry, people.' He started the car once more.

Kat said 'What do you – ?'

'Shhh, later.' Ashton gave a quick shake of his head. 'Let's get this over with, first, then I think we might have a quiet chat with him. Can't do it right now. How are you doing back there, Billy?'

'Being good, like Mel said. Can I have an ice cream?'

'As many as you want when we get to the fair,' offered Ashton. His attention was on the herbaceous quartet in front, the proud advance guard of their huge army. 'I promise.'

'Boys, too? They want ice cream, too. And Winnie.'

'Yes, okay.'

'Maybe the boys would prefer Gro-More,' Kat sniggered.

The parade perked up as the fairground calliope hove into view behind the cloud of hamburger and hot dog smoke wafting across the field. Kat inhaled the heady scent of burnt onions. The woody quartet triumphantly led the parade across the builders' slip road with a sense of an expedition bursting out of the rainforest. Three-quarters of an hour behind schedule, their arrival was greeted with wild applause. Except for the two opposition councillors, who demanded to know who gave the boys permission to cut chunks from the recently planted leisure centre hedge to make their fancy dress.

CHAPTER 44

Surely they didn't expect Kat to join them on the Big Wheel? Just looking at it made her stomach churn. By some standards, it might not qualify as a bare-knuckle ride, but for someone who got seasick going over speed humps, it was not her idea of paradise. Crammed into nothing more sophisticated than a glorified chair-lift, they took off with a helicopter-style swoop, leaving her stomach behind. Billy whooped with delight. Kat kept her hands gripped tightly on the crossbar and her eyes fixed on the horizon. Two units ahead, Winnie and the boys were divesting themselves of greenery. She could hear their shouts over the fairground music. Not content with conning ice creams from Ashton, Billy had also negotiated a ride on the wheel for them all.

'So, Billy, tell us about your dad,' she invited, switching her brain into work mode to take her mind off plummeting to her death.

'Daddy gone bye-bye.' Having finished his ice cream, he was inspecting the contents of a packet of liquorice allsorts Winnie had given him. Most of them had bite marks.

'Yes, I know,' said Kat. 'When did your dad go away?'

'Not gone away,' he tutted, and returned to his allsorts.

Mel had been sure about her brother and his *Daddy's gone, bye-bye* phase. The boy was brain damaged. Who knew how his mind worked?

'Billy, did you really see your dad?' Kat tried to engage him, eye to eye, which was not easy with that squint of his.

''Course I did.'

'Where was this?'

'Looking for Livingstone's supper. Sometimes daddy helped. Sometimes Cosmo. Sometimes Bernie, too.'

'Who's Livingstone?'

'Salamander. I forgot to feed him. He died.'

'Your salamander. Right, I see. And Bernie?'

'He's Cosmo's friend.'

Now they had the full pack: Cosmo King, Bernie Delaney, Livingstone the salamander, and Jeff Rampart, the policeman father. Was Jeff's son there and saw what happened that night or was this going to be another red herring?

'You were collecting food,' Ashton said. 'For Livingstone. And your dad was helping. Is that right, Billy?'

'Livingston likes slugs and snails. But he died. *Slugs and snails and puppy dogs tails, slugs and snails*.'

'And where did you look for these slugs and snails?' Ashton asked.

'There.' Billy pointed to the Julie Andrews site. 'Cosmo says mustn't tell or Daddy get in trouble. Me, too. Not allowed out at night.'

'Why would your dad be in trouble?' Ashton asked.

'I never told anyone,' Billy said sulkily.

'No, of course you didn't. Can you remember when this was?' Kat asked, but she knew Billy was unlikely to be able to identify a particular day at this late stage. Thirty years would be a hard task for anyone, impossible for someone as brain damaged as he.

'Not allowed out without a grown-up.'

'You did go out, though, didn't you?' said Ashton.

Billy nervously licked his lips and avoided eye contact.

'You won't get into trouble,' Ashton said, loosening his grip on the rail and placing a reassuring arm on Billy's shoulder. 'I promise.'

'So you sneaked out without anyone seeing,' Kat said. 'Gosh, that was daring Go on, you can tell us.'

Billy seemed to be debating within himself, nodding his head from side to side and giving small grunts. Finally he rocked forward.

'All right. But you mustn't tell. Promise? I got insects for my tin, and Daddy came. Said it was our secret. He always knew good insect places.

'Did you tell anyone else the secret?' Kat asked.

'No. Daddy said not to. Then he fell down. Bernie and Cosmo came but Bernie went away again. Cosmo said Daddy was tired cos he works too hard. Told me to go home. He burst into song with *Chitty Bang Bang, Chitty Chitty Bang Bang, Chitty Bang Bang...*

Kat closed her eyes to help her think despite the tuneless singing.

'This isn't going anywhere.' Ashton said.

'Gotta go bye-byes now,' Billy said, clutching his safety harness. 'Not fall down.'

'Don't worry, Kat and I will see you don't fall.'

'Hey, hang about,' Kat whispered, sitting up in her chair, forgetting she was thirty feet up in the air. 'I don't think he's talking about falling from this contraption. He's talking about what happened back then.' She turned to Billy. 'When Daddy went bye-byes, can you remember, were Cosmo and Bernie there, too?'

Billy screwed up his eyes, squinting, trying to remember.

'Told you. They came afterwards. Then they went away when the lady came. She had yellow hair. And shiny teeth. Can I have some more ice cream?'

'Yeah, soon as we're on the ground,' Ashton said.

'Okey-dokey, pig-in-a-pokey,' Billy said, letting his head go back at an awkward angle. His eyes had stayed slightly open.

Kat pinched his arm to check he hadn't died. He'd better wake before the ride ended. She didn't fancy lugging his dead-weight.

'How far have we got?' she mused. 'Bye-bye seems to mean going to bed, not going away. It was always assumed Billy was talking about his dad going away.'

'His dad went to sleep? That's bye-byes, not bye-bye,' Ashton said.

'How does Rampart end up in the hole dug for the foundations,' Kat asked.

'He could have fallen in accidentally,' Ashton suggested. 'He had been drinking that night.'

'Heart attack, stroke?' Kat wondered. 'No, that doesn't work.'

The big wheel was slowing, disgorging riders as each rack of chairs reached the ground. Kat stroked Billy's arm. He woke immediately and continued chatting as if he'd not taken time out for a sleep.

'Going on the tea cup now?'

'Wait for us,' called Ashton as they clambered out.

Kat trotted to keep up, and stopped dead at the tea cup. She'd rather book a weekend break with Dignitas than go on that thing. She'd disgraced herself before on one, throwing up over a half-mile radius.

'Nope, sorry. Can't,' she said, shaking her head. 'You go.'

'Oh, come on. I'll – ' Ashton stopped. 'Right. Okay. We'll let the old cowardy-custard watch,' he joked.

'Yes, boys only; like Daddy and me.' Billy clapped sticky hands delightedly. 'Can Cosmo come? And Mel?'

'No, Cosmo's busy,' Kat said. 'I'm not sure where Mel is.'

'Last seen heading for the Radio Wazzoo van and a mayoral Desert Island Discs,' Ashton said. 'Best to wait.'

'Okay,' Kat replied. 'Off you go, fellas.'

She timed the ride. It had been only four and a half minutes, but she saw Ashton cover up a stagger when they disembarked. Billy was looking around, his head going right and left, scanning the fair.

'Mel says you have to take your tablets now,' Kat said before he had time to decide which ride he would try next. 'We'll leave plenty of time before the fireworks. Shall we get some tea?'

'Yes, Pepsi and cake,' Billy replied, immediately docile. He trotted heavily off to the tea tent ahead of them.

'Did you get any further forward?' Kat asked.

'Some. Looks like he sneaks out when the granny's tucked up with her hot water bottle. His dad's already out on the tiles.' Ashton kept his voice low. 'He's poking about under stones and dropping slugs and creepy crawlies into a tin when he sees his dad roll out of the Stargazer. Rampart shows him this big hole and says he'll help him, but shortly after that he falls into a hole.'

'The hole excavated for the Julie Andrews foundations.'

'And this is when King and Delaney come along. Doesn't look like they were there before he fell in, so we can assume they didn't shove him in the hole,' Kat said.

'But why didn't they haul him out?' Ashton asked.

'Maybe they didn't like slugs and creepy crawlies. Ha! Sorry. Are you putting all this in your pretend notebook?'

'It's a lot better than some statements I've seen, pretend notebook or otherwise,' Ashton said calmly, seeming unfazed by her having sussed the trick he'd pulled on her two months earlier, using his diary as a police notebook. 'We didn't get any further, cos the ride ended.'

Billy had reached the tea tent. He was droning tunelessly:

'Nana nana, Nana nana, Nana nana, Nana nana, Batman,
Nana nana, Nana nana, Nana nana, Nana nana, Batten-buuuurg.'

'I think he's decided which cake he's having. On your toes, Kat-woman, we can't afford to lose our star witness,' said Ashton.

CHAPTER 45

Billy ate like a washing machine on a slow spin cycle. Mouth open, jowls wobbling, he filled his mouth with chunks of marzipan-coated pink and white chequered cake and chased it down with a gulp of cola. Ashton was as usual stuffing himself, also with cake, but in a marginally more refined manner.

'This hole your daddy fell into,' Kat said. 'How did he fall? Did somebody push him?'

'No. We played jumping games,' Billy spluttered through layers of Battenburg. 'Daddy made funny jokes.'

He clapped delightedly forgetting he had cake in each hand. Surprised, he examined his fingers carefully, then licked the cake off, digit by digit, alternating between the colours. They watched, and waited for him to finish.

'Daddy made Billy laugh,' he said, and leapt sharply to his feet, rolling his body, windmilling his arms. With exaggerated surprise, he suddenly reared back.

'Ohhhhh, Shiiii—' he wailed theatrically. As he fell backwards, he almost took the side of the tea tent with him.

Alarmed, people jumped to their feet. An elderly gentleman fell off his chair. Billy opened his eyes and laughed. He was having a whale of a time. Once they had him upright again, they took him out to sit on the grass where he could cause less damage.

'Daddy said bad word when he fell down,' he said. 'Not allowed.'

All three were sitting facing each other on the grass, legs crossed. Billy beckoned them closer.

'When Daddy fell down, he said *shit*!'

'Yeah, shit would cover it,' murmured Ashton. 'All those years and nobody sussed.' He turned back to Billy. 'Then what happened?'

'I couldn't see him. Bernie came and said where's your daddy and I said he'd fallen down the hole, and Bernie said stay there, and then Cosmo came and they went to see Daddy, and they were gone a long time and Cosmo said not to worry cos Daddy had gone bye-byes and best not to disturb him. and he said he'd take me home, but they had to empty Cosmo's lorry first. But they didn't take me home like they said, cos the lady came and they went away without me.

'What lady was this?' Kat asked, wondering why, if King and Delaney hadn't had a hand in Rampart's death, the former had remained silent for thirty years. No wonder he had been anxious to encourage the view that it was a death entirely divorced from the affairs of the estate.

'Told you before. Nice lady from the pub. She had yellow hair and big shiny yellow teeth. She said someone sicked-up on my dad's coat. She gave me things and said I should take them home for him.' He began picking up and eating crumbs from his clothing.

'What did you do with the things she gave you?' Ashton asked.

'Put them in my special tin, for when my dad wakes up.'

'Your special tin?'

'Yes. You want to see it?'

'Er, yes, please. Is it at home?' If it ever existed.

'Not home now.'

'With thirty years to lose it, who knows where it is,' muttered Kat.

Billy reached into his canvas mailbag and lifted out a battered shortbread tin. The colours were so faded it was not possible to pick out which of the terriers on the worn lid was white and which black.

'It's a lovely tin.' Kat said, feeling a surge of adrenalin. 'Could we see inside?'

Billy hugged it close, but finally, with great reluctance he gave up his treasure. 'Careful, it's my special tin.'

'We'll be careful,' Ashton promised, gently lifting the lid.

Kat held her breath. The tin contained a sad collection of memorabilia: a dead spider, a *When You Are Three* musical card, Rubik cube, Pokémon cards, two Subutteo figures, and a tiny broken penknife tacky enough to have come from a Christmas cracker.

In the bottom of the tin there was a brown ten-shilling note and some loose change, including a yellow threepenny bit. It lay alongside rusted keys and a miscellany of old coins. Inside a leather wallet was a small spiral notebook and a broken pencil, seven £1 notes, and some photographs once held together by a perished rubber band. Lastly, there was a gent's wind-up wristwatch, a big multi-dialled affair, which showed the right time. The last item was a battered warrant card, all that was left of Jeff Rampart, PC ZX801.

Ashton handled the warrant card with care. Kat picked up the photographs and turned them over. A child's hand had written on the backs. *My mum and me* showed a beaming bottle-blonde in a sixties mini skirt, beside a happy, before-the-accident six-year-old Billy who smiled proudly from a shiny two-wheeler. There was a pair of abandoned stabilisers on the ground beside him. In another, a slim young driver posed against a glistening Ford Capri. Lastly, there was a laughing group hanging onto each other so as not to fall off the bonnet.

It took Kat some seconds to decipher the childish scrawl. She turned the picture over.

'Jack, there's a picture here –' she began.

'Hang on a second.' Ashton put the watch to his ear. 'Billy, how on earth did you manage to do it?'

'Not my fault; pencil just broke.' Billy was almost in tears.

'No, not the pencil, old son,' soothed Ashton, 'Your dad's watch. It's working perfectly.'

Billy was relieved, but the strain was showing.

'I was careful,' he said. 'The pub lady said I had to be. I wind it every Sunday after tea like my dad. Can we go on another ride now I've taken my tablets and finished my cake?'

'I've a better idea.' Ashton eyed him reflectively. 'How about I give you a ride to the police station in a real police car. We can show them the things in your tin and they'll take some photos of everything and you can have it all back straight away. What do you say?'

'Can we have sirens and lights?'

'Yes, as many as you want.'

'In the elephant car.'

'Not the elephant. I'll get us a proper police car.'

'Is there cake and lemonade there?'

'I'm sure we can fix that,' said Kat.

'In the elephant car. With lights and sirens, you promised.'

'We'll take the elephant off, for safety,' Ashton said.

'We'd best tell Mel where we're taking him, or she'll think we've kidnapped him,' Kat suggested.

'No! I want the elephant on the car. Elephant car. Elephant car.' Billy was gearing up for a tantrum.'

Ashton turned to Kat. 'How am I going to drive down to the nick with half the windscreen blocked and a pink elephant on the roof?'

'Kat coming, too,' Billy pouted.

'Yes, I'm coming,' she hurriedly reassured him. 'Come on, Jack, let's get him in the car before he changes his mind.'

They all bundled into the Land Rover, where Ashton ripped a hole in the elephant's foot which covered half the windscreen and clamped a magnetic emergency light bar on the front of the car. No simple Kojak light this time

'They're going to love this at the nick,' he sighed.

With the Blazebuster strobing, the wah-wah wailing, the pink elephant flapping, and Billy carolling *'nana-nana-nana-nana'* they screeched out onto Warp Drive and off the estate.

A pink plastic elephant straddling an ancient police Land Rover, even with all its lights and sirens going, is nowhere near as cool as a puce-coloured bus trundling across a red-hot Australian desert in high summer. But it was camp enough to give the lads and lasses down at Bickeridge nick a good laugh.

CHAPTER 46

Kat didn't get back to the carnival until half-way through the grande finale. In her absence, amidst much confusion and accusations of cheating, the talent contest had been won by the harpist. The presentation had to be paused awhile when, in her excited rush to claim the prize, the winner ran slap into the drinks machine in the lobby and was briefly unconscious. St John Ambulance performed the necessary in the absence of the elderly duty-GP, who had gone home early. Karen told Kat afterwards that this was because the doctor had imbibed so much of the council's free booze that he'd fallen asleep in his deck chair in the VIP tent. Awaking to find a wet patch on his clothing, he had jumped to conclusions, privately blamed old age, and quietly taken himself home. Nobody had bothered to tell the old soak that the sticky stain on his crotch was only affectionate drool from Shardonnay's dog.

In view of Billy's condition, it was decided that Kat should remain with him as a responsible adult until they finished at the police station. Which meant that she also missed the biking vicar's piece de resistance on the wall of death which he'd performed, to the unrestrained applause of his parishioners, in a diamante-trimmed leotard.

The mayor had presented the winning princess and runners-up each with a colourful sash in six languages reflecting the multicultural nature of the estate. But the girls found themselves in trouble when the Catholic priest said it was disrespectful for some to have worn their First Holy Communion dresses for a secular occasion.

'Holy Mother,' he said. 'Whatever will the Bishop say?'

But a pattern had been set. Friends of the Earth complained that the royal conveyance was belching smoke in a designated low emission zone. Councillor Picket, in the mayor's absence, had with misguided fervour and a sense of his own importance, requisitioned the rugby players' float for the princesses' victory lap. This led to a punch-up between supporters of the two factions. To rub salt into the wound, the boys were subjected to a Maori victory Haka by the winners' mums, incorporating a whole range of rude gestures. The lady in the saffron sari locked her ice cream van and joined in, as any self-respecting granny of a carnival princess naturally would. Soon the protagonists lost track of who had done what and to whom, or why. Nobody seemed to care as long as they packed in their punches.

A tattooed football mum, who by coincidence was also one of the disappointed talent show participants, accused the judges of rigging both the float competition and the talent contest. The judges denied their decision had any bearing on the harpist's relationship with any member of the panel. The ensuing battle demolished two floats and an extremely expensive harp and was directly responsible for the tailback at the dentists the following week.

Police took the opportunity, with attention elsewhere, to make another of their hitherto unsuccessful garage swoops. This time, without the leak of advance disclosure, the raid had resulted in the discovery of the biggest collection of fake registration plates south of Watford, and enough spare parts to set up in competition with Nissan Motors.

Meanwhile, detectives were brainstorming over Jeff Rampart's possessions. Noses out of joint at Kat's involvement, they claimed to be awaiting DNA results and refused to confirm whether or not the skeleton was Mel's dad.

Kat left Ashton at the police station and took Billy home to Mel's place before going back to the estate on her own to catch the last hour of the carnival. Ashton appeared preoccupied by the time he eventually returned to the estate as the finale, to a delighted chorus of applause and oohs and ahhs, was getting into its stride with a cluster of rockets. He didn't show much enthusiasm, either, for the huge blue cartwheels shooting into the sky or for the Catherine wheels hissing and snapping and throwing their tails out and twirling coloured sparks into the night.

The fireworks had been Barry's creation. He was in his element, but couldn't resist making a self-deprecating joke about it.

'Silly me - I spent a fortune last year going to see the northern lights and I didn't catch sight of so much as a candle watt,' he told them, pretending to be pissed off. 'If I'd had any sense I'd have stayed here. It would've been cheaper than forking out for blooming Norway.'

Toddlers straitjacketed into their pushchairs screamed and bounced up and down in synch with the bangs; parents laughed with delight that their offspring were having such a good time. Simultaneously with the colour fest they let off the big bangers. Nobody had warned the local hospital, where the first bangs had them thinking of rolling out emergency planning measures in anticipation of casualties. Karen screeched at the bangs and grabbed mock-amorously at any passing male. Lee said she didn't get out much, what with work and the baby.

Fireworks over, the crowds dispersed. Word had gone around that the skeleton was the mayor's dad and that detectives were squeezing more information from the hospitalised Cosmo King.

'They've not finished with me at the nick yet,' Ashton told her. 'The locals are narked that I muscled in on their territory. They're making noises about your involvement, too. I agreed to go back in, tonight. We could always have a Chinese, if I don't finish too late and they haven't chopped my legs off.'

'I've had enough for one day, I'm knackered,' said Kat. She felt drained. Too much rushing around, too many late nights, not enough vitamins in her food. Things were catching up.

Ashton said he'd let her get an early night and give her a bell next day. Whilst she was glad he could be so understanding, she was nonetheless a trifle miffed that he hadn't put up much of a fight.

CHAPTER 47

Now the police had released the Julie Andrews site and the area around both the burnt-out community centre and the housing office, redevelopment was shooting ahead. Labourers were being taken on by the dozen. The cumulative effect of the fire, Kat's hard work and what people were calling the Magaluf effect meant the project was going to come in on time, and financial disaster avoided.

As often happened towards the end of a project, Kat was working into the early hours. She was not concerned, therefore, that Ashton was preoccupied with his own work. Late nights and irregular eating habits had left her with bags under her eyes and nervous indigestion, but she was on the home straight. After counting the tenants into the two airport-bound coaches she would follow behind, by car. Requisitioning a fifty-seat air-conditioned coach for the return journey all to herself was hardly an option. Once she had put them on the Magaluf flight, she would use their absence to tidy up loose ends.

She was temporarily without her own transport. Shardonnay had lent her own, Shitty Shitty Bang Bang, to get her to Gatwick, with an admonition to keep the engine running as long as possible or the battery would lose its charge. She also suggested Kat parked the clapped-out VW Beetle facing downhill, for a jump start should it prove necessary.

Kat opted for the non-motorway route, convinced that she was a target for the bullying tactics of the convoys of lorries driving at great speed and veering into her path with indicators and horns full on whenever she attempted to overtake. Because most machines or gadgets coming Kat's way seemed to have a self-destruct button, it came as no great surprise when twenty minutes after setting out, a knocking started from under the bonnet. Shardonnay had warned her that the car was inclined to make funny noises that may or may not come to anything.

She had been adamant, however, that as long as the engine was kept running, then so would the car. Kat hadn't worked out how she was going to get the car to re-start once she'd parked at the airport, but suspected she might need a push. She'd sort that out as and when.

It would be Billy's birthday two days hence; she had bought him a card. In her hurry to leave, however, she'd omitted to post it, and it was now lying on the passenger seat.

Ignoring the engine racket, she drove slowly along the A217, keeping her eyes skinned for a kerbside letter box. A post office, should any remain extant, was out of the question. Posting the card could only be done from a sitting position, keeping her feet on the pedals. Any post office was going to have to be very close to the road to manage that. She could not risk stalling. She was close to the airport before she saw the familiar red box on the kerb in a small parade of shops just before the A23 junction. She turned into the service road and gently kept the brake down with the engine still running, hanging onto the steering wheel with her left hand, ready with the card in the right.

At the exact moment that she leaned out, the engine noise changed into something a little more threatening than hiccups. The angle of the letter box opening was all wrong. The card skidded across the side and disappeared out of reach onto the pavement, narrowly missing some dog poop. Kat banged her head on the roof when the car bunny-hopped forward a couple of inches. As she took her hand off the steering wheel to rub her head, the car gave a final cough, and died.

'Buggeration,' she muttered, and rubbed her head again.

The good news was she no longer had to remain welded to the steering wheel since any damage was now done. She slid out and retrieved Billy's card from the pavement, dusting it off on her T-shirt before dropping the envelope in the box.

When she returned to the car, inevitably, it refused to start. No amount of kicking, shoving, pushing or as a last resort cursing would persuade Shardonnay's useless heap of scrap metal to budge.

There was no-one in sight who looked as if they might have the strength to give her a push. In film or fiction the heroine would have used a pair of tights and some eyebrow tweezers to cobble the engine together and get the thing going again.

Kat clambered out. It was a purely symbolic gesture, because she didn't know anything about the inner workings of cars. She had no idea what she expected to find. There was nothing that looked like it might benefit from a pair of tights or eyebrow tweezers under the bonnet of

Shardonnay's heap of junk. Just as well: Kat had neither tights nor tweezers. She did, however, have an RAC sticker on the windscreen. He'd better be quick. She was pushed for time.

The RAC recovery vehicle rolled up in under forty minutes, hazards flashing brighter than alien spacecraft landing lights. He hauled her into his cab and the car onto the back of his recovery vehicle, and insisted on continuing the short distance to Gatwick, where he parked illegally across six bays at the drop off. She almost had to abseil from the recovery vehicle cab which was three times her height. She left the RAC man making placatory gestures at a traffic warden speed-walking towards them. The queues at the check-in were longer than a wet weekend but there was no sign of her tenants. According to the screens, the Magaluf gate had closed.

'Damn, damn, double damn, and buggeration,' Kat said.

A middle-aged couple in matching Burberry outfits straight out of *Rupert Bear* turned up their noses and commented loudly in rasping Afrikaans, or bad Dutch, at her choice of language. Catching her expression they hurried off, worried perhaps that she might take them on.

Gatwick, paranoid about security, like other airports world-wide, had closed its observation deck to the public. She made for the multi-storey. There was a spot at roof level from where she could see passengers trailing across the apron. A quick head count confirmed they were all there. In Cosmo King's unavoidable absence, Karen and the big vicar were co-ordinating the excited band of travellers.

Kat rang Karen, who craned up and spotted her; she was all smiles and waves. Kat waved back. The rest of them waved. Kat waved again. Drivers in the car park waved. Travellers heading for other planes on the apron waved. They waved from planes waiting on the runway. And some say the English aren't friendly.

'See you in a month. We'll keep a sexy Spanish waiter on the side for you,' Karen shouted into her mobile, and, shrieking with laughter, they all trotted up the aircraft steps. Karen's back of the bus sing-songs were the highlight of the South London bingo-trip charabanc crowds; the cabin crew didn't know what a treat they were in for.

Although Kat had agreed to go out to Magaluf to resolve last minute issues with the tenants before they moved, beaches weren't her idea of a holiday, and even though they were paying for her to travel business class, she would not be tempted to think of it as anything more than work. In any case, the nuns at the home had left her with a mediaeval approach to such things as holidays: simple accommodation, food for energy, and something to keep her occupied. A strenuous back-packing expedition taking in a dozen ancient or religious sites, building a school or a well in some Godforsaken poverty-stricken village in India or Nepal, or, for the pious, a silent religious retreat with uplifting reading broadcast to all during meagre meals. She didn't fancy lying around watching the English frying under their knotted handkerchiefs and straw umbrellas as they flicked through two-day-old tabloids printed on thin paper and shouted the odds down mobile phones. If all went as planned, by the time the wanderers returned, the final tranche of homes would be waiting.

All her charges having successfully enplaned, she turned to leave. A Surrey and Sussex Bugle, mother-ship of Bickeridge's local rag, lay discarded on a baggage trolley. The front page was taken up with a picture of the late 'Teflon' Ted Delaney skewered to Kat's bed. The caption read 'Gang Boss dead in freak accident'. The headline was accompanied by a picture so out of focus that it must have been taken by one of the paramedics or a policeman at the scene using a mobile.

She picked up the paper and skimmed the article. The shattered bedroom window was explained. Apparently it hadn't been the blast from the explosion that had caused the glass to break. It appeared that the explosion had startled Delaney into firing his gun at something the paper called a hotspot in the window above him, causing the glass to shatter in the way it did. Well, one more question answered.

For the rest, there was little she didn't already know: the missing Bernie had been in Sitges all along but was avoiding close encounters with those seeking him. Delaney's two muscular sons were rumoured to be hot on Bernie's heels, and were last seen getting into a cab at Barcelona airport. Another episode in the colourful cavalcade of London gangland history. Let the Delaneys sort it out amongst themselves. That's what families do. Isn't it?

CHAPTER 48

Kat's new flat over the leisure centre was an improvement on the old. Decorated and furnished at no cost to her because once she was gone it would be used by the council for twin-town visitors.

She and Barry had spent a happy afternoon exploring IKEA, discovering that the names were more exciting than the stuff they sold. But it was simple and functional, and easy to maintain. There had been some initial confusion with locating chairs called Lindved off shelves labelled Lillberg or Linnarp. Barry suggested it might be something to do with living half your life in twilight that gave the Swedes their odd sense of humour and weird filing system. Kat assured him that she had watched enough mind-numbing Scandinavian films to conclude that they didn't do humour as we know it, only weird.

In the IKEA car park Barry produced tools to assemble their purchases, refusing to leave until he was confident that everything was present and correct and they would not need to return.

Ashton admitted he had been put on suspension awaiting a disciplinary hearing for having given her details of the police investigation. Hardly a hanging offence, but it had left him increasingly ambivalent about remaining in the police force. Some of his demolition-day pictures had been published, and now, with time on his hands, he was roaming London with his camera.

It would be time to start scouring the classifieds when she returned from Magaluf. With instructions from Ashton to have a good time she gritted her teeth, stocked up on sun cream and flew out to discuss the final arrangements with the happy holidaymakers.

The flight was predictable. Despite the council forking out for her to go business class the only thing missing was the scenario where the entire crew come down with acute food poisoning and a large inflatable doll named Otto must land the plane. She arrived damp and sticky from coke sprayed by a girl in killer heels staggering along the aisle during the only patch of turbulence on the entire trip. A hairy mammoth with bad breath had kept leaning across to peer out of her window. She knew better than to argue with a dog collar and a big crucifix. The in-flight coffee had tasted no better than in economy and the only good thing about the Spanish omelette was that it came on a proper china plate. On the up-side, there were no children in the row behind to kick her in the kidneys, slam the food trays up and down, and no-one in front keeping their seat reclined while she ate, as they did back in cattle class.

She spent her first afternoon in Magaluf being sociable with tenants, parked on a lounger under an umbrella, covered in little more than an English newspaper. She managed to stick it out for the day. Duty done, next morning she had put her clothes back on and moved her centre of operations to the hotel's atrium where coffee and mineral water on demand and the soft whirr of the air conditioning kept her company while she juggled colour charts and finishes and received visitors.

Karen was trawling the island for religious fridge magnets for Lee's mum, and hand-crafted jewellery for Shardonnay who, having moved house earlier, was missing out on the council junket.

Predictably, the tenants were divided roughly into two halves: those who had to be prised away from beach or pool where, flopped out slathered in sun oil, they guzzled sangria until tea time, when they could dump the kids with the hotel minders and sample the night life. And those who, when they weren't eating and drinking or disco-ing, were on a perpetual market dash, amassing leather, flamenco shawls, and bullfight posters with their name on. One step ahead, Kat rose sufficiently early to catch them before they dispersed.

Ashton rang regularly. His picture of Kat in a deluge of pigeon feather confetti had been nominated by a photographic magazine for an award. He told her the three boys were behaving themselves so well that Meccano Mickey had now had his wheelchair restored permanently. Skateboarding mastered, Winnie was being instructed how to ride a bike. To date, there had been no complaints.

An ecstatic Shardonnay also rang to let them hear her good news. Her DNA had come back, ruling out Cosmo King as her father. Rosie Delaney had instantly sunk into a decline.

After ten days of sun, sand, and last-minute requests for changes to bathroom suites and front doors, Kat almost jogged onto the plane to come home. She had a terracotta pot for her new kitchen: an incentive to experiment with proper cooking. On the other hand, she might use it as a fruit bowl if she ever got around to buying more than the occasional banana. For Barry, who liked to drape furniture with theatrical touches, she had found a particularly dramatic silk shawl with an eighteen-inch fringe. Mel wanted a dress-length of embroidered organza. For Ashton she had a leather-bound early edition Elizabeth Barret Browning. A dark little bookshop down by the docks had beckoned, and she had recalled he liked both Brownings. His birthday was soon. It made her feel awkward, giving him poetry. Giving anybody poetry. Giving anybody anything. Maybe she'd hang onto it.

'Good journey?' Damp from the shower, Ashton was draped in one of her new bath towels when she struggled in juggling her luggage with the groceries and ready-meals she'd picked up at the airport M&S.

'Fair to middling,' Kat gasped. 'I wasn't expecting you.'

'Might as well make the most of it, since we are both here –'

She never knew when he would turn up, with or without his camera. Un-policeman-like, he had taken to turning his mobile off when he was working. She had become used to the pattern of their relationship: a quick shuttle in from another galaxy, then back into the old spaceship and away again. An hour after she got home, the microwave suppers were still on the floor where she'd dropped them.

'Good timing,' she said. 'I'm glad you came.'

Ashton snorted with laughter. 'I'm glad I came, too.'

'How are you, apart from the obvious?'

'I'm fine. The disciplinary looks likely to end with a rap on the knuckles, loss of rank and a spell back in uniform, which is not my style. I'm going to call it a day and take my chances with photographic work before I get too old to switch horses. Financially, I can manage a few lean years while I get established. It isn't as if I have a family to provide for, this time around. But you don't want to hear all that. Why not put that stuff in the freezer and we'll go for a meal down on the river'

'A meal down on the river sounds fine.'

If Barry got his way, there would soon be a restaurant on the estate. Kat's idea for an integral community centre within the leisure complex had been taken up with enthusiasm, particularly once councillors realised there would be no alcohol licence at the new centre. Instead, there was to be a substantial eating facility. Although nothing had been settled, Barry wanted to turn the place into a BYO restaurant.

The development had indeed speeded up once the tenants had cleared off to Magaluf. The architects and engineers, job done, moved out and the painters and decorators moved in. Apart from a two-person outreach office that would function mainly as a one-stop advice shop, the council's staff would be moving back into the town hall and leaving the day-to-day running of the estate in the hands of the tenants. Karen had been shortlisted to manage the one-stop office. Following Kat's focus groups and training sessions, there were now enough residents sufficiently capable and willing to run their own show on the estate.

With all the old buildings gone, for the short time remaining of her contract Kat commuted between an alcove in the library and home. Her flat above the leisure centre was seeing more traffic than Hyde Park Corner. Barry was on leave, waiting for the replacement community centre. With time on his hands, he'd taken to cooking meals for her because, he said, she never stopped long enough to eat properly. He also tried to give her cookery lessons. They had become good mates. Without any sexual buzz to complicate matters, their friendship had grown into something special.

Cosmo King continued to be remanded in custody, and was undergoing plastic surgery after the damage inflicted by Winnie. An election was to be held for a new committee and chair person for the residents' association. With their alcoholic perks removed, many of the old committee had lost interest. Meanwhile, the tenants had developed a taste for secret ballots since the Magaluf vote. They'd picked up the jargon: the estate echoed to the sound of breaking moulds, hustings and talk of tactical voting, and simple majorities.

With a number of the estate's more challenging households already evicted for significant rent arrears as well as the large number now tanning themselves in Magaluf, the estate was quiet. Kat had anticipated being able to spend more time with Ashton. However, apart from their one dinner by the river on her return, that hadn't happened. When he wasn't tidying up the loose ends of his disciplinary proceedings and waiting for his suspension to end so he could resign from police, he was toting his camera hither and thither. There had been no more picnics in the park or riverside meals by either moonlight or midday sun.

Just as well, perhaps. He wouldn't have appreciated how Kat's attention to the minutiae of getting the project home and dry in time was taking so much of her time and energy.

CHAPTER 49

Kat had taken to crawling into bed earlier and earlier each night. Her mission had, however, been accomplished: the regeneration would come in not only on time but also within budget. In addition they'd had the go ahead to market any new accommodation not needed for tenants. Words such as profit and capital income were being bandied.

'You've done well, Petal,' said Barry. 'But you've been overdoing it. Too many late nights burning the midnight oil, a dodgy diet, and the stress of getting the estate sorted. Your moods are going up an down faster than a tart's drawers. Take a break before your next job. What about Mel's Spanish place? It'll be free now the season's ending. You could chill at the villa, renew your energies, and if you were that desperate to keep in touch, take your laptop.'

'Too tired. In addition, I'm barely back from Magaluf,' Kat said.

'Yeah, but that was work. Hardly comparable.'

'Not sure I can be arsed.'

'What d'you say I give the cordon bleu a miss tonight and get us a takeaway? Crispy duck, gingered squid with peppercorns, and loads of vegetables. My treat. Noodles or rice?'

'I haven't been able to face squid in any shape or form since I had food poisoning. The idea makes me queasy.'

'That was three months ago. You're forgetting the squid in question had been in your fridge for almost a week.'

'Be that as it may, apart from all the upchucking and downloading it caused, that squid must have damaged my insides. I've had heartburn from nose to kneecaps ever since.'

'That's job stress. I keep saying you need a break. I try to get you to eat regularly, but you don't always co-operate. If you're not up for a couple of weeks at Mel's place in Spain, why not get a tonic or something useful from the doctor? Either way, stop sitting around, go into town, get some fresh air. You haven't had any proper exercise, either. Stock up on fresh veg while you're out and we'll give the crispy duck a miss. See if you can find some really fresh white fish, and I'll conjure something bland for supper. Can you pick up a couple of limes, too? Asparagus if you can find it. I'll make a list.' Barry never gave up. It was easier to do what he wanted.

Half an hour in the supermarket resulted in a sizeable haul. Her few days in Magaluf had added a kilo to her weight, most of it on her bust. She decided to stock up on fruit and veg in an attempt to curb her appetite and cut down on carbs. Barry wanted coarse-cut marmalade, three types of lettuce, ginger root, celery hearts, a whole cod. Wine. The last few bottles of Rioja had tasted bitter, metallic; she switched to white, to go with the fish. Imitating Barry's habit, she gave the fruit and vegetables a good sniff and an exploratory squeeze before bagging and weighing.

That week's BOGOF offers in the health and beauty section were hair repairing conditioner, denture tablets, lip gloss and pregnancy testing kits. Her hair sucked up conditioner, she was out of lip gloss, and the denture tablets would come in handy for getting stains out of mugs and lavatory bowls. She had no idea what prompted her to throw in the testing kit, except that it was on offer.

Before leaving the mall, she tunnelled through the lingerie racks at M&S to get a new bra. She didn't usually bother trying things on before she bought them, but she felt like having a break, the middle-aged assistant was enthusiastic, and they offered a free fitting. Just as well, because she now found that after five years of wearing the one size, she needed two cup sizes larger. A diet and exercise regime beckoned. Meanwhile, she would have one bra that fitted properly.

Barry had left a note to say the shower in his new flat was having teething problems and he'd used hers while she was out. While in residence he appeared to have tidied the place, mopped the floor, and arranged a single geranium in a plain glass holder on the hall table. Pity she'd be moving out soon. Otherwise the tidying up and flower-arranging relationship might have turned into a long-term arrangement. Meanwhile, the place was a hymn to hygiene.

On the way to the bathroom with her spur-of-the-moment two-fors it occurred to her that apart from the hair conditioner, she didn't need any of it. She popped a denture tablet into the lavatory to bleach the bowl, had a shower using the gel Barry had left behind, washed and conditioned her hair, applied lip gloss, and filed away the pregnancy kit in the medicine cabinet. She really had no idea why she'd bought it. She didn't know how they worked. She'd seen them on the pharmacy shelf. Now she was curious. Taking out the instructions, she put the lid down and sat back against the cistern to read it. It didn't look too complicated.

The sun through the window was warm on her face and hair. The rattle of coin jewellery and exotic Egyptian music drifted up from the belly dancing class in the leisure centre below, soothing, soporific. Her eye caught a black hole of spotty mould growing on her new shower tiles. Cowboy builders. The flat was less than six months old. She stopped herself going through a mental snag list of other other things that might prove substandard. Her job on the estate was finished. As good as. She needn't worry about builders' faults anywhere on the Moor. No longer her problem. She'd be moving on.

She came to with a start, recognising the steel drum riff of Crank Dat Soulja Boy and realised she must have dozed off on the loo. An hour had gone by. The belly dancers had finished while she'd been napping in the sun which was coming through the bathroom window. Surely she had more important things to do with her time.

Two for one. She shivered as memories of her attack of diarrhoea and vomiting came unbidden into her mind. It had kept her housebound for three days before she had recovered sufficiently to stagger down to the chemist for a morning after pill. But she'd got away with it. And if not, it was a bit late to be worrying now. Wouldn't do any harm to make sure, though. Just to be on the safe side, so to speak.

She took a deep breath, slid out one of the plastic bags, and tore it open. The instructions were easy enough. Pee, wait, read.

Peeing on demand was harder than she'd thought. All last week she'd been passing more water than the Aswan Dam. Now, when all she needed was a splash, her waterworks had gone on strike. She hated sitting around doing nothing. If she hadn't been using one hand to hold the stick, she could have multitasked. Something to take her mind off it. Like, for instance, finish reading all twelve hundred pages of tiny type and turgid prose of Les Miserables. It was nothing like the musical. Painting a different pattern on each of her toenails would break the monotony except that the one bottle of nail polish she possessed was transparent, for minor repairs to her clothes, and for invisible mending. She gave an involuntary laugh and drenched her hand and her watch in warm urine, which would have been handy if she'd been stung by a jellyfish. She told herself to get a grip. and began counting aloud.

'One elephant, two elephant,...'

Thirty seconds is longer than most people realise: longer than a whole scene in a TV soap, for instance.

'Three elephant,...'

As long as she kept counting, she could believe anything.

'Four elephant,...'

Back in the Neolithic Age, didn't they use mice or frogs or rabbits for this exercise, and send it off somewhere? No news being good news, she could have waited in blissful ignorance for two weeks.

'Five elephant,...'

Maybe she could do a litmus test, instead; the one where they work out the density of the blue colour and usually have to have a number of tries before they get it right.

'Six elephant,...'

She sighed. Mental wandering would get her nowhere. Some positive thinking wouldn't come amiss. Failing that, as a last resort, prayer. Or threats.

'Twenty-nine elephant,... thirty.'

This was such a waste of time. She sighed, opened her eyes, and examined the urine stick.

PREGNANT, in capitals, full banner headline: PREGNANT. She blinked, narrowed her eyes, and squinted closer, expecting something different. The end credits, maybe, scrolling up the screen. For preference, something a little more explicit, such as NOT. She shook it, forgetting it was not a mercury thermometer. It didn't change. PREGNANT, it still screamed in giant obscene graffiti.

If she was to be honest, the pee-on-a-stick exercise shouldn't have been necessary. Barry was right about the mood swings: they weren't normal. No more than the tetchiness or the acid reflux. Everything she ate except raw vegetables, crackers or custard creams had been making her queasy. Also, her recent fad for giant tubs of tzatsiki should have alerted her. The yo-yo moods and weight gain had not been chronic anaemia, or overwork. Had all that decorating and furnishing been part of a primitive, instinctive nesting process? Shit.

What next? Knitting needles and balls of wool? Or knitting needle and bottle of gin?

Kat examined the stick in her hand once more, looking for the sell-by date. It might only have been on a buy-one-get-one-free offer because it had been on the shelf too long and might not be working properly. Kat's monthly cycle invariably became irregular whenever she worked herself into the ground and didn't eat properly. That would be it, she thought. It's the sort of thing that happens to women on a bad diet or in captivity: their periods often disappear altogether. She gave the stick a shake. It was all a question of faith. The nuns at the home put their trust in the power of faith. If she willed it to change, it would. She only had to believe hard enough.

But it didn't change. Okay. Since it was a two for one offer she didn't have to go for the first estimate. She took out the second stick and repeated the process, taking extra care this time, suspecting something must have gone adrift with the first test. A second would show the correct result. Good. No problem. This time she peed to order. Good sign. She counted down, waiting, no change. Not so good. She wasn't great on technology but she had to allow there wasn't much that could go wrong with a simple pregnancy kit. She slumped heavily on the council's best Armitage Shanks and almost knocked herself out on the faux-marble tiles.

It was her bad luck to end a long sex drought by getting knocked up. She'd been on the Pill for so long, she had taken for granted that it would always work. Surely there was a backlog with these things, a build-up, an accumulation, a stock-pile or whatever in her bloodstream, to carry her safely through any little slip ups involving diarrhoea and vomiting and tardiness in taking a morning after pill. Three days, for heaven's sake. Three rotten days. Safely on the Pill for ten years and pregnant after one night of sex and a stingy three days of gut rot.

A wasp was buzzing annoyingly at the bathroom window, going round in circles. She squashed it with the toilet brush.

Kat knew she wasn't mummy material. She wouldn't be. Not with her role model, a mother who could dispose of her child and walk away. She didn't stand an earthly. What was done was done. She'd deal with it, quietly, on her own. There was nothing to be gained by whingeing. Be good if she had someone to talk to, though.

Mel was not expected back from the end-of-season clean at her Spanish villa for another couple of days. Ashton was, to take a linguistic lead from Cosmo King, a different kettle altogether. She toyed with the idea of nipping along to the clinic and getting sorted before he was any the wiser. End of story. Alternatively, she could play dumb and go on as usual, overworking, eating badly, running, jumping, never standing still, and hope for a spontaneous miscarriage. No, that was pathetic.

She couldn't sit there waiting for the world to end. She risked a permanent lavatory seat rim on her backside. She heaved herself up. The strong sun pouring through the bathroom window sapped any remaining energy she had left, forcing her eyes shut and inducing a relentless torpor. She had no idea of the time. Her crap watch, after its dowsing with warm pee, had well and truly stopped. She had been stuck in the bathroom for well over an hour. She was so good at strategic planning when it concerned others. Time to plan a strategy for herself, for a change. Stupid, stupid, stupid. A bit of common sense, and this could have been avoided. She would have to reach a decision before Ashton showed. He was out there somewhere with his camera, his phone switched to voicemail. She re-charged the battery on hers. Closer inspection of her watch showed it was steamed up with still-warm pee. Thick headed, she rose; it was as sapping as fighting a quicksand.

Clinic, chemist, or bottle of gin and a hot bath? She was having a hard time working things out. Her brain was packing up. She'd wait until tomorrow. Get some rest. Her brain would work better, that way. One more day wasn't going to make much difference.

CHAPTER 50

Kat knew Barry would bang on the wall when he was ready for his shopping. Until then, there were messages and emails to be going on with. As usual, upon examination, much of it was junk: Amazon were advertising a ghosted autobiography of a minor celeb, the library had sent renewal details, there were offers to enhance her genitalia, invest in Nigeria, send cash to an old friend stranded abroad, except that she didn't think any English language graduate she knew would write *plise send mony.* A disliked ex-colleague wanted a job reference. Let him whistle.

Slipping out of her shoes, she massaged her feet against the chair legs. Her head was tight and raw. Her sinuses were blocked, her skin was flushed, her throat sore, the sort of feeling she had after a long-haul flight. People who talk about the glow of pregnancy are lying. She'd felt a darn sight better before she'd found out.

Nausea swept over her as she caught a whiff of tobacco through the open window. Absently she rubbed her stomach with one hand and her neck with the other, a party trick of independent hand movements. She couldn't concentrate on emails. Her skin was damp. She was bloated and miserable and someone had parked a bulldozer on her bladder. It occurred to her that the one place she'd feel comfortable for the foreseeable future would be in the weightlessness of a full tub. She never had baths in the middle of the day.

She trudged back into the bathroom, stripped off her sweat-soaked clothes, and stared at her naked body in the mirror. She touched her stomach with her fingers, trying to see any small sign of what was happening. Her stomach seemed harder, rounder lately. How could she have thought the cause for her clothes becoming a little tighter had been caused by grazing on custard creams and tinned macaroni cheese when she was too busy to stop for a meal. Her breasts were definitely larger, no ambiguity there. She just hadn't been looking. She'd already had to buy a bra two cup sizes larger. Next thing she knew, they'd turn into over-inflated party balloons.

She sank into the bath after filling it with the rest of Barry's shower gel and enough water to keep an Indian village going for a week. Rats to the hosepipe ban. It was time to think about herself for a change. Because you're worth it, she told herself in a silly American voice.

She could imagine herself, as fat as a house, unable to bend or kneel comfortably, fending off enquiries about her waterworks. Worse yet, she'd be expected to sit through endless tales about the agonies suffered in labour and hear blow-by-blow descriptions of TV series about East End midwives in the Fifties. She'd get heartburn if she so much as walked past a curry house or a takeaway Chinese. She'd be sentenced to wear one-size-fits-all tracksuit pants with stretchy waistbands and strings of waist extenders from a mail order catalogue. Her ballooning thighs would rub together, her ankles would no longer squeeze into boots, she'd get splodgy feet. She would become short of breath. Her skin would be so greasy she'd only have to touch a door hinge to stop it squeaking.

If she managed to navigate through that, she'd graduate to broken nights, dawn feeds, the twenty-four-seven stench of nappies, sour milk and regurgitated baby food.

That would be followed by months of teething, night-time screaming, and all-day drooling. Kat wasn't the sort to dote on offspring. She couldn't see herself as the sort who'd perform and volunteer and help out with a Stepford smile, supernatural patience and a play-school voice. She could not see herself following up on school notes, always having the right supplies and costumes and right money for the book club and school outing. She was convinced that people had to be profoundly disturbed to be able to live in that way.

There would be sleepless nights worrying about playground accidents, bullying, and perverts, then teenage tantrums and worries about promiscuity and drug abuse.

More immediately, she was not ready to cope with the inescapable presence of another human being wanting, demanding, her attention. Kat valued her independence, and had always managed to avoid commitment. No point chucking all that.

What the heck was she going to tell Ashton? He'd already had one dodgy pregnancy foisted upon him. He wasn't going to be too keen about another. No-one would blame him for thinking he'd been made the fall guy once more. He'd assume she'd lied about being on the Pill.

She really had no option.

Abortion was no big deal. She'd be just another statistic joining the fifty-two thousand abortions in London each year.

There was a soft tap at the front door. Not Ashton. She knew the rhythm of his knock the way wartime Morse code operators knew each other's tap. In addition, he had his own key. She stayed quiet, and soon heard the quiet sounds of Barry letting himself in to collect his shopping from the kitchen. Moments later she heard his stereo. He was playing his Cole Porter album again. He'd left her a post card of Millais' death of Ophelia. So appropriate, so Barry.

'Petal, fallen asleep in the bath again? Trying out a new tarragon cod with asparagus, mashed pots, guaranteed comfort food par excellence. Good choice of wine. Will give it ice time. No hurry. Timing not critical. B.' Copperplate, green ink. He'd drawn a smiling daisy.

She couldn't keep going round in circles. What to do next? She opened the wardrobe. Looked like she was in for another wild spree at the charity shop. She jumped as a wire coat-hanger became entangled in her hair and something wrapped itself around her neck. The door began to swing to behind her. She leaped away, slamming the wardrobe door. The last thing she wanted was for people to think she had died in some sort of autoerotic game by herself, hidden in the wardrobe.

Barry had ice-cold glasses ready. He actually preened because the wine had reached the right degree of coldness. As if Kat knew the difference.

She hadn't intended telling him she was pregnant. It must have been the wine. He said he'd guessed, and what did Ashton think about it?

'He doesn't know, yet,' Kat said, without going into detail.

'You sound worried

'Yes, I am. I can't have a kid now – the timing's all wrong. It's not just me or my job. It's the wrong time for Jack, too. There he is, about to chuck in the police with all the financial certainty that goes with it, to go into an uncertain career in freelance photography. The last thing he needs is to be saddled.'

'So he's definitely leaving the police, then?

'Very definitely,' Kat said. 'Using the stuff he's already taken of London street life, he's found an agent who's helping him put together a portfolio. He'd be living off his savings while he tries to make it in photography. This is something he's always wanted to do. Last time he considered going into photography, he got lumbered with a wife and child. It would be cruel to make him go through all that again. Shit,

Barry, why didn't I suss out that manky squid earlier? I've rather buggered things up.'

'But you told me you'd taken a morning-after pill.'

'Yeah, three mornings after: a trifle *trop tard*.'

'*Zut alors*, as they say. How far gone are you and what's the cut-off date for decision making, so to speak?'

'Well, it all happened back in May. I'll need to think about doing something soon.'

'There's always adoption.'

'Nope, definitely not adoption.' She was adamant. 'Despite what they say, most men don't want some other man's kid.'

'Well, you've ruled out adoption and you don't want to tell Jack,' he said, opening a second bottle. 'That only leaves the clinic job. A quick scoop, couple of Aspirin, home again and feet up in front of Torchwood re-runs, all done and dusted.'

'Torchwood?'

'Well, whatever takes your fancy.'

Barry made it sound an easy option, but Kat thought abortion sounded so calculated. Those blessed nuns had much to answer for.

'I could just do myself in,' Kat said. 'That'd solve things.

'What were you thinking of, specifically?' Barry asked. 'A quick slash of the wrists? It'd mess up your decor. You've no idea how hard it is to scrape blood out of tile grout.' The wine was going to his head.

'You're right. Wouldn't want to leave a mess behind.'

'Saw a film, once,' said Barry. 'The slasher covered the floor with a plastic sheet beforehand. Could always try that.'

'There's a tarp in the boot of my car,' she said.

'No, Petal, you haven't got your old heap any more. Somebody cremated it.'

'Buggeration. Slipped my mind. I thought it was kids who fired my car,' she said. 'But now I come to think about it, it was more likely to have been the gruesome duo.'

'What? Delaney and King? Who cares? It's done, now.'

'No tarp, then. Another door closed,' she said, crinkling her nose. The wine was making her sinuses fizz. 'Suffocation by cling film?'

'Take ages. You'd have to pirouette endlessly inside yards of the stuff before you got it sufficiently airtight.'

'You know, I don't think I've got the energy,' she said. 'It'll have to be wrists in the bath, easy and comfortable. When it's over, you'll have to haul me out and pull the plug.'

'And give the place a going over with Barman's Friend so they can re-let your place. Will do.' Barry poured more wine for himself.

'Nice wine. Give us a top up; more of this rather perky little vino and a couple of packets of Paracetamol might do it. What do you think?'

Barry pursed his lips. 'Imagine waking up in hospital having your stomach pumped out. Where's your sense of style? Pills and overdoses went out with prawn cocktail and baked Alaska. You wouldn't do anything so passé. Would you?'

'Maybe not. With luck, there's been a rift in the space-time continuum, and all this is happening in a parallel universe.'

'You wish.'

'I feel I've been sucker punched. It's slowing my thinking.' She leaned her head back and closed her eyes.

'Seriously, Kat, if a termination is what you want, go for it.

'Not much choice. There's his job, my job, his history, mine.'

'All that baggage doesn't help, I agree.'

'Oh, sod it,' she said. 'Life's too short. Give me another top up.'

'Did you see that piece in one of the Sundays last week?' He said as he refilled both their glasses, his with wine, hers with mineral water. 'Someone's done a survey of gender and parenting. and found that not only do gay men make good parents but they are also the best godparents. Apparently, the typical gay never forgets birthdays or special occasions, likes shopping, cooking, dancing, and gossip, and is gentle, creative, and sensitive. Oh, and the clincher is we tend to die rich and childless, leaving all our worldly goods to the kid. So why not forget about an abortion, have the kid, and let me be fairy godmother?'

'Gosh, Barry, sounds like you're thinking of coming out.'

'No, I'm staying where I am, hovering in the doorway. One beating is enough to persuade me to keep my sex life, such as it is, very much an undercover operation.

CHAPTER 51

Mel arrived home unexpectedly, ahead of schedule. Barry admitted to having texted her while Kat was out shopping. Abandoning her end-of-season landlord chores, Mel had locked her villa, exchanged her ticket for an earlier flight and flown home, arriving to find her friends well into their second bottle. Barry put another one on ice.

'You must have had some idea that one day you might want to settle down and have kids,' Mel said. 'This has just brought it forward a little. At least with your skills you will always be in work.'

'Work's no bother,' Kat replied. 'It's the settling down with kids that's the problem. To be honest, a husband and a houseful of babies has never featured in my annual letter to Santa.' The wine was making her talkative. 'My wish list is rather different. Tops, I want to continue being paid for doing the sort of job I enjoy best, then I want to get my hair permanently straightened, and last, I want to win enough on the lottery to buy a customised Morgan Roadster. Not gonna junk all that. Or risk making the same mistake as my mother.'

'Your mother?'

'Oh, yes,' said Kat, in the over-careful manner of someone who believes they've had exactly the right amount to drink. 'Must've told you about my mum. No? The one who tried to drown me. That mum. My mum, she used to get through a lot of sweetcorn. It kept defrosting, you see, so we had to eat it before it went off. You can't keep refreezing stuff until the cows come home. We had sweetcorn fish pies, sweetcorn tuna and mash, sweetcorn soup, sweetcorn lasagne, sweetcorn pancakes, sweetcorn fritters, sweetcorn purée on toast, sweetcorn with everything. Where was I? Oh, yes, my mum. Give us a top up.'

She still hadn't noticed that for some time now Barry had been refilling her glass with fizzy mineral water.

'Ta. Nice wine. My mum. Here's how it goes. She'd get into a relationship, and I'd have to make myself scarce. No problem. I got used to curling up with a book in a boiler room in winter or the lift inspection hatch in summer. I'd disappear even when I didn't need to,' she said. 'They'd be all over each other for a while, then I'd come in from school one day and she'd be in the kitchen, broken crockery, torn tights, bag of frozen sweetcorn clamped to her face, mascara down to her chin as if she'd staggered home after a bomb blast. If anyone came knocking, she'd concoct some bullshit about being short-sighted and walking into a lamp post and warn me not to say anything. He'd usually be in a better mood when he came back from the pub, but to hedge her bets, she'd sling me outside so it wouldn't piss him off seeing me there.'

'You're not your mother. Nothing like. And not all men are shite. Jack's okay,' said Mel. 'Listen, if you're toying with the possibility, however remote, of going ahead with this pregnancy, maybe you owe it to yourself and the child you're carrying not to drink yourself silly.'

'Thank you for sharing that with me, Oprah Winfrey. Just fill me up and stop being a pain.'

It ended, as it was bound to, in tears, with Barry the loudest wailer of all. They draped his new gypsy shawl elegantly across him and left him sprawled on the sofa in a fair imitation of the dying swan. Mel, assured Kat would be okay, went off home, albeit with some reluctance.

Back in Kat's flat Winnie was in residence once more, his creepy chimpanzee fingers grooming the panda Kat had picked up at Oxfam. He perched on the kitchen windowsill, waiting for her return, his bright, calculating chimpanzee eyes catching anything moving on the ground below. Her flat was otherwise empty. No steady background hum of familiar domestic machinery, fridge, computer, TV on standby, it was disconcerting. She could almost be in a flotation tank. She dug out a ready meal of chicken korma with egg fried rice and an onion bhaji and zapped it in the microwave. As the fumes began to permeate the flat she went off the idea and instead dumped it on the floor for Winnie, who grinned and rolled back his lips, showing his teeth in a gigantic gummy smile. He must have thought it was his birthday as he detached himself from his panda, and dug in, giddy with pleasure. Kat made do with a single-egg plain omelette, which she didn't finish. Her panic was diminishing, but she needed space.

At three am, with the neighbourhood tucked in for the night, she had the streets to herself. There was a heaviness in the air, an atmosphere that often comes before a storm. The air was redolent with last night's wood smoke despite the London-wide ban on solid-fuel fires. The scent of burnt pine had dissipated a little during the night, and was pleasant. Apart from the drift of the river the only thing moving was a faint mist rising off the water. She followed the towpath until she came to a bench with a brass inset which informed her that the seat had been installed in memory of one Carol Flutter, *'a wonderful wife, mother and grandmother, always loved, always missed.'* Well. bully for her.

Across the river, one of the houseboats had balloons strung along the rail. A figure came out to sit on the deck, and she saw the glow of a cigarette. She had stopped getting withdrawal symptoms whenever she saw anyone light up. After a while, the smoker threw the glowing tip into the river and went inside.

Kat headed back uphill and slipped into bed convinced that after all that fresh air and exercise she'd sleep.

A jagged spear of lightning made her jump. There was a long rumble of distant thunder, followed by silence. She had never understood why anyone would want to waste energy trying to gauge the distance of the storm from the time gap between thunder and lightning.

The thin curtains sighed back and forth in a gauzy film over the open windows. A dog barked in the road and a hundred and one others immediately set up an answering chorus. Her land-line rang. She pushed off the bedclothes and picked it up but there was nobody there, only the hollow silence of an empty line. The storm must have brought down a cable somewhere.

At half six it began to rain, a sudden deluge that came in through the open window. She closed it. Outside everything was grey, morning shadow. She shivered, waiting for the the sky to begin to lighten the trees. Summer was over.

With the noise of the storm shut out by the double-glazing, the flat was completely silent. Time was, she'd have been perfectly content with the sound of silence. That was before Ashton had come along and disrupted her life with the rustle of Sunday's newspaper or the dulcet tones of radio pundits wittering on about the collapse of England's middle order in Ahmadabad. She'd even got used to Pavarotti from the shower. The fridge had joined the conspiracy of silence; having reached temperature, it had switched itself off.

It hadn't taken long for the pigeon population to reassert itself on the estate. Winnie, back once more on the kitchen windowsill, had discarded his panda and was absently scratching his balls as he watched a pair of birds the size of terriers trying to perch under the eaves out of the rain.

Noticing her standing there, he hopped down from the windowsill and came over to give her a hug and a bit of a groom. She must be looking a total wreck if the blooming monkey was feeling sorry for her. She hugged him back, until he decided he'd had enough of being squashed, and scampered back to the windowsill to continue out-staring the birds.

Ashton had finished tying up the loose ends resulting from his resignation from the police force, and was engrossed in his photography. Both of them could do with a break. Maybe they'd both take up Mel's offer to spend some time doing absolutely nothing in Spain. Her passport was still in date. She emptied her bag out – all the usual odds and sods, including birth control pills – useless damn things. She made a face at her passport photo. The holographic vulture on the page made her appear worse than could a portrait in any Wildean attic. As ever, there was an up side to every down: somebody would have to be seriously pushed to want to steal a passport with a picture like that. She was safe from identify theft there.

Soon it would be winter, with its unremitting grey skies, winds, rain, and no chance of seeing the sun again until the spring. There was already a smell of dying vegetation in the air. Mel's Spanish villa was sounding better by the minute.

By ten o'clock the rain had settled into the seeping, penetrating, light grey that the English, with their blotting-paper skin, understand so well. Buildings and streets and sky blended together in misty dampness.

Kat stood by the window, resting her forehead on the glass, and doodled childishly in the condensation with a finger. Silly patterns, erased as quickly as she formed them. She could see the wet street and the yellow light of street lamps which remained on even at this time of day reflected in the rain.

Outside the still-closed Chip'n'Chopsticks takeaway, the Moor's token homeless person sheltered swathed in sleeping bags, in the doorway among the discarded chip papers and polystyrene burger boxes that had blown into the doorway overnight. He put away his mobile to talk to a rain-caped community support officer who had to bend down to pat the man's dog. The policeman offered the dosser a cigarette and the dog a toffee, both of which were accepted with the speed of light.

A bus trundled into view, empty. Not in any hurry, it stopped to let a sodden street cleaner drag his cart across the road. The hard rain had beaten the plants in the council's hanging baskets to naked stalks. The steps below were littered with broken blossoms and cigarette ends bucketing downhill, miniature barrels going over Niagara. The commuters and school kids had gone past more than an hour earlier, but it was still too wet for any but the strongest of the Twirlies, in their see-through macs and pleated plastic rain hats, flourishing their Freedom passes in jazzy plastic holders from the 99p shop.

The kettle whistled. Kat was about to turn away from the window when she saw Ashton's car draw up below. She watched his tall figure unwind from the car. Now she'd moved in above the leisure centre, he was content to leave his Merc in the car park immediately below her flat. The preponderance of CCTV cameras did not, however, deter him from setting the alarm each time.

As he hopped out of the car, it looked as if he was about to break into a little dance routine, but he was no Gene Kelly. And anyway, he had no umbrella, no coat. Lightning cracked and sparkled as he hurried across the road.

Kat ran a brush through her hair, whipped on her new lip gloss, sprayed a cloud of fabric freshener in the air and walked through it before she heard Ashton's signature rap on her door. Crunch time. She took a deep breath and a last look in the hall mirror.

All right, Mr DeMille, I'm ready for my close-up.

'Ta-dah! Late breakfast!' Ashton waltzed in, toting a bottle of Champagne, and looking remarkably pleased with himself.

'Breakfast?' Uh-oh. She sounded like Little Miss Echo. Champagne at this time of the morning wasn't his usual style. But hey, gift horses and all that. He'd brought her Champagne, for Heaven's sake. Special treat. Be grateful.

'Yup, we're celebrating,' he said, grabbing her for a quick boogie around the room. 'Fantastic news,' he told her, excitedly. 'I've landed the trip of a lifetime: a year in Antarctica, on a sponsored scholarship, photographing an expedition. It's the most extraordinary piece of luck. They rang this morning. The guy who was going to do it had already reached the Falklands with them before he discovered his wife was expecting after years of unsuccessful IVF. Right now, he's somewhere over the Atlantic on his way home, and the expedition is without a photographer. That's where I come in. I'll have to get my skates on to catch up with them before they leave Port Stanley, because if I miss that slot, I'm stuck with hanging around for the next plane or getting a civilian flight to Chile and travelling down from Punta Arenas.'

'What a fantastic opportunity for you, Jack,' she managed. Her mouth was dry but nonetheless she kept the smile going. 'When do you have to leave?'

‘Well, that’s the down side. They want me straightaway,’ he said, a touch rueful, but only a touch. ‘They’re rushing the paperwork through and arranging a psychological screening and a medical. Luckily I had my appendix out when I was a kid so that’s one less thing to worry about. They’ll carry the insurance for anything else. I’ll be back before you even know I’ve gone. I thought we’d have champagne to celebrate. Don’t suppose there’ll be much alcohol where I’m headed. Got any oranges? We can make Buck’s Fizz.’ He was manipulating the wired cork, not looking at her.

Kat focused on her fast-dwindling options. There’s a time and a place for everything. She needed to make a decision. What if she were to dump her news on him now? An argument about termination or whether or not he was the father would serve no useful purpose. He’d been down that road before. She’d lay odds he’d be less than enthusiastic about repeating the exercise. Tell him now, and if he hadn’t already been leaving, she probably wouldn’t see him for dust. But wait. What if he felt obliged to give up this dream job? What if he felt honour bound to stick around, offer to make an honest woman of her? History repeating itself, or what?

He’d almost prised the cork off. That Moët must have cost him a small fortune.

‘Hold on, Jack. I’ll fetch some glasses.’

o0o

ACKNOWLEDGMENTS

My heartfelt thanks to fellow authors who acted as my peer review group and so generously provided me with their advice and insight throughout.

I am grateful to my family for their support and encouragement without which this book might never have been begun in the first place, let alone finished:

Owen Saunders, who willingly read draft after draft and was unstinting in his advice.

Alex Grover, for sharing with me her expertise with the technology and dealing with my constant demands on her time with goodwill and patience, and, of course, for the cover design;

And in particular a very special thank you to Glyn, for his painstaking final checks of the manuscript which have spared my blushes by weeding out my mistakes and inconsistencies. Any remaining errors or omissions are mine own.

Want to know What Kat Did Next?

If you enjoyed Kat Among the Pigeons, you can find out what happens next in the second novel in the Kat Shakespeare series, an extract of which appears in the following pages.

CHAPTER 1

Kat struggled to force oxygen into her lungs. Her arms pumped, her lungs laboured. Sucking in warm air through her open mouth she forced herself to keep up the pace against the defiant pitch of the hill.

Aside from an occasional tinkle of neck bells in the scrub which alerted her to keep an eye out for the goats that could leap out on the unwary, she had the mountainside to herself. She looked a sight, but this early there was no danger of offending any fashion gurus with her ancient Lycra shorts and two-sizes-too-small sports bra that was tighter than body armour and almost cut off her oxygen supply. In addition, she'd picked up a pebble-dash finish from the grey dust that hovered around the silent cement quarry which scarred the hillside.

Later in the day the trail would be clotted with fitness zealots, booted and backpacked, and with families chattering over to Los Alamos for Sunday lunch.

She felt the relentless drag of gravity as the zigzag trail steepened. Her calves were pulling. She was wheezing audibly when she reached the little enclave of concrete barbecue stands with their blackened grids. Bending from the waist, she sagged against a wooden picnic table. She blinked hard a few times to clear the sweat from her eyes. The morning sun was hot on her head. Upending her water bottle over her face for an instant, she swilled and spat a mouthful before drinking. Her scrunchie had jumped ship earlier on the trail, and now her hair flopped against her neck in slick-with-sweat coils.

Beyond the terraced rows of sparkling white beehives, the sun reflecting off the sea was dazzling. On a clear day you were meant to be able to see North Africa. Maybe, but you'd need a ladder and some glasses. And only on a day of exceptional clarity. She dragged in air, letting it out little by little, enjoying the view down the valley while she waited for her heart rate to slow.

She must have overdone the water stops; her bladder was bursting. Trying not to disturb the bees foraging amongst the swathes of rosemary, she squatted in the scrub with her pants hitched around her knees and peed into the dust. Across the hillside she caught the glitter of the lake above the dam.

A little higher she could see the cave, little more than a crack in the rock, where it was said a handful of civil war freedom fighters had sheltered while contemplating whether to fight and die, surrender and be executed, or make a run for it. Gary Cooper had done it beautifully, propped up on the mountain with his machine gun while his comrades rode safely into the end credits.

Gamely, she set off once more, head up, feeling the sun on her face.

'What the f—?'

Kat stumbled, kicking out as an animal shot across her path. Startled, it yelped and lolloped off, tripping over its own ears. It was a small black and tan, with a fancy diamante collar. She was lucky; a bigger dog could have had her leg off.

Beside the path ahead, sunlight sparkled off a little waterfall. The soft noise as it splashed onto pebbles was a perfect accompaniment to the constant hum from the bee-hives. That, and the sound of her wheezing. She looped a towelling sweat strip around her neck, took another slug of tepid water, and watched the antics of a pair of large birds floating on a thermal overhead. She guessed they might be the endangered Bonelli's eagles the birdwatchers had been nattering about. Kat wouldn't know a red kite from a red cabbage, but it did not detract from her enjoyment of the birds' performance as they caught their thermal and waltzed in silence together.

Setting off again, she slipped through a v-shaped livestock squeeze that only two weeks earlier she'd had trouble with. Her exercise regime was working.

Ignoring the mule track leading steeply uphill and towards Granada, she continued along the trail to La Esquina. A casualty of the civil war, the tiny village had been rebuilt as eco-homes for tourists tired of the villa-with-satellite-TV-and-pool scene.

Kat wasn't knocking tourists. They were the ones who provided most of her income. She, too, had first come as a tourist, but she'd had to be different. Other thirty-something singles backpacked in the Himalayas, cycled between Thai villages, or trucked across Australia. Instead, with flights to Malaga frequent and cheap, a more-than-working knowledge of the language and a free villa on offer from her friend, Mel, Spain had seemed the easy option for a short break while she contemplated her options at what had been a tricky time in her life.

A year on, she was still there. The metamorphosis from community activist to expat Brit, one of the crowd who gravitate to the Costas, had been relatively painless. She didn't miss England: the queueing, the binge drinking, the Saturday night street fights, the whingeing. Some things, maybe: summer rain, toad-in-the-hole, second-hand book shops, baked beans and Worcester sauce on toasted white sliced.

She did, however, miss a decent transport network. The village had only two buses daily to and from the coast from where one could pick up a motorway express to the train stations at Malaga or Almeria.

The other thing she missed was being near a gym. There were chic fitness centres in the towns along the coastal strip where zumba and Pilates reigned, but the Spanish didn't go for weights or circuit training. In the villages, the fitter ex-pats walked their dogs for exercise and those less fit gossiped over coffee and two-day-old newspapers. Amongst the locals, those lucky to be in work dumped the kids at dawn and disappeared, leaving Grandma to take the kids to and from school. Elderly men, survivors of the Civil War, or the regime which followed, hobbled painfully to and fro with the aid of sticks and moaned about dog shit, short skirts and the Euro, and left their womenfolk scrubbing and cleaning until you could perform open heart surgery on their floors. Sports enthusiasts juggled the Spanish language TV channels for 24-hour football coverage.

Rather than confuse those who asked, it was easier to describe Kat's morning exercise as jogging. Having long ago concluded that the health benefits were at best minimal when weighed against the mortality rate, she had developed her own style of interval training. It was a tad down the athletic scale, but it was better than no exercise at all. It also seemed to keep half the village amused. Today, half-way up the sierra, aside from the avian Fred and Ginger cavorting in the sky above her, she had no audience to entertain.

Swinging downwards, she touched her toes a dozen times, smug that she could do it without bending her knees. Grabbing both ankles, she felt the strain as she pushed and stretched half a dozen times before setting off again.

She'd been vaguely conscious of the yipping from the firebreak. Thus forewarned, when the dog ran across her path once more and dropped a shoe in front of her, expecting her to do something about it, she ignored him. Undeterred, he followed, nipping playfully at her ankles. She stopped. He stopped. She flung the shoe back along the path and broke into a lope. Ignoring the shoe, the mutt trotted beside her, long ears flopping along the ground.

Aside from the danger from wild boar in this area, the wretched animal could fall into any number of holes in this terrain. She had almost sent him over the edge earlier. She aimed her electronic dog scarer at him. Apart from a perplexed rub of his left ear, she got no reaction. That had been another five Euros down the drain. She was going to have to stop buying stuff off the internet.

'Go away! Buzz off!' she yelled, sending the animal into the air and disturbing a cluster of goats grazing and farting audibly in the scrub.

The dog wrapped his body around her ankles. She'd never lose the stupid mutt. His owner was most likely still in bed. She did a U-turn, heading for a cluster of villas she'd passed twenty minutes earlier.

A sign of the times: the first three gates were padlocked. Two of the houses were ambitious renovations halted in progress. The third was a sprawling bungalow with a drive-through portico supported by pale pink Styrofoam pillars. The bungalow had a kidney-shaped pool set to the side, a visible statement of wealth.

The fourth villa, which must have had an effect on property prices in the otherwise upmarket enclave, was a two-storey untidy jumble of once-whitewashed stones. Kat had no problem imagining the tastefully tinted, slightly-out-of-focus, picture in the estate agent's window: '*original features, lots of potential - good investment*'. In close-up, the wall was generously coated with graffiti in more than one language. Windows gaped, glassless. Weeds sprouted on broken sills. Tall iron gates hung on rusted hinges. A mustard BMW with Malaga plates sat under a sagging metal vine frame in front of the house.

'Hello-oh, anybody at home?' she called.

With places like this, there was usually someone shovelling cement or sawing beams nearby. The dog scampered off. Kat followed its yapping to the edge of an empty pool lying between the villa and unkempt terraces of over-ripe fruit.

'Noisy boy. What are you making such a fuss about?'

She leaned over, and immediately jerked back, her skin prickling, hardly registering her mobile falling into the empty pool. Oblivious to the gummy smell of pine and the warm scent of rosemary and mint, she gazed down.

The woman who lay spreadeagled on the cracked dry tiles of the empty pool was well past Kat's help

'Aw, shit,' she said. 'Not another one.'

Kat had been brought up in a children's home run by nuns, where attendance at the open casket funerals had been mandatory. On those occasions the deceased, aged nuns, had the cosmetic services of a pious undertaker before such viewings. However, this was not one of those occasions. This woman lay amongst the detritus of summer, her arms outstretched, one leg buckled beneath the other. Her blonde hair was spread like bleached seaweed. The one foot in view was shod in a smart navy pump. The heel had broken off.

Kat saw no sign of anyone else. There were no shoe or footprints. No tell-tale cigarette ends, drinks cans, condoms, chocolate wrappers. No litter of any kind. Only a few sun-scorched leaves. And her mobile scattered around in bits.

With her phone gone, and all the villas seemingly empty, she'd have to go back to the village to alert the police. On the other hand, it didn't seem right to leave the woman alone. She'd have to put her mobile back together. She groaned. That meant getting down into the pool. She peered over the side to see how close the phone parts were to the woman's body, and was reassured. Slightly.

'Hallo? Was ist los?'

Kat gave a startled squawk and almost shot out of her trainers.

A man built like a bunker had appeared on the hillside opposite amongst the un-harvested fruit that hung heavy on the trees and littered the ground on the terraces of citrus, avocado and olive. And pomegranate, by the look of it. Anything else was grown in huge plastic greenhouses. The man was wearing the sort of tan leather shorts and red and white check shirt that looked as if he was en route to or from an Austrian folk-dance. His grey-blond hair was worn long.

The man was wearing tan shorts and a red and white check shirt. His grey-blond hair was worn long.

It was only when his voice cut through the sharp buzz that Kat became aware of the flies around the woman's body.

'Hello,' she called across the divide. 'There's been an accident.'

That wouldn't do: he'd spoken to her in German. Hers was school standard at best, but she was game. to give it a try.

'Wir müssen die Polizei telefonar?' *No, that was wrong. Telefoniert. That was the word she wanted.* 'Wir müssen die Polizei. telefoniert, aber mein mobile...' *Mobile? Handy.* 'Mein Handy ist kaput,' she yelled. 'Can you call the police? Rufen Sie das Polizei, bitte?' It wouldn't get her a part in a Das Boot remake, but he'd get the gist. She'd run out of steam, but failed to produce the hoped-for response. She did an encore, this time in English. For all the good it did, however, she might have stepped out of an alien spacecraft shouting *Klaatu barada nikto*. The German took off.

Resigned to the inevitable, she stepped down into the pool. Staying well out of range of the body and its attendant flies she picked up the pieces of her phone as rapidly as she could and got out again, fast.

As she reassembled her mobile with unsteady hands, her eyes flickered over the garden, the brush, and the nearby houses. Anything to avoid looking at the body.

Waiting for the police, she was aware of each rustle although she knew it was the dog snuffling in the undergrowth. Now and then she caught a reassuring glimpse of his upright tail.

Her awareness had sharpened so acutely, she imagined she could smell putrefaction. There was no sign of the big German. The place was deserted, aside from Kat, the corpse, the dog. And the relentless buzzing of the flies.

2885083R00142

Printed in Great Britain
by Amazon.co.uk, Ltd.,
Marston Gate.